Black Ivory

by

Jo Squire

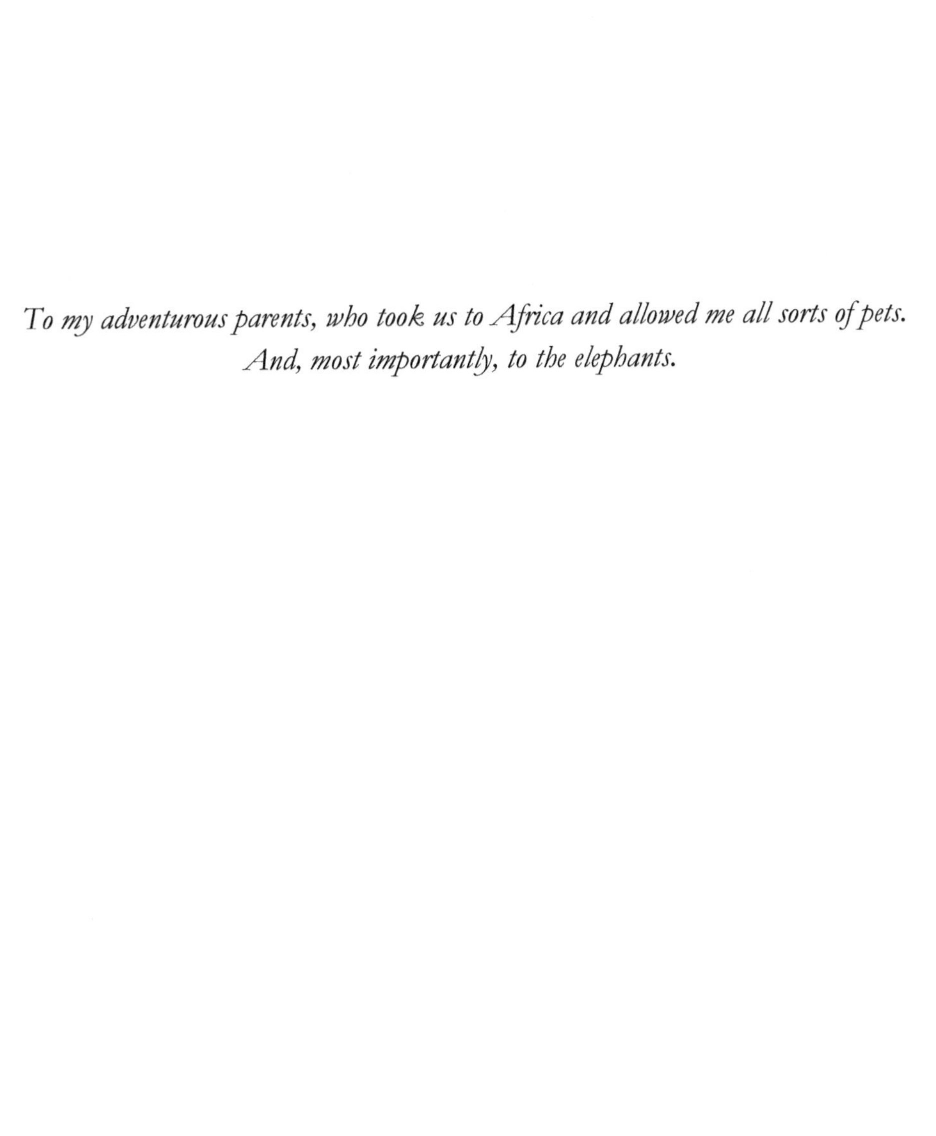

To my adventurous parents, who took us to Africa and allowed me all sorts of pets. And, most importantly, to the elephants.

One

If the poacher could see the future, he'd think twice about why he's out here alone on the hottest of days. But his horizons are limited by the anger that drives him blindly onward. Meanwhile the curtains of his desires shift endlessly and obscure his perspective, blocking any prospect of clear vision.

All afternoon, the elephant has searched for water and found only dry riverbeds. At dawn, on the other side of the plains, a dominant bull chased him from the herd and familiar territory. Now thirsty and tired, he rests under a shady acacia. Initially, the human presence nearby was a mere irritation, enough to make the elephant alter course. But now he just wants to be left alone and doesn't yet understand his vulnerability. More than once, the man came close enough for him to charge and trample. But this elephant had no reason to be aggressive. Experience has not yet taught him how dangerous humans can be. He wants to find water before the dark closes in. Even animals as large as elephants have more to fear at night.

As the poacher loses track of his prey, he halts in a patch of shade. "Fucking elephant!" His words hiss into the quiet of the savannah. It's late, and he's eager to make this kill and get out of Masaranga Park.

Ahead, a rocky outcrop is just visible through the mopane scrub, and the poacher pushes toward it through thorny vegetation. Athletic muscles strain under his sweat-soaked shirt as he hoists himself to the highest point, grunting from the exertion. Silently the poacher curses again and rubs the deep scar on his thigh, a reminder of a score he will one day settle.

Not long ago, the bull was almost in range as it crossed the dry riverbed, its ivory virtually within grasp. Balanced on the rocks, head above the canopy, the poacher narrows his eyes against the sun and searches for his quarry. No tell-tale patch of a gray hide visible anywhere below. This hunt has been far too hard, and he's exhausted. Usually, a challenge inspires him, but he's out of patience. A surge of rage erupts as he assesses his failure so far.

The poacher hates being out here and has honed anger into a weapon that keeps him hard. On this scorching day, he's been taken to his limits, and his fitness and strength have not proved enough. He scans the savannah for the slightest movement and deliberates. Whatever it takes, his mission is to always come out on top. There's so much that he does not yet have, and this failure frustrates and disappoints him. The elephant has out-maneuvered him. Long before now, he'd anticipated his prey nicely lined up in the sights of his gun, but it's unpredictable and difficult to corner.

"Motherfucker!" American movies have expanded his vocab, and the poacher usually gets a kick from hearing the word roll off his tongue. To vent properly, he silently follows up with a stream of Swahili profanity. It's best to keep a lid on it and avoid giving himself away. The elephant must suspect his presence. Why else would it have changed direction so unexpectedly? It's a crafty beast, not the dumber, easy to kill animal he thought it'd be.

The poacher drops from his vantage point and stalks back to where he last sighted the elephant. He treads carefully to avoid dry twigs. Those tusks looked perfect and would be worth a year's wages slaving in some dead-end job. That the elephant must die means nothing to him. Its ivory will buy plenty of diversions.

But he can't sight the bastard. "Son of a bitch!"—an apt curse picked up long before he cleared out from that backward village of his childhood. Usually, he'd consider it super-cool to swear in English instead of Swahili or even his native Kikuyu, but his confidence has fled for now.

The poacher tucks the gun under his arm and trails back and forth through a dense thicket. Surely it's he who should be able to hide easily.

Where has his prey gone? How can a massive elephant disappear? The bastard is tougher to kill than he ever imagined. This is not at all how the Nairobi black-market punter described it. The poacher reflects that he despises that man anyhow. His contact had probably never come near an elephant, and certainly never tried to shoot one. Despite this sudden insight, he pushes on doggedly. With the rewards so high, and the likelihood of punishment low, he'd be a fool not to apply all his talent to this kill.

Spiked branches scratch through his sodden clothes. As he stumbles on over uneven terrain, sweat runs into his eyes and blurs his vision. He wipes it away, but more forms immediately. It was a crazy decision to hunt without support. His village archenemy was recently jailed, so he could easily find a couple of offsiders from home. The truth is, he prefers not to split the profit.

The visibility is down to a few meters when the poacher hears a movement to the left and chases the sound through the thorny scrub. An insect bites the back of his head, and he flicks it away without checking what it is. At last, there's a motionless gray shape up ahead. Would the elephant have heard him close in? He freezes and readies his gun, aware that the bastard is smarter than he gauged. He's got close enough to at least injure it and won't miss his chance, though, at this angle, it will only be wounded. Not to worry. A perfect shot is impossible, and he's unlikely to get so near again. As lust for a kill overrides all caution, he abruptly takes aim and fires at the patch of hide.

The blast rips through the silence of the savannah and sends hidden creatures scampering for cover. The poacher hardly notices the noise or the weapon's kickback. He's proud of his fast reflexes, and, with a gun in his hands, he's usually lethal.

🐘 🐘 🐘

Deafened by the blast, the terrified elephant wants to escape, but a searing pain rips up his thigh, and raw instinct overrides fear. He swings toward the danger, his movement surprisingly fast for his size. The second bullet just misses as the elephant's fear and pain merge into self-defense. He faces his assassin and perceives only a man. Unfortunately, he's not yet learned about guns and the advantages armed men have over their prey.

The poacher falls back from the charging bull, but he's swift to act and gets another shot in as it turns away. Charged with adrenaline, he chases his prey, gun reloaded. There's almost a clear shot across the riverbed! But, at the last moment, the elephant turns and vanishes into a patch of dense scrub.

The man follows the blood trail until his breath comes in gasps, and he's forced to slow and assess the situation. What chance is there of tracking the elephant? It might lose enough blood to slacken pace, and give him the chance to get back into firing range. Streaks of his own blood crisscross and dry on his skin.

For a while, the poacher persists. His sweat drips into the elephant's dusty footprints until the trail thins and disappears. The light fades as the sun drops below the tree line. Exasperated by this unexpected failure, the poacher vows that only this once will the elephant get the better of him. To lose like this is unacceptable. His keen sense of self-preservation forces him to admit temporary defeat, and he returns to his vehicle. The bastard elephant never faltered enough that he could finish it off.

The poacher halts and violently curses as he registers how much money he's just lost. He uses the long walk back to his well-concealed Land Rover to plan. Next time, he will bring offsiders and they will clean out many elephants. Had he brought help, that animal would already be dead, and he'd be cheerfully hacking the ivory off its head. In future, he will recruit fit men like himself but manage them carefully. They will need to be kept in control as workers under his command. He'll pay them well enough, but he's the brains and the lion's share of the booty will be all his.

Two

As Lou strides across the browned paddock, a hot breeze gusts against her bare arms, and blows her loose khaki pants around legs fit from hours of walking. Across the African savannah, a red dust haze filters the slanted light of dawn, a guarantee of another scorching day. There have been no clouds for months, just this steel-blue sky. Lou stops and squints toward the sun's early rays, her shadow stretched tall behind her. As sun-bleached hair blows into her eyes, she makes an irritated gesture and reaches up to twist it into a ponytail. So far, it hasn't been a good year.

Soon black dots will spiral upward as vultures catch rides within columns of rising air. *When will clouds arrive and deliver the rain needed to end this relentless drought?* After months of scrutinizing the empty Kenyan sky, Lou's patience has run as dry as the bushland.

The horses watch her approach, their tails switching the first flies away. As Lou lifts the lid off the food barrel, the roan mare shoves in and almost knocks her over.

"Roma, get away!" Lou pushes back against her.

Oliver is equally annoying. Anxious for rations, he nuzzles his bowl. Finding it still empty, he strikes the battered metal repeatedly with his hoof, as if his message to her is not already clear enough.

Lou elbows both horses out of her way. Oliver nickers as if to say "At last!" when she begins to scoop out oats. After a night of disturbed sleep, Lou feels at the end of her tether and understands their anxiety. She's in a hurry to get her early morning chores done and wants to work on her thesis, which is behind schedule again. It's about time to reclaim her motivation and catch up, as this debilitating drought has drained her energy. Always now, she clings to a futile belief that the drought must soon break.

The rough texture of the oats softens between her fingers as Lou mixes in molasses. Roma steals hungry mouthfuls.

"There you go!" Lou pushes bowls toward the horses, and they take a step back out of her way. The horses wouldn't survive solely on the savannah's sparse grazing, whereas the hardy wildlife has been forced to evolve several degrees of drought tolerance. Lou's concern for the wild creatures, especially the elephants, is at the forefront of her mind.

She returns past the scattered buildings of Masaranga Park Headquarters, their run-down condition seeming especially evident today. At the moment, Lou feels pretty run-down herself, but a censoring voice tells her she has no excuse. Of the buildings she passes, only the visitor's center is freshly painted—a cheery facade for the outside world.

An energetic wolfhound bounds toward her from behind the vehicle shed.

"Zebu. Good morning!" Lou's mood lifts a little as the dog smiles—a wide jaw of perfect teeth. Around headquarters, Zebu is the easiest to please. Lou hugs her tightly until, abruptly, the golden canine breaks free and runs circles around her all the way toward the kitchen. There, outside, Zebu settles and waits, sure that better things exist on the other side of the screen door.

Inside is freshly ground coffee and a screaming kettle but no sign of Grace, who is family but not family, a mainstay when others have deserted. As Lou pours the scalding water into the pot, the pungent aroma reminds her how bitter Kenya's coffee has been this year.

Zebu has fixed her with a stare. Lou grins at her beloved dog and yanks a frozen shank from the deep freeze. She hands it into those gentle jaws and laughs as Zebu skulks off toward her den under the mango tree. As if anyone is going to steal it! Recently, Zebu is the only one able to cheer her up.

Almost ready to tackle her pile of notes, Lou sips her coffee. Voices drift down the corridor. A few Swahili words from Grace end with a sharply enunciated "Hapana"—No! A more subdued male voice follows, a grumbled response as if an intruder has been dismissed. Grace is an expert at sending people on their way. Seconds later, she bustles in with a satisfied smile on her round face.

"Kikuyu man came looking for work in the garden. I tell him no water to make plants grow, so no need for a gardener!"

"Ah!" Lou gives her a wry grin.

It's all the reply needed. Grace is Kipsigus and biased against the Kikuyu. She's sure that Kenya's government favors them. Secretly, Lou agrees.

As Lou tops up the sugar in her coffee, her attention drifts. A torrent of thoughts carries her past the bougainvillea hedges and out to the plains. There, each day the savannah creatures struggle to stay alive. Though her eyes rest on mauve and red flowers high and brilliant against a clear blue sky, Lou is aware only of what lies beyond. Out there, in the vast wilderness of Masaranga National Park, is a poaching epidemic with no end in sight. The elephants and rhinos have suffered the most.

Last week's loss of a pregnant rhino to poachers added to Lou's despair. *Where have we gone so wrong?* Absently, she slices and eats a mango, hardly noticing its cinnamon taste, and then wipes her hands clean on a damp cloth to save water.

"When did Dad leave?" she asks Grace.

"Before sunrise. He will come home tonight or tomorrow."

"Oh!" Lou was unaware her father might be away overnight. Why didn't he tell her? Sometimes it's as if she's not here. He's also become infuriating in other ways. When she asks his advice, he often replies with, "Well, what do you think?" As though he no longer wants to venture an opinion.

Lou had planned to stay up late last night to consolidate her backlog of notes on elephant movements, but she had procrastinated and gone to bed instead. As her sleep was more broken than ever, a complete waste of time. She feels more exhausted now than if she'd worked through the night.

A fleeting impression of a nightmare returns. Her absent brother was entangled with trouble, not entirely of his own doing. In the same dream were elephants and rhinos they'd tracked and known as individuals, but hadn't seen for ages. Chances are that the poachers have killed them. If only this part of the world, stretched to breaking point, could be fixed. How? Lou has no idea, but not from a lack of worrying about it. She sits at her desk and resolves to decipher meaning from her copious notes. Above her sits a watercolor, a graduation gift from her father, and inspiration for her to continue. Within its carved frame, an elephant stands sentinel over arid savannah of yellow grass and red earth, the landscape a reflection of current conditions.

When a gecko chirps noisily from a hiding place behind the painting, it sounds more cheerful than Lou feels. Her task seems suddenly insurmountable, and Lou escapes to the bright light outside, all commitments shelved. Her rifle and binoculars are already stashed in her old Land Rover. She glances at the blazing sky and returns to fill her water bottle from the filtration urn. At least her father's absence means he can't criticize her revised plan, so she can temporarily escape from her obligations. For a moment, Lou is assailed by a pang of guilt—she really should focus on her thesis. But … So what if Dad considers her impulsive? She's also a hard worker and will continue to review her notes tonight.

"You need me to drive, Memsahib Lou?" Peter calls out as she loads the bare essentials into the Land Rover.

"No, thanks!" Today "memsahib" irks Lou so much she fails to consider his offer. By now, he must know she loathes that title, which artificially elevates her above him. Peter is her lifetime friend, and nothing should change. She can hardly believe her brother enjoys his recent title of Bwana David.

Lou drives her Land Rover out of the compound, trailing a cloud of red dust behind. Earlier today, her father also left through the only gap in the bougainvillea hedge on his way to discuss Masaranga's management with Nairobi bureaucrats. Not that he's likely to get far. Considering the severity of the present drought, the thought of their comfortably detached lives exasperates Lou.

Her favorite herd, the Mbane elephants, were by the western waterhole at dusk yesterday. The mothers and their teenage calves seemed unsettled. In the herd is a younger female, Tumaini, who is particularly interactive and one of Lou's favorites. She trusts Lou and often approaches her vehicle as if she's happy to see her again. The herd has probably moved on, but the waterhole seems a sensible place to check, one of the few not yet dry. Lou's affinity is for the elephants, even more than the gorgeous big cats, with their sought-after pelts. Elephants have a vibrant social life and are playful with their calves. They don't have a deadly hunting instinct. Hours of field study have proved to Lou that they're not aggressive unless threatened. She knows they're capable of complex thought and deep emotions.

As the Land Rover rattles along the dirt track toward the waterhole, Lou's thoughts return to her brother. Before his interests shifted to city life, David usually drove, and they'd argue good-naturedly, just for the hell of it. Driving flat out, he'd tear across the grassy plains, dodging wide-topped acacias. The ride was always fun. Lou misses his company. When she recalls her extra duties since he cleared out, her foot inadvertently pushes harder on the accelerator. Savannah plains and woodlands stretch out all around, and Lou's spirits rise as she leaves headquarters far behind.

Near a termite mound the size of an elephant calf, Lou stops at a staff-only gate, through which she takes a narrow shortcut that winds across an expansive area of grasslands. A hot wind blasts through the open windows, and the Land Rover jars over potholes, but Lou doesn't mind the rough ride. She loves the savannah with its dramatic scenery and spectacular wildlife. There's always something fascinating and new to be found out here.

The banks of the waterhole have widened further, and it's now mostly a basin of cracked mud. Through binoculars, Lou checks the water's edge for signs of wildlife, but the place seems deserted. Elsewhere on the plains, the picked-clean skeletons of casualties testify to the cruelty of the worst drought since her father took charge fifteen years ago. President Moi survived a coup attempt only to be faced by the starvation of his people. Even maize flour is in short supply. Outside the park, crops fail, while inside, wild animals die.

For a while, Lou continues along the road which enters thick scrub. She searches for the mothers and their calves, as the herd could still be close by. Her attention shifts constantly between the track and the bushland, but she sees no sign of them. Almost ready to call it a day, Lou rounds a bend to find a massive bull elephant blocking her way.

As Lou slams on the brakes, the vehicle stalls. Briefly winded, her chest smashed against the steering wheel, she manages to restart the engine with shaking hands, her fingers fumbling. The elephant hardly slows. Unperturbed, it continues towards her as if expecting right of way along the narrow track. Elephants don't frighten Lou, but this is a dangerous way to meet one. Thirsty elephants can be irritable, and this one seems on a mission.

As the dust plume from behind the vehicle overtakes and engulfs everything, a sense of panic takes hold of Lou. The sound of her own ragged breathing reminds her to calm down. She revs the engine in an attempt to scare the bull, now shrouded by dust and invisible to her. Behind her, dense scrub lines both sides of the track, and she has no memory of a suitable spot to pull into along her escape route.

The dust thins and the elephant takes shape again, unaffected by the din from the engine. Huge ears billow with each step as he fills her windscreen view, the deep wrinkles in his leathery skin all too visible. Lou sights the track behind and lets the clutch out too fast. Her head hits the window frame as she stalls again. A set of tusks towers above her.

"Shit!" Lou again crunches the gears into reverse. She's never been attacked by an elephant before, and this bull has no reason to be aggressive, but she needs to get away before she's trampled. Thank god, the vehicle is moving! It lurches backward. Lou inhales sharply and feels dust roll down into her lungs. She mustn't lose the track and crash. For a few hundred meters, Lou manages to stay ahead of the tusks. She keeps an eye out for a gap behind to pull into and escape danger. The last junction is too far back. As she switches her attention between the track behind and the elephant in front, a wheel drops into a pothole …

The Land Rover veers crazily left. Lou spins the wheel against the pull, but feels the vehicle pitch abruptly back over a bank. It slides alarmingly, and she swings the wheel back again to avoid a tree, losing control completely. As the vehicle slams sideways, Lou is thrown hard against the door. Sudden pain radiates along her leg. Thorny bushes scrape and squeal against metal outside. The Land Rover tilts and slides and its front wheels leave the ground as it skids to a halt, hood tilted skyward.

Clutching the steering wheel, Lou holds tight within the protection of the cab. Through the windscreen, she sees mostly blue sky. The passenger door has swung open below her. For a long few seconds, she catches her breath, aware of her heart jumping wildly within her ribcage. Outside, the bush is suddenly ominously silent under the hot sun. Then Lou hears the soft pad of enormous feet and the swish of air behind huge ears.

Time suspends. Enveloped by shape and movement, Lou loses coherent thought to hold them together. The elephant doesn't alter pace or even turn his head toward Lou as he passes. Each footfall releases a swirl of dust as he moves on as quietly and quickly as he appeared. Dust settles behind him. A thick scar on his thigh stretches and twists with each step along the track. Lou knows most of the elephants in the park, and the injury identifies him as Tembo, one of the upcoming tuskers.

Tembo's droopy haunches vanish around a bend. With his disappearance, the bush becomes surreally quiet. The sun's heat bores in through the windscreen. Beads of sweat drop from her arms onto the dusty passenger doorframe. Her throat feels on fire and her mouth tastes gritty. Lou eases herself down through the passenger door, but still winces as her feet touch the ground. Her thigh burns. She's painfully aware the situation is her fault. So stupid of her to have come out alone on a little-used track, without adequate provisions.

"Shit!" A wave of self-directed anger and frustration passes through Lou. With such a long walk back, Lou considers starting the Land Rover. But at that crazy angle, there'd be no traction. Her mechanical knowledge is limited and she can't solve this alone, not without a winch to drag the vehicle out.

For a moment, Lou tests her weight on her sore leg and considers her options. She decides to walk and retrieves her rifle along with her pathetically light supply of essentials. After closing the vehicle to keep inquisitive animals out, she drops back down again, misjudges her landing, and flinches as another jab of pain radiates upward.

No one will worry about her until dusk, so the chances are she'll be stranded here all night if she waits for help. The only option is to go the same way as Tembo. Her choice to leave alone this morning was dumb and impulsive, especially as Peter volunteered to come. If she'd not been so easily riled, he'd be with her now.

Her lack of water is another oversight. Lou swallows a mouthful that tastes metallic as well as being warm and gritty. She's made every mistake in the book. This scorching heat won't let up for hours. With an imminent bruise on her thigh and a fuzzy head, Lou limps away from the vehicle's relative safety. *I have no foresight. What made me so mindlessly confident when I know the importance of caution out here?*

The silence weighs heavily as Lou hobbles along the dusty track. Most wild animals shelter during the day's worst heat, which is why the elephant took her so unawares. She wonders why Tembo was on the move when he should have been resting in the shade.

Perhaps she should have stayed with the vehicle, but her father is more likely to return tomorrow than tonight. She's wary of a night alone in the bush, though had she prepared adequately, the situation would be less daunting.

With each step now, her boots sink into dust, and her shirt and pants had turned ochre a couple of hours ago. Fortunately, she's fit and used to trekking through the bush. Though Lou bitterly regrets not asking Peter along, this walk doesn't seem impossible. Once back beyond the junction, there may be a tourist vehicle to give her a ride.

She's given up trying to calculate her progress in terms of distance. Her headache makes it too hard to even try now. Instead, she focuses on the next bend as the trail weaves through the scrub, each turn similar to the last. After a while, her leg begins to throb in sympathy with her head. Away from the vehicle and exposed, she must remain alert for danger. At least Tembo should be far ahead and isn't predatory.

Perhaps Grace might send Peter to search at nightfall, as he's the most likely one to find her. Lou wishes Peter were here now. His familiarity with how she works would help him guess where she'd gone. As well as fieldwork, they often work together to intercept poachers from villages near park boundaries, who set cruel traps and snares but rarely use guns.

Her father does not yet take Peter out to chase the well-armed gangs that slay the elephants and rhinos. Those patrols are riskier—the poachers hostile and dangerous, and after higher stakes than food for their families. Though Peter is impatient to help, it'll be a while before her father allows him to go. Lou is glad about this, as she'd hate to see him hurt.

An unexpected childhood memory comes to Lou—her mother interviewing a young Grace, who hoped to become their nanny. Alongside, Peter waited politely, one hand on his mother. News had spread about the arrival of a new family that might provide employment. Peter kept quiet and didn't yet speak English, but he smiled shyly and accepted treats from Lou's mother. That they were pocketed rather than eaten suggested he was on best behavior. The village kids were rarely so restrained.

After Lou's mother left for greener pastures, Grace was a lifesaver. Usually fun, and never too strict, she always manages to be cheerful, whatever the circumstances. However, there's much Lou can't discuss with her—or anyone for that matter.

Again, Lou wills Grace to send Peter, and then she remembers: one of the two functional vehicles is behind her on a bank, while her father has the other. A third languishes in the shed, waiting for the tardy mechanic. Her heart sinks, and she tries to pick up the pace, but a slow limp is as good as it gets. As she forces her legs along, the relentless heat sucks her dry.

The harsh reality is that she alone must extricate herself from this situation. But her thoughts become erratic, alighting on memories. One comes of a misunderstanding. Her mother had sent Grace home when she came to work the day after she'd given birth to Peter's sister. When they visited her a week later, her breast milk had run dry because she'd self-rationed, assuming her job lost. The concept of maternity leave was foreign to her. They assured Grace otherwise and left her simple home feeling terrible. A year later, Grace was stoic when her baby died unexpectedly from an infection.

As the light dwindles, so do the memories. Lou's shadow walks on the road ahead of her. She turns to see the sun low over the flat-topped acacias and a baobab silhouetted against the empty sky. All around her, patches of shade expand and coalesce across the landscape as Lou hobbles sluggishly onward. The endless afternoon has not proved long enough.

Her tongue has stuck to the roof of her mouth when Lou takes her last mouthful of water. It's cooler now, but the junction is still too far. She shouldn't have left the safety of the Land Rover. With her legs like lead weights, it takes all her resolve to put one foot in front of the other.

Without warning, an impala steps out from the bush onto the track ahead. His cover blown, the startled antelope freezes briefly at the strange sight of a human outside a vehicle, and then leaps sideways and crashes away through the dense scrub, horns first, its sleek neck arched.

Lou wonders if it was headed for an evening drink. Fuzzy-headed, she tries to recall close by water sources, but her thoughts are frustratingly slow, and she has no memory of water nearby. Though with her raging thirst, any muddy puddle would suffice. Close to where the impala disappeared, Lou crouches and searches the bush for a track that might lead to a water source. She's forced to bend lower to search beneath an overhanging shrub, where there's a gap in the vegetation. As she steps toward it, her foot catches on a dead branch submerged in the dust, and she trips headlong into the warm, powdery surface. Without strength to recover, she lies there coughing weakly as the dust catches in her throat.

But somehow, the ground beneath her feels comfortable, the dead branch a suitable pillow. Lou decides to rest, now that she's down in such a cozy spot. It's a relief just to lie still. Shadows of her brother and distant mother wander through her mind, and then an image of her first and only boyfriend boarding a plane for life elsewhere. To no avail, Lou tries to communicate with them along with the other foreign people inclined to inhabit her dreams. But this isn't a dream. Instead it's her normally resilient self, collapsed on a deserted track.

Briefly, Lou summons the energy to lift her head and finds her vision blurry. She tries to focus on the reality of her present situation where it's important to stay on guard. With night so close, so is the risk from predators. She reaches for the rifle butt on the ground beside her, although she'd never kill an animal except in self-defense. A single shot into the air would chase a lion away.

But a murky consciousness engulfs Lou, and it suddenly seems pointless to struggle anymore. She's on the dangerous outskirts of Nairobi with her brother, David, and desperate people are closing in. There are no escape routes anywhere. At last, she manages to retreat into the dark, peaceful space beneath the dream, where there's no need to try so hard. It's an enormous relief to be in this calm place, entirely passive and still.

Three

For some time, Lou remains on the dusty ground, unable to deflect danger as the last light fades. Close by, a nightjar calls in the bush. Then silence until some part of her becomes aware of a distant rumble. The sound intensifies and tugs at her consciousness and pulls her away from that other place. Doggedly, Lou clings to her peaceful space even as the ground begins to vibrate under her body, though it would be sensible to roll over and see what's going on. Perhaps a thunderstorm has arrived, carrying the much-needed rain. But she scrunches into the fetal position and returns to her serenity.

Forceful hands yank Lou up out of comfortable darkness and shake her resistance away with an annoying determination. A sudden stab of pain radiates from her thigh. Harsh reality returns. A jolt of fear floods through her as she's lifted upright into the glare of headlights. Then, an unexpected but familiar voice.

"Hey, sis. Wake up and get your act together! What the hell do you think you're doing?"

Unbelievably, her long-absent brother has shown up just when she badly needs help, the last person she guessed might rescue her.

Another jab of pain assails Lou as she tries to stand. The world spins, and she staggers sideways. David breaks her fall and lowers her back to the ground. He runs concerned eyes over her as if looking for broken bones.

"I'm OK!" she assures him.

"Stay where you are. I'll get some water."

As he strides back to the vehicle, Lou notices he's lost his fit suntanned physique. A Nairobi lifestyle has taken that from him. Then her vision blurs again, and she slumps back until he pulls her upright with a water bottle against her lips. After a mouthful, she takes it from him.

"Thanks. I'm really OK!"

"You could have fooled me!" David snorts in amusement. "You're lucky I had the spotlights on and the lack of ground cover made you easier to see."

Lou forces a smile and guzzles a bellyful of the sweetest water she ever tasted. Her sluggish blood vessels greedily soak it up. Incredible relief floods through her. She's so glad to see her brother.

"Thank god you finally showed up with great timing," she says. "What have you been doing all this time?"

"Surely that's what I should ask you! Where's the Land Rover? Did you break down?"

"I backed away from an elephant and went over an edge. I've walked for ages."

"On your own?" His incredulous expression indicates no answer is needed.

"Mm," replies Lou, dazed but defensive. "I hit my head. I wasn't thinking straight." She adds churlishly a moment later, "Seems like I've been left mostly alone in Masaranga anyhow!"

"Yes, Dad's not home, and for some obscure reason you left Peter behind," he replies, missing her point about his desertion.

"Dad's in Nairobi again," she answers wearily.

"Grace was right to worry. You were just curled up on the ground. It's almost dark for god's sake!"

"I needed to rest!" says Lou, aware her brother has every right to be cranky.

As she climbs into the passenger seat, the rearview mirror reflects her face: bloodshot blue eyes in a mask of red dust. Her skin feels grimy.

"God, I look terrible!"

"A bit scary!" he replies and starts the engine. His eyes are the same blue as hers and his blonde hair is stylishly cut. A moment of understanding passes between them. She's missed him. Glad to see him and grateful he rescued her, she again wonders about his Nairobi life and hopes he's OK.

David hands her a piece of biltong from the glove compartment, and she chews it hungrily as they drive. The headlights pick out a thickset, sparsely leaved baobab, a landmark she noticed before her sense of time vanished. The tree is not at its best and has lost the green leafiness and heavy, white, pollen-filled flowers present in times of plenty.

"We're almost there!" says Lou.

Minutes later, her Land Rover appears out of the dark. Only its bonnet is visible, protruding from the thorny scrub at an ungainly angle.

"Good work, sis!" David sizes up the damage. "My crazy sister! You're bloody lucky you didn't get eaten by a lion! Why did you leave the vehicle?"

"I don't know."

She feels like an idiot.

"Never leave your vehicle! You know it's rule number one!" David opens his hands in a gesture of disbelief. "I'm astounded that you tried to walk. You must have gone soft in the head out here on your own. Have you lost your mind?"

Usually, Lou finds it fascinating to watch him work. Tasks that frustrate her come quickly to him. But she struggles to pay attention as David hoists himself up, unlatches the hood, and shines his torch in. He's an old hand at this, and life always appears effortless for him, though her father reckons he's overconfident. For some reason, David is reticent about his Nairobi life. When Lou asks him about it, her questions mostly go unanswered. Perhaps he'll let go of that disturbing secrecy now he's here again. That's if he sticks around. But right now, all she wants is to get home.

"All good! I'll pull you out," he shouts. "Grab the tow rope!"

She hobbles around and helps him hook things up. The dead-tired part of her hoped to go home first and that he'd return tomorrow with Peter. Never mind, she's had plenty of practice at this.

Twenty slow minutes later, Lou climbs into her seat.

"Got it in four-wheel-drive?" David shouts from his vehicle.

"Of course I have!" Lou grumbles as she holds tight to the steering wheel. Does her brother think she is that useless? But, on second thoughts, perhaps he has reason to assume so.

"OK, here goes." David revs his vehicle, and the slack is taken up. As the ropes begin to strain, Lou releases the clutch gently, careful not to stall again. The engine roars, and, with a jolt, her vehicle surges forward over the bank. Thorn bushes squeal against her sides, and the wheels get traction, until suddenly she's free. For a moment, as dust obscures everything, Lou laughs, cheered by the ease of their success, until a moment later when a fit of coughing takes hold.

Her father arrives home within minutes of them, and his joy at seeing David overrides any obvious annoyance at her idiocy.

"Treat it as a learning experience. Lucky David arrived to sort you out!" he says.

Lou didn't expect sympathy. She hobbles toward the fridge and raids it for leftovers before making herself scarce.

Four

Hot light slants through the gaps between the curtains. Dawn has come and gone. Her body tired, Lou wakes slowly, surfacing in stages. Her muscles feel stiff, and a dry mouth reminds her of yesterday's stupidity.

Silence outside. Expertly, she wraps a blue sarong around herself, the same way the local women tie theirs. Wearing it reminds Lou of long-past holidays on the Kenyan coast and how it felt to be carefree.

The stone floor is warm underfoot as Lou searches the house to find no one home. Her brother and father have left without her. It's David's first day home, and she wishes they'd woken her. No sign of Grace either.

Lovely chilled air rolls out as Lou opens the fridge and helps herself to the water jug. *Where have the men gone?* Though her sleep-in has allowed her to recover, she's disappointed at being left behind. Grace is outside, where the passion-fruit vine is tangled on the fence around the vegetable patch. As Lou waves to try to attract her attention, Grace bends down and disappears below the fence line. Though it's an ongoing fight to keep the wildlife out, she always manages to coax vegetables out of the soil even during droughts.

"Zebu! Zeeeebu." Luckily, the dependable dog is always available for a cuddle and, within seconds, she emerges from her mango-tree den. While Zebu chews on a bone, Lou devours stringy mangos, glad that nobody's around to observe her poor manners. She'd rather be out with the others, but may as well return to her notes and make up for zero progress yesterday.

Lou sips the bitter coffee and forces herself to work, immediately engrossed as her thoughts return to Masaranga's elephants. Hours later, she looks up to find the sun already low. She's been totally absorbed. *Where is everyone?*

A quick search, and Lou finds David on their wide veranda. It overlooks a waterhole now busy with evening visitors. Impalas and Thompson's gazelles have congregated to drink. Zebu is snuggled up against David, taking advantage of his absent-minded pats. She senses Lou and spins around to greet her with a yawning whine and a downward-dog stretch.

Yesterday, when her vision was a bit hazy, David seemed well enough. Now, the impression is different, and it's not positive. Dark smudges underline his eyes, and, as she quickly hugs him, something new seems contained within them.

"Recovered?" he asks, with a wry smile.

Lou nods and grins. She wants to know what his new life is like.

"How are you? You didn't answer me yesterday. Are you OK?"

As if he'd tell her!

"As well as ever," he replies, non-committal as expected. Her confident brother briefly holds her questioning look. "Just got a lot to deal with right now. I'm working hard!"

"You look tired," she insists.

"Yep, I am. Could do with an early night, but Dad wants some company to check the southern waterhole tonight."

Lou nods abstractly and recalls how often she's asked to go on a night patrol. Her father always knocks her back. Already mild envy of David mixes with her pleasure of having him home.

"He won't take me!" she complains.

"I wish he'd leave me here tonight. Still, it's good he protects you."

"Protects me!"

"Come on, Lou, you know it's dangerous."

"I'm as good a shot as you."

"For someone so frightened of leaving Masaranga, you're oblivious to the dangers around you."

Lou wants to ask why he thinks she's frightened. But Zebu starts banging her tail on the deck and their father steps out.

"You ready? We need to leave," he says.

His hand rests on David's shoulder.

Lou smiles, glad to see them like this, despite her gripes.

"See you in the morning," she says.

Already, they're on their way. Her words bounce off their retreating backs as they head off across the dried-out lawn, the dog on their heels.

"Zebu, come back here!"

Too excited to behave, Zebu ignores her. Neither of the men notices as Lou runs to catch up and grabs her collar. Their Land Rover accelerates out of the compound. The ensuing dust cloud makes Zebu sneeze, before she plants an energetic doggy kiss on Lou's cheek. Lou giggles and holds her tight until the vehicle is out of sight. Another upside of David's visit is that father is cheerful now he's home. Her dad came out to Africa with high expectations but never envisioned his wife's dislike of the isolation. Left at home again by the men, Lou feels a twinge of sympathy for her mother, despite the way she deserted.

Semi-lucid dreams wake Lou in the early hours, and it's a relief to escape that dense dream-space, where her memories and imagination tangle. The stone floor is cold underfoot until Lou reaches the living room with its thick rugs and smells of leather and wood polish. The security lights are off, so she navigates by touch, past the old furniture, and lets herself out through the French doors. Outside, moonlight glints off the waterhole below. Lou waits until her eyes adjust to the night, and she can see the outlines of the valley floor. It's a touch eerie, but she's used to it. The silent African night feels entirely safe. Through her binoculars, she checks for wild animals.

The present drought forces the animals to come to water left in deeper waterholes. It makes them easier to locate, which exacerbates the threat from poachers. Partly hidden in the dense shadows below is a creature Lou can't identify, perhaps a jackal or a similarly shy nocturnal animal. She hasn't yet worked out why elephants hardly use this watering spot. Only occasionally, even in this drought, does thirst force them to visit. But from here, she never sees them let their guard down and play. They're wary, as if old memories of the place are stored in their genes. Lou wonders if the elephants were heavily hunted from this vantage before the area was protected. Was that knowledge passed on through the generations? As the old adage says, elephants never forget.

Long before Masaranga became a national park, this part of Africa was elephant country. The more data Lou collects for her thesis, the more she understands the way man's maps and borders have been detrimental and restricted the elephants' ability to find not only enough to eat but also the right mix of food. Her interviews with village elders leave Lou surprised by the speed of change. Like many other animals, elephants relied on migration channels, but, as Africa tamed down, ancient migration paths used for centuries have been cut off.

Fences and farms block off wild bushland as the human population expands exponentially, and people encroach on the last elephant habitat. By the time Lou finishes her research, there will be even fewer places left for them to survive. Along with the earlier decimation of elephants by white hunters for their treasured ivory, it's no surprise the last of the gentle giants are under such threat.

In days past, the savannah's balanced ecosystem supported generations of elephants. They spread seeds over vast distances. Their calves learned the ropes from the grown-ups and graduated through the matriarchy. As sentient beings with complex social networks, elephant families are similar to those of humans. The teenagers learn both their roles and the migration routes from the elders, the knowledge handed down from one generation to the next.

Once, Lou observed an elephant revisit the place where her elder sister had died a year before after ingesting toxic bacteria from a soupy waterhole. The elephant gently touched the old bones with the sensitive tip of her trunk as if remembering and paying respect for her lost companion. It was a special experience for Lou and confirmed other records that elephants have long memories of the birth and death events of their own kind.

Lou makes a mental note to search old records and discover what went on at this home waterhole. For practical reasons, her research is usually focused inside Masaranga, whose boundaries have become almost physical barriers to elephant movement. She has been recording how such confines affect the herds' ability to survive, and their effect on the elephants' emotional well-being.

Even in modern times, a trophy hunter would consider this vantage point as no more than a prime spot from which to shoot. There are still people who have not evolved mentally from the days of colonial rule when men postured in safari jackets, over gin and tonics, bragging about the creatures they'd killed. Lou can almost hear them.

"Jolly good show what! A perfectly splendid set of tusks to mount, old chap!"

Nowadays, grasping trophy hunters rely on the ego boost of the kill. The women who cling to the hunters have their own self-interested motives. What do those fly-in people know of the real Africa? They've never seen how elephants greet each other after being separated, their joyful trumpeting at finding each other again. In their ignorance, those people are unaware of how elephants form the same social bonds as humans. Either that or they just don't care.

It's arrogant for humans to imagine themselves as the only self-aware beings. To do so fails to credit elephants for their emotional life and sentience. Like humans, elephants learn as they come up through the ranks. They are continually forced to adapt and survive experiences of persecution and restricted boundaries created by mankind. To make the situation even worse, even where the wildlife is protected, it's rarely safe. Modern poachers are so well armed. Colonial invaders supplied the weaponry for the corrupt to take up the plunder where they left off.

The Africans who grew up in the bush are the only ones who really understand what it means to live so close to wildlife. They are the ones who once fitted chameleon-like into the country. Their reality has more relevance than those past and present invaders who consider the territory theirs to pillage. So much water has gone under the bridge, the damage irreparable. Lou hopes the time has come to stop the losses and save what's left.

Kenya was given back to her people when she became independent twenty-five years ago, in 1963. That year was also Lou's year of birth, though she was born elsewhere. Strangely, the matching of dates makes her feel an irrational affinity for the country. It's an illogical whim of her making, but Lou feels part of the country and it's where her life began. Her memories originate here, but she's a guest rather than a citizen. Not being born in Kenya is why she can't safely envisage a future in this country, where her heart will always remain. This dislocation seems to have lodged in her psyche, and it always drives her right along.

Though the night is warm, Lou pulls her nightshirt more tightly around her shoulders. Outlines of trees emerge along the water's edge as her eyes adjust to night vision. She likes the idea of being the only person awake for miles. Remnants of her waking dream filter back into her mind, where she struggled to talk to her mother in another place and time. But her words got lost in the space between them. She's glad to have woken and escaped from the dream. It's so serene and quiet here, and she can safely watch the creatures of the night.

Five

"Hey, David, do you remember that shady camping spot?" Lou asks, over a period of days.

She makes sure to drop enough hints to remind him how much fun it is to go on safari.

"How about a campout on the Lumbawa River?" he suggests one afternoon while they're repairing the door on a wildlife hide.

"Great idea!" Lou agrees, and before he can backtrack or change his mind, she starts preparations. He suggests the shady campsite under some huge old trees where they've camped before. It's an obvious choice considering the drought.

It's a day's drive, and, on their arrival, Lou prepares dinner while Peter and David set up camp in the clearing above a sandy riverbank. From this campsite, the track disintegrates into animal trails. They erect tents close to the Land Rover for safety should wild animals come in search of food. Too often, tourists break the no-feeding-the-animals rule and create a nuisance for the next group of campers. Baboons can be dangerous and frightening when they're accustomed to free handouts.

But a different nuisance wakes Lou. During the night, a thorn punctures her sleeping mat and it slowly leaks air. She manages to ignore the discomfort of the hardening surface until the ground-chill seeps insistently into her sleep. Half-awake, she drifts in and out of consciousness, readjusting her hips against the cold earth. Her dream takes her down below the ocean's icy surface, deeper and deeper, until she's out of air. Suddenly jolted back to reality, Lou gasps a lungful of air. The content of the dream surprises her as it's unlike any other she's experienced. *It's years since I've seen the ocean, so where did that come from?*

After a restless night, Lou wakes to orange light filtered by her tent. From the treetops, birds announce the dawn. It's a relief to escape her nightly demons.

She crawls from her tent and stretches her cramped muscles. Close by, Peter crouches over the beginnings of a fire as he coaxes a yellow flame up through the kindling. Thin spirals rise from the crackling twigs, and their wood-smoke puts Lou at ease as she watches Peter balance a saucepan of water over the flames.

Defying the chilly night, the sun climbs into an inevitably cloudless sky, its fierce rays deceptively beautiful as they penetrate the canopy and dapple the leafy forest floor. Delighted by these patterns, Lou watches the shafts of yellow dance across the clearing. Soon, unrelenting heat will infiltrate even this shade.

A quick smile from Peter. He's pleased with the fire. His skin gleams dark and wet from an early morning wash on the riverbank. Lou can't believe she failed to hear him collect wood and water. Perhaps she slept for longer than it felt.

"Good morning, Peter. You're very quiet out there!"

"Yes, that way, I see more."

He means more wildlife. Suddenly, Lou wishes she'd also got up earlier.

"What did you see?"

An astute accomplice makes all the difference. Peter knows this country and its creatures well from his childhood spent in the bush. Also, he often borrows her reference material, unlike others, who fail to use such opportunities. Peter has an incredible sense of the savanna. He may laugh at her collections of scats, but he can match them to the right species.

Lou shares everything she knows with Peter, and she ensures his access to more, to equip him to look after Masaranga. His prospects of being part of the country's future far outweigh hers. She also wants to be a part of it, but her chances are slim as she's considered an outsider, neither born here nor a citizen. This recent insight depresses her. She was so young when her family moved from England that she hardly remembers it. Kenya is her only real home, but the chances are she won't be allowed to stay forever.

"A leopard came through in the night!" says Peter. On the edge of the clearing, he crouches to examine the red dirt, the flames behind him forgotten. The earth is cold under her bare feet as Lou hurries past the boiling pot toward the pawprints that disappear into thicker vegetation where the ground slopes toward the slow-moving river. The claws are retracted, so they don't belong to a cheetah, and they're too small for a lion.

The fact that a leopard has passed by doesn't worry Lou. Probably it's after an antelope and would avoid the dangers posed by humans. Peter could help her track it.

"Peter, could you …"

"I followed a short way earlier. We can try after Bwana David wakes up."

A thrill of excitement passes through Lou. Leopards are elusive and hard to spot. She hurries to get ready and puts shoes on before she wakes David. Only yesterday, he criticized her for going native. Strange, as they both used to go barefoot before he left to become a city slicker.

"Yes, I'm awake. Stop shaking the tent!" David sounds cheerful despite his complaint. "I'm just lying here, listening to the sounds. I'd forgotten how good it is to wake with the birds!"

"There's plenty of stuff you seem to have forgotten," says Lou, glad he seems happy back out in the wilderness.

They skip breakfast, and Peter leads them off, a rifle slung over his shoulder. He follows the prints into the dense riverine scrub. They duck and weave behind him, their progress slow.

"Many times, this leopard stops! Maybe she's hunting," Peter whispers over his shoulder. For some reason, he's deduced that the cat is female. For one hundred meters, they clamber over fallen logs on the sandy riverbank until again impeded by the dense vegetation. They push sideways up the bank from there through narrow gaps in the bush, occasionally stopping to talk in low voices. When they start again, twigs snap underfoot and branches swoosh back into place behind them.

As Lou scrapes past spiky bushes, thick thorns jab her. Her skin prickles, and her shirt is soaked. She's thirsty, but the prospect of a glimpse of the leopard spurs her on. Some of the signs that Peter finds are easy to see, occasionally even a paw print. But other clues he discovers with a sense

Lou seems not to own. Ahead of her, David is panting from the exertion. He's no longer lean and fit like he used to be.

They stop for Peter to examine the ground, then backtrack. Tiny duiker antelopes hide in the bushes, invisible until they take fright and explode into flight right next to them. Lou can't help but jump away, even though there's no danger.

From upstream comes the sound of branches snapping, perhaps a bolder animal, less in need of concealment. A loud crack halts them. Instinctively, Lou crouches. Ahead of her, Peter cranes forwards, hands cupped behind his ears to listen for trouble. For a few long minutes, they wait.

"Buffalo, I think," Peter whispers over his shoulder.

"Are you sure?" says Lou.

Hopefully, he's wrong. Lou listens intently. How close would it be, and is it approaching them? She imagines it enormous and bad-tempered.

Peter beckons and swings his rifle off his shoulder. They move sideways down the riverbank to better see their surroundings. With the leopard trail forgotten, they step out from the thicket onto the sandy riverbank. The river is a mere trickle, but its water is clean. From its banks, there's a line of sight toward the disturbance.

A set of black horns pushes out of the scrub ahead. Instinctively, Lou takes a couple of steps backward along the river, aware of her boots sticking in the damp sand. Ahead, a buffalo emerges and immediately spots them.

They freeze. A rifle shot might scare it off. Lou's heart begins to race. The massive head and curling horns lift higher, and the glistening muzzle twitches to test the air. Then the bull snorts, a noisy bad-tempered sound.

"Don't move!" says Peter as Lou takes another step backward.

"It's cranky!" she whispers, obeying him.

But the buffalo seems to assess an absence of danger. He steps confidently right out of the thicket and crosses the sand to a pool of water. One eye on them, he drinks greedily. They're close enough to see his muscular neck rippling as he swallows. Sunlight reflects off the water droplets on his wet muzzle. He snorts again and abruptly retreats along the bank. His hooves kick up sand as he crashes through the bush, and briefly comes back into sight at the top of the bank. Then he's gone. Today, he has no reason to challenge them, no herd to guard. Suddenly, they're all grinning at each other. Peter slings the rifle back over his shoulder.

"You want to go back to the leopard trail, Bwana?" he asks David.

"Better not. Could be another buffalo close. Anyhow it's too hot now."

Lou is glad of his decision, though it's out of character with the old David. City life has drained his willpower. She hopes this new brother is not permanent. Yesterday he accused her of being overly resistant to change. It's not something she's ever considered. Does he have a point? She scowled and failed to find a suitably cutting reply. But despite his criticism, it's good to have her sparring partner home.

When they return to headquarters, her father is restless and preoccupied, though he jokes with her brother over several sundowner whiskeys. David laughs a lot and seems not to notice their father's distraction. Though both are incredibly practical, they can be emotionally detached and abstracted in other areas.

Lou understands the fragility of their position. There's evidence all around that her father may be forced out. Nearby, colonial landowners are also being forced to relinquish their farms. But it's not as if his position resembles that of a landholder farmer. He looks after Masaranga's wild country for everyone. Someday, they will have to leave all this, but right now, they must hold tight like limpets clinging to rocks. She wonders how long they will be able to resist Kenya's changing currents and turbulent waters. Sensible others have already let go and joined the flow downstream to new lives. Lou finds it hard to envisage life elsewhere, and there's so much to do here. Until Masaranga is again a haven for wild animals, she wants to stay and protect this precious stretch of wilderness.

David's line of conversation along these topics exasperates and frightens Lou. He's unusually defeatist and convinced their days here are at an end. It's true the manager's position will eventually go to a local, but surely not just yet?

Six

On a shadowy bend of the river, the leopard drops from a high bough, silent apart from the soft thud as her pads hit the sandy ground. Her sleek form remains still as her emerald eyes search the terrain for movement. She listens for the faintest rustle in the undergrowth. Self-indulgent people deceive themselves when they purchase a pelt like hers as, inevitably, they fail to capture that natural elegance. When they grasp at that wild beauty, they only destroy what they hope to seconder.

A gnawing hunger has this leopard on the hunt earlier than usual. She needs to fill her belly with meat to feed her three young cubs. So far this time, she's lost none to predators. This second litter benefited from her previous attempt at motherhood when none of her kittens survived the first few weeks.

She hears the dik-dik push through bushes downstream, though she can't yet see it. The cautious antelope smells water but not the leopard. On slender legs, he takes a couple of dainty steps out onto the riverbank and stops to again check for danger. But he's upwind and unaware of the leopard as she watches him, utterly still, her dappled spots blending with the shadows.

More confident now, the dik-dik drops his head to drink. He's thirsty, and his field of vision is reduced. Stealthily, the leopard shifts position. Her attack is fast and silent. Flattened close on the ground, she twists sinuously through the undergrowth, and hardly disturbs the vegetation.

Suddenly unsure, the dik-dik freezes, his eyes wide and aware, and then, on tiny hooves, takes a few quick steps towards cover. He feels exposed in the bright sunlight of the open bank, but his intuition comes too late to save him from the final rush. The leopard startles him as she lands hard on his back, knocking the breath from him, her teeth already sunk deep in his neck.

The leopard holds on until the antelope's eyes dilate and dull, and his body loses rigidity. As the cat waits, she watches for other predators or scavengers that might have heard his short, terrified gasp. She's afraid her meal might be stolen.

Unchallenged, she drags the carcass up the riverbank to a tree. With a single leap of incredible strength, she hoists the body several meters up to the first fork. Ravenous, she gulps down her first meal in days, still watching for competitors. By the time she returns to the den, this feast will have made her stronger, and the rest will feed her hungry cubs.

The drought has forced her from her usual territory to hunt along Masaranga's boundary. Her belly heavy and her body slow, the leopard chooses a direct route back to her den, and she skirts a new maize plot that encroaches the park boundary.

Its devious owner has surreptitiously expanded his farm, planting an extra few rows each season, so it protrudes into the park. He's cunning and keeps a gun, partly because he mistrusts his neighbors, but also to kill unsuspecting creatures that venture too close.

Today as he relaxes by his back door, with a view across his expanding land, he wishes something exciting would happen. All alone, as is often the case, he's bored. To pass the time, he daydreams about making love to his neighbor's young daughter, who has recently grown a tantalizing set of breasts. He's sure she sets out to deliberately lure him; why else would she walk past so often in her cute little dresses?

For a moment, when he glimpses the spotted pelt in the scrub, he can hardly believe his eyes. But, wily and quick, he never lets a chance pass. From a life lived close to easy poaching, he's a practiced shot.

When the leopard reappears in a gap between the vegetation, he's ready for her. She's exposed for half a second, just long enough. A single bullet explodes through the air, and her body briefly suspends in shock. She twists unnaturally and falls to the ground.

The man moves quickly. He must haul the cat back to his house before his neighbors get wind of what he's killed and demand a piece of the action. If they ask, he'll lie that it was a mousebird. Nevertheless, his elation runs high; he knows exactly where to sell the leopard's pelt for an excellent price. He also has a Nairobi contact who will love those long feline canines.

Seven

Early in the day, a party of photographers visits headquarters, and Lou takes them over to see the home waterhole.

"Wow, some view!" they agree in unison and immediately become busy. One couple starts to boast about their wildlife experiences. Others put their cameras to use. Above, a hawk passes by in search of rodents only visible to sharp eyes.

"Can you mark the best viewing-hides and waterholes on our map?" Their leader speaks with a drawl. "Between us, we've enough camera gear to solve this country's debt problem!"

Lou smiles at him and wishes they would. She discusses the plight of the elephants and adds hints on how they could spread the word. Her intent is not to sound fanatical and bore them or spoil their experience. Somehow, the welfare of wildlife must touch their hearts. Perhaps, after they've collected photographic records, a few might want to save the real animals. Genuine involvement might inspire them more than just taking the images home. If they knew the truth, they might feel able to help.

Lou would appreciate some sort of help. She's always exhausted, and time never stretches enough for what must be done to safeguard Masaranga's wildlife. The constant threat from poachers pushes her long past when she should stop. If only she felt more at peace with the world, but her mind continuously tracks ahead, dragging her toward the unknown. It seems crucial to be occupied and useful. Ingrained within her is the expectation that if she keeps up the pace, then, eventually, things must resolve. Only then will life be less painful.

Another tangle of dreams occupies her sleep, her night filled by disconnected, nonsensical scenes that lack clarity. Lou wakes from a vista of vast plains, dotted with gazelles. A pride of lions prowls among the herds. Two Masai warriors stride across the grassland, dressed in traditional reds, with long spears held ready. They have a long walk ahead to reach the edge of the plains and safer territory. Reluctant to lose the images, Lou comes conscious slowly, unsure whether she was accompanying the warriors or whether she was one of them.

Today her brother needs a ride into Nairobi, a fact he sprang on her last night. As a little more warning would have been handy, frustration with David displaces the dream, and Lou loses her awareness of its space. The vista merges with the savannah in her elephant painting. With the warriors gone, her thoughts take precedence, and she's disappointed to return to familiar surroundings.

At least a few hours on the road might provide time enough to talk to David. Apart from their campout on the river, his stay has been short and busy. Lou has resolved not to complain about the brevity of his visit nor to pry about his life, though she's sad Masaranga now occupies such a small part of it.

"Morning, sis!"

Unlike her, David rarely feels afflicted by the morning blues. As he overtakes her in the corridor, she gets a quick, supposedly comforting squeeze of her shoulder, before he hurries energetically ahead, past paintings of wildebeests and buffaloes. Once, she'd have told him her dream, but not after yesterday's advice.

"Stop dissecting everything! You ponder life too much," he'd said. "It's a waste of time and drags you down!"

"Maybe the dreams tell you stuff you need to know."

Around him, she's quick to defend herself.

He rolled his eyes in an expression of amused disdain.

"Dreams are just your brain getting rid of stuff. You always let your imagination get the better of you!"

He seems to judge her harshly, and Lou tries not to take it to heart. Is she equally quick to cast aspersions? Perhaps so, though she sincerely hopes not. In any case, it doesn't matter as she's almost fallen off his radar. But does he have to leave so soon? He's only been home a week, and she's going to miss him.

"Why so long-faced?" he asks as she sits at the breakfast table.

"There's no one much to talk to when you're gone."

"A loner's choice to stay here all the time!"

"I can't leave while we're losing so many elephants."

"And you think your presence makes any difference?"

The probable accuracy of his statement stings, just as it hurts to see him act so detached from the crisis.

"But you could stay; that might help!"

Lou doesn't mean to sound so angry, but, anyhow, he hardly notices.

"I doubt it. Dad's got rangers to patrol the place."

Perhaps David is right. So far, her presence has made little difference. Lou fights back the tears as she tries to disguise her disillusion. That's best kept under wraps.

"What time do you have to be in Nairobi?" she asks.

"My plane for Mombasa leaves early tomorrow, so we have all day! Sara's invited us to stay. You can drive home fresh in the morning after you off-load me."

Why hasn't David told her his plan before? He must have a group of tourists to accompany on the coast. A visit to Sara is not a bad idea, but she'd have appreciated being asked earlier. Her brother is often like that now, entirely on his own trip and forgetting to inform others. But, anyhow, she remembers liking Sara, and a visit to her acreage on Nairobi's outskirts sounds exciting. She wonders if Sara's daughters still live with her.

"Carla or Lexi likely to be there at the moment?"

"Lexi is popular and has a fancy apartment now. She rarely goes home. Not sure about her sister. You want to stay there?"

"Yes, of course. I'll tell Dad."

"He already knows."

"Thanks for not letting me know sooner!"

"Well, you don't have to stay. It's your choice."

Of course she'll stay with Sara! With David's help around headquarters this last week, Lou is up to date on her thesis. By his judgment, she's not useful here in any case. She tells Grace, who hugs her tightly and says, "Good. I look after Bwana, and you enjoy to visit friends!"

"I'm only away overnight!" Lou replies. "Do you remember Sara?"

"Yes, I remember Sara and her girls. You were together here, many years ago. You were like this!"

Palm down, arm outstretched, Grace measures her memory of Lou's height on that occasion, but Lou can't recall it. Sometime, she must ask Grace for more and retrieve some memories. Others she'd rather avoid, like her years at boarding school. Not that university life was fantastic either. Institutions make her feel like an alien, and she hates city life. Perhaps she's just downright weird, but the wilderness seems more worthwhile. Elsewhere is noisy and crowded, a congested version of reality.

"Come on. We've got a couple of stops on the way." Pausing at her bedroom door, David tries to hurry Lou up while she throws an overnight bag together.

"I've only just discovered your plans! What sort of stops?" says Lou, but he's already off. She hears him shout goodbye to Grace on his way out.

David wants to drive, which suits Lou. He skillfully negotiates the roughly sealed road that drops along the Rift Valley toward Nairobi. She knows the route well from her many trips to the university. Many of the potholes have merged after years of disrepair. Her brother drives fast and manages to avoid the worst. Occasionally, he swerves to miss errant traffic approaching on the wrong side of the road. Lou knows not to complain about his speed and annoy him. Despite her concerns, she has to admit that the drive, with the dust-free wind against her arms, makes a welcome change from Masaranga's dirt tracks. She's surprised to feel her spirits lifting.

Eight

The outskirts of Nairobi at last, although Lou always feels overwhelmed by the multitudes crowded along the streets. Kenya must have been a scary and dangerous place when the Mau Mau uprising raged. After the rebellion, when independence was granted, Kenyatta became president. That was twenty-five years ago in 1963. Lou was born in March that year and often she wishes it had been in Kenya.

Fortunately, David knows the intricacies of these back streets. Alone, Lou would be lost out here. Life seems safer at Masaranga, far away from the densely packed city. She likes the natural order of the bush, where every creature plays its part. On this busy road, amidst the impoverished throngs, she feels exposed and uneasy.

"Nearly there?" Lou tries to keep the concern from her voice. With the sun headed toward the horizon, it's not a good time to get lost. She's frightened of being caught after nightfall out on this poorly lit edge of town.

"Yup." David's focus is on avoiding potholes and people, and he's strangely unfazed by the crowds.

His lack of concern should comfort her, and his casual reply does settle her nerves somewhat. However, Lou is less reassured than she'd once have been. He was unforthcoming when she asked about his Mombasa assignment, so Lou is left to guess he has visitors to show around. She won't ask again.

"Ah, here we are!"

Abruptly, David swings the steering wheel hard left and narrowly makes the turn.

A gang of youths leaps sideways off the road. Simultaneously, Lou is flung against the door, her thigh taking the impact.

"Careful!" She grabs the seat. Outside, the young men laugh and hang on to each other for balance. They stare into the Land Rover, curious to see who almost ran them over. Lou is amazed that they don't seem angry.

"Sorry, sis." David grins recklessly. Lou rubs her thigh and smiles.

This final stretch of road is off the main suburban route, past the ornate gates of upmarket compounds. It's less crowded and quieter, and Lou's spirits rise at the familiar landmarks. Finally, the flower-laden branches of the enormous jacaranda tree by the entrance to Sara's compound. Inside, bright purple and pink bougainvillea flowers hang off dense spiky bushes.

Immediately, a guard leaps down from a shelter inside the gates. He hurries to the entrance and raises his hand to greet them. After a quick glance into the car, he swings the curled metal railings open. Behind him, two energetic Dobermans bound back and forth. Sleek and shiny coated, they bark at the car, while their stumpy tails wag vigorously. The moment David pulls up at Sara's house, Lou jumps out to pat the dogs, but sharp Swahili commands from the guard banish them to their quarters. They trot away, their enthusiasm dampened. Lou is sad to see their muscled haunches disappear around the back of the house.

The massive wooden front door opens, and Sam, the houseboy, flashes them an even-toothed smile and then hurries away to find the memsahib. Lou catches her brother's eye and grins happily. They used to be inseparable when their isolation made them fellow adventurers. In those earlier carefree days, their exploits taught them a lot about the bush.

"The twins. How wonderful! It's been a long time, Lou." Sara's smile is warm, and her hair is bleached blonde from the sun. She often travels to the coast to buy antiques from Mombasa traders. Suddenly, Lou glimpses how attractive her host must once have been. Sara was born and raised in Kenya, which makes her and her equally blonde daughters all citizens. Lou envies them for their right to build their entire lives out here. She's reminded that her father's long-term position is tenuous.

Sara sweeps Lou up in a hug, which takes her by surprise. It's ages since anyone but Grace has done this. David gave it up long ago, and Lou has no memory of her father hugging anyone. She holds on for a few extra seconds, stepping back awkwardly as she realizes Sara has let her go.

"Garden looks fantastic!" As usual, David sounds confident and entirely at home. "You're a miracle worker. Such colors in a drought!" he adds cheekily.

"Just a matter of knowing your desert plants, David." Sara winks at Lou as if she understands David's disinclination to notice details.

"Never know, it might rain tonight! Save a week's water supply on the flowers." David overdoes the banter.

Lou follows his glance toward the darkening sky, still empty of clouds, and then instinctively checks their hostess. Why does David have to be so rude? But Sara shows no signs of any offense; to survive out here alone, she can't afford to be oversensitive.

"Anyone for gin and tonic?" asks Sara, and then switches to Swahili to send Sam for drinks. She strides decisively ahead of them, and a quick flick of her chin indicates they should follow through to the living room. They walk under the whoosh of ceiling fans, past wall-hangings that depict stylized African figures. Heavy wooden doors fold outward and Sara leads them out onto the elegant old veranda with carved furniture.

Below them, a wealthy Nairobi suburb stretches across sparsely vegetated hillslopes. All around are high fences, mostly topped with strands of barbed wire. Lou thinks of the patchy half-wall of bougainvillea around Masaranga's headquarters. It's all they've ever needed as protection from wildlife.

When the drinks arrive, the cold ice soothes Lou as much as the shot of gin. After the long drive down the Rift Valley and through Nairobi, it's a relief to have arrived. She watches the bands of light change across the sky as the sun sinks toward a horizon streaked red and orange. The intense heat diminishes, and the air softens. The drink eases Lou's concerns and her mind loses focus as her thoughts wander from one thing to another.

David inquires after Sara's daughters, and an irrational pang of misgiving surprises Lou. Carla always seemed genuine and engaging, but now Lou guesses her sister, Lexi, is part of the reason her brother comes home so infrequently. This unwelcome insight slams into Lou's awareness. Instinctively, she prefers Carla. However, it's been a while.

Her secretive brother tends to scatter false clues when interest is paid to his personal life. Now, as Lou focuses briefly, she guesses he's hung up on Lexi and has passed over her more interesting and appealing sister. Hopefully, she's wrong. Lou lets her thoughts meander around this possibility until David starts to discuss an upcoming trip with the sisters.

"Why don't you come to Mombasa?" David suddenly asks her. "You need a break as well, Lou. You've got far too serious!"

Lou raises her eyebrows, non-committal, and then notices Sara's interest in her response. Sheepishly, Lou smiles. She does need to become more sociable.

"I'd love to go," Lou hears herself reply. "Is it true you can dive the reef now?" She talks fast to cover her awkwardness and experiences an unexpected rush of anticipation.

"Why not just snorkel?" Sara asks.

"Why weight yourself down with all that diving gear?" David shakes his head derisively.

"My ears give me hell when I free dive!" Lou replies.

As well as stretched eardrums, intense pain from compressed sinuses are embedded memories for Lou from years ago whenever she tried to duck-dive down toward the sandy ocean floor. She gave up, only to watch David drop deep below the surface without apparent effort or discomfort. Even back then, Lou fantasized how it would be to swim freely down below the surface.

Sam returns carrying an antique tray, loaded with chinking ice-cubes and gin straight from the fridge. The bottle glistens with condensation as it hovers above her glass. Lou briefly considers sticking to tonic water on the second round but relents and accepts a generous splash of gin. To hell with it! She's rarely sociable, and she senses an ally in Sara. There seems to be no need to feel wary inside the safety of her house. The drink tastes quinine-tangy and delicious as Lou watches the shadows lengthen across the slopes until the last arc of the sun slips below the plains beyond the edge of town.

Dinner is cold game meat from a shooting reserve with home-grown salad and avocado. It's not the first time Lou has eaten antelope meat from a managed hunting block. There, at least, there's money to properly manage the wildlife and keep poachers out, perhaps a reasonable trade-off.

"My brother manages the hunting block," says Sara. "He complains that elsewhere, dishonest managers use legitimate channels to sell illegal goods. The crooked spoil what should be a workable system."

"Do they shoot elephants on the hunting block?" Lou asks tentatively.

"Not sure. I'd rather not ask as the idea upsets me too much!" replies Sara.

"They'd have to. The blocks need to pay for themselves. They're run like businesses," says David. The idea doesn't seem abhorrent to him.

The meat is lean and tender, sliced thinly, and well salted. It tastes better than beef. Cattle are poorly adapted to the harsh climate in comparison to the wild animals that evolved here.

Lou detests the idea of rich men shooting game as a sport. As if you can call it a competition when the men have the guns and the animals are labelled as dangerous should they defend themselves! With corruption and poverty rampant, Lou can't decide how best to protect wildlife.

"Do you remember those clients, who were caught in a park near a hunting block. They'd shot a rhino," she asks Sara.

"Of course. That particular incident was over the newspapers for days," replies Sara.

"What happened in the end? Were they charged?"

"Oh, it was all hushed over! No doubt, the right money put in the right pockets."

One school of thought is that practicality must override distaste for killing wildlife. Lou understands the logic of compromise, and the land does remain more productive when grazed by wildlife rather than cattle.

"That's impala. The darker meat is waterbuck," says Sara.

Lou dutifully takes a piece of the thicker dark meat and compliments her host.

"Can't understand why they don't farm the wildlife," says David as he tucks into his steak.

"They cull the antelope when their numbers increase beyond the land's capacity to support them. It's much the same as farming," replies Sara. She too is practical.

"How's your antique business going?" Lou switches subjects.

"Busier than ever. Plenty of people selling up and moving out or being forced out. They often sell beautiful old pieces they can't transport halfway around the world. It's sad for them, but it keeps me busy. However, the supply won't last forever. I'm already starting to trade in modern carvings and—"

Outside, one of the dogs barks noisily from the darkness. Lou hears a frantic shout from the far side of the yard. Sam comes running through the house. His feet slap on the stone floors. His voice is agitated, the Swahili so rapid Lou can't keep up. Something about the dogs and a call for security.

They hurry after Sam through half-lit rooms. Lou's vision swirls as she runs through the shadows behind the kitchen toward the kerfuffle. In the torchlight, one Dobermann still barks furiously. The other lies in the dirt. His body is kicking, shaking and twitching. He starts to convulse. As Sara squats by the dog, his limbs stiffen, and his body becomes a hard mass of clenched tissue. Saliva drips from the pulled-back lips. Lou kneels by Sara and puts her head low on the dog's chest, where the heart should beat, and listens. All she hears is a muffled gurgle. Under her hands, the muscles lose some of their stiffness. As the final convulsion subsides, the dog becomes motionless.

A few seconds of silence ensue and then a rapid interchange in Swahili between Sara and Sam.

"What's happened to the dog?" Lou interjects, unable to follow.

"He says poisoning, but I'm not so sure." Sara's voice sounds thick as she chokes back tears. "Poor, poor Kaiser. He's the quiet one of the two." Then, suddenly, Sara turns away from the dog and calls out. "Hapa, hapa (here, here)."

Torch beams approach from the driveway. Through the disorientation of the gin, Lou experiences a pang of terror. First the dead dog, and now lights that bear down on them. For a moment, she wants to run for cover and bolt back into the house.

Khaki uniforms materialize from behind the torchlights. Insanely relieved, Lou remembers the residents here share security guards. Sam must have set off the alarm the moment he sensed danger. Otherwise, they'd never have arrived so fast on foot. The guards are fit, muscular Africans, their guns held mid-shaft, barrels pointing at the black sky. Sara speaks with them, and her voice's natural authority takes control of the situation. She suggests a snake is responsible, not a person, though she agrees Kaiser could have been poisoned. Who would the culprit be? Kaiser was a healthy-looking Doberman only hours ago. The guards look to Sara for instructions and automatically agree with her. Their torches sweep the ground all around as shafts of yellow light search the compound for a snake.

Nobody pays attention to Kaiser now. Kneeling again, Lou feels compelled to touch his face. Her hand moves quickly away from the wet saliva to the chest area. She runs it over the sleek, soft coat. The still-warm dog feels almost alive. All around Lou are loud voices, though the other dog has finally stopped barking. Sensing the danger over, he wags his tail stump and assumes Lou has squatted down to fuss over him. He pushes his face against her and looks up, his eyes hopeful as if he's not yet aware his companion has gone. Lou rubs his face with her spare hand, feeling the same sleek coat. Absently, she thinks a snake would be long gone now; too much noise and too many feet stomping around, vibrating the ground. No snake would stick around so much activity.

Sara slips the guards a few extra shillings for their rapid response and sends them home. The two men smile happily, their white teeth flashing briefly in the muted light. They've been well rewarded for the false alarm—a better outcome than having to deal with a real break-in or attack.

The men gone, Sara again squats by her dead dog. Now practicalities have been dealt with, silent tears run down her cheeks.

"Good alarm system!" David comments, his eyes on the departing guards.

"The last time the security guards came was a break-in. Luckily, I was in bed, in the barred section of the house. The guards arrived just as the thugs got in!" Sara's voice has cleared. Her arm around Lou, she steers them back into the house. Lou feels shamed by her own lack of coping skills. Why is she so upset? Kaiser wasn't even her dog.

"Things have got a lot worse in Nairobi of late," says Sara. Back on the veranda, she pours them another drink without asking. "Have a look at the extra precautions I've taken inside."

They follow her down a corridor towards the bedrooms. An internal gate of iron bars barricades off the sleeping quarters.

"If intruders collect enough of value from the house, they're less likely to hurt anyone back here. Otherwise, they're quick to use their knives."

Lou envisages burglars in the night wielding the curved blades of sharp steel, the pangas customarily used for harvesting maize. It's well known that people are often carved up by those blades, but Lou is shocked to see how close Sara lives to that reality.

Perhaps they live closer to such dangers, even in the bush, than her father lets on. He reckons that sort of savagery only occurs close to suburbia and that life is safe in Masaranga, as long as you take precautions and have respect for the wild animals. Though a black mamba could be the culprit, Lou knows Kaiser would have to threaten it first. A snake kills in self-defense or to eat. People are different enough to feel hate and act on it.

"You don't think Kaiser was poisoned?" Lou asks.

"No," replies Sara. "He's killed many snakes in his time; never could leave them alone." Sara grins ruefully at the memory, her distress well disguised. "David, could you help Sam move Kaiser down the back. We'll dig a hole in the morning." Sara's ability to suppress sentimentality is impressive, and Lou admires her strength.

The food on the table no longer appeals to Lou. When David returns, he sits down and munches on the last slices of meat. They watch as he eats in silence, chewing and swallowing, cleaning up the remains. Lou thinks about their future out here. She wonders where they'll all end up, and if Sara will see her days out, sleeping in a bedroom barred off from the main house. Lou feels safe but imprisoned as Sara shows them their rooms on the safe end of the corridor. This event reflects only a small part of life and Lou doesn't want to view Africa negatively because of it. She's sure it will all seem better tomorrow in the bright light of another day, but it will be a relief to return home

Nine

A ripple of fear runs through the wildebeests as they become aware of the predator—a man hidden on the edge of the dry plains. Moments later, the herd stampedes, the disturbance radiating out from the source of danger as the wildebeests flee. As hooves hammer against the hard ground, a wall of dust rises across the plain.

The poacher silently curses and ducks back undercover. He wants to hide from the animals but also because hunting is prohibited here. The brainless wildebeests must have spotted him. Furious with them, he listens to the noise from the herd as panic travels from the nearest wildebeest to the next, and the following, faster than a vehicle could travel this rough terrain.

The mother that set off the stampede pushes her gangly calf ahead of her and shields him with her body. Mother and calf move as one with their typical ungainly gallop. The man considers using them as target practice.

Incensed by the easily spooked mother that started the alarm, the poacher raises his gun to line her up and then her calf. As far as he's concerned, the dumb animals can go to hell. He could shoot them without remorse but manages to restrain himself. His gunshot could give him away unnecessarily. He's entered Masaranga illegally and does not want to be caught here with his firearms and a pile of ammunition. Besides, he considers the wildebeests valueless, of use neither as trophies nor food. The money from past poaching trips already stocks his fridge with food more appealing than a stringy wildebeest calf.

Frustrated, the poacher rubs the scar on his leg as he watches the panic and bides his time. The dimwitted animals have probably warned the elephant of his presence. He anticipates far greater rewards than meat, and his hunger is for more out of life than it has so far delivered. On his last trip, he scored two pairs of tusks and sold them to a slippery acquaintance, a man he despises, who probably sold them on for several times his price.

Often now, the poacher schemes to bypass the fat-cat middlemen, who profit from his hard work and the hazards he faces. But, as yet, he's not connected enough to grease palms and transport the illegal merchandise, the black ivory, out of the country. This thought causes bitter resentment to rise like bile in his throat, and his jaw tightens. It's he who risks his life out in this harsh terrain doing the dirty work. The hardest job of the whole black-market operation is to shoot the elephants. He's the one who runs the gauntlet and is most likely to get caught and thrown in jail.

He'd prefer to be seated in a bar, drinking beer with a long-legged piece of ass at his side. Truth be told, he does get a strange enjoyment, a motivating kick from these angry rages. When adrenaline surges through his arteries, his focus becomes acute. He listens for the sounds of his gang members, who are supposed to be close behind.

Bull elephants with decent tusks have been hard to find recently. Other poaching gangs have probably beat them to it. The poacher knows the competition is severe, and that his gang has been forced to compromise and hunt poorer pickings. They were closing in on a half-grown elephant, whose small tusks would still make the kill worthwhile. Such a juvenile usually makes easier prey than a solitary bull.

The wildebeests have almost certainly alerted and spooked the elephant, a fact that infuriates and frustrates the poacher. Had he resisted the urge to step out of the scrub for a clear view, the worthless animals would still be grazing peacefully. Angered by this mistake, his resentment toward the evermore wary elephants escalates. His task of shooting them has become difficult. As the rest of the gang catch up, he ducks further back into the shade to hide his blunder. To keep their respect, he must conceal that he's blown their cover.

The wildebeests settle, less skittish now with the threat out of sight. The dust raised by the stampede irritates their lungs, and they head toward a muddy stream for an evening drink. The calf trips, but recovers quickly and attempts to drink from his mother even while she continues to walk. Still watchful, she stops and allows him to nuzzle in. Tourists that pass by in vehicles are familiar, but a man on foot is strange and threatening. She cuts the drink short to keep up with the herd, anxious at being separated. Her udder is almost dry, and she's thin from the drought. By now, the rains should have started, providing fresh grass across the savannah and plenty of milk for the young. Unless this happens soon, her calf won't survive.

The poacher and his gang skirt the edges of the dusty plain, careful to stay hidden. A couple of daylight hours remain, possibly enough for them to pick up the trail of the half-grown elephant and dispatch it

Ten

From high above the plains, the view stretches across a vast expanse of the savannah to a starry horizon. In a clearing below Lou, a herd of elephants approaches a lake. She thinks it's unusual for the waterhole to be so full during a drought. Its surface mirrors the night sky so that a full moon shines out from the watery depths.

The matriarch arrives by the water's edge first. Her calf romps by her side, and she protectively nudges him closer. Briefly, the pair are perfectly imaged against the night sky. Then the mother extends her trunk to drink and, as she touches the surface, ripples bend the light and distort her reflection. The herd catches up and wades into the shallows. Delighted by water, the elephants communicate with low rumbling sounds of contentment.

The elephants in this herd have experienced death early and are young survivors of previous hunts. Their half-grown tusks gleam like white gold in the moonlight. Around their watering hole are grasslands where alert antelopes group together, wary of predators that hunt under cover of night. Beyond them, dense vegetation grows along the sandy river, its thick-leaved canopy snaking across a patchwork landscape.

Unknown to these elephant survivors, a band of men approaches downwind, their guns carried with deadly ease. They lope almost silently across the moonlit plains toward the herd. They've ambushed elephants many times, and it means nothing to them that the animals are so young. These lethal hunters would argue that if they don't take out the elephants, someone else will. Practiced and proficient, their entire focus is their own gain, completely careless of what they destroy. A high reward ensures they kill and supply ivory to temporarily satisfy human craving and desire. Even immature tusks are worth killing for.

The calf responds to the worry in his mother's deep rumble and moves closer to her safety. He has yet to learn to survive a dangerous world. Lou must warn the elephants of the criminals. Only she can alert them to the menace and save the massacre. Terrified, she screams over and over again, emptying her lungs to no avail. The killers are so close. Stealthily, the predatory men close in, downwind of the herd.

It's almost too late. Dread consumes Lou as the empty space swallows her screams. The carnage seems impossible to stop, the air between her and the gentle elephants thick and impenetrable. Exposed and vulnerable, they remain unaware of the threat. A last silent scream empties out of her as the gang leader steps into the clearing and lifts an automatic to his shoulder. The others follow in rapid succession.

Unleashed chaos as explosions rend the air and drown the screams as elephants fall, trapped within walls of bullets. Unable to escape, the mother swings around to protect her calf. Bullet holes puncture a line along her chest, and she drops. Caught between the fear of leaving her and of the men, the calf extends his trunk toward her sprawled body. A bullet slams into his side. Another takes him down. His death arrives seconds after hers, his anguished scream audible between gunshots.

As the savannah rips apart, Lou jolts awake. She lurches off her bed; the slaughter scene horribly real; her yelp of fright muted by gunshot outside. Like a hunted animal, Lou waits for the nightmare to recede and gathers her senses. Even before she reaches the window, she understands that the mousebirds are again raiding the fruit trees. Peter fires another shot overhead to scare them off. Wings flap as birds begrudgingly fly to safer perches. Accustomed to being moved along, they're cheeky and will return the moment Peter is off guard.

Her heart still pounding, Lou feels an irrational surge of anger at Peter and the pesky gray birds with their routine raids. Thank god it was only a nightmare, but still an ominous start to the day. Lou scoops water over her face. She rubs hard around her eyes to dispel the lingering images and remembers David arrived yesterday; it's not all bad. Her father crosses the compound outside with Zebu at his heels, her fat tail wagging lazily. The dark patch of sweat on his shirt indicates it's already hot.

By her bed, a stack of field notes on the Mbane herd reminds Lou of her schedule. She tries not to rerun her nightmare. Her observations confirm how elephants learn from each other, and that loyalty is essential to their survival. They grieve at finding the bones of a poached elephant and appear as aware of the concept of death as humans. Not only do they regularly revisit sites where their relatives have died, but they also return to places where their human friends have been lost.

But poachers and land encroachment leave no secure places for these intelligent beings. Wild areas become denuded maize plots. People born a generation ago took the last of the productive land.

A wave of frustration takes hold of Lou as she dusts off her paperwork. Red smears streak across the rough draft. A perfect final copy will provide the credentials for her to push for better protection. What sets Africa apart as unique is fast fading. She must hurry up with her thesis. Once it's done, her opinion might mean something. Until then, she can only bide her time.

For a long while, her hand moves pen over the paper as Lou sorts facts into a meaningful order. The distraction of her work is meditative. Masaranga's creatures are written into documents. She refers to papers by other researchers. Antelopes, zebras, and wildebeests take their turns to graze the fresh pasture. As they migrate in waves, each species takes advantage of the different growth stages. Left alone, nature balances itself.

Eleven

A descending spiral of dots appears up ahead, and a jolt of fear runs up Lou's spine. The sense of dread from her nightmare comes rushing back.

"Hey, Peter!" Through her binoculars, she identifies vultures gliding down in a spiral.

"Let's check it out." Peter keeps his voice matter-of-fact as he slows the Land Rover to search for a way across country.

Please, not like my dream, Lou thinks, unable to keep a sense of dismay under control as they bush-bash through acacia scrub.

But squadrons of vultures have congregated at ground level. As the vehicle enters a clearing in the bush, Lou and Peter are faced by a massacre worse than her nightmare. Huge gray carcasses sprawl across the ground as if the elephants were in full flight, while poachers indiscriminately gunned the entire herd down. The air is thick with the stench of death and decay, and pervasive clouds of flies hang over the carnage. As Peter eases the vehicle closer, a silver-backed jackal slinks off.

"My god." An expression of disbelief across his face, Peter jumps down from the vehicle.

Lou half expected devastation, but she's mentally unprepared for the scale of it. She clung to that slither of hope, which delays shock right until undeniable reality smacks a person in the face.

Her gut turns. Nausea and anger rise as Lou fights to control an already broken heart. She follows Peter toward the nearest dead elephant. As her emotions escalate, Lou wants to scream and rant, but instead cries out, her throat constricted. It's an agony she can't bear and impossible for her to stop. The fury and frustration fuse into something indefinable, and she begins to sob quietly, her devastation complete. These extraordinary creatures, the elephants she knows so well, murdered and butchered so close to home. No way exists to deal with such pain. This slaughter can't be fixed. What's been done here can never be undone.

Lou forces her jagged breaths to slow and turns to Peter. Evidently, he's struggling with similar emotions.

"So many! We've never lost an entire herd," she says, her voice sounding thin and small.

"We will catch the bastards," replies Peter.

But how? Lou could gun down the perpetrators with her own hands. Suddenly, she feels a rush of determination to follow the trail right back to the corrupt fat cats behind these poachers.

As they approach a dead calf, a lone hyena makes a run from behind it. He's a bulky male with a powerful chest, his muscled forelegs and jaws bloody after scavenging the carcass. The hyena lopes away toward a gap in the vegetation, and Lou sees a flash of wary eyes as he turns for a last glance at the abandoned meal and then melts into the shadows.

Hyenas look scary, but they're not malevolent. The evil here has been perpetrated by humans. Lou loves the weirdness of the hyenas and the way they live in structured communities. Their shy skulking behavior and strange gait don't worry her and are part of their fascination. This wilderness is their place, and they clean up carcasses when other creatures die. But the greed-fueled carnage in front of her is a man-made catastrophe and a symptom of his ability to destroy indiscriminately, without regard for nature and her self-regulating cycles.

"This little guy had the tiniest tusks. But they still killed him!" Lou's voice breaks mid-sentence as she approaches the dead body of a juvenile that she knew as a boisterous teenager, whose antics were tolerated affectionately by the herd. His face is a mass of wounds and congealed blood. Grim-faced, Peter examines the bullet holes and rent-apart skin.

In a daze, Lou scrambles over the uneven ground behind his carcass to reach the fallen matriarch. Of course, her ivory would be coveted by poachers and those ignorant enough to buy it. Sprawled dead against her mother's hindquarters is an even younger calf. This time, Lou makes no effort to stop her tears. She waits by the murdered calf for her vision to clear. This herd was part of Lou's study, and the calf was a shy female, guarded by her mother and the other adults.

"These butchers were brutal and heavily armed." Peter's voice is thick with grief. He continues on to the next dead elephant and disturbs a disheveled marabou stork that stalks away from its sentry over the bones, its red head like a bald old man who has now seen the worst.

Hearing Peter's sadness, Lou nods, unable to trust herself to speak. They both know the calf wouldn't survive without his mother, but the fact he died needlessly like this makes it harder to stomach. His body is small beside his dead mother. Bullet holes ooze along their sides. Twenty-three of them have been killed, the whole herd. None escaped.

Three bald-headed vultures with bloody breast feathers hop heavily away along the flank of the next carcass as Lou approaches. A frantic flapping of wings and the gorged scavengers rise on the hot air, only to land on the bare branches of a dead tree nearby. From there, they keep a lookout from the safe vantage point. They've plenty of time and food. Like the hyena, the vultures clean up after the killers.

When Lou studied this herd, the elephants never threatened her. After a while, she was allowed to tag along on the edge of their highly social existence. She took notes from the Land Rover, and meticulously recorded their lives and how they protected their own, with the belief her work would help protect them. What a joke! Somehow, she must ramp up her efforts. Her work suddenly seems way too passive, and it's patently obvious that all her records haven't helped these elephants.

The ivory will decorate houses and add to the status of the rich or the ignorant, while these mothers will never walk these plains nor rear calves again. Lou recalls how this matriarch would lift her trunk to detect danger, her curved tusks catching the sunlight. Protective of all the young elephants, the matriarch took a while to allow Lou closer. Now, Lou feels that trust has been broken. The loss sits as a dull, leaden lump inside her. One brutal, savage act and a whole herd of inherently gentle creatures dies.

"It's such a waste of life, of all we've done," she says.

"Yes, we have spent many hours with these friends. And now they are gone." Peter's voice is resigned, as if he has already accepted this loss, while she's still stewing on it, unable to accept it.

"How are we going to stop this?" Lou asks him. She mustn't wallow in these emotions now the damage is done, as it won't help the remaining elephants. But Peter shrugs his shoulders. How indeed? For years, Lou has watched her father struggle to control poaching. There must be better ways to protect the elephants from such savage acts.

Peter checks the oozing holes in another gray mound. He better knows how to gather information on the weapons used. Lou watches as he tries to reconstruct how the poachers approached the herd, his eyes narrowed against the slanting sunlight. Abruptly, he strides across the clearing and disappears into the shadows. Lou remembers the hyena and lifts her binoculars to keep guard, but, almost immediately, he reappears along the perimeter. The vultures turn their heads to watch him closely from their vantage points. Otherwise, the bush is strangely silent. Under different circumstances, savannah creatures would be more active at this time of day.

"These men were wasteful with their bullets," says Peter when he returns. "They entered from the west, near where the road cuts the boundary."

As Lou turns to face west, she doesn't need to ask whether they could follow the trail or what they would do if they caught up with the men. The first angry red streaks of the sunset have already cut across the horizon.

Her tears have caked dry, and Lou's rage solidifies into cold hate. They should get out of here before dark. They need to relocate the dirt track they left to follow the vultures here. Otherwise, they're lost. She wants to follow the poachers' trail, even this old, but they're unprepared for a chase after armed men. Her eyes meet Peter's, and she doesn't need to remind him it's time to leave.

"When we reach the track, we will check along the western boundary road," he says.

A sensible suggestion.

"OK," she agrees. Once they have their bearings, it doesn't matter how long it takes to return home.

In the morning, Lou wakes early, her mind blurry from anxiety-ridden sleep. Below her thoughts are dreams of the dead elephants and jubilant poachers, and it's difficult to discern between real and imagined.

They're busy outside. Her father shouts sharp instructions, brief and to the point as two rangers load the vehicles. Otherwise, they're unusually quiet. None of their normal cheerful chatter. Their Land Rovers roar out of the compound as Lou pours coffee, bitter from sitting too long. Today they will search for the poachers' escape path after last night's failure to find the trail. Lou tries to banish images of yesterday as she struggles to stem the flow of tears.

"Eat some porridge!" Grace pushes a dish toward her.

"I can't yet. I feel sick." Lou is used to this and knows what's coming. The bowl is placed firmly in front of her.

"How can you stay strong and fight if you don't eat?"

Grace is right. She has no choice but to toughen up, especially now the poachers have become bolder than ever.

For years the park patrols worked reasonably well. Poachers mostly took one animal at a time. Now a whole herd has been taken out with only the vultures to alert them. Lou is aware that the new breed of poachers is indiscriminate and wasteful, that they kill entire families, including the elephants with almost no ivory. But this is her first experience of it. The new turn of events frightens her and sets her stomach churning. Suddenly, she understands they need outside help to block this new wave of crime. Unless they learn quickly, similar slaughters will soon follow.

Twelve

As the python searches along the water's edge, she flicks her forked tongue to taste molecules carried in the morning breeze. The air is heavy with scent. Observers might mistakenly imagine the python sees her surroundings in the same way as other animals that share her territory. But her taste buds tell her more than her eyes. Ravenous after a night's unsuccessful hunt, she weaves across the cracked mud surrounding the lake. Her previous meal was small and digested quickly, and she's already burned that energy. Recently a male wrapped his coils around her and fertilized her eggs. Since then, she's been hungry and focused on the pursuit of food.

As she begins to swim, submerged in the shallows, her wake disturbs the muddy water. Stilts, plovers, and bright white egrets flap frantically and lift off the surface to avoid her. They glide far enough to skirt around her sinuous progress and land again on delicate legs behind. Today she ignores them; her tongue tells her of more available prey up ahead.

"Do you see her over there?" Eagerly, Joshua jabs a finger toward the lake.

Through binoculars, Lou scans the swamp and reeds that grow thick in the shallows. She stops at what she took to be a small tree trunk. It's a python!

Joshua's vision leaves hers for dead. When Lou lowers the binoculars, nothing suggests the log is a partly submerged python. She hears the alarm calls of the wading birds and guesses they helped Joshua pinpoint the snake. Beyond the reeds, thick lily pads spread out across the water, and startled lily-trotter birds use them as stepping stones as they escape the commotion.

"You have good eyesight!" Lou compliments Joshua as they watch the snake speed up.

"Yes, I've been told this before." He laughs cheerfully, without affectation. He's easygoing and unashamed by his lack of modesty.

Joshua was at Nairobi University with her two years ago, and he was an encyclopedia of reptile facts and figures right from the start. There's been a smile across his naturally open face all morning. He's stayed fit and fascinated with the outdoors, despite his government paper-pushing job. Snakes were the main focus of his study, just as elephants were her passion. Lou considers him an ally. His parents were poor and made Joshua promise to take a safe government job after he won a scholarship and became the first university graduate in their family. Lou thinks it unfortunate he kept his word, though, of course, he would. Since then, he's been stuck behind a Nairobi desk.

A month ago, Lou called Joshua in his office to beg for help to get an interview with the Environment Minister.

"But I'm in Mines and Development!" he'd replied.

"Well, the people I spoke to in the Environment Department don't appear to have your interest in the environment!" Lou half teased him, hoping he'd get the point. "Like you, they're not defined by their job descriptions."

"Few people in these offices are passionate about their work. Rarely are such things as they should be." Joshua sounded sad, and his apparent resignation surprised her. Could a couple of years behind a desk have so dampened his enthusiasm?

Not so long ago, he wanted to save the world, but it now sounded as if he'd lost some of that fighting spirit. Early in the conversation, she decided a visit to Masaranga might cheer him up. Her invitation was immediately accepted, but it took much longer to organize this brief escape. It seems a pity for someone so attuned to the wilderness to have to spend life so far from it.

But her mind has wandered as it often does.

"Look!" exclaims Joshua as the water seems to boil over by the reeds. The python is coiling and now balling around a victim that thrashes only briefly. A startled squeal subsides into a short piggy grunt, and, in the ensuing quiet, a white heron gracefully glides from its hiding place within the reeds to a safer spot along the lake.

"She's caught a warthog!" Joshua's tone is admiring. "A young one, only small."

Lou lifts her binoculars to see and wishes her vision were so good.

"Amazingly fast for such a big snake!" Joshua's enthusiasm is palpable.

"If only I had your eyes!" she replies.

She's sad Joshua can't work where he's inspired and passionate. They watch the python reorganize her coils around the warthog that has lost all its fight.

"Perhaps you could study and earn money as a ranger at the same time."

"My father would be disappointed and angry, my mother less so. Also, I have a family to support and ranger wages are low. My wife is pregnant with our third child."

"But Joshua, you can't be more than twenty-three years old!"

"I am twenty-two. We start our families young here. You know that!"

Lou does know, so she shouldn't be surprised. But for some reason, she'd imagined there'd be other things Joshua would choose to do first. To start this young, with so many kids, deprives him of choices.

"What about you, Lou? When will you have children?"

"One day. Sometime far in the future. Maybe!" Lou can't yet envisage herself busy raising a family. "I want to change other things first!"

"One person can't save the world," he replies in a quiet, almost gentle voice.

"Well, I can at least help save Masaranga's elephants. That would be a start."

"Yes, it may be possible." He smiles.

Is he humoring her? It's hard to tell.

"I will help you as best as I can," he says, suddenly serious again. "I will try. But please understand that government institutions are resistant to change. Everywhere, people put their private interests above all else. Often, even those who want change refuse to pay the price."

Lou thanks him, overjoyed that he wants to help and follow his real instincts though they seem at odds with his career. It must be hard for him to match his choices with his ideals. As she drives the Land Rover further along the water's edge, she considers how lucky she is to be here, studying what matters to her, doing what she believes in. It's something she won't forget in a hurry again.

"Joshua, you're brilliant!" Lou slaps him on the back as he spots their second snake in twenty minutes, his ability uncanny. Usually, she'd be lucky to see a couple of snakes a week, and that's better than most. In his element, Joshua grins and points out that this snake is easier to spot. Two plovers are boldly dive-bombing it to impede its progress along an exposed bank, as if they're unafraid of retaliation.

As the birds are fearless, Joshua suspects the snake is sick. Lou follows him across the dry mudflats, and they creep towards where the plovers continue to hassle it. Wings flash black and white over the reeds as the plovers flap away to safety. Their alarm calls penetrate the quiet morning. As Joshua reaches the snake, he slows briefly to size it up and then pounces, cat-like, and grabs the writhing creature behind the head. The python only fights momentarily. When Lou catches up, it's already less frantic as if ready to surrender to its fate.

"No wonder the birds aren't scared!" Joshua says. His thumb and forefinger move adroitly along its triangular head to open the scaly jaw. The diamond markings are light and washed out, making it less attractive than the earlier python. It twists as Lou examines it, and she jumps sideways to avoid a loose coil not yet wrapped around Joshua's arm. A wound extends along one side of its head. From the appearance of the granulation tissue, Lou guesses the injury to be several days old and relatively free from infection.

"It can't catch food with a damaged mouth," says Joshua in a concerned voice, confirming her thoughts. She wonders how long it might take to die. Injured wildlife either starves or is saved from a slow death by a predator.

"Let's put him in a sack. You can feed him until his jaw heals," says Joshua, as if it's the only option.

Lou was taught not to interfere and let nature take its course, but it's sad to see the python injured and helpless. In the Land Rover is some fine-mesh netting, which she converts into a sack. Lou holds the makeshift pocket open and helps unwind the snake from Joshua's arm. It writhes as they drop it in and tie the top with string. Nature has taken such a hiding,

Lou can justify her interference as acceptable. It won't hurt her to learn more about snake husbandry either. At least pythons aren't venomous

Thirteen

For a moment, Lou stands by the door, shocked by the state of her room. While she was out, monkeys must have snuck in through the open window. They're the only creatures bold and inquisitive enough to wreak this sort of damage. On a previous occasion, she caught them in the act, and the mischievous monkeys swung back through the window with breathtaking alacrity.

Her possessions are scattered randomly, and her painting hangs askew. Had her door been open, they'd have invaded the house as well and gone to town on it. She retrieves an unraveled roll of toilet paper and rearranges her bathroom. They must have done a fast raid for their approach across the compound to go unnoticed by Zebu. Not even a bark!

Even as Lou worries about the damage and what's missing, she grins wryly. The investigative monkeys would have enjoyed such exciting new toys. Her rhino lampshade is sideways on the bed and undamaged, unlike the smashed glass by her table, its water spilled across the stone tiles and a mat. Her files form a haphazard pile on the floor close by but avoided a soaking. Had a person done this, Lou would be angry, but the mischievous monkeys weren't malicious, though their antics have made a considerable mess.

Lou gathers up paperwork on her knees. Damp from the mat soaks up through her slacks. Only now does she notice the photo of her mother, smiling at her from better days. Its glass is cracked. A wave of anger and sadness assaults her as images rise of her mother helping her onto her first pony and teaching her to ride. Lou grits her teeth and forces back tears, allowing anger to take control. It's the first time in ages she's looked at this photo, and her reaction takes her by surprise. Distracted by the mess, her guard is down as she stares into these familiar but distant eyes.

Lou wonders if her mother still smiles this way at the person that stole her from them. What made that man so much more important than her own flesh and blood? A much more glamourous lifestyle that enables her to live around the embassies of the world? But why break off all contact with the family? Was life really so bad here? Not for the first time, Lou commands herself to let go of it all.

Cautiously, she picks up the photo, examines it for the last time, and puts it face down in the bottom drawer of her filing cabinet. Lou is angry that she allowed it to stay out at all. Then she collects the broken pieces of glass carefully, one by one, so the sharp edges don't cut her skin.

Lou still feels cranky with her father. When her mother left, he failed to talk things through with them. Perhaps Dad was too British, or just thought they were too young. But there's been plenty of time since and hardly a word from him. The romance of a diplomat's lifestyle must have enticed her mother, the lure of a dashing man with a foreign embassy posting. Life in Kenya failed to live up to expectations, the outcome being that Lou's dad inherited the job of bringing up Lou and her brother.

Now her father has again distanced himself from their neighbor's recent tragedy, and he's volunteered Lou as a stand-in. Today she must drive Brad's children to the Nairobi airport. They, too, have lost their mother and are about to start a new life.

Brad lives fifty miles along the Rift Valley, and the long drive up the escarpment seems slow today. Lou's thoughts return to the photo of her mother that, weirdly, broke only days ago, a timely reminder of how fast things can change. Lou used to enjoy this drive with the anticipation of time spent with Kate, female company being rare in this remote male-dominated territory. On her last trip, six months ago, when Lou waved her friend goodbye, she never imagined it would be the last time she'd see Kate.

Her visit today is more of an errand. With Kate gone and her family torn apart, what sort of condolences should Lou offer Brad? It's especially hard as the present situation stems from his infidelity, and it's a case of truth being stranger than fiction.

Though upset at how her father distanced himself from all this, Lou knows Masaranga really needs him right now. She's glad to help, but her trepidation rises as the car roars around each switchback, its engine ever more labored along the endless climb. Expatriate company is scarce out here, and her father hasn't openly allowed the tragedy to dismay him or affect his relationship with Brad. Since her mother's departure, calamity rarely seems to touch him. The panorama opens below Lou, layer on layer of hillslopes rising above the plains.

Was her father always so distant? Only a few memories remain with Lou of how he was before her mother left. Her parents were full of hope for a new and exciting life when her father made the decision to give up a perfectly good career in England. Her mother was as keen as her father and they made the choice together. Africa seemed to hold so much of interest that it was worth risking everything. Then, just when he'd proved himself and been trusted with Masaranga's management, her mother left them. Had the idea of a step further into isolation scared her? Lou guesses it could have all have been nothing more than bad timing.

But all that is past. It's best to forget the broken photo and develop a cheerful outlook. Lou rarely comes this way, and the scenery is a change from the savannah. A slow trip, but she's finally up high, the road clinging to the side of the valley. The dust is gone, and the temperature has dropped. Here the harsh sunrays are muted by the altitude, the light softer. The plants have suffered the drought better.

Kate's outlook on life was quite different from hers, but it's easy to guess how alone she'd have felt. A wave of sadness hits Lou as she rounds the last corner before the property. She gets a new sense now of Kate's life. Straggly pot plants and disorderly chairs have replaced the well-kept entrance of the Dutch-style homestead. Lou pulls up by the arched entranceway and takes a deep breath. She's angrier than ever with her father for his lack of support. A moment of déjà vu as the doors swing open, and Mary, the nanny, steps out, a brave smile across her tear-streaked face.

"Thank you for coming," Mary says politely, though, obviously, she'd have preferred for no one to come and the children to stay. Packed and ready, they wait forlornly, their faces perplexed. Suddenly, Lou recalls her own father telling her the bad news all those years ago.

Unlike Lou, Tara and James were born here and have less sense of how it will be to live elsewhere. Mary tries to smile at them but breaks down and sobs noisily. Her attractive face becomes swollen as the tears roll unchecked from her bloodshot eyes.

"You mustn't worry. The children will be OK." Lou attempts to calm her, but her words sound hollow. About to continue, she hesitates and then, instead, hugs Mary. It's best to stick to the basics. The only way to help is to drive Tara and James to Nairobi and get them onto the plane home. However, it's strange how the English here still call England home when hardly anyone views it that way.

"Thanks for this, Lou," says Brad.

"I'm so sorry about Kate," she replies, unsure exactly of his head-space right now. He stands slightly apart in a detached manner as if he wants to pretend the farewell is not real. Along with his family, he's lost his driving license. His drink-driving offenses must be severe, otherwise he'd have bribed his way out of the situation. Perhaps, all things considered, he's not yet got around to that option. Stony faced, he steps closer and quickly embraces his children.

"Keep your chins up, kids, and behave well for your grandparents!" With his stern voice, Brad is the polar opposite of the distraught Mary. It must weigh on their consciences that their relationship started the chain of events that ended Kate's life.

Mary may never again see Tara and James though she's cared for them since they were babies. Her own baby is their cute coffee-skinned half-sister. Lou waits as Mary holds the children tightly against her chest and kisses them fiercely one last time. They cling to her as she pushes them away. With her supple young body and flawless skin, Mary is hardly an adult herself. She's central to the problem, but it's not her fault. Had Brad not chosen her, his eye would have wandered onto another susceptible young woman. Perhaps had he taken a lover less attached to the family, all this could have been avoided.

When her own life was upended, Lou didn't lose Grace. Nor did she have to leave home and live in a strange new place. Her own mother chose to do that. She's grateful not to have been sent "home."

Faced with the present fallout, Lou keeps her views under wraps. What's done is done, and her opinion counts for little. The consequences will continue in the minds and lives of these children. When Lou agreed to deliver them to Nairobi airport, for their first-ever plane ride to the UK, she never guessed how much stuff would come up for her. The children's grandparents demanded their return so they'd grow up "civilized." But is that really the best place for them?

How well Tara and James will cope with entirely new lives is anyone's guess.

"It will be a whole new adventure for you two!" Lou tells them.

"That's for sure," says Brad. "You kids are more adaptable than the rest of us." He glances at them briefly as he tells them, his own emotions tightly under control. Has he taken much responsibility for their misfortune on himself? Is he burdened by the knowledge his actions inadvertently killed Kate?

As Brad follows them out, his face expressionless, Lou suppresses her aversion to his treatment of his family. She shouldn't judge so harshly. Mary loads their pathetically small bags into the car. There's nothing else to do or say after Mary steps aside, and it's time to leave, so Lou eases the car slowly off down the bumpy driveway. It gives the children time to watch their home shrink to a flash of sunlight off the glass doors. She turns onto the road, and the house is swallowed by the landscape. Such a miserable way to leave, but they seem too dazed to comprehend their last view.

With the house lost on the hillside, Tara turns toward Lou with troubled blue eyes. Her world upturned, the child attempts a shy, hopeful half-smile. But a memory reinstates itself and the moment disappears as her eyes focus back within.

In the back seat, James remains enveloped in the stunned silence that comes after a period of emotional upheaval, a state Lou recognizes from long ago. No energy remains for further protest, and all feeling has been cried out. For a while, the siblings stare quietly out of their respective windows. It's hard to know if they're aware of the villages and maize fields that flash by outside. What thoughts and memories occupy their minds?

"James and me are going to England for a holiday," announces Tara suddenly.

"Yes, that's good, isn't it?" Lou smiles and ruffs up Tara's wild hair. The girl feels hot and bothered. "Would you like a drink?" asks Lou. She checks the rear mirror and catches James's eye. "What about you?"

Tara nods quietly, but James averts his eyes and looks back at the passing acres of yellowed maize crop.

"Mummy's waiting for us in England," he says to the window.

"Your grandma is definitely waiting for you over there!" replies Lou.

She fights to contain her tears. The boy clings to the hope that his mother is alive. He wants this to be a lie and her death an illusion. The last time they saw Kate, she was alive and well, distraught perhaps but not ill when she slipped away to the hospital and left them in Mary's care.

In a patch of roadside shade, Lou pulls over and pours cold lemonade from a thermos. Nearby, under a tin-shelter bus stop, a group of giggling children in raggedy clothes stop their game. With inquisitive dark eyes, they watch Lou's waif-like charges drink.

"Now hold tight, so they don't spill!" she says as the siblings gulp down the sweet liquid. Lou pours the remains into two paper cups and hands them out the window to the others, now waiting closer. They take turns sipping the treat, arguing about whose turn it is, and then wave as Lou eases the borrowed Peugeot back onto the road.

The last time Lou saw her mother was over fifteen years ago, and her skin was pallid despite her permanent tan. Perhaps it reflected her mother's doubts at the prospect of deserting. *Not enough misgivings to leave a path open for communication*, thinks Lou angrily. Surely it must have hurt to split off from her family. But Lou has already been through all this muddled thinking where she wonders and assumes and guesses but fails to get closer to reconciliation. Again, she sinks her unresolved thoughts back down to a safer hidden place. But immediately, her anger at Brad and the injustice resurfaces. She takes Tara's empty cup and notices James's eyes are fixed back on a point outside, blind to the cultivation and ramshackle villages.

On the rare occasions when Lou visited, Kate seemed highly strung but kind, while Brad had a reputation for being drunk and awkward. Only they knew exactly what brought them to Kenya. Maybe, like many others, they dreamed of a more exciting life or an escape from a disappointing one back home. Perhaps they imagined they'd reinvent themselves in Africa. Vaguely,

Lou remembers her father's eager descriptions of the wild country that would be their new home. Too young to completely understand, she found it irresistible. But what was life like for Kate and Brad before disaster struck?

But Brad shouldn't have chosen the closest target for his wandering affections. If he'd kept his affairs out of the home, Kate mightn't have known about the coffee-colored sister and naturally surmised who the father was. Being pregnant again herself, she reacted poorly.

Isolation made her predicament worse with no one to confide in. Just this fact makes Lou feel negligent. Sometimes Kate made slightly offhand comments about her husband, but Lou was taught not to interfere in other peoples' affairs. Now Lou ponders how life would be, stuck out here with her kids and a straying husband.

Kate fell to pieces and went alone to Nairobi for an abortion. Did she have no support at all? If only she'd made contact and let her friends know. An awful sick sensation runs through Lou as she imagines Kate, anxious and distressed, driving alone through this same landscape to the hospital.

Lou was ignorant even of Kate's pregnancy. Unsurprisingly, the news came via Grace, her word-of-mouth telegraph often the swiftest information source. Kate bled badly during her abortion and needed a transfusion to save her life, except it didn't. The hospital gave her incorrectly labeled blood. The mismatch caused an anaphylactic reaction, and she died. How often do fatal mistakes happen in the hospitals here? As the miles roll past, Lou envisages how it would be to die alone in a strange place.

"Lou, Lou!" Tara's high voice breaks her tunnel vision. Suddenly aware she's on automatic, seeing only the mirage above the hot tarmac, Lou jams her foot hard on the brakes. The kids have pivoted around, their faces pressed against the window. In the red dirt by the road, baboons huddle in disordered groups. Lou continues at a walking pace. They pass a couple of baboons that pay little attention to the vehicle as they meticulously pick parasites off a dominant male.

Across the road, a group of juveniles squabbles over mango skins, thrown from a passing vehicle. Lou counts at least twenty baboons all up. She stops the car, and immediately all the baboons pay attention. The troupe lacks the frightened, ready to flee attitude of most wildlife. Instead, they're obviously accustomed to getting food from passing cars; they wait, hoping for handouts. Lou knows how detrimental it is to feed wildlife like this. Heartfelt gestures can turn wild animals into dangerous beggars. With no treat forthcoming, the baboons lose interest and resume squabbling over the spoils from the last vehicle.

As Lou pulls away, Tara points to an undersized mother, alone on the far side. "That one's all floppy!" she wails. A lifeless baby hangs limply under the mother's arm as she searches for morsels on the dirt verge, still unready to relinquish her dead infant.

It's too ghastly. Lou accelerates the car into the heat haze, and Tara starts to cry. Once out of sight of the baboons, Lou pulls over again and lifts Tara onto her lap. Sobs wrack the child's small chest as she puts her arms around Lou and hangs on. Her face remains pushed against Lou's shirt until the tears run dry. The frailty of the six-year-old makes Lou want to keep her safe. If only she knew how to make up for things.

"Tara's a crybaby." From behind, a whine of complaint. Lou turns sharply to see his eyes are wet. She leans back to comfort James, but, unlike his sister, his body is stiff and unyielding. Only a year older than Tara, he's twice her size. Lou feels powerless to help.

Growing up without their mother is going to be tough. Lou considers what her mother never told her, all the things she had to learn on her own. But she must hurry along and keep moving toward Nairobi international airport, or the kids will miss their plane.

Fourteen

Monty the snake is hard to feed, but he's a survivor and, slowly, the wound heals, helped by antibiotics from the first-aid kit. As he becomes more robust and harder to hold, Lou becomes faster at grabbing him behind the head when necessary. The day she returns Monty to the waterhole, she calls Joshua again.

Predictably, it takes a while to put the call through and tell him the good news about Monty's release back to the wild.

"That's wonderful. The best news all month!" says Joshua. "Absolutely nothing of interest happens here!"

The phone line is erratic, and Joshua sounds as if on the far side of a noisy ocean. But something of interest *has* happened. He's wangled an appointment for her with the Assistant Minister for National Parks. It's a huge win as all other leads have failed. Joshua must have called in a favor.

"I'm eternally grateful. Thanks. I'll make it up to you!" Lou promises.

"No need for that. Just please don't be too outspoken," Joshua warns her. "Remember, despite his position, the minister doesn't know much about wildlife."

"I'll be polite and not say anything radical!" Lou answers, grateful for the opportunity. This is her chance to push for change.

"You're the last whites permitted to manage a national park here, and you're not permanent residents," he reminds her.

"But we've been here for twenty years!" she replies, and then quickly tones down her indignation. Joshua doesn't make the rules, and she understands his misgivings.

He cautions her again. "Much has changed in the last few years."

Lou is not in denial. Most of her school friends left long ago, many for the UK. A few emigrated to further away places, like Australia and Canada. Their parents often chose countries with wide-open spaces, in an attempt to fulfill their yearning for uncrowded places where nature still survives.

Not so long ago, Kenya evicted the last white landowners from their farms. Their meager payouts bought little in the Western countries, where the farmers had to start new lives. It was considered proper punishment in the eyes of many but was harsh treatment nevertheless. Many of their old farms were distributed within the political old-boy network. The rest were divided into subsistence maize plots for Kikuyu families. In theory, this provided a home and food for them, but not for the huge families they continued to have. If the government spent money to educate and support women, particularly around birth control, then the burgeoning population of hungry people might not spiral ever upward, dangerously ahead of the land's ability to sustain them.

As Lou listens to Joshua's cautions, she watches Grace hang bright dresses on the clothesline outside. As a Kipsigus in Kikuyu country, Grace is not entirely at home here either and prefers to live at headquarters rather than the nearest village.

"OK, Joshua. I understand," Lou assures her friend.

"I don't think I can help you much more," he says. "Government employees are often unhelpful. They're either frightened of losing their jobs or just too lazy to care."

"Maybe they're not used to your ability to speak openly," says Lou. "Perhaps, they don't understand sincerity!"

"Anyhow, I better stick to my job from now on."

"Sorry." Now Lou feels worried for him. "Please remember to visit anytime you want. I wish you could follow your heart."

"I must go now. Good luck. Please don't be disappointed."

"I'm not disappointed. I'm very grateful."

"No, I didn't mean it in that way. Goodbye, Lou."

She replaces the receiver and sits for a while, wondering what angle to try on the minister. Outside, Grace moves on to other tasks. Behind her, a colorful row of clothes hangs motionless in the still air against a hot blue sky.

Fifteen

The offices and corridors of this government building are like meerkat warrens. As Lou hurries past open doors, employees stare out as if she's more interesting than their paperwork. Nervous and out of place, she finds the door of the "Assistant Minister for National Parks" at the end of a brightly lit corridor, below an etching of a buffalo. A secretary with high cheekbones and braided hair beckons her into a waiting area.

"Mr. Lonnegan won't be too long." After a quick perusal of Lou, the secretary returns to her paperwork.

Lou glimpses Fred Lonnegan in a smaller office off to one side. Anxiously, she waits while her mind runs possible scenarios. As the wait stretches out, the secretary sneaks glances at her. Lou tries to catch her eye, keen for a chat to break the ice, but the woman just types faster and refuses to engage. Lou takes a few deep breaths to settle her nerves. She mustn't ruin this opportunity to get her message across.

It's so long before Fred Lonnegan waves her through that her jitters have almost gone. So stupid to be uptight, she thinks, especially when he's not the imposing man of her projections.

This man doesn't match up to the formidable official she'd imagined. Tiny veins pattern his pasty skin, and his belly bulges over creased pants. Lou has plenty of time to absorb this because he leaves her standing for a while, his attention on a document in his plump hands. He reads as if alone in his office, while she wonders if she should sit down. Even his bald patch is pale, an unusual sight in a country that sits right on the equator, where it's no easy task to avoid the sun.

Fred Lonnegan mightn't be as commanding as she expected, but she needs his help. Joshua pulled strings for her, and she must make the best of it, particularly after her own futile attempts to get an interview. She wonders if he could exert enough influence to help Masaranga, even should he want to.

Finally, with visible effort, he stands to shake hands. He's short and his handshake soft, but something about him tells Lou she'd be smart to toe the line. Her father's parting words were, "Don't expect the Environment Department to care about nature." If only his views didn't reflect Joshua's sentiments.

Lou sits and watches as he carefully lowers his bulk into the leather chair. The bags under his eyes make him look exhausted, though it's only 11 a.m. Outside his open window, a manicured lawn stretches toward benches and tidy garden beds.

"Terribly hot day," he says. "What will you have to drink?"

His accent makes her think of posh private schools.

Not waiting for her reply, he summons his secretary. "Tonic water for the memsahib and a beer for myself, *tafatali*."

His voice softens into exaggerated politeness when he tags on the Swahili—"please." With a quick nod, the secretary hurries off. Office protocol must be slack for beer to be drunk so early in the day. Lou is glad to be let off with tonic water.

"Now, young lady, you've come all the way from Masaranga. How interesting! I rarely find time to leave town."

"I'm sorry you don't get much time. We'd love you to visit," she replies.

He fails to answer, and she's unsure how to continue. Despite warnings, she naively assumed Fred Lonnegan visited territory relevant to his job.

"I rarely leave Masaranga!" she adds.

"Oh!" He raises an eyebrow. "Well, I hardly spend any time in the bush. A quick trip to Amboseli and the like, nothing too far. I'm busy. It's quite a job keeping tabs on these blacks."

He winks conspiratorially. Uncomfortable, Lou grins and keeps her conflicting thoughts to herself. She's here on a different mission; other battles can stay under this, so-called, civilized surface.

Outside, a gardener tends the flower beds, his shoulder muscles flexing as he digs the dirt. Further away, barefooted youths play football by a freshly painted fence. The ball thuds dully as it hits the wooden palings, and good-natured laughter drifts into the office.

"How are things out there?" Fred Lonnegan provides an opening.

"The place is parched. Even the large waterholes are drying up," she answers. "We're also having quite a battle with poachers."

"Yes, my dear, an ongoing problem. Nothing new about them," he replies, with a dismissive gesture of his hands. "Our resources are inadequate," he continues. "It's been twenty years since I came out to help these people, and I've not seen a worse drought."

"So, you must like it here?" Tentatively, Lou searches for common ground.

"Bit of a backward place," he counters. "But there are benefits of living here. Ah, right, the drinks!" He winks as the secretary places the tray between them. Condensation drips off the glasses and soaks the placemats.

Her problem is his lack of interest, not the intimidation she feared. Lou wonders how, as a foreigner, he's kept this position. He must be sympathetic to the people here, despite his condescension. Otherwise, why was he not moved along with other whites? Joshua suggested Mr. Lonnegan had influence. Too white to be appointed minister but, as assistant, able to exert influence from behind the scenes. Lou needs his help, so it's best to keep an open mind, though evidently her preparations for a formal interview were unnecessary.

He lifts his glass and indicates for her to do the same.

"Wonderful!" He swigs the beer with appreciation.

She takes a sip of her tonic water. Perhaps she should start again.

"Mr. Lonnegan, I don't want to waste your time. I've come because our elephants and rhinos are being wiped out. My father manages Masaranga, where I study them. I've brought data to demonstrate the extent of the problem."

"My dear, you're not wasting my time at all. I hope you like tonic water. It can be hard to get a decent drink, even in Nairobi!" The label on his beer distracts him for a moment before he continues, "So you keep track of the elephants?"

"Yes, as well as I can. The population is on a downward spiral. We just had an entire herd slaughtered." Lou hates describing individual elephants that she knows merely as quantifiable commodities.

"I hear black-market ivory is at a premium. It's big business," says Fred Lonnegan.

He studies his glass intently, as if it were a crystal ball.

"Masaranga is no longer a haven for wildlife," Lou replies. "We've lost half our rhinos."

"You're obviously a capable young woman. How did you envisage my help?"

His eyes leave his glass of amber liquid, and he looks at her again.

"I'm not sure." Lou is relieved to have his attention. "Perhaps extra rangers. We need to run constant patrols."

He considers her request, as she waits quietly, her heart heavy. He seems almost bored with the interview.

"The poachers may just be hungry men from surrounding villages. Little can be done about Kenya's population explosion."

Lou disagrees. There's plenty that could be done in terms of empowering women so they can make better choices. But that's not his arena.

"The poachers are well organized," she replies. "With high-powered guns, they kill whole herds. Villagers poach one at a time, often with snares, not guns." It frustrates her to point out the obvious. Fred Lonnegan should know this!

Disconcertingly, he studies her. She's unable to guess his thoughts or to gauge his level of interest. Will he forget the interview and her request the minute she leaves?

"If this is true, we must treat the situation with utmost care," says Fred all of a sudden. "Heavily armed men are dangerous when the stakes are high, and the poachers have little to lose."

His words make her shiver, but Lou hangs on to the "we." It's a shred of hope, and an ally in the Environment Department is essential.

"Loss of wildlife means fewer tourists. Long term, Kenya has a lot to lose," she reminds him.

He nods, as if he's understood her.

"Thank you for the interview. You're our main hope," Lou says. "I'm grateful."

Again, she's out of words, and none seem forthcoming from him. Then he smiles suddenly and says, "Of course I'm sympathetic. You've come to exactly the right place. Please keep me updated on all aspects of the problem, so I can work out how to help."

Fred looks at his watch and smiles, his eyebrows raised slightly. The interview over, Lou tucks her unused notes away. As he sees her out, he says, "I must introduce you to an ambitious young man in my department. A job like this would be perfect for him to sink his teeth into."

Inexplicably, the tide has turned for the better. False promises perhaps. Why did his attitude suddenly change? Lou leaves quietly and feels the secretary's eyes follow her back down the long corridor.

Perhaps Fred does understand the tragedy of losing what's left, now that Africa's vast wildernesses have shrunk into comparatively small areas. Only the inhospitable, impossible to cultivate areas became national parks. If people knew how poachers plunder these last vestiges, they'd be incensed. Lou carefully stuck to the elephants and said none of this to Fred. It's always hard to know how or why a person's opinion sways, and whether his is on the other end of the spectrum from her.

Obviously, opinions differ. Many consider it their right to conquer and use as suits their interests. They'd consider man-made destruction merely as survival of the fittest, with humans the top predator, though their harsh egocentric view will ultimately take humans out with the rest of the planet. And should people survive their own violence, how will they exist amid depletion? Once the wild is conquered down to what is directly "useful," how will they feel then?

These thoughts make Lou feel weak with defeat. She's hardly started to do anything useful, and she must snap out of this mindset. Otherwise, it's all too daunting, any effort pointless.

As her mind takes another turn, she wonders if David is right? Shouldn't she just lighten up and enjoy life more? But from where she's standing, he's not benefited much from that approach.

When Lou comes to her senses, she's seated at a roadside café, a waitress at her side. She orders and pays, unsure why she stopped here.

"Memsahib, your coffee!" The astonished waitress returns just in time to see Lou hurry off down the street, her need for a drink already forgotten.

Sixteen

David is home again, and, for a few days, he strides around with a couple of rangers in tow. His new, confident look irks Lou slightly, considering how little time he's spent here recently. She envies his sudden self-assurance. If only she were so sure of her capabilities. With the world shifting under their feet, her inability to see downstream frightens Lou.

David has embraced change better and, in his time away, stepped back from Masaranga and her troubles. His apparent indifference makes Lou feel more alone than ever. Even their mother deserted for someone keen to move on to "better places."

She watches now as her brother cracks a joke with the rangers. They all laugh and move off towards the workshop. Half-smoked, handmade cigarettes dangle loosely from their fingers. Zebu trails behind.

Red dust hangs in the hot, still air, the fine particles suspended in the sunlight across her room. Lou dusts them off her typewriter and sits down ready to continue her work, her mind not on the job. She'd have preferred that her brother invited Lexi's sister, Carla, to visit Masaranga rather than her pushier sister Lexi. A guilty twinge accompanies her attitude, and, to compensate, Lou attempts to rustle up more enthusiasm. *Perhaps it will be fun.* Lexi's layers of make-up and revealing dresses make Lou feel they have little in common. *No need to stress as she's David's guest.* Carla left for Tanzania last week to interview Masai women for her research project, which is a pity as Lou could have done with some like-minded company.

Lexi's main interest seems to be men, and David's self-assurance reaches unwarranted heights around her flattery. Her brother's blindness to Lexi's shortcomings makes Lou weary, and she makes a mental note to call

Carla after her trip. As long as Carla comes to Mombasa, Lou plans to go along. Meanwhile, David's visit home will most likely be cut short, as, under Lexi's influence, any excuse will have the two of them rushing back to the city.

Her brother is sickeningly chirpy at breakfast the next morning. He grins at her across the breakfast table, which he's dragged out onto the veranda. His back is to the view down the valley, where rays from the sunrise reflect off the waterhole. A herd of Thompson's gazelles drinks in the relative safety of dawn. The lovely scene settles Lou and reminds her of her small-mindedness. She loves this view and landscape.

As Lou piles her plate with pawpaw, she remembers how much grunting and shoving it took to shift this table out here. David insisted the relocation was for the breeze, not the view, though clearly it's to impress his visitor. Even so, it's a great idea, and Lou wonders why they've not moved it before.

"The table looks good out here," she says.

"Ah, it speaks to me!" replies David.

"I've just woken up. Give me a break!"

"You're always an ogre in the morning."

"You're the monster," she retorts and then grins. "Can't think why you're so cheery today."

David ignores her as he cheerfully butters toast, loading the thick slices with marmalade. Everything he does is in excess these days. It's weird for her to watch this reinvented brother.

They've always eaten inside and used this area for sunset drinks. The outlook is especially gorgeous when the sky is awash with color. Once only, Lou suggested they move the table out, but her father was against it. She realizes that her brother no longer waits for approval. He just goes ahead and does what he likes. Perhaps she'd be smart to follow his lead, but, somehow, it's easier for him. Lou wonders where to start. One day, she will just go ahead and suit herself, irrespective of what everyone else thinks and wants.

"Another scorcher on its way," David says half to himself, his tone expectant. As Lou glances away from the peaceful valley, she sees both anticipation and agitation, but at least he's enthusiastic about something, even if the reason grates her.

Whatever the circumstance though, Lou loves the unique magic of the mornings here, when the air is clean and crisp, even though, recently, the early sun sucks up any last drops of moisture, and the days unfold into the reality of an ongoing drought.

"If you like, I'll help Dad today."

"That would be great, sis."

He beams at her and devours another slice of toast.

It's late when Lou and her father return from the waterhole. Lexi's giggles reach them all the way over at the vehicle shed and continue unabated as they unload the Land Rover and walk to the veranda. Lou hears ice clinking and David's voice as he recounts a story about life on safari.

Lexi greets Lou as if she is a long-lost sister and then turns her full attention to the men. Lou pours two double-ration gins and takes a decent swig of hers, before handing a glass to her father. He rarely makes time for social visits, and, evidently, he's not seen Lexi since she was a child.

"It's so lovely to be here!" their guest enthuses. "Life in Nairobi can be a bit of a bore sometimes. Same old people all the time." The tan line along her bra opens up when she leans forward.

"David seems to have taken to it!" her father replies.

Does Lou detect a note of cynicism in her father's voice? She takes the end seat and sips her tangy, bitter drink.

"David always enjoys a good party. He's very popular!"

Lexi winks at David, and he puffs up instantly at the flattery.

"I hope he's made some useful contacts." Their father plays along.

"Oh, I make sure I introduce him to all the right people!" Lexi replies, her hand protectively on David's arm.

Lou wonders who exactly are "all the right people" as she helps Grace bring out dinner, an extra effort made for their guest.

"It looks delicious!" Lou hugs Grace quickly and helps her cut the roast meats. Grace's ever-ready smile reassures her. It's hardly changed since that first day.

They plan as they eat dinner. David will take Lexi out early to see the game. Lou doesn't really mind that she's not invited. She's behind on her notes, and, anyway, she hates to hear the wild animals described as game. Hours after she goes to bed, she hears the laughter continue into the night.

In the morning, her father looks exhausted. He insists he's OK; just a late night, that's all. David and Lexi are not yet back. Lou pours coffee and worries about her dad. His approach to exhaustion is to just buckle down and get on with it. He never was one to shirk responsibility.

Grace's rooster crows noisily outside as Peter chases the chickens from their night enclosure into the yard. Lou grins at their general alarm, even though it's an everyday routine. Besides providing food, the chickens eat the ticks that would otherwise plague Zebu and the horses. The oxpecker birds help as well, searching the horses' hides for juicy morsels, plucking the parasites off. When the birds are at work, Roma always prances around the enclosure. Despite her quivering flanks, the birds hang tight and flap to balance, only letting go to relocate away from her switching tail. The chickens and oxpeckers save Lou a job of de-ticking the animals.

As if summoned by Lou's thoughts, Zebu appears by the breakfast table, her mouth open in a smile. She's not allowed to beg and has snuck onto the veranda. Lou hugs her, enjoying a brief cuddle, ready for what's to come.

"Zebu. Off you go!" Grace's tone leaves little space to maneuver.

Zebu's energy drains. Suddenly stationary in Lou's arms, she takes a few steps, then stops to glance back, hopeful of a mind change.

"Go on, Zebu. Good girl! I'll get you a breakfast bone soon." Lou encourages her to behave.

A half-hearted tail-wag, and Zebu leaves.

"You spoil that dog!" her father complains. "OK, get her a bone!"

As Lou follows, Zebu exuberantly spins through 180 degrees and lands to face her mistress. After a quick face rub, the dog gallops circuits around Lou, and her toenails scrabble wildly on the hard earth as she narrowly misses a collision. Finally, in a crouch on the ground ahead, she waits for Lou to play, ready to pounce. Lou feigns as if to run away, and Zebu rushes past. Lou laughs until she's out of breath, unexpectedly happy again. "Come on, let's get that bone!"

Zebu trots ahead now. Every few steps, she looks over her shoulder to check Lou is still behind her.

They pass Peter, a headless chicken in his hands—tonight's dinner. At least she doesn't have to kill and skin their food. He saves her from such tasks. Her father promised to buy Peter and Grace a plot of land near their home village should they be made to leave Masaranga. That way, they'd grow vegetables and chickens in case work becomes scarce. They're of the wrong tribe to easily find other work close to here.

Amazingly, two whole days pass before Lexi insists David return her to the city. He tells Lou he misses her, and she manages a smile.

"Come to Nairobi again. You should spend less time mooching around here!"

It's pointless to explain how she feels, and he should know her by now anyhow. He always criticizes her choices.

"I'll visit you," she agrees, but there's a lack of intention behind her words, and he knows it.

"He can take you on a tour of the city!" Lexi says. "It's always fun to return to civilization!"

That depends on your definition of civilization, thinks Lou, unable to see the upside.

"We'll make that trip to the coast." Her brother fills the gap in the conversation, and Lou nods to show she's keen.

"Good luck with everything," she replies and hugs him quickly.

He shakes hands with their father, who slaps him playfully on the shoulder. "Don't be a stranger, son!"

"More coffee, Dad?" asks Lou once they've gone.

"Good idea. I'll be in the office." Her father immediately heads off to work.

When Lou returns, he's preoccupied with the pile of mail that Grace collected from town. She waits and sips coffee until it's obvious he's forgotten she's there.

It really doesn't matter that he's not in the mood to talk, as Grace and Peter have arrived with bulging bags of vegetables. This reminds Lou she should help prepare lunch for a party of government officials. With the distraction of Lexi, she'd forgotten. A guilty pang assaults Lou as she considers her self-absorption. Their visit must run smoothly. How could she have forgotten this critical event that could officially put Masaranga back on the map?

"Here, let me take some of that!"

She grabs a bag of earthy potatoes off Grace's precarious load and follows them into the kitchen.

"Hey, Peter. It's your day off!"

It is, but Grace woke him early. She considers his primary task is to help his mother. "My son is a strong man. He can rest once the work is done," she always says, her voice proud.

Seventeen

From a great distance, female voices infiltrate Lou's sleep. Busy and persistent, they chatter in a tribal tongue. Unwillingly, Lou rises through layers of awareness to a hot morning. As shafts of sunlight bore through the curtains, Lou squints and rolls away from the light and disturbance outside. If only she could learn to wake up cheerful. Today, a convoy of government officials is due for their free lunch.

Ultimately, once the demons have fled, the familiar chatter settles Lou. For a moment, she lies still and tries to remember her dream. But, instead, she envisages the scene outside, where women gossip and tease one another as they erect makeshift stalls. Tradition still allows the women to set up at headquarters. On busy days, they arrive early to arrange their carvings and beaded jewelry on vividly colored tablecloths in an effort to tempt visitors.

Considering the big day ahead, it's good that the chatter woke her up, but, inexplicably, she wants to burrow under the covers. What is it that makes her want to return to the dark space she's just escaped? Lou sinks back down and catches the tail of an unsettling dream, until the chatter drags her back to reality. A wave of frustration rises, and, in a single abrupt movement, she throws back the bedcovers. And it's hard not to smile. Word has got out, as always, that wealthy visitors are on their way. Potentially prosperous shoppers might be persuaded to buy the work of these artists.

In the bright sunlight, the dresses are vibrant and complement the women's skin tones. One of the five gossips is older, without the plumpness of the others, and her skin hangs in loose folds. Lou watches her hold a scarf of boldly patterned material against her face, demanding attention. When her friends turn to look, she laughs, a gutsy exuberant sound, her gapped teeth exposed. A young woman with plaited hair claps her hands in delight and answers in a jaunty tone. The rest smile indulgently and continue to arrange soapstone carvings on vividly colored backgrounds.

Later, a burst of more affected laughter erupts from the veranda while Lou sets down plates of finely sliced meats. Grace follows with salad bowls and home-baked rolls, and her friend Mary ensures alcohol flows freely. The officials arrived in a convoy of shiny black cars and aren't shy of indulging. The men wear well-cut suits, and among them are two stunning women, their intricate hair braids accentuating high cheekbones.

Lou feels her social ineptitude must be entirely visible. This is not her scene, and she found the introductions too fast to recall names. To compensate, she keeps busy and only occasionally stops to talk to one of the intoxicated visitors. The safest course seems to remain occupied. The title of party-animal has never applied to Lou; quite the opposite. She's clueless when it comes to chit-chat, and today is no exception. An evening by a campfire would suit her so much more.

Though her father also dislikes these rare visits, he's deep in conversation with an angular-faced man, whose gray-speckled hair and trimmed beard give him a distinguished air. In theory, this visit is a friendly drop in on their way upcountry. Lou was appreciative they requested to come. She wants to swing extra help toward Masaranga, despite her gut feeling that this is unlikely to happen.

But a bit more warning would have been helpful. Such visits are free rides for officialdom. Lou wonders if there are other reasons why they've come to Masaranga. None plan to tour, and not a single eye has turned toward the plains and waterhole below.

However, it's essential to treat them as royalty. Quite apart from needing reinforcements in Masaranga, her father's position is precarious and they need to buy points. Lou dreads the likelihood they'll be forced to follow those who've lost privileged jobs and left the country for uncertain futures.

Talking of privileged positions, Fred Lonnegan is here, and Lou made a significant effort to welcome him. He's entirely at ease, and the other officials seem to kowtow to him. Lou wonders how she could have differently handled their meeting a couple of months ago. He heads a table, where the laughter is loudest, and Mary is kept busiest, the glasses emptying as fast as she can fill them.

Lou takes her first drink off a loaded tray and asks Mary to get more bottles out of storage. No one's holding back. The champagne makes her edgy as she sips it too fast, a rare treat. Before long, she's almost as cheerful as the rest of them. She smiles at an attractive man, suddenly aware he's been watching her. Immediately, he raises his glass and approaches her confidently through the crowd.

"Sam Watchiri," he introduces himself when close enough to be heard above the din. Compared to the drunken group, he's calm and composed. They shake hands, and his grip is firm.

"Lou Hopkins. It's lovely to meet you!" she replies with a grin. Sam is attractive, and the champagne has given her confidence a rare boost. Lou notices the expensive suit on his athletic body as she leans closer to hear above the chatter.

"So, Will is your father," he says. "Excellent! I hear you study the elephants."

Ingenuously, she forgets the small talk and comes to the point. "Yes, I do. I've documented how human settlements block wildlife migratory corridors."

"How interesting!" Sam replies in a less than interested voice.

"But heavy poaching has made the herds skittish and hard to study." Lou talks faster now so she can, at least, have her say before he turns away. "Their social structures are disrupted, and they're too stressed to breed."

"That's a pity. I'm sorry it's compromised your work."

Lou almost replies, *Yes, a problem for me, of course, but what about the damage to the elephants?* when Sam continues, "In fact, Fred briefed me. He indicated we might fund some rangers for you."

"Really?" Hardly able to believe her ears, Lou glances towards the lively crowd at the head of the table.

"Plenty of time to talk to him," Sam assures her. "Let me introduce you to a couple of my associates." His hand lightly on her back, he steers her towards a couple of the younger men.

Lou goes obediently with him, her mind on a tangent. She must try to sound less desperate for help and allow him to bring it up. Perhaps Fred took her request on board.

"How do you spend your workdays?" Lou asks Sam as he leads her around.

"Just like this!" he replies evasively. "My life is very boring."

But as Sam reminisces about his early days in Mombasa, it's obvious he prefers the coast to the savannah, which is unfortunate as the inland country has been her whole world. To Lou, though, he still seems smart and exciting.

As Sam steers Lou around the party, he tells her she has beautiful blue eyes. Suddenly, she's self-conscious, though it's become easier to mix with this group of strangers, who greet Sam with jovial slaps on the back. No one else feigns much interest in her research, which is no surprise. Few politicians have wildlife conservation on their radar. Their official focus is to represent the people, but, too often, it's more a matter of feathering their own nests. The immaculately dressed women seem amused and sympathetic at how Lou spends her time. The men are less obvious, and she notices a couple of them surreptitiously check her out.

Sam is easily the most charming, and she's flattered by his attention.

"You've chosen a remarkable project," he says. "The elephants are important for our economy. People love to see those big tusks."

Lou abstains from expounding how much more they are than a set of tusks. Neither does she beg for the help they need. It's great to have his attention and the rest can wait for now. The champagne has done its job, and she's enjoying the experience.

"Lou, how perfectly delightful to see you again." Fred Lonnegan materializes at her side, the veins on his cheeks accentuated by alcohol. "Sam, I see you're taking care of our lovely hostess!"

Embarrassed, Lou drops her eyes and smiles and replies politely. "Yes! Sam's doing a great job, especially as I hardly know anyone."

Fred is more than tipsy. At such close quarters, he's quite domineering, as if used to having his way, but his help is vital. He, too, gives Lou a once-over, which makes her squirm. Her long shirt and slacks were a good choice. She hopes Sam has it right about the extra rangers.

"Not such a bad part of the country. What a treat to come inland!" Fred's words are slightly blurred.

"It has its own special beauty!" Lou answers. "I can't imagine living anywhere else."

He's genuinely surprised by her reply. "Well, you might have to live elsewhere one day," Fred chides her. "A young woman like yourself would become terribly lonely out here."

"Not so far!" Lou replies, but his attention has already moved on.

"Sam, I'm afraid we need to hurry everyone along," he says. "It's a long drive up the valley."

"Certainly, sir. I'll let the drivers know," replies Sam respectfully, his tone confident. Sober and at ease, he seems more switched on than his superior.

For a moment, Lou watches as Sam glides agilely around the tables with a brief stop to answer the older man, still with her father. He disappears behind the house towards Grace's quarters, where the drivers are having lunch, and Fred turns back to her.

"Sam's an astute man. He'll go far! Thank you for the delightful luncheon, Lou. Oh, did he tell you we have two new staff for your anti-poaching unit? Your father knows the details."

"Thank you. Thank you very much. I can't tell you how much this means to us." Suddenly grateful, Lou is annoyed with herself for not liking him.

"Pleased to be of service," Fred replies, smiling. "Do pop into my office whenever you're back in civilization. Now, I must get this mob moving!"

He winks and brushes past her, patting her back as he shuffles away, his legs unsteady from the drink. He stops for a quick word with one person, then another, before he leaves ahead of the group. He must surely be a clever man, despite her first impressions. What confounds Lou is how he's kept his position when so many outsiders were forced to go back to where they came from.

Eighteen

Backlit by the evening sun, the massive nest hangs heavy and dark, enveloped within an orange halo. As the weaverbirds worked to expand it over the years, the tree bough warped under the weight. Late in the afternoon, its community of birds is always busy, and their silhouettes dart in and out of the multiple entrances. As Lou passes by on her way to the vehicle shed, she follows a kink in the track that developed to protect the weaverbirds from disturbance.

If the weight of the woven-grass structure were to snap the branch, years of work would crash to the ground, and a generation of weaverbirds would probably die, even if Lou were able to strap its bulk back in the tree in a belated attempt to save the chicks. About sixty couples use these well-insulated chambers.

Shadow and light catch their wings, making it hard to distinguish individual birds. The spectacle creates beauty in a mechanical corner of the compound that's otherwise dominated by hard lines and angular equipment.

As Lou loads spotlights into the vehicles, she can hear Peter briefing the new staff members. Naturally delighted with his new responsibility, he's doing a great job. He's attractive, with dark, flawless skin and perfect teeth, and has a ready smile today, apparently cheerful in his new role of educator. With rifles slung over their shoulders, the rangers divulge little of their thoughts while they listen quietly.

The new rangers are from Nairobi. Surprisingly, Sam sent them two city boys. However, any help is welcome, and they've been put straight on the job, with the hope they might quickly develop bush-survival skills. Of course, Peter will need to train them well as they go, but he reckons they're already skilled shots and comfortable with their rifles. The more time wasted, the more elephants die.

Paul, the taller man, grins frequently. He's interactive with intelligent eyes and broad cheekbones, which makes him likable at first sight. John, his co-worker, lacks confidence and waits slightly back, fidgeting quietly, with his eyes firmly fixed on the ground. In contrast, Paul nods every now and then to demonstrate his absorption of Peter's information barrage.

But despite his attentiveness, Paul also appears amused. Lou guesses he's not used to being instructed by someone obviously younger and less worldly. She makes a mental note to suggest her father send Paul out with the older rangers—although it's unlikely he'd consider her opinion worthwhile on such matters.

Lou sighs and wishes she could go on the run along Masaranga's northern border tonight. She'd like to be more involved and useful, and it's always exciting to head into the bush at sunset with spotlights ready and the anticipation of sighting predators on the prowl.

Peter has finished their initiation, and the men head toward the Land Rover. Without a moment's hesitation, Paul takes the passenger seat. John vaults into the open back, and, as his skinny legs swing over the tailgate, he grins shyly at Lou for a second before ducking under the canvas back.

Peter accelerates away, and the weaverbirds' noisy din is briefly banished by a wake of swirling dust that engulfs their nest. As the vehicle leaves the compound, thorns in the overgrown hedges catch on its canvas back and send dusty red and purple flowers swinging wildly. In an energetic last-minute chase, the dog gallops past Lou toward the gap in the hedge and becomes a moving shadow within the dust cloud.

"Zebu, come back here!" Lou shouts.

Each bound becomes shorter than the last. As the cloud clears, Zebu turns sheepishly and wags her tail gently on her return, head low, ready to roll submissively, should it be necessary.

But Lou rubs the soft folds of skin under her neck, and Zebu opens her jaws in a contented smile as she gets more of a cuddle than she deserves.

"Naughty girl!"

Zebu's tail wags harder, and she follows Lou back to the corrugated-roof building that serves as the office.

"Hi, Dad."

The dark smudges under his eyes seem permanent.

"Outside," he growls, and Zebu bolts from the theoretical no-go territory. Her gaze shifts to Lou and she lies down, head resting on her paws, watching and waiting.

"The dog has got too bold for her own good." Her father's tone is matter-of-fact.

Lou ignores him as she knows that, on long afternoons, he's inclined to weaken and let Zebu sleep by him in the office.

When Lou glances at Zebu, she gets an instant tail wag of acknowledgement, which makes her father roll his eyes in mock despair.

"Peter's gone with the new boys?"

Yes, she nods.

"Your brother with them?"

She shakes her head and wonders if he will criticize.

David returned from Nairobi two days ago and has not yet been out.

"Those new rangers are cheeky looking," he says. "The trouble with those city boys is they think they know it all. A year out here should sort them out!"

"I hope so. We need help. You look tired, Dad."

"I'm used to tired." He shrugs his shoulders and smiles.

On the map of Masaranga behind his desk, two large blue areas are marked along with several smaller waterholes. The blue is deceptive as the real water sources are rarely that color or size. A spidery pattern throughout the rest of the open space depicts winding riverbeds and dirt tracks. New bright red stickers sit mostly in the northern and western areas, inside elephant country as reminders of where they've been shot. Lou averts her eyes, the memories of those massacres too painful.

"I might go out and camp on that shady stretch along the river tomorrow. It's too far for a day trip, and I could do with some time out." She points to the spot on the map.

Lou's statement is more of a question, and her father glances sharply at her.

"Only if you take Peter to keep an eye on you. The new boys can accompany me tomorrow. You're not to go alone anywhere after that last episode. Take your brother as well. He's doing little enough around the place."

Chastised, Lou nods and says nothing. It's taking ages to live down how she failed to stay put and wait for help. Any defense on her part seems pointless as no excuse exists good enough to ignore such a fundamental rule of survival. Quietly her heart gives a little leap of joy as he's basically agreed to her plan. Peter won't need any persuasion, and neither will David with any luck.

Her father hunches back over the aerial photographs spread across his carved wooden desk. In this permanently makeshift office, his elegant desk always seems slightly out of place, with animals etched along the edges, and its polished surface smooth under Lou's fingers as she leans closer.

"Don't camp anywhere near this section." He points toward the highest focus of red markers. "Poachers use bush tracks that cross all over this area. They'd probably see you first and clear out, but that's not the point. It's risky. Stick south of the river, on the tourist tracks."

Lou hides her disappointment. She'd planned to go through that remote section of elephant country and get an updated overview of the area. Fortunately, it's off season for tourists so the roads won't be busy. She sighs inwardly and wonders if they might make a couple of low-risk diversions once they've sussed things out.

"What's going on in that head of yours?" Her father sounds suspicious. "Lost in thought again, I can see! You should come down from the clouds. I'm surprised I let you out anywhere."

"Don't know where I get it from!" she replies with a mischievous grin.

For a moment, his face is blank. Then he smiles and chuckles, but his amusement fades as he leans back over the photos. Streaks of gray run through his previously jet-black hair, and crows' feet now line his eyes, more from constant worry than smiling.

But her dad does sometimes smile, considering the disruptions to his life. He's remained steady through a multitude of difficulties. Now with Masaranga so severely impacted, he feels responsible. Lou understands him because of her complete empathy for the park and its inhabitants. They'd both be lost without the place and what it stands for.

When Lou slips from the office, he's absorbed entirely elsewhere. Only Zebu notices her leave and faithfully trails her to the house, where Lou kicks off her shoes and heads to her desk to write up the last lot of notes before her camping trip generates more data. Though she must compel herself to start, once she does, the movement of her pen across the paper reassures her. Her mind focuses, and her thoughts no longer wander the well-worn channels that carry her toward anxiety and fear for the future. Lou now keeps that dark place to herself for fear that others will again judge she takes life too seriously.

Nineteen

Long before dawn, the lions start to hunt. When Lou wakes in her tent, the guttural growl outside seems unreal, as if part of a dream, until another primal call sends a jolt of fear right through her. She rolls onto all fours like a frightened animal. The canvas tent seems flimsy, as a burst of hooves shakes the hard earth of the savannah. Suddenly, she realizes she's not the only one scared.

Crouched motionless on her heels, Lou listens to the hooves slow. She should have pitched her tent closer to the Land Rover. Instinctively, her hand touches the cold metal of the rifle by her sleeping mat. The sounds of the hooves slow and then stop to be replaced by a chilling quiet.

"David," she whispers.

"Definitely awake, sis," he replies immediately, his voice far calmer than she feels.

"Where's Peter?"

"Yes, I am awake also. The lions are not as close as it seems."

"How can you tell?"

"I hear how the wildebeests run. Lions are not so fast. They have been stalking them for—"

A massive roar cuts him off. Lou gasps and pulls her rifle under her arm. Her head touches the A-frame roof. The ground vibrates as terrified animals run for safety. Another roar, further away this time. Thank god, the hungry cat has moved away—but, on second thoughts, the second roar must be another lion. She tries to rationalize. The lions are focused on their natural prey out there, and humans aren't part of their regular diet.

A shiver runs through Lou as she unzips her tent and pushes the rifle muzzle ahead through the flap. Backlit by the moon, jagged silhouettes tower above camp. Above the trees, bright stars glint in an inky sky. Only the outlines of the other tents and Land Rover are clearly visible as dense shadows obscure all that lies beyond.

"What're you up to, sis? Stay put for now!"

"Can't we get in the car?"

Just asking this question makes her feel pathetic.

Another primeval rally of feline grunts reverberates through the night air. Again, the ground shakes under hooves. The sound intensifies until it sounds as if the wildebeests will stampede through camp. Despite David's caution, Lou is ready to run for the Land Rover, when another massive roar halts her. The vibrations build into a chaotic flurry of ambushed animals, trapped and running every way. Lou focuses on taking slow deep breaths. She reassures herself that the lions have already bypassed the campsite and easier prey.

However, the equally scary prospect of being trampled by frenzied mobs of wildebeests makes her heart pound as violently as the ground outside. Then, suddenly, out there on the savannah, the petrified herd quietens. Lou imagines the wildebeests hemmed in on all sides, terrified as they listen and wait for the final rush.

"Stay put and keep your rifles ready," says David in a low voice.

"OK."

Lou is too afraid to move anyhow. It's not far to the vehicle, but to run now and expose herself as frightened prey would be madness. To stay inside the thin-walled tent seems equally crazy. The lions must be aware of their camp and have smelt them long ago. Usually, only weak or injured lions come after people, but this rationale doesn't entirely settle her.

Abruptly, out beyond the silhouetted trees, the sounds of a sudden violent struggle ensue. The strident distress call of a dying animal cuts the darkness. A horrifying sound so close. Then the thud as the prey hits the ground. The agonized grunts of the wildebeest give way to the roar of lions as several cats call together. Their triumphant echo reverberates through Lou and imprints her memory, its ferocity stamped into every last cell.

Her fear drains slowly as the tension across the savannah is released. The predators have made their claim. Lou becomes aware of her trembling hands only when they stop.

Dawn brings dramatic change to the savannah. At first light, David drives them out to search for the kill. Almost straightaway, they discover the pride, rested and content, bellies full. Viewed in daylight from the Land Rover, the predators are gorgeous cuddly cats, whose golden coats contrast starkly with the bloody carcass. Intense yellow eyes return Lou's gaze, the lionesses untroubled by the vehicle. From safety, the sleek cats are magnificent. With the day not yet heat-sapped, the scene is sharp and vital. Hearing the kill firsthand has altered Lou's perception of it. The chilling uncertainty of the dark bears little relation to these satiated cats, so unbelievably close to camp.

As usual, Peter was right, and a wildebeest has died, its existence extinguished to sustain the lions. Along with the others, this animal's hooves pummeled the hard ground, but it was the unlucky one, its attempt to escape futile. For many animals, survival involves horrific episodes and the daily terror of being stalked, each day's existence a gamble. Only a stripped carcass remains of what was a life, hours ago. But it's a reprieve for the rest of the herd, all probably grazing quietly, not far away. For a while, the sacrifice will sustain these top predators. Soon, scavengers will clean up.

David eases the vehicle closer, and Lou positions her camera. Now lazy, the cats guard the remains of the corpse, undisturbed as the shutter fires repeatedly. The kill has fed six adult females and three juveniles. A half-grown lioness methodically licks at the remains of the bovine head, and Lou can hear the rasp of her rough tongue against the freshly exposed skull. Birds call from the shady treetops, oblivious to the gruesome scene. Survival of the fittest sometimes seems more like survival of the luckiest, the fortune distributed unfairly, much like the artificial world that humans have made for themselves. Lou's thoughts tease around the concept as she watches the red tongue work the bone.

The largest lioness arches her back and stretches lazily, her muscles rippling under sleek fur. When she approaches the cat with the skull, the smaller cat snarls, but defers and slinks off, as the Queen claims her right. Besides humans, lions have little to fear, as long as they know their place. A cheetah cub is fair game, as killing it saves the lion future competition for resources. Nature is sometimes as cruel as man, though never as perverted. Lou watches as the Queen's long canines sink into the skull, which cracks noisily. Segments dislodge and a slow regular crunching sound begins as her molars finish the job. With the fragments swallowed, the cat methodically works the groove behind the eye socket.

Peter drove them out early to catch this scene. As the day heats up, these lions will move away and find shade, so that a group of tourists might later discover the carcass and wonder what they've missed. Not many people get an inside experience of the savannah, and for many an African adventure is mere entertainment. They pay up, and then move on to the next holiday, a new destination, another continent. They take their memories home and forget how little wildlife really remains. But at least the tourist dollar encourages the people to preserve their wild heritage.

Perhaps only what is perceived as directly useful to people might survive an overpopulated planet. Self-preservation for some and greed for others makes people destructive. Will this continue until the earth becomes stripped of magnificent animals such as these lionesses, replacing them with overpopulation, crops and concrete?

David becomes irritated when Lou harbors anxiety over all this. He judges she should stop agonizing and get a life. He's a bit grumpy this morning, perhaps from lack of sleep. The boys were up before dawn and made tea over a fire. Snuggled in her sleeping bag, Lou listened to their voices rise and fall. At first light, she crawled out and drank her tea in silence while she recalled the sounds of the hunt.

When they return to pack up camp, David teases her about her first impulse last night to run for cover, and Peter fails to defend her as he used to do. Lou gets the funny side of her humiliation, but she's also tired, and the kill was close. Even Peter was surprised by the proximity of those lions.

Twenty

All around Lou, vast expanses of golden dunes stretch toward the distant horizon, where they meet the bruised blues of a stormy sky. The immense empty scenery lacks a point of focus within its patterns of sunlit curves and scythe-shaped shadows. The realization that this strange landscape lacks reality causes Lou to wake, but she keeps her eyes closed in an attempt to recall the dream sequences that led her to such a superb and barren place.

A memory of her mother slips through, and she bats it away immediately. Her distant mother leads an alternative life and long ago lost any rights in this realm of existence. To make life lonelier, David deserted for Nairobi again, despite the fact he's needed here. His neglect of Masaranga saddens Lou, as she's sure his heart really lies here. On the bright side, their holiday with Carla and Lexi is not far off, and David generously organized her a lift to meet them in Nairobi.

But what was that dream about? Lou retreats under the covers, wraps her arms around her knees and puts her mind back there. But the dunes stretch endlessly with nowhere to go and no place to retreat or hide; a vast impassionate space. A background roar begins to intensify until it's loud enough to engulf all other senses, and she wakes just as a vehicle pulls up in the compound.

Outside, the sun has broken the horizon, and two well-dressed men wait by the office. Though people often arrive early to catch the dawn wildlife before the heat sets in, these official-looking Africans don't seem to be tourists. The tall, athletic one contrasts starkly with his stocky companion, whose bulging belly is visible even from this distance. Still drowsy, Lou tries to place the tall one. Then her father has joined them, and the men converse briefly in a patch of pale sunlight while he finds his keys to let them into his office. Her heart lurches as she wonders if this has something to do with her father's position.

But a dove coos calmly on the roof above her, and immediately another one joins to start the dawn chorus. At the same time, Grace crosses the gap between the kitchen and office with a tray of steaming mugs. Lou quickly throws on clothes and hurries to the kitchen, where Grace's coffee helps her mind to clear. With sudden anticipation, she guesses one of the visitors is Sam, the handsome official who was so friendly the day they had visitors for lunch. Lou is indebted to him for encouraging the Department to provide extra rangers.

Optimistic now, her mind gives a leap of relief at this opportune visit. Sam was a touch full of himself, but Lou didn't mind as he was so charming and willing to assist them. She curbs an instinct to listen in at the office and instead helps Grace prepare breakfast before taking a shower. The warm water feels good as it washes across her skin. Lou lathers quickly, keeping it short to save water and time as she hurries, not wanting to miss anything.

The men are already at the breakfast table when Lou arrives, her hair wet and combed back off her face.

"Good morning, Lou!" Sam stands to shake her hand and gives her a friendly smile.

"Good morning, Sam." Lou grins back at him, glad she remembered his name, as it's not one of her strengths. He introduces her to his companion, who shakes her hand but is otherwise dismissive.

"Hi, Dad!"

"You're late," he replies. "No doubt you stayed up late and worked on your thesis!"

Lou grins at the backhanded compliment.

"Our visitors have government business in Nakuru," he says.

"We've dropped in on our way through to see your new rangers," explains Sam.

"Of course!" says Lou. "We're very grateful. Thanks. It's much appreciated. You must have started early to fit us in!"

"Oh, we've not come far today," Sam defers politely. He actually seems uncomfortable, and Lou hopes she's not overdone it. Does her gratitude sound a bit over the top? Her father changes the topic with a question about the management of Lake Nakuru.

Lou spreads butter on her toast and watches it melt as she listens to the conversation. Sam's job must be high profile judging from his confidence and expensive clothes. Her father dresses poorly in comparison, even on his Nairobi days. Sam must be on his way up. Lou catches him sneaking glances at her and averts her eyes each time, the attention making her shy. He's solicitous, but she feels strangely uneasy. Later, while their visitors meet with the new rangers, Lou tells herself to get over it and that she must have got out of bed the wrong side this morning. It's completely obvious that Sam is extremely intelligent and motivated.

Twenty-One

Now that Lou is familiar with this Nairobi suburb, she spots the outline of the jacaranda tree long before David pulls up in front of Sara's gates. They've arrived early, but Carla is already out the front. The exuberant Doberman bounds in circles around their Peugeot as they load her bags. It would be fun if the dog could accompany them to Mombasa, but that's out of the question.

True to form, Lexi keeps them waiting, and some repacking is needed to make space for her large bag. The moment it's stowed, Lexi slides into the front seat next to David. They flirt shamelessly, and David's subsequent high spirits are infectious. As they set off, he sends them into fits of laughter, which reminds Lou why their safaris were always so much fun. David navigates the crowded outskirts skillfully and, before long, they turn onto the coast road for the long drive to Mombasa. After months of drought, a swim in the Indian Ocean seems like a long-awaited dream.

As Lou listens to her brother flirt, a forgotten memory of a childhood adventure surfaces. She'd tagged along with David and Peter to explore a stretch of bushland along the Nwasi River. Always the ringleader, David was ahead, and Lou had to hurry to keep up.

"Keep up, Lou. Don't be such a slow coach!" he called over his shoulder as they took turns jumping down from a high bank onto a trail leading toward the water's edge. She landed awkwardly and was rubbing her ankle when his next command came with a ramped-up urgency.

"Let's get out of here!"

Ahead of them on the narrow trail was a hippo with muddy water dripping off its huge head. As it ambled toward them, the massive animal seemed unaware of their presence. Hippos deservedly have a reputation for being dangerous at close quarters as angry chomps from their giant jaws have undone many people.

The only escape route was to dash back up the steep bank. At the rear now and closest to danger, David started to pull himself up on tree roots, grunting and cursing. Lou managed to scale the boulder she'd just leapt down from and then grabbed saplings to haul herself higher up the slope.

"Get a move on!" David bellowed as he stormed past and then slipped directly in front of her. Despite his handicap, he reached the top first, covered with scrapes and grazes. Once safely on their way home, Lou and Peter giggled as they recounted David's antics and they ribbed him mercilessly for how fearful he looked as he overtook them.

Nevertheless, many such incidents have failed to dampen David's desire to lead. Always dynamic, he applied plenty of pressure to coordinate everyone and make this trip happen. Lou was last on board and took some persuading considering her other commitments. Also, while they're away, there are fewer eyes on the lookout for the elephants.

The highway traffic is as chaotic as ever. David has developed the attitude of "if you can't beat them, you may as well join them," which is perhaps a poor survival tactic considering the live-or-die fanaticism of other drivers. But on the less frantic stretches of road, his cheerful spirits rub off on Lou. He's shed his sarcastic shell and his old spark seems to have returned

Along with the erratic drivers are the impossible-to-avoid potholes that inevitably puncture right through the bitumen into the dirt below. The miles shudder by, and Lou hopes the road won't be this bad the entire trip down to the Mombasa. On the upside, though, they're about to cut through the open country of Tsavo National Park.

As hours clock by, a heat haze begins to shimmer above the asphalt. Their spirits wane. Hot air roars through the open windows and drowns out the banter between Lexi and David upfront. Carla seems occupied with her own thoughts, her eyes on the passing landscape.

Buildings and cultivated plots give way to savannah. Beyond the drone of engines and petrol fumes, the plains stretch toward a distant horizon. Silhouettes of elephants shelter in the shade of sporadic, wide-branched acacias.

The car swerves alarmingly. Temporarily inattentive of the road, David has leaned toward Lexi. He touches her neck and lifts her necklace into his hand. Has he only just noticed the ivory trinket? Lexi reveals it's a gift from a besotted admirer, possibly one of David's wealthy clients. Lou wonders if all his clients are rich. She wonders if they come on any other business apart from tourism. Trust Lexi to use the opportunity to brag, even at the expense of wounding David. But he's quick to dismiss her admirer's poor taste in choosing ivory as a gift.

His criticism falls on deaf ears as Lexi pouts. "The ivory looks even better on me, and anyhow, I couldn't hurt the poor darling's feelings," she says to David.

A privilege she apparently doesn't extend to him.

"Who would the poor darling be?" he asks Lexi. "Not a recreational hunter-type, I hope."

In place of an answer, she drops her sulk and winks at him instead. In a flirty voice, she asks what sort of gift a man with superior taste might pick. He grins and touches her cheek gently, outwardly happy to let the matter go.

Her heart suddenly heavy, Lou wishes he'd have the good taste to fall for Carla and surrender Lexi to the other poor bastard. She wonders what sort of tourists David is usually involved with. Not trophy hunters, she hopes. He's never actually told her. So much for listening to other people's conversations. Is she just jealous of losing her brother to other people who care only for themselves? Lou realizes how much he keeps to himself and that she can no longer confide in him.

On an embankment, they pass an overturned truck, the wreckage twisted, the tires already scavenged by humans. Carla raises her eyebrows as if to say: someone was unlucky that day. Most likely, a crazy driver like so many others, who pushed it that bit too hard, though that's not the point. Lou settles back into her corner again.

The drive drags out. Eventually, even the front-seat chatter dies down. On the last run down to the ocean, David stops at a rustic café. Lou stretches her cramped muscles, glad of the opportunity to escape the car and her thoughts. The moist breeze smells refreshingly different from the dusty inland air.

The others disappear into the cafe's dark interior, and Lou wanders across to see the view from the outside deck. It's ages since she saw the ocean, and the lookout is breathtaking. The hillside drops down sharply in front, and the vista beyond stretches toward silhouetted palm trees at the line where the land gives way to an iridescent sea. A sense of endless possibilities in an infinite universe suddenly washes through Lou.

Luxuriant vegetation covers the slopes below her. On the edges of the emerald forest, tropical birds dart between light and shadow. Lou has an illusion that if she fell over the edge, the thick canopy of leaves and vines would save her, the patch of jungle below so dense, the plants so bound together as to be impenetrable.

Carla returns with two coffees and fried snacks with soft centers that taste of banana.

"Thanks. I really appreciate it. My shout next time." Lou grins, grateful to her friend.

"You always find the viewpoints! I'm glad we took a break, though we're almost there," Carla says between mouthfuls.

"Yes, it's a long hot drive!"

"David and Lexi want to check we're happy to share?"

"Of course. I expected we would!" Lou smiles, painfully aware that what she feared for David is a done deal.

"My friend Steve can teach you to dive." Carla changes the subject subtly, her voice determined. "You'll like him. And you already said you wanted to learn scuba."

"Sure, I'm keen!" Lou admits, her mind's eye sinking for a moment below the blue surface on the horizon. "Do you like my brother?" she adds casually.

"Of course! But I'm not my sister."

"That's for sure!" Lou keeps her voice even.

"Anyhow, Steve's nice and he's popular with his clients," says Carla.

"You coming diving?"

"Of course not! The idea terrifies me!"

They're giggling together almost conspiratorially, though neither could pinpoint precisely why, when an expensive car draws up. David would immediately identify its make and model, but Lou has no clue. An elegant

African woman steps out in high heels. On her way into the café, she glances at them as if to ask what's so funny. When she reappears with coffee, Lexi and David are close behind.

Lexi seems distracted and not quite as possessive of David as she usually is. Lou only notices because it bugs her. She notices Lexi's surreptitious gesture to acknowledge the driver of the fancy car. The man is little more than an outline behind tinted windows, and it's impossible to see if he reciprocates. No one else notices. Wouldn't he'd wind the window down if he recognized Lexi?

They watch as the glamorous woman leans in to hand the driver his coffee and then slides elegantly into the passenger seat.

"Don't think much of her necklace," says David to Lexi, who is already back on his arm.

"What do you mean?" she replies.

"A line up of leopard canines. Beautifully set, mind you!"

"Oh, I never noticed."

"Unusual for you not to notice something like that." David takes his opportunity to tease her. "Her husband and your admirer must have similar taste!" He laughs good-naturedly. Lexi gives him the strangest look that he somehow misses. He's already headed toward the viewpoint. Lou turns to get another glance at the couple in the car and notices the two kids staring out from their comfortable back seat as the vehicle eases quietly away. It's too late to observe any more.

A shrill giggle distracts Lou's attention from the departing car. David has his arms around Lexi as if he might throw her over the rails into the jungle, while Carla must have gone back inside for another drink. Though sometimes unsure of Carla's take on life, Lou knows it often matches hers.

Their shared room opens onto a gorgeous view across the ocean. As they drop their bags off on the way to the beach, Carla tells Lou not to worry too much.

"What do you mean?" Lou replies, already at the window. She can't wait to get back into the water.

But Carla is inclined to keep things close to the chest, and she changes tack, her voice overly reassuring as if she needs to convince herself more than Lou. "We're going to have a fantastic time. First stop tomorrow is the dive shop."

Twenty-Two

$\mathbf{L}$ ou was happy to go for a walk alone, seeing the others were hell-bent on a shopping spree, which was easy enough to avoid. She remembers this stretch of coastline as idyllic before ramshackle development took over. But even with the massive changes here, the elements remain constant, and the tropical breeze today has wrinkled the ocean's surface into a gorgeous mosaic of blues and greens. Yet the shoreline bears little resemblance to her teenage memories as makeshift houses have mushroomed along the coast. Last time she walked here, there were no buildings, and it was possible to sprint straight down onto the sand, and then swim out past the breakers.

Up ahead of her, three ragged boys romp out from their dilapidated home. Lou slackens pace as they tear toward her along the uneven walkway. They carry sticks and use them to keep homemade wheels rolling, the toys ingeniously crafted from salvaged materials. Lou laughs and steps aside to avoid a collision with the unruly kids. Their shrieks of laughter are briefly dampened, but they giggle together once they've passed, their expressions open and interested as they take her in. Their radiant complexions suggest health, despite their poverty. Food grows plentifully in this warm, wet climate, and these kids look as if exercise is just a normal part of life, unlike many of their Western counterparts.

After months of drought, the moist air against her skin feels lovely. Small clouds dot the sky, and an expanse of water stretches all the way to a hazy horizon. Being near the ocean reminds Lou of the eternal cycle of elements, of how this timeless coastline has seen multitudes of people come and go.

They spent several family holidays on the coast. Silversands campground at Malindi was a favorite spot. Another time, when they went more remote, the car got stuck in the dunes, and they had to camp and wait right there until a vehicle came through two days later. The driver was a tough, wiry man.

"Been here long?" He'd grinned wryly at them. Even at that age, she'd felt embarrassed by their predicament though relieved to see he had a tow bar and winch.

Her best memories are of the times she followed her brother through the shallows to where the sandy floor dropped away.

"Hurry up, Lou!" he'd call, always in a rush to escape the heat and hit the water. They waded in waist deep as far as the drop-off and then pushed out from the ledge into deeper territory.

When her father taught them to snorkel, his favorite spot was around a headland with no road access, so it was a long swim to get there. On a good day, when the water was crystal clear, the underwater landscape was surreal. The echo of the ocean around her was interrupted only by the sound of her breath. Waves dumped seawater down her snorkel, but he taught them to how to pinch the mouthpiece and blast it back out. Each time, she'd take a deep breath afterwards and return to the comforting sounds of the sea.

Later, older and more confident, she went alone. Sometimes further out, it took every last drop of her reason to overcome a fear of imagined dangers such as the possibility of a shark lurking nearby.

As Lou hurries along, waves curl, catching the sunlight, and break across the beach below. She anticipates all that is hidden beneath the surface. In her mind, and in the calmer waters beneath the turbulence, kaleidoscopes of memories and fish glide through parallel worlds. Oblivious of the irritation of a man who steps around her, Lou stops to imagine how the underwater world now looks out past the headland.

Do huge red anemones still cling to the underwater rocks out past the craggy headland? Their sticky tentacles once carpeted that underwater landscape. When touched, they stuck to her fingers. If the waves carried Lou too close, she'd twist through the water to avoid them brushing against her bare skin. She often body-surfed behind David through narrow gaps between anemone-encrusted rocks, their challenge to race through too fast to be grabbed by their soft tentacles.

So much has changed. Her invincible brother was a fearless swimmer, and Lou trailed him wherever. Her trust allowed her to follow him into deep water, devoid of handholds. The ocean floor drifted far below them, dotted with colorful coral outcrops. It might be confronting when mouthfuls of saltwater made her gasp and cough, but then she'd lift her head above the surface and roll with the swell. Her view would shift between the sandy shore and out where the waves met the sky, and the ocean's wildness inspired her. In those moments, Lou felt she could float forever within an alternative world.

When physical exhaustion overrode their combined enthusiasm, David would call it a day. "I'm bored now," he'd say. "And I'm hungry."

Bedraggled, Lou reluctantly struggled out of the sea. Sand stuck to her legs as she followed him up the beach to the campsite to raid their food supplies. They slept outside the family tent so they could watch the night sky.

But there's no time for this today, nor to feel the sand and water on her skin. As Lou walks along the pavement, she suppresses an urge to rush down onto the beach. She wants to run wild with the elements, to kick up sand and leap into the ocean, to swim below the surface as long as her breath lasts. *Later!* Lou assures herself, her feet firmly enclosed inside sensible walking shoes.

There's someone Lou wants to see. Of course, the men would disapprove, in their own tolerant sort of way.

"What should we do with our superstitious, scientific girl?" They'd roll their eyes, and David would shake his head to express exasperation at her antics as he sided with her father. Only she knows that he once visited an African psychic, though he'd never admit to it.

The market is already bustling with people, their clothes sweaty from the humid heat. It's such a pity that the wet season refuses to move inland and relieve Masaranga's drought. Tourists generally avoid the rainy season, and Lou is the only white face in the crowd. A couple of men give her the once-over, and a woman squeezing sugarcane juice smiles. Hopefully she doesn't resemble an unsuspecting tourist who might be persuaded to exchange foreign notes for just about anything.

Lou is as at ease here as at the local markets outside Masaranga due to a life spent here. With her roots planted firmly in African soil, a smidgen of local superstition has also infiltrated her. Undercurrents from the other side are active in these places, and sometimes the sixth senses of the "uneducated" outstrip other methods for gathering information. Years of scientific study have not completely knocked this out of Lou, and she's aware there's more to things than her five senses can tell her.

Her desire to return to the seer seems quite natural to her, though she'll keep it a secret. As well as being curious, she wants to use everything possible amid such uncertainty.

Over ten years ago, Lou and David visited the seer as inquisitive teenagers, and Lou was nervous and giggly. David was enthralled initially, but something the fortuneteller said spooked him. If only she could reach back and remember what. However, David has moved on to other things, and he'll roar with laughter if he ever hears about this.

She asks for directions from a heavyset woman seated behind a display of red beets and wilted greens. Perhaps the woman won't know where to find the seer or will say that she's long since gone. But her eyes smile at Lou's request, and her lips compress and thicken as if she's intrigued. Using a tribal language instead of Swahili, she calls to a woman at a nearby stand that's piled high with spices. Her answer is accompanied by a giggle and a curious glance at Lou. Once the directions are given, Lou is dismissed with a flick of the head towards the path she must take.

Twenty-Three

Lou pushes aside a curtain patterned like python skin and ducks through the doorway, where she hesitates. Her eyes take a moment to adjust to the dimly lit room, where, in an alcove, a stout woman waits cross-legged, a question on her face. She gestures for Lou to take a place on a stool opposite.

"You have been here before."

The seer's voice contains both interest and detachment, and Lou hears this as a question and not the statement it really is.

"Yes, quite a long time ago," she answers.

"I remember you."

The seer's hands are cold to touch when Lou hands her the payment. Actually, this woman appears more human than the one from Lou's memory, and her profession hasn't protected her from the passing of time. All those years ago, the whites of her eyes seemed brighter, her skin blacker, which made her seem formidable. Time has weighed her body down, though evidently her mind is as incisive as ever.

Over the top of a wooden chest that sits between them, the seer studies Lou intently, which is disconcerting. The shadows and angles of her face are accentuated by flickering candles, whose wicks have burned uneven rims, allowing columns of wax to spill out like tiny waterfalls. Lou breathes in the strong smell of evaporated wax. Strange ebony carvings and spirit faces decorate the walls, and they give Lou the creeps. To avoid them, she looks straight into the seer's fathomless eyes and another existence.

Years of science haven't precluded Lou from crediting mystics with abilities to see beyond barriers closed to her. She manages to keep her gaze steady and is drawn closer to that strange and unnerving disconnected place.

Suddenly, the seer is with Lou and all her memories. So similar to that other time when she was much younger. The memories that hurt most are little changed, and she remembers this weird, alarming sensation that accompanies such a mental undressing. What's next? Lou almost regrets her decision to come.

With a decisive sweep of her arm, the seer empties a pouch of strange items onto the chest. Lou recalls that quick flick of a wrist that scatters the pieces in a pattern. A polished fang lands dead center, its ivory glimmering in the candlelight. At a signal from the seer's long fingers, Lou tentatively picks it up. Her fingers glide over the smooth sharp point and then catch on the bulkier unenameled part, usually hidden away in the jawbone. Lou guesses it belonged to a large cat, a leopard perhaps. This canine, set within an equally resilient jaw, once wielded enormous strength as its point sank into the flesh of its prey.

All of that is past now. Lou wonders how this wildcat met its fate.

"You will need the intuition of a leopard." The words break a long silence.

Lou follows a sudden urge to look up and search for an explanation. The seer's eyes return her gaze, intensely aware.

"You already have what you need. It will come when you ask the right question."

Lou waits but no more is forthcoming. A drop of sweat rolls down her spine. For a second, she glimpses a leopard before it slips away through thick forest. Gold and black spots merge with the dappled light. Camouflage. That's the key. Transparency won't help. Her actions and choices must stay hidden. Some things are best done alone, the same way a leopard would. Small and solitary compared to the gregarious lions, leopards use different tactics to survive—stealth rather than physical strength.

As Lou emerges from this mental space, she realizes the thoughts are not entirely her own. The seer helped her interpret. With those eyes on her, she feels naked as if her mind is no longer her secret place. Lou remembers how her intuition was once close to the forefront of her awareness, where now opinions and rationalizations roam randomly. They stop only when she endeavors to take control and focus. She hopes she is not as judgmental as her brother.

"Your brother is not with you."

Another statement rather than a question. This time, Lou remains quiet, unsure whether the seer remembers David or if she still has access to her thoughts.

"You are anxious and unsettled. To be alone is most useful. Use that sharp mind well, otherwise it will be a long struggle." The finality of the seer's words suggests the session is already over.

A sick tight sensation wraps around her neck. The woman suddenly seems ominous, the room suffocating. The strange carvings stare from the dark recesses behind her. Lou swallows hard and uses all her self-control not to leap to her feet and escape through the thick folds of cloth behind her.

"You hide your fear well! That is necessary and good."

The seer always speaks generalities. Though Lou knows a particular question won't supply a specific answer, she can't help but try.

"How do I protect the elephants, and those close to me?"

"Move alone. Others have separate paths."

The undersides of her dark hands are pale in the candlelight as the seer picks up the scattered objects, one at a time, in some methodical order. The session is clearly over, and Lou's thoughts empty out. Her conflicted emotions remain: relief that she's apparently capable of dealing with whatever comes, but also alarm that the session seems unfinished, and a fear that things will get worse, with no simple way out.

Now it's hard to move, the world outside as frightening at this den. Lou waits as those surprisingly delicate fingers pick up the last item, the canine that she held in her own fingers, the leopard's ivory. Abruptly the woman looks up at her.

"Don't trust the man who pretends to be black. Now, time to leave!"

Her flick of the head is so dismissive, her words so decisive, that Lou retreats as if she's overstayed. She backs out and bows her head, mouthing a thank you. But the woman has already turned away, the session clearly erased. The python hangings fall into place behind Lou, and she's back on the street again.

Outside, in the blinding light, Lou squints and blinks, watched by curious bystanders. Sound fills the space all around: the noisy chatter of young voices, a man's angry shout, a dog's terrified yelp. Strangely, none of this was audible only moments ago.

Lou walks away along the dirt street to escape the onlookers. What did the seer mean by that last comment? Last time Lou and David left together. He was right next to her and wouldn't stop laughing, which was infectious at first. They ran through the streets, and she'd giggled crazily until she caught on that his laughter was false bravado.

"Scary Mama!" he said eventually, and she stayed quiet to cover her unease. The stranger knew inaccessible stuff, things Lou was hardly aware of herself, like how their mother was just before her departure. Despite her initial trepidation, the act of sitting quietly in front of the seer had helped Lou put together forgotten pieces from her past. But her brother's subsequent unease frightened her. They never spoke much about it afterwards.

A friendly vendor calls out a few words as Lou passes his stall. She gives him a few shillings, and he weighs mangoes. His bony hands add and remove little weights until the scales tip evenly. When Lou signals for him to keep the change, he selects another ripe mango and adds it to her bag.

"Ready to eat!" His eyes crease merrily. Lou grins back and her heart lifts a little.

"Asante sana," she thanks him.

Typically, Lou would want to immediately peel back the yellow skin and bite into the ripe fruit, but, right now, the idea of it makes her queasy. What would David make of such superstitious nonsense now? She might never be able to tell him about her second visit.

Twenty-Four

Carla's friend Steve seems easy enough to get on with, and Lou imagines he'd need to be to make a dive operation like this successful. Cliché, but those gorgeous, blue-green eyes hold her captive. Instinctively, she likes him, but he looks like the popular type who should make a sensible girl wary. One thing she learned at university, besides her studies, was to be cautious of the good lookers. Even so, those eyes and the wild-looking sun-bleached hair suit the surroundings.

If only Carla had not left so quickly after introducing them.

"How long have you had the shop?" Lou asks Steve to quell her anxieties about his experience as a scuba instructor.

"Nearly eighteen months. I'm Mombasa's first dive operator and it's not always smooth sailing!"

"That's to be expected, I'm afraid." Lou notices a photo of a shark on the wall behind him. "What brought you out here?"

But Steve immediately starts to describe some of his successes to date, as if keen to counteract his initial negativity. On the walls of the cluttered room hang wetsuits, fins, and other equipment, the uses of which she will doubtlessly have to master. The hoses, gauges, and lifejacket-like objects make Lou wonder if this is going to be complicated.

"I don't get enough divers yet to warrant buying more stock." Steve frowns as he searches for a wetsuit to fit her. "Actually, most people prefer to snorkel." He gives a broad-shouldered shrug, and Lou immediately wants to reassure him.

"I've snorkeled a bit, and I rarely get cold," she says.

"Great!" Steve seems pleased. He holds a wetsuit alongside her. "This should fit. It's cooler below the surface and you'll lose more body heat, so you'll need this. It's also protection against corals and stings."

Usually there are fewer dangerous creatures than people imagine. Lou lowers her eyes as he gives her a once-over, and she's slightly uncomfortable as he sizes her up. But his assessment is fast, and he drops the suit into her arms.

"Try this one. Let's kit up and get into the water straightaway. Otherwise, we'll fry."

Suddenly brisk and business-like, he rummages through a pile of masks.

Steve seems to be in a hurry as he selects equipment off the walls. Lou wrestles with the wetsuit, while he carries tanks out from the back. The exercise has made him fit, and he works effortlessly. The wetsuit seems snug enough to keep her warm, which is great. Despite her reassurances, she hates being cold. Steve shows her how to clip a buoyancy jacket to a tank, and then link it up with the regulator hoses. Lou envisaged a lesson in a pool. She seems to have got that bit wrong. Instead, she follows him from the shop across the sandy beach and straight into the ocean.

Sunbathing tourists watch from deckchairs as Lou wades into the shallows, the tank heavy on her back. Warm seawater begins to seep into her wetsuit. Steve's rapid instructions are hard to keep up with as he demonstrates how the air hoses work. The information about this new life-support system comes thick and fast, while Lou focuses and tries to absorb it all. At the cost of sounding stupid, she asks him to slow down.

"Don't try to remember it all at once." Steve quickly brushes her concerns aside. "Just get a feel for it. The theory will come easier then." The barrage of facts continues as he rearranges the hoses and then tightens her buoyancy jacket.

Steve maneuvers Lou so her back is toward him and turns her tank on.

"OK, breathe through the regulator. Let's see you swim!"

Tentatively, Lou pushes forward into the swell. As she sinks below the surface, the weight of the tank lifts off her back. A wonderful sense of freedom comes to her now she's able to breathe underwater and glide under the waves. Around her, sunlight twists and wrinkles through layers of water, while below, rippled sand stretches away across the undulations of the seafloor.

Steve stays close but does nothing to guide her.

"You're a natural!" he says, when she finally surfaces for the first time.

He seems genuinely pleased and his approval buoys her. Still on a high, Lou grins. He probably says the same to every new student.

"No, I'm serious." Steve picks up on her doubt. "People are usually uncomfortable at first, and a few get claustrophobic."

He's making it so easy for her, and she's grateful. Already Lou knows this is going to be a lot of fun.

"Let's try a few safety exercises," Steve says. "I'll talk you through them before we submerge and practice."

Lou nods cheerfully with new-found confidence.

They swim underwater out deeper until Steve stops on the sandy seafloor and indicates for Lou to kneel opposite him. The wrinkled surface is five meters above her, and sprays of sand hang in the seawater, scattering the sunlight. It's surreal and otherworldly below the surface.

Caught up in her new surroundings, Lou begins to space out and enjoy the experience. Steve has other ideas and abruptly pulls the regulator out of her mouth. Though startled, Lou was warned they'd practice an out-of-air situation, and Steve immediately hands his own mouthpiece to Lou. She takes a couple of breaths and returns it to him. He sucks in a lungful and gives it to her again. They practice for a while and Steve demonstrates how she should relocate her own mouthpiece, which is out of view. Then he switches it around so they breathe out of her mouthpiece and share her tank of air.

As Lou gets the hang of it, they grin at each other as best as people can underwater. Steve signals for her to try another recovery exercise, and she maintains her calm as he pulls her mask off. Saltwater stings her eyes, and Steve is a blurry shadow when he hands her mask back. As shown earlier, Lou pulls it onto her face and blows air through her nose with her head tilted back, so the mask fills from the top. It's simple enough to learn these techniques with Steve's straightforward tuition. There's an intimacy about being down here with him, unable to talk but dependent on him. He's totally focused on improving her skill with the equipment. Lou doesn't care how long it takes and would happily stay down here all day.

Silvery shapes of shoreline fish cruise into sight until startled by her bubbles. They detour effortlessly, gliding away on perfectly adapted fins. A sense of calm pervades Lou and she loses track of time.

When their tanks are low on air, Steve takes her arm and they surface slowly. In the brilliant sunlight, they swim on their backs toward the shore, while Carla watches from a beach chair, a book by her side.

"That was a long first lesson! I'd lost hope you'd return from the depths!" she exclaims as they wade toward her.

Lou is relieved her friend doesn't seem to mind the wait.

"Really sorry. It didn't seem that long." She's apologetic and massively grateful Carla talked her into this. With the tank's full weight again heavy on her back, Lou is suddenly tired.

"We did a bit of safety practice," says Steve. "I got the feeling Lou didn't want to come up!"

"You're right!" Lou beams at them both. "It was fantastic. Thank you."

Impatient customers wait by the dive shop. They surround Steve and bombard him with questions as he shows Lou how to rinse the equipment.

"Classroom theory tomorrow," he says.

She nods and grins, inordinately happy, as Steve turns toward his new clients.

Later, as they relax over beers, Lou hesitates when Carla asks her opinion of Steve. To be honest, her last relationship has made Lou wary of attractive men, so she's reticent and just happy to be in such stunning surroundings. Over a stretch of sand and saltwater in front of the bar, shades of pink and red streak the horizon, while behind them, a pregnant sun sinks below luxuriant slopes, her orange rays silhouetting massive old trees. The new learning curve has Lou excited, and she feels strangely happy.

"No sign of David and Lexi?" Lou asks to distract Carla from more questions. The others were going to meet them an hour ago.

"No. Are you surprised?"

"Suppose not."

"My sister's always been a bit unreliable."

"David never used to be!"

But Lou doesn't want to discuss any of that either. She drains her glass and says, "Let's go for a walk along the beach." Right now, she'd rather not take anything too seriously.

Twenty-Five

Steve's first impression of Lou is that she's aloof. Well, maybe not aloof but sort of distant as if her mind is elsewhere. Her blue eyes meet his only briefly, a quick smile, and then she turns to say goodbye to Carla. Steve watches her now as she examines the gear hanging on hooks around his shop. He always likes to gauge a person before exposing them to a strange environment. Some are inclined to panic, so it's smart to work them out ahead of time.

"Ever dived before?' he asks.

"No," Lou replies, and instead of expounding, she gives him an impish grin.

It's left field from his initial judgment of ice-queen and leaves him with no real clue as to her thoughts.

Aware of her eyes on him and suddenly self-conscious, he selects a couple of wetsuits. Just another pretty girl here to learn to dive, he tells himself. There's always plenty around, all tanned and sun-streaked and in holiday mode. Nothing new, really. Except she's not in holiday mode. Her approach is no nonsense, almost business-like, and she asks a lot of questions as he goes through his spiel.

"Don't think too hard about it. Just let it come naturally," he says. This is usual advice when clients are stressing, though she's not yet at that stage.

Turns out, Lou is a natural in the water, which is a relief and makes the whole exercise and Steve's job relatively easy. She seems suddenly more cheerful as if enjoying the process. Steve remembers that Lou lives here, and he's the relative newcomer for a change. It's certainly a tough world out here and business is difficult without decent connections. Maybe a survival instinct is what makes Lou a bit different, more like her friend Carla. Though Steve remembers that other sister, Lexi, as a whole other kettle of fish.

Steve watches Lou swim around a couple of meters below him. Some fish scarper ahead of her, their silvery sides glinting in the clear water. Lou chases them toward him so they're forced to dart around him. Then, in a rush of bubbles, she stands up in the shoulder-deep water and pulls her mask off.

"I think I've got the hang of it," she says and pushes the mask up onto her forehead, her hair a gorgeous tangle. Even with all the ungainly dive-gear on, she's alarmingly attractive. Although Lou's obviously comfortable in the water, Steve reflects that she's got a lot to learn.

"It's quite a bit harder when buoyancy really comes into play," he replies gruffly. "OK. Let's submerge again, then sit on the bottom and practice a couple of things."

Another impish grin, and Lou sinks back underwater. Perhaps a little too confident, he thinks, for a beginner. Maybe it's all bluff. Put to the test, the truth always emerges. Let's wait and see.

But the exercises go like clockwork, and Steve's mind wanders now, as it often does on the rare occasions when the students catch on quickly. It's been tough since Jed reneged on his share of the investment in the shop and took off. Steve never factored that in as a weak point. At least the discovery his supposed friend was a piker came sooner rather than later and before they got locked together in business. But it would have been a lot easier to run the show as a two-man operation. Fortunately, the local lad he's put on has been a great help and useful for Swahili practice as well. It's not a hard language to learn, and the young bloke is funny as hell.

But Steve needs another business partner if he's to stay here longer term. Jed's citizenship was his ticket. Despite the shortcomings of life here, both the money and the diving are good. Besides that, it would be a pain to go home and have to admit his father was right and that he should have put his marine science degree to better use. Although the old man might consider that his son is frittering time away on the Kenyan coast, he no longer owns him, whatever he thinks, however astute he is.

A shoal of striped fish whir by, and Steve realizes Lou is paying more attention to them than his hand signals. Their air supply is low and it's time to finish. He doesn't like to leave the shop with the new employee for too long, not at this stage anyhow. The lad is just learning the ropes, and this is not a place where you can trust people unconditionally, no matter what sort of rapport you have with them.

Carla is waiting for Lou, so she takes off pretty fast. Steve is a bit disappointed to see them both go. Nice girl, Carla. A really good sort. A bit less wild and out there than Lou seems to be. Carla's mother, Sara, was his point of contact when he first arrived in Kenya. Her hospitality and graciousness put him at ease instantly in the strange new territory. Steve recognized how strong Sara was, and respected her hard won independence. He was grateful for her old-school hospitality, not something he'd experienced back home. There's much about life in Africa that either brings out the strength in people or sends them packing. He guesses that Lou's life out in the bush is just another step removed from normal life. Perhaps that's what makes her so different, and not in a bad way.

Steve tries to imagine a life spent mostly out on the savannah. Lou must have spent a lot of time following the elephants around the bush. You'd think it would wear thin after a while, but it's obvious she finds it fascinating and loves them. Admittedly, his own elephant experiences have been memorable. The funniest was a female calf, who'd trailed behind the herd and not kept up with mother as she crossed the road in front of Steve's car. On noticing her absence, the mother trumpeted noisily and kicked up the ground with her hindlegs, sending grass and dirt through the air. This alarmed Steve until he realized the problem. Suitably reprimanded and in a hurry to catch up, the infant came running, her tiny trunk flapping wildly. She didn't take the shortest course back to his mother, and instead completed a wide half-circle like a naughty toddler who knows it's in trouble.

Steve's safari experience with a couple of his mates was unreal. They camped for a month, moved on every couple of days, and drank a few too many Tuskers in the evenings. At first, they worried whether elephants and lions might be unwelcome visitors to camp, but it turned out they were never a problem. It was more the baboons either stealing food or openly demanding it. In one campsite, a troupe of baboons watched from the trees by the campsite, bold as brass, as Steve and his mates set up tents. They'd joked that it was like being at a zoo, just with the humans as the source of entertainment.

The baboons took turns coming down from the high boughs to sit on the bonnet of the vehicle. Steve chased one in an attempt to make it drop a loaf of bread. He'd backtracked pretty fast when the baboon turned and bared its huge canines at him. Scary bastards! It reminded Steve of people at their worst. His mates got a bit smarter about stowing the food after that, though it wasn't as if he hadn't warned them.

A safari experience chasing after elephants through the bush with Lou would be an experience in itself and whole lot of fun. She's named most of them and knows their relationships with each other. But it's hard to envisage taking time off, as he's in over his head with the shop now that Jed's bailed. No chance of a break for a while. Just the thought of the tourist season ahead has Steve stressed. So much for the cruisy tropical lifestyle he'd planned. The diving has been great, but the tourists are hard work much of the time.

Twenty-Six

Even on a clear day like this, the ride out to the reef is rough, and Lou finds it difficult to believe that the dinghy is headed for the sheltered spot promised by Steve. Weighed down by three divers, the boatman, and their scuba gear, the boat bounces wildly as they punch through the water. With each wave choppier than the last, the conditions bear little resemblance to tourist brochure depictions of a calm Indian Ocean.

A stray wave from a low angle throws Lou against the side of the boat, where she clings tightly as more saltwater arcs over the bow and smashes through them. The wetsuit does protect her from some of its force, and from the boat's hard edges, as another breaker slams the dinghy back the other way. Despite the discomfort, the wild ride is strangely exhilarating. She's already completely soaked, and it's exciting to be exposed to the elements but protected from them at the same time.

An overly severe Hans opposite her in the dinghy appears to disagree. He turns her way, and Lou smiles, but Hans is too distracted to respond. It's his first off-the-boat dive as well, and he balances awkwardly as if not enjoying any of this. His jaw set, he squints toward the horizon until the next wave throws him forward. Steve helps him back into position.

"You OK?" He gets no reply.

Again, Lou smiles reassuringly at Hans, but he looks straight through her. She glances back at Steve, who shrugs his shoulders helplessly and grins at her. Suddenly they're conspirators, their amusement at Han's grim demeanor shared. At least she's not yet frightened. Hopefully, her strange sense of invincibility will remain when it's time to drop below the surface into deeper waters.

From the moment Hans arrived at the shop this morning, he was cranky and uptight. Admittedly, his annoyance at the wild ride shouldn't be comical as it's partly justified. Lou readjusts her position just as another curl of spray drenches them again. With wet hands, Hans angrily wipes his face and scrunches his eyes against the salt-sting. Steve offers him a towel, but Hans is too preoccupied to notice. Instead, he dons his mask ahead of time as protection against the spray. Though ashamed by her own lack of sympathy, Lou notices Steve struggling to stay straight faced.

The boatman throttles down, and Steve clambers over fins and weight belts to reach the bow, where he stands and points out submerged reefs to guide the boatman.

"Polepole," he shouts, urging the driver to slow further.

Under the boat are pale-green shallows, stretches of pastel coral, and bright flashes of color as fish dart toward the safety of submerged bommies. The swell has dropped out and this patch of the ocean is amazingly calm. Lou wonders if sharks patrol out where the reef drops away.

"All OK?" Steve asks, and Lou hopes she's not given her trepidation away. She smiles confidently back and shelves all her reservations. It's finally time to sink below the safety of the surface into a new space, where she's reliant on her gear.

The ocean doesn't frighten her, but Lou has a healthy respect for it. She balances on the side of the dinghy and rechecks her gauges, she doubts she's ready for this. Now that the wind has dropped, the heat from the sun bores through her wetsuit.

"OK, Hans and Lou, I'm in first. You two follow together on the count of three." Steve's voice is business-like and leaves no space to indulge in second thoughts. He rolls back over the side, and the water explodes in thousands of bright droplets. The boat rocks alarmingly. Across from Lou, Hans waits, ready to go. There's no time to procrastinate as Steve surfaces in the swell and begins to count them down. At two, Lou pushes her mask on tighter and holds her mouthpiece in place; at one, she needlessly sucks in a lungful of air and rolls backward.

The tank breaks her fall, and she drops into an explosion of bubbles. Her reflexes complete a somersault through a watery world. With each breath, columns of bubbles swirl all around her. They rise faster than she does, gaining momentum on the way up. Lou rolls upright inside an expanse of blue as her buoyancy jacket also pulls her upward. As she breaks the surface, her delighted laughter sounds strange and muffled through the regulator.

Refreshing seawater has seeped into her wetsuit, and her reservations have evaporated. Lou slightly deflates her jacket and sinks back down into the stunning scenery. As always, everything is strangely surreal below the luminescent surface of the ocean.

But close by, Hans grapples blindly as he attempts to adjust his gear. Instinctively he dog-paddles, though it would be easier to just hang still in the water. He struggles unnecessarily, still fighting the experience, his movements ungainly. Steve swims over and helps him re-clip a loose buckle. At the moment, Lou's equipment seems fine, and she likes the added dimension of freedom. Her snorkeling experiences have missed much with their confinement to the thin interface between air and water.

Steve looks under the surface and waves for Lou to swim closer. She resurfaces next to him.

"You seem comfortable. All ready to go?" he asks.

"Yep!" Lou drains her mask.

"Don't tighten the strap. You'll give yourself a headache," Steve cautions. "Deeper down, the pressure will seal it."

Carefully, he checks her gauges and straps. Reassured, she floats in the boat's shade, her eyes squinting against the reflections from the waves.

"You OK?" Steve asks Hans, who nods, his regulator firmly in his mouth.

"Almost no current. That's good. Ready?" Steve asks.

Lou nods and hopes she looks confident. Though, truth be told, she's no longer anxious.

"OK, let's go then! Breathe out and relax as we go down. Empty your lungs, and you'll sink better."

The boatman leans over to watch them descend, and his silhouette ripples and shrinks as they drop down below the surface. As the ceiling of their new world rises, the boat's engine revs, and the curved underside glides to safer waters away from the reef. Behind it trails an inverted wake that looks weird from below.

Steve's hand is on her arm as they sink further. Water squeezes her forehead. Lou swallows in an attempt to release the pressure from her ears, but the pain intensifies as seconds pass. She pinches her nose and blows hard. At last, a high-pitched whine and her sinuses equalize, releasing her from the vice-like grip of water pressure.

As they touch down on a stretch of sandy seafloor between craggy coral domes, Hans gestures violently toward his ears and makes a somethings-not-right hand signal. Suddenly, he starts for the surface. In a panic, his arms and legs flail as if trying to climb a rockface as he heads for the surface. Steve indicates for Lou to stay put and chases him. Halfway, he catches up and holds on to Hans tightly in an effort to slow his out-of-control ascent. Hans kicks and struggles as bubbles swirl all around. If he fails to exhale on the way up, the expanded air could burst his lungs. But the men rise more slowly above Lou now. Steve looks down toward her and makes a quick "are you OK" hand signal, and she signals back that all is well.

Lou doesn't mind being alone here. She swims over the sandbanks between coral outcrops. The sound of her breaths soothes her, and her bubbles expand up towards the men silhouetted on the surface. Ahead, a coral wall rises from the seafloor, its caverns safe territory for secretive fish. They hang under ledges and flee through the spaces within the reef as she approaches. Fifteen meters overhead, the boat motors towards the men.

Down here is a realm of surreal calm, and the gaps between her breaths lengthen. A school of mauve parrotfish approaches until Lou exhales and startles them with her bubbles. Pectoral fins whir in unison as the fish veer off. Like birds, they retain formation as they glide safely away.

Steve sinks suddenly into view, gesturing to catch her attention. Lou had lost track of the world overhead. He shrugs his shoulders, points to the surface and makes the hand sign for a boat. Perhaps Hans isn't OK. Lou assumes they're to cut the dive short, but Steve's hand signals indicate she's mistaken, and her heart soars as he gestures for her to follow him.

He leads her down over a rocky ledge, and they drop into deeper water along a descending coral ridge. Distracted by the scenery, Lou fails to add air to her jacket against the increasing pressure and suddenly drops like a brick. There's a moment when she's falling even as she swims upward, fighting the weight, her buoyancy lessons forgotten.

Immediately, Steve is alongside, and he holds her to prevent her from sinking deeper. When she steadies, he adds air to her jacket to make her float weightlessly again. Aware she's disregarded her lessons almost as quickly as Hans, Lou feels embarrassed, but relieved. Quietly, she resolves to focus more on practicalities from now on.

Her ineptitude doesn't faze Steve, and he grins, his lips distorted by the regulator. For practice, he makes her add air to her jacket and then dump it again. They rise and fall in the water until she's able to keep her buoyancy neutral. In her theory sessions, he taught her that poor buoyancy wastes valuable air.

They swim on through passages between coral walls. Awestruck, Lou becomes aware of each breath. As her exhaled bubbles head for the surface, she remembers Steve's advice and slows her breathing. "Always conserve your air," he said. "One day, the reserve will save you or someone else."

Now, between breaths, she hears ocean life and the distant roar of moving water. She imagines currents surging along channels and rolling over reefs, the same way the wind blows past trees and through forests. Close by are the rasps of parrotfish teeth against coral as the force of their jaws causes their bright bodies to twist sideways with each bite. Even closer than the fish is the sound of Steve's breaths, regular and more widely spaced than her own.

So much activity to absorb at once. Red coral trout with blue spots chase smaller competitors off their patch of reef. The younger trout flee to find themselves in other occupied territory and trailed again. As slim cleaner-fish dance toward their hosts, their blue and black stripes glint in the sunlight. The larger fish become stationary, a signal to start, and they go to work, biting microscopic parasites hidden between shiny scales. Lou watches as a bulky grouper muscles in to displace an angel fish, and then hangs with its mouth open and gills extended as an invitation to work safely within.

Lou has only just got East Africa's thousand or so bird species more or less sorted in her memory. Now there's all these fish to get her head around, never mind multitudes of other sea creatures. Her knowledge of this watery domain seems massively limited as she sinks to check under ledges and hovers over the tops of the enormous coral plates. Thumb and forefinger circled, Steve signals to check she's OK. Lou nods and does the same signal to say "Yes, all is well." Her passage through the water feels clumsy compared to Steve, and Lou judges she's got a long way to go.

Steve stops and points into a half dome of coral. Nestled within an alcove is a dark red anemone with delicate, mauve tips. Clownfish dart bravely between tentacles, only to rush to safety as the divers move closer. Lou watches them wiggle deep within the soft folds until almost hidden from sight.

A shadow passes over them as a vast circle of schooling barracuda swirls overhead, a cylinder of life drifting off the edge of the reef. Steve leads her on past crevices, where crabs and shy fish move back out of sight. He points out bright nudibranch flatworms that look like slugs with tiny antlers. This marine encounter is strange and exhilarating but also dreamlike, the underwater world a blend of anticipation and tranquility.

When Steve holds her air gauge in front of her mask, the needle is on the red. So much for her promise to pay attention. He points to the surface, where the boat floats above a school of trevally. He's navigated a circuit, and they're almost back where they started.

They ascend slowly, following the bubbles up to where they break on the surface. Lou is slow to release air, so her jacket expands and drags her up too fast. She grapples for the dump valve, but again Steve is a step ahead. He catches her and slows her, so they break the surface together. Encircled by the blue of sky and sea, they float effortlessly, laughing, Lou embarrassed at getting it wrong again.

"Happens to most people," Steve assures her. He's guessed her thoughts. She floats back in the water, her face against the heat of the sky as Steve passes their scuba gear to the boatman. Seal-like in his wetsuit, he pulls himself into the boat.

"Good dive, Memsahib Lou?" the boatman asks as he takes her weight belt. She nods happily. Floating on the surface, she's as comfortable as a sea mammal inside her buoyant wetsuit. It's a balmy, sunny day, and life feels fantastic.

"You went really well!" says Steve as he heaves her over the side of the boat.

Lou feels he's being too kind. She manages an ungainly frog-leap and almost lands face first on the floor of the dinghy.

But Steve's attention is on Hans, who looks bored, safely wrapped up in a towel.

"Sorry about the wait," Steve apologizes. "And don't worry. It's common not to be able to clear an ear."

Hans seems uncomfortable and slightly disbelieving.

"Is it painful now?" continues Steve. "Good. Try and equalize the moment you start to go down, well before you feel any pressure. Not to worry. If you like, we can try again tomorrow. I won't charge you again."

Lou shivers slightly, despite the warm breeze on her face and the sun on her back. An hour in the water has dropped her body temperature. Poor Hans, having to ditch the dive. It's a pity, and she wishes they'd not had a private laugh at his expense on the way out.

"Great dive. You were relaxed. That counts for a lot." Steve smiles at her. "Pretty good buoyancy too."

She laughs, skeptical, considering the glitches, and says, "Not really, and I used my air too fast."

"Can't be perfect the first time!" He gives her a curious look and then turns back to Hans, who seems miserable.

Twenty-Seven

It might be fun to daydream occasionally, but Steve is somewhat annoyed that Lou dominates his thoughts as he heads down toward the ocean. Right now, the last thing he needs is a distraction, and he has a feeling she might be more than that.

He arrives to find a shell vendor on the low stone wall out the front of the shop.

"Take those things elsewhere!" Steve shoos the man away. Have these guys not yet learned he hates the way they earn their money? He's never even been polite on the topic. They just don't want to get it. Their prices go up as the supply goes down. Steve is with Lou on this one, as angry about how they plunder the ocean as she is about the elephants. There she is, back in his mind again. He sighs.

The security doors squeal as usual when he pulls them back, all the time ignoring the gaze of the vendor, who has refused to scarper. Almost immediately, a group of Germans walks in. Great. As a rule, they're not time wasters, and before long he's signed them up for the day. They have scuba tickets, so hopefully all he has to do is take them out and keep a sharp eye on them underwater.

One of the women is a stunner and flirts openly with Steve as he checks her dive ticket. Though apparently not attached to anyone, she's definitely not his type. In theory, these divers are a seasoned bunch, but time will tell. It's not until you get them underwater that the truth emerges. The worse braggers often have the poorest skills, immediately apparent from the way their limbs flail about underwater. Steve always keeps such divers away from the prime coral bommies, as their fins are liable to knock off great hunks of the coral he wants to protect. The introverted, quiet types seem to have more awareness of their surroundings and are generally better able to fine-tune their buoyancy.

By the second dive, Steve has relaxed as the divers turn out to be OK. The visibility is over fifty meters and the view incredible, with a coral wall stretching out of sight. There's nothing new at the site, but he doesn't care. There's something special about being underwater with the sound of the bubbles and the ocean all around. Light rays penetrate from above and change with each moment as they dance through the water. It's the site he bought Lou and Hans out to, one of his favorites. This reminds Steve. Hans has booked again for tomorrow. Poor bloke. He was angry more at himself than anyone else and should do better the second time around. Steve knows he shouldn't have encouraged Lou to find it amusing, but they just seemed to feed off each other that day. That's what worries him. She has an infectious restlessness that makes him feel quite reckless. Not the end of the world, he supposes. His parents consider his decision to come out to Africa and set up a business as irresponsible, so who is he to talk? He wonders if he's not so different from her.

Later, when the wetsuits are hung, and Steve is partway through hosing the saltwater off the dive gear, he hears the young guy shout out that Lou is here.

"What?" He must have heard wrong; got her too much on his brain.

"Memsahib Lou. She has come!"

Lou looks embarrassed, which only seems to add to how attractive Steve finds her. Apparently, she's walked for hours and has some story about being irritated by her brother's shopping expedition with Lexi. That's no surprise.

"Lexi could talk most men into buying her a gift!" Steve says and laughs, remembering the exposed cleavage. Not his type, thank god.

"I wish it were not David." Lou's voice is sad and she sounds almost, but not quite, resigned.

Quietly, Steve's opinion is she should worry less about her brother and more about herself. It's a man's world out here, and she needs to be careful. He keeps quiet on the subject now, not wanting to take a step wrong as she's so visibly upset. Instead, he hurries to finish the wash down and shut up shop, all the time wondering if she has any plans for the evening.

The young bloke hits him up for a pay advance. Partly because Steve is in a good mood, but also because he's in a hurry, he gives it to him. It wouldn't look good withholding it in front of Lou either. For some reason, Steve gets the feeling she might sympathize with his offsider. Truth is that the wages are so low here, an outsider might consider him to be almost engaged in slave labor. Most of the locals aren't hard workers, though this does not apply to his offsider, so Steve doesn't really mind that these advances might go on forever. Then he remembers that Lou would be used to the low wages that go along with fringe benefits such as free accommodation in this country.

The rangers at her bush camp probably don't earn much more than his bloke, and some of them would have families to support. Birth control doesn't seem to be much of a thing here, despite the poverty and their inability to feed so many extra hungry mouths. It's one of many factors that keep everyone so poor; eight to fifteen kids would also keep all but the most affluent Western families well below the poverty line.

Steve won't have the heart to dock the young bloke's wages the amount he's borrowed. He considers it money well spent considering how the energetic and good-natured help has saved his skin and cheered him up. At one stage, Steve thought he wouldn't have a hope in hell of staying on alone, at least not for the extra year he envisaged.

Twenty-Eight

Jewelry never was Lou's thing, and she's had enough. After an hour, Lexi is no closer to a decision on which necklace David should buy her. Time to call it quits. Lou promises to meet them later, and they hardly notice her leave.

Without a plan, Lou wanders past upmarket shops, until a sculptured jade head in a window display draws her closer. Too expensive for her, but the shop offers an escape from the hot, busy street.

Narrow stone steps lead down to its glass door entrance with fancy gold writing. Lou enters the den-like interior, where more steps descend to the secluded shop floor. Now Lou wishes she'd ignored her impulse to enter. A quick look and a hasty escape will do. That way, she won't have to explain she can't afford anything.

The Indian proprietor is busily scurrying back and forth, commanded by a woman used to calling the shots. Suddenly Lou is curious to see her. On a spending spree, the woman has taken charge of the eager shopkeeper, who unlocks glass cabinets and hands her ornaments.

Lou's eyes adjust to the muted light. A gold belt with a dragon-head clasp fastens a blood-red silk dress around the client's waist. Her glossy black hair coils back into ivory hairclips. Lou passes crammed displays of carved chests, antiques, and wall hangings as she comes closer. The place resembles Aladdin's cave.

With a dismissive gesture, the woman indicates an ivory tusk, stashed behind the counter. "No, not an old, stained one!" she says. "I need a perfect white pair for my entrance hall."

"Of course! We most definitely have!" The proprietor's lilting voice warms encouragingly. "But they are surely at my brother's place close to here. My boy will find him for you, no problem!"

"He must hurry then. My guests fly in today." The woman checks her watch

"Of course! Would you like some chai?" His long fingers summon his son, at a guess from the similarly hooked nose. A surreptitious glance at the fashionable client as the lad listens to instructions in rapid Hindi, then, quick and agile, he scales the steps, his slim form silhouetted at the top for a second, where sunlight briefly spills in before the gilded door shuts it back out.

"Memsahib, some chai?" The proprietor sizes Lou up. The client turns to reveal Chinese features, heavy makeup, and lipstick to match the dress.

"No, thank you." Lou smiles to show no hard feelings.

"Of course, Madame. It is not necessary for you to be buying. Perhaps something cold?"

"OK. Chai will be lovely. Thanks."

Lou accepts now because it seems rude not to, though she's incensed by the ivory. Her initial refusal should have been firmer. The man vanishes behind patterned rows of camels on a silk curtain that probably arrived in a crate of luxuries from Calcutta.

Lou is about to leave, but he immediately reappears. The client returns an ivory elephant to the counter and takes the first glass. She cast an expert eye over Lou's casual shirt and lightweight pants and addresses her like a familiar friend.

"My darling, are you looking for jewelry? Good quality is hard to find. You need something to bring out your face!"

Lou watches the woman caress the carved elephant made from ivory hacked off the real animal. The fingernails match the dress, blood-red against white. Her mascaraed eyes narrow in concentration.

"I prefer to see the ivory on the live elephant," Lou replies, shocked by her sudden rudeness as she speaks her truth.

"If you want to deprive yourself of ivory, there are other rarities here," replies the woman. "But buy it if you like it. Otherwise, someone else will have it rather than you!" Her lacquered nails indicate a tusk carved into a row of elephants, joined by trunk and tails.

"How much is that one?" she asks.

The proprietor examines the ornament minutely and calculates his highest price.

Lou scalds her tongue on the chai. She notices a chest made from densely grained wood. Where was the tree cut from, and how long ago? She has no idea. Her aversion means nothing to this woman, who either doesn't understand or is willing to ignore the fallout from her choices.

Lou wishes her curiosity had not enticed her into this den, where comfortable deals are made without regard for their far-reaching consequences. Such places beguile people into helping the ruin of Africa.

As Lou slips back up the stairs, her departure goes unnoticed for the second time today. Outside, petrol fumes fill the congested street. The heat from vehicles and the sun engulf her. Even so, this mayhem is preferable to the reality behind her. Her sunglasses cut the glare as she walks, oblivious of her destination. Too many shops here strain at the seams with animal products. Lou walks fast and her thoughts churn. Her anger settles, but then she reverts to concerns about her brother. Meanwhile, her feet carry her through winding streets and alleyways that lead her toward the waterfront. She lets them choose their own way and continues without a plan, her mind on other paths.

Eventually, now desperately thirsty from her long walk, Lou stops to buy Fanta at a rickety stand and hands her shilling over to a man with a toothless smile. She swigs down the cold drink and looks around for a kid who might want recycling money. It's a shock to find herself by the dive shop.

Her instinct is to leave before anyone notices her, but it's too late.

"Hey Lou, how are you?" Steve's young employee springs out from the shop, all muscles and youthful energy. "How did you get here?" He glances around, evidently expecting to see a car.

"I was just walking, and I ended up here," she replies.

He seems taken back. "It's a long way and not so safe to walk!" Before she can stop him, he calls out. "Bwana Steve! Your friend Lou is here."

Steve beams at her and shows no sign of surprise. Mortified, Lou grins back. She shouldn't have just turned up like this.

"Sorry to disturb you. I had no idea I'd come so far." Inwardly she cringes, imagining how this must sound.

"I'm glad you did. Where are your friends?"

He smiles again. Lou drops her eyes, embarrassed, and then looks at him awkwardly, wanting to explain. "I had enough of David and Lexi, so I took off on my own, and then got angry in a tourist shop. I walked to let off steam."

"Sounds like you had an interesting day! What made you angry?"

"Just about everything!" she replies, unwilling to immediately rehash her thoughts. Unloading on Steve won't change anything.

"Was that your brother who picked you up last time?" he asks.

Lou nods, aware of her social ineptitude. She forgot to introduce them. Lost for words, she glances toward the ocean and sees an orange horizon. It's late.

"You can't walk back." Steve indicates the darkening street. "It's not safe here at night. I'll give you a lift. I've finished anyhow."

"I'd be really grateful, thanks. My brain seems on strike today!"

Usually, Lou would be determined to walk, if only to demonstrate her arrival here was unplanned. But he's right about the danger. With that raised, she's glad he's escorting her back.

It's dark when they shut the security bars, and the street seems deserted, though elsewhere, the bars and restaurants will already be busy.

Steve backs his old Peugeot out, and Lou gets in, strangely relieved at the idea he'll look after her. He's exchanged T-shirt and shorts for a decent shirt and jeans and seems entirely different. It makes him look older, but she likes the change. She guesses their age gap could be as much as ten years.

"You must enjoy your business. Is it fun?" Lou asks as Steve flicks the headlights on and frightens a stray cat. It bolts across the street and vanishes down an alley between white-washed houses.

"Yes, but there's always a downside. A friend and I set the shop up, but he got cold feet and went home. He might have been the smart one!"

"What are the drawbacks?" asks Lou, though she partly knows the answer.

"I'm over having to bribe everyone just to stay in business." He laughs good-naturedly and suddenly swerves as a taxi hurtles out of a side street. Their car ends up over the sidewalk. A moment of shock, then suddenly they're laughing.

"Bloody madman! Sorry about that!" Steve grins. "Another reason to get out of the place. We're all bound to die on the road here. Nobody learns the rules. And you know why?" He doesn't wait for her reply. "Because anybody can buy a license with baksheesh."

The car jolts off the rough edge back onto the road. They drive in silence. Lou is taken aback that he's not happy here. Surely most people would envy him.

Lou's concerns that the others might worry about her prove unfounded. On the outside deck of the bar, Carla waves to attract her attention. David and Lexi remain mutually engrossed. Behind them, bright lights illuminate rows of waves breaking across an expanse of yellow sand.

"I think I owe you a drink," says Lou. She's glad Steve's with her.

"I'll get you one!" he replies.

When Steve arrives with their drinks, Lexi runs her eyes approvingly over him. For a moment, Lou wishes they'd gone elsewhere. Her brother is such a pushover.

"Where have you been? I was worried." Carla's eyes search her face.

"A boring story!" Lou replies. She wonders what Steve's thoughts are.

"Just relax for a bit." Carla smiles at her.

"I'll be back in a moment," Lou replies and walks to the edge of the deck, so only sand separates her from the waves. She breathes in the salt air and watches the light catch the white tips of the breakers.

Behind her, chair legs scrape noisily. David has rearranged the table closer to the view. Steve brings her gin and tonic over and then returns to sit by Carla. The ice clinks as Lou takes a sip and turns back to the sea.

Two kids lean through the railings and chatter excitedly about seahorses. Their mother calls them back to safety. Lou returns to the table, where Carla immediately elbows her in the ribs while interrogating Steve about the diving. Lexi giggles out by the railing as if David has told the funniest joke ever. Lou feels like the odd one out, a fringe dweller at the edge. If only she fitted into life better.

Her drink has some kick, and she's thirsty. It vanishes, and Lou laughs, embarrassed when Steve shakes her empty glass in mock disbelief. She uses her long walk as an excuse.

Another drink and her spirits rise. Still overly aware of Steve, she starts to relax. He laughs at one of her quips and winks. She resists an urge to lean over and run her fingers through his hair. It's weird to feel this way. To break her internal turmoil, Lou jokes with Carla and notices Steve frown slightly. He gets over whatever it was, joins in again, and watches her as the conversation jumps around the table. The idea of behaving in any way like Lexi appalls Lou, but she also hates the idea that people might find her weird.

Foreign tourists drink beer at the next table. Lou hears their laughter as they rib one another. Between them is none of the awkwardness that consumes her. She listens to their camaraderie and feels unsophisticated, an odd one out.

"What's up? You seem sad!" Steve's voice breaks into her thoughts. He leans over to ask the question so only she can hear. In the background, Lexi noisily describes a Nairobi bar she claims to know well.

"Nothing! Sorry, I was miles away," she lies.

"You look down all of a sudden."

"Just listening to them!" She indicates the next table with a sideways glance. One man wraps his arm around his girlfriend's shoulder. She giggles as he whispers into her ear.

"And you're not one?"

"Not what?" Lou is completely distracted.

"Not a tourist?"

He laughs again, and the sound of it makes her smile.

Twenty-Nine

Below a jagged headland, the heavy swell breaks over rocks sculpted by water. Lou adjusts her mask and pushes off from a submerged ledge into the cool of the ocean. Underneath her, as she snorkels out, mushroom-topped corals stretch toward a drop-off, where a clear blue panorama opens up. She swims hard against a strong current to reach the scenery that she first saw with her father and brother.

Unlike the newly developed coastal strip, the underwater topography seems hardly changed. Ahead of Lou, just below the turbulent surface, are the giant anemones that she remembers well. They hang off the same giant boulders, their tentacles shifting in the current. Captivated as a child by this underwater world, Lou often begged her father to let her stay in the water.

"Five more minutes, Dad," she would plead time and again, whenever he tried to call it quits.

Now, Lou drifts in the current as she approaches an underwater window between dark boulders, its edge lined by the tentacles of orange anemones. Through it, cobalt-blue water beckons, calling her out deeper. She inhales deeply and dives down, using the current to carry her, angling toward the opening. Her body streamlines as she flies through. Tentacles briefly brush against her arms. A few strokes in the deep blue, and then Lou rises through the water, gasping as she hits the surface. Exhilarated, she swims back to the rocky entry point. Although brightly patterned fish hang virtually motionless below her, she has to kick hard to make headway against that same current.

At the water's edge, Steve waits, crouched on his heels. She'd expected him to follow her in. Ridiculously happy, Lou smiles up at him.

"Now I see why you took to scuba!" he shouts above the waves that swirl and break around him.

"Come in, it's fantastic!" she calls.

Lou watches him tighten fin straps. Already soaked by the breakers, his tanned skin glistens.

Steve catches the final rush of a wave and rolls into the water next to her. He floats effortlessly on his back, letting the current take him. Tropical fish flee ahead as they drift for a few seconds and then swim with the tide along the rocky shore. The current is a wind that carries them across a hidden landscape. Everything seems so simple as they silently glide past scenery filled with strange sea critters. Sea stars, fluorescent sponges, crinoids, and other nameless things pass by below them.

Lou catches onto a ledge of an exposed reef to watch a banded sea snake search inside coral crevices for hidden prey. Steve returns and tugs her fins to get her attention.

"Hurry. We should stay together!" His voice is just audible above the sounds of the ocean. He spots small bright nudibranchs that she misses. But occasionally she notices things that he passes over, so it's her turn to show him.

Close to where the headland slopes off and gives way to a sandy beach, the water shallows out enough for them to touch bottom. The current has eased. Exhilarated, they stop and push their masks off.

"That was some drift!" Steve sounds breathless from the swim, as she is.

Had Lou been on her own, she might have pulled out a while back, but there's always safety in numbers, even if small. Water drips from Steve's hair onto his shoulders. She again resists an urge to run her fingers through his hair. But he pushes her hair gently back off her cheeks, and his fingers brush her skin as he lifts her face to his. Their lips touch, the kiss so natural that she's not even sure who initiated it. She catches her breath, laughs, and kisses him harder, all thought suspended, her hand wrapped around his neck. All of a sudden, she tastes saltwater again as they sink below the surface. The kiss rudely broken, they surface together, laughing and holding each other, his body hard against hers.

"I've wanted to do that since the day you came into the shop," he says.

"Yes," she replies. Then suddenly embarrassed at sounding ambiguous, she covers. "Let's go back and rescue our stuff off the rocks. The current is changing."

She kicks off ahead of him and swims fast through the water, acutely aware of how close behind he is.

She lets him help her out at the entry point. Some of the rocks have submerged, reclaimed by the sea, its power undisputed. They stand and watch the waves break over the smoothed edges.

"Better get back to the shop. My clients will be there soon," Steve says after a while.

Relief and disappointment wash over her. "Yes. We should. Let's go."

At night now, when she closes her eyes, underwater scenes play on the back of her eyelids. Above acres of bright coral, fish glide through watery blue spaces. Thousands of purple and orange anthea fish dance on the screen. And somewhere within that world is Steve, showing her all that she's missed. There's something so elusive she can't find it to save herself? But her attention keeps catching on the small things, like the nudibranch flatworms, their minuscule lungs exposed like antlers on their multi-colored surfaces.

Thirty

In the shaded bar, off the crowded street, Lou orders a drink and picks a quiet table to wait for Steve. The place is packed. Above the din, noisy laughter and occasional high-pitched giggles erupt from tables all around her. More uptight than she'd like, Lou tries to ignore the background noise. Her eyes focus out toward the ocean, and the light breeze off the water cools her skin. It won't be long before she has to return to the reality of Masaranga.

Her drink arrives, the glass clinking with ice, and Lou gulps it down. If only she could settle her mind. Her thoughts are wildly out of control, and her restlessness is back. Fortunately, the gin has started to kick in and ease her anxiety. A little light-headed, she sips more slowly. The waiter returns and casts an inquiring glance at the empty seat across from her.

"Sparkling water, please," she says. The last thing she wants is to get tipsy and act like an idiot.

Because Steve is late, Lou fears he's forgotten her, or, worse, decided not to come. A weird sense of relief accompanies these thoughts. In some way, it'd be a whole lot simpler if he failed to turn up. What a stupid mindset! Suddenly, she's frustrated with herself. What's wrong with her, and why is she tormented by this self-doubt?

This bar was Steve's suggestion, and she's not been here before. It's obviously popular with tourists and locals alike. But the cheerful commotion all around makes Lou feel strangely alone. Her seat is partially hidden to one side, and she unobtrusively watches people come and go. It's interesting to observe from a quiet spot, and Lou likes being away from the crowd.

But the last person Lou expects to see is Lexi. Suddenly, there she is across the crowd at the side of a well-dressed man. He's briefly in profile as they walk toward to exit. Lou's chair scrapes behind as she quickly jumps up to attract their attention.

"Hey, Lexi!"

Her words vanish in the din, and Lou starts to dodge between tables toward them, navigating the crowd. They're a stand-out couple. Lexi's black dress sits low across her back, while her swaying hips suggest high heels. The suave jacket of her companion hangs as if well cut and expensive. His arm settles around Lexi's shoulders with a lover's intimacy as he steers her through the throng. As they walk confidently away, Lou recalls the car by the lookout only days ago. She's suddenly glad Lexi failed to hear her.

As the man turns again to open the door for Lexi, Lou tries to catch a better glimpse of his face, but to no avail. Once they've stepped out onto the congested street, her chance has gone. Partway across the bar, Lou comes to a halt, her thoughts in overdrive. That man is familiar in some other context. Lou stands there, hesitant, her indecision unnoticed.

The bar where the couple must have been was out of her line of sight. Annoyed, Lou returns to her beach-view table. So much for her supposed observational skills! So, what is Lexi's real agenda? She's never mentioned meeting anyone here, and that was definitely more than just a friend.

Lou wonders how to make sense of the way Lexi unashamedly flirts with David when she's obviously less smitten than it appears. After her initial flare of anger, Lou finds relief in this revelation, followed by a twinge of guilt as her brother is evidently being misled. Her hands shake when she picks up her drink.

Briefly, Lou considers letting David know about this and then reasons against it. He's a grown man and will tell her to mind her business should she bring this up. He wouldn't like her meddling in his life and might interpret it as sisterly jealousy. Maybe he'd be less upset than Lou imagines. With David so cagey, she's lost insight into his thoughts. But best leave it alone. Lou vows to put Lexi's antics out of her mind. Her glimpse of the man's profile might irk her, but that doesn't mean she knows him. It's not her business, and she'll stay out of it.

Her thoughts continue to roller-coast. Isolation has made her introverted, and Lou feels on an emotional ledge faced by this new reality.

Perhaps she's too easily thrown by what should and shouldn't be, a deficiency to fix. Also, how does she feel about Steve?

On the one hand, Lou can hardly believe Steve likes her; on the other are her reservations about the popular types. Perhaps he's one of those players. Although, at least Carla respects him. The fact she introduced them should possibly be proof enough he's OK. Steve does seem to share some of her passions, and this almost wins her internal argument. She wills her mind to settle, but, seconds later, it's off again.

Would it be smart to invite Steve to Masaranga for a behind the scenes experience? Most tourists rush through, the wildlife merely entertainment. A casual invitation, in case he's not interested. Lou would hate for him to have to make excuses or feel pressured.

"Lou. Hey, Lou!"

Steve is with her, trying to get her attention. Her concerns recede. He kisses her quickly on the lips, surprising Lou enough to silence her.

"Let's sit on the deck?" He indicates a shaded table, just vacated by a sunburned couple, who look as if they've come from a cold climate.

She nods, and they push past people onto the deck.

"It's strange," she says. "I saw Lexi here a moment ago."

"I hope she was in a hurry!" Steve seems amused. "Your brother reserved a spot for them at that fancy new restaurant. He came by the shop an hour ago."

"You sure? What did he want?"

"Just a chat, I guess. I was in a hurry. Running late, as you can see!"

She grins and decides he's utterly charming.

"Did David ask about my diving?"

"Of course. It was our main topic of discussion!"

Lou laughs self-consciously, silenced by his teasing, and wonders about all the glamorous girls he meets from around the world.

She's light-headed again later when they weave through the throng and climb down onto the beach. Across the sky is a span of rippled clouds, their underbelly pink and purple. It seems uncomplicated to hold Steve's hand and be led past a belt of lush vegetation onto the expanse of sand. The tide is out, the sunset reflected in silvery puddles of seawater.

They kiss as naturally as if it were inevitable, his lips gentle at first, then harder against hers. Their tongues touch, intense and electric. He pulls Lou against himself, and she goes quickly, without her mind interfering. When they break for breath, they laugh and hold on to each other.

"I wasn't sure you liked me," says Steve, still holding her.

Lou looks at his handsome face as different replies flash through her mind. None seem OK, and then it's too late to answer.

"You don't say much!" he says.

"No. Sorry!" Lou laughs self-consciously and wishes she'd said the first thing that came to her. Anything would be better than nothing.

"Where do you want to eat?" He's serious all of a sudden.

"I don't mind. I'm easy."

"No, actually, you're not. Do you like seafood?"

Embarrassed, she nods and replies, "Truth is I don't know the local restaurants. Just let's not go to where my brother is taking Lexi!"

Generally, she's more decisive, but it's different with him around. For the moment, Lou wants to let him lead the way. It feels good to temporarily relinquish all responsibility.

Thirty-One

After an afternoon scouring the shops, Carla sounds relieved when they source a weekly anti-malarial for her research trip.

"Great. At last! The daily tablets are a pain and don't prevent Tanzanian strains of malaria."

"I had no idea! Let's go for a walk on the beach." Lou is keen to escape the shops.

"Sorry. I'm tired. I envy your energy!"

Lou's feet ache as well, but the ocean inspires her. Across the water is a jagged ridge of coral outcrops exposed by the receding tide. Enclosed within this inner reef is a calm lagoon, its water shimmery and silvered.

As Lou wanders along the beach, she worries about why she didn't go home with Steve last night. Now she's lost her opportunity to know him better. Is his place sparsely decorated, unlike her own messy room jammed full of artifacts she couldn't resist? He'd be justified to consider her messages mixed. Her thoughts niggle away. Perhaps her uptight attitude put him off. What's he doing right now? The memory of her afternoon snorkeling with Steve makes her smile, and a young woman passing her returns the smile. Lou wishes she could be so natural and uncomplicated.

And underneath all her anxiety sits the memory of Lexi sauntering through the bar. The image resurfaces like an annoying insect whenever Lou drops her guard. It bothers her that she's no closer to an answer. The evidence Lexi has another man jars badly, though Lou feels more relieved than angry. Maybe David might break his trance and come to his senses. But right now, he'd laugh if she brought it up.

"Lexi is popular and knows a lot of people," David would say. Perhaps he'd even consider himself lucky to be dating one of the in-crowd. Again, Lou decides to put the matter aside, and instead worry over Steve's impressions of her own behavior.

The fading mauves and pinks of sunset, the breeze and the balmy ocean are not enough to settle her apprehension. Like an irritating grain of sand in her eye, the memory of Lexi and the well-dressed man returns. Lou feels she shouldn't discuss it with anyone, and she again warns herself to stay out of other peoples' business.

Above the newly washed beach exposed by the receding tide is an expanse of powdery sand. Thick-stemmed creepers invade the highest sections. Just below them is a group of fishermen. They huddle together, their hands busy, the fine sand sticking to their ebony skin. Their knives twist back and forth as they methodically sort and dissect contorted mounds of material.

Lou alters course slightly to pass discreetly closer to the group. As she draws near, the mounds become open hessian sacks. Inside are glinting, spotted cowrie shells that only recently were part of the reef ecosystem. With mechanical efficiency, the men gut the still-alive cowries, forcefully eviscerating the life forms from their lovely homes. Soon, the tourists who buy these shells will have inadvertently ransacked nature, not cognizant of the many better ways to support these men and the systems that support them. Instead they unthinkingly reward untenable destruction.

Halfway through gutting a cowrie, the closest fisherman looks up and grins. Briefly, Lou pauses, alarmed by how many cowries are piled next to him. So much damage caused by a single person in a day! The man selects a largish shell and dusts off the sand with expert fingers.

"You like?" he asks, his expression expectant.

"Sorry, no." Lou indicates the sea with a wave of her arm. "I like to see them alive in the sea, not dead like this!"

In response, he shrugs as if to say, "Oh well, never mind," and glances curiously at Lou, his amusement barely concealed as he turns away to select another dying cowrie.

Lou's father taught her to push any occupied shells she discovered out of sight under coral ledges, temporarily hidden so they might survive a while longer. An ephemeral safety, but hopefully worthwhile. Their concealment might extend life long enough to create another generation of cowries.

Further along, tourist stalls dot the high-tide mark. The sand underfoot is as soft as the evening light, whose silvered rays illuminate rows of carvings artistically arranged to attract attention. Lou expects that nothing will interest her among the displays. She's seen so many similar before, and, although individually crafted, the artworks usually follow comparable patterns that no longer draw her in.

Nevertheless, the shapes fascinate and attract her attention. Over the years, Lou has acquired so many artifacts that they've spread out from her bedroom into the house. Her favorites have human faces entwined with animal torsos, and they sit like totem poles inside the main entrance.

At first, each carving was treasured. But new acquisitions crowded out the previous ones. Lou plans to dig them out and polish them up when there's time to reminisce and reorganize, the events of her life marked by how each item became hers. For now, they rest chaotically and quietly accumulate dust and scars, their aged surfaces marred by splashes of liquid.

Nowadays, Lou resists any urges to buy more, but, despite this, the glossy black outline of a hippo and calf catches her eye. They rest on the yellow sand as if wallowing, their bellies hidden below an imaginary waterline, only their backs and heads exposed. With a friendly headshake, Lou dismisses the vendor's sales pitch, her intent not to buy.

But the acutely observant vendor expertly spots a hint of interest. He knows that willpower can be weakened, even though a visitor may end up with more than can sensibly be carried home. The owner of the hippos notices Lou's hesitation. To negotiate a realistic price, Lou must hide where her interest lies; otherwise, the starting point will be ten rather than five times the vendor's minimum. Out the corner of her eye, Lou sees him follow her gaze. Deliberately, she ignores the shiny black hippos nestled on the yellow sand and instead focuses on a collection of rhinos.

She touches a rhino carved from grainy wood, sculptured to show every skin crease. His horn would, she reflects grimly, be the death of him in real life. The piece is adorable, but not unusual.

"How much for this one?" she asks and smiles at the vendor, a young man with serious brown eyes. He examines her face, her fingers on the carving, and returns to her face. His price is the predictable multiple of the going rate, and Lou laughs, cheerfully but not unkindly. She always barters like this, so no hard feelings remain once the deal is done.

"Too much!" She gently returns the rhino to the soft sand and picks a darker one with smoother outlines.

"What about this one?" His price halves, but she feigns a loss of interest and starts to point randomly as if getting a feel for the prices which immediately become more reasonable.

When Lou touches the hippo and calf casually, as one of many, the figure is three times the going rate. But it's unique, and she likes it. Lou offers him a third. He drops to two-thirds and won't budge. To haggle further won't gain her enough to make it worthwhile, so she agrees. He seems anxious, and, for a moment, Lou feels unsure about the purchase, but she hands the money over anyway.

He eases the hippos into a padded paper bag for protection, though Lou tells him not to bother. He insists and hands the purchase over. It's heavy under her arm as she shakes his hand. Though the cost is a bit high, she's glad to own it.

The sunset fades and the sky fills with purple-bellied clouds. As Lou follows the waterline, her concerns drift away. The breeze off the ocean cools her skin, and warm sand crunches under her feet. Along the beach, artists roll their creations into protective strips of old clothing or newspaper before stowing them into hand-woven baskets. A man holds up a painting and shouts out a last, special price of the day for Lou. She waves and indicates her padded bag to say she's spent her money. When sales are so essential to them, her lack of interest makes her feel mean.

As the light fades, Lou thinks how the sea creatures will now change stations below the ocean's calm surface. Steve described the reef at dusk when he promised her a night dive. Soon, parrotfish will secrete protective cocoons and hide in coral caverns, while crustaceans emerge from safe crevices. Predatory nocturnal fish will hunt daytime stragglers too slow to take refuge. In the dark, the deep-water sharks will swim shallower to where soft pastel-colored corals open like night flowers.

Lou imagines this underwater realm, where hidden life ventures out under cover of darkness just as it does on the savannah. It's a new world for her. She wades into the lukewarm saltwater and hears the murmuring of deeper currents farther out.

Past a stretch of shallows, she reaches a place where the beach gives way to dark shadowy rocks. Five exuberant children giggle and chatter as they splash out of the water toward her.

"Jambo!" the smallest girl calls out boisterously, and then innocent smiling faces surround Lou. Seawater streams out from their curly black hair. One of the boys wears a raggedy T-shirt emblazoned with "Free Tibet."

"Do you know where Tibet is?" Lou asks him. She sits on her heels and encourages them over, but they giggle harder and move further off, suddenly too shy to come closer.

Then, as the kids dart around Lou, a jolt of recognition arrives. Lexi's friend. All day the knowledge has prodded her from just below the surface. It was the handsome Sam who came twice to Masaranga. On their official visit, Mr. Lonnegan described him as needing something to get his teeth into.

Surely my imagination is out of control? Lou struggles to reassure herself. A sideways glimpse is not enough to tell. But suddenly she's sure. It was Sam, the confident charmer, who was so friendly and free with his compliments! Of course, Lexi would find him attractive. Lou liked him and was grateful for his part in providing extra rangers. He'd seemed uncomfortable when she'd thanked him so profusely on his return. Lexi must know him from one of those infamous Nairobi parties she always enthuses over.

Lou sinks onto the wet sand, not caring that the saltwater has soaked her clothes. The watchful kids see she's forgotten them, and run away in search of other diversions. The last rays of sunlight vanish below the horizon as Lou stares abstractedly across the dark water and recalls the fancy car at the lookout. The fact Lexi and Sam are in a relationship disturbs her irrationally, more than it should.

Lou returns through the busy evening streets to her hotel and finds Steve's car outside. She hurries upstairs. *Has he been here long?* Her concern allows Steve to tease her about the wait before he asks her out to dinner. She decides to show him the hippo later.

The following morning, Lou eases the shiny black carving out of the bag. The hippo will look perfect placed on a glass table as if floating on a pond. Her hands smooth over the dome of the mother's back as she rubs off the complimentary sand. She puts it on a table in the sunlight. Now Lou understands why the vendor was nervous and insisted on a bag. Part of the baby hippo's shoulder has broken off, and it's not in the bag. The broken, exposed section needs to be sanded. She's not angry as the scarring should hardly show.

Thirty-Two

Aburst of laughter wakes Steve up. It's Lou, on the outside deck of her hotel room. He wants her back in bed, up close to him. What's she doing out there when all he wants is to make her his again?

Lou shakes her head with an expression somewhere between amusement and irritation at something she holds in her hands. It looks like a carving.

"What's so funny?" he asks.

"The hippo calf's shoulder is damaged," Lou replies and places the piece on the bedside table to show him. Actually, he'd prefer to look at Lou, still wet from the shower. Steve has slept in. He makes an effort to focus on the carving.

"And that amuses you?" He's angry at whoever sold it to her damaged.

"He beat me at my own game. My bargaining technique actually worked against me!"

"How?"

"I liked it so much I feigned indifference and never picked it up for a proper look."

Crazy psychology! How often does she feign indifference? Is that why she's so hard to read, and what gives her that aloof quality when she's clearly quite emotional? It suddenly occurs to Steve that Lou is introverted rather than indifferent, and he's been slow to realize it because she's so out there in other ways.

Steve gets her amusement. It's nice she doesn't hate that the guy beat her. After all, the vendors get a whole lot of practice. He'd be angry, but she shows no trace of that as she re-examines it. That good-natured aspect is a refreshing side that she sometimes hides, especially when on a roll about human attitudes toward wildlife.

"Just needs to be sand-papered back and polished up a bit!" Lou climbs back into bed. Steve pulls her close and hears her intake of breath at his touch. Her skin is soft as she rolls into him. He can't remember feeling this good about anyone before. Even in bed, Lou has a quiet intuition of how it is for him. Her hands slide down his back and over his buttocks, making him so hard he aches with the need to be inside her. Her body molds and moves with his. Steve hears her cry out only seconds before he does, the sound carrying him toward that blinding light he desperately craves.

It's late when he gets to the shop, but the young bloke has already opened up. Good job he trusted him with the keys. The lad is a fast learner. Pity he's not older and cashed up enough to be a business partner. Truth is, his employee should be at school getting more of an education. He's too smart for this. Steve suddenly realizes these are partly his father's thoughts, rehashed as his own. The old man would be surprised how well his son has done financially in his time here, despite the loss of Jed as a partner.

Tourists are already trying on wetsuits, which is good. The faster this is done, the more time he has to prepare for a visit from a prospective partner from Nairobi. The man knows nothing about the dive industry, which worries Steve, but with his choices limited and his visa about to run out, he can't be choosy. At least the man's got money and the right connections.

It's just snorkelers today, and Steve sends the young lad with the boatman. His thoughts track back to Lou. He'd waited impatiently for her in the lobby yesterday evening, and she'd not feigned indifference. Thank god! A bloke likes to feel welcome, and it seems he is. Actually, Lou has never played him or acted as if she has hidden agendas around him. His initial ice-queen judgment was misplaced.

Last night was pretty special, and Steve can't wait to see Lou again. She'd wanted to avoid her brother and the sisters. When she hinted at being a bit over it, Steve filled in the spaces. He understands her better now. To be honest, the way her brother is all over Lexi makes Steve worry about David's judgment. Though, to be fair, there always seems to be plenty of apparently smart businessmen with short-sighted taste in that department.

Thirty-Three

Her time at the coast has been far too short. As a sense of emptiness wells up inside, Lou forces back tears when she hugs Steve goodbye.

"I'll be back!" she says to him.

"You better be!" he replies jokingly. "I haven't even started to show you around."

The others are in a hurry to leave, and everything is too rushed to tell him how sad she is. *Probably a good thing.*

"Come on, Lou! We're ready!" Lexi's voice is insistent and she's already in the front seat with David.

The long drive provides too many hours for reflection. Lou watches the landscape pass by, the potholed road splitting the plains into ragged halves. David and Lexi chat upfront. Carla reads a book on tribal cultures, and occasionally looks up to throw sporadic comments into the conversation.

With the steamy coastal air left far behind, the country dries up around them. Vast tracts of desiccated savannah stretch to the horizon. Wide-topped acacias dot the plains, and in their sparse shade, impalas and gazelles seek relief from the morning heat. The car bounces along the rough tarmac. It carries them back across areas too dry for human habitation, territory better left for wildlife evolved to tolerate harsh conditions.

In places, where farmers run cattle, water is stored in thick concrete tanks. These ranchers often battle with the thirsty elephants that migrate in search of water from even more desolate areas not yet taken by humans. During droughts, elephants are desperate enough to risk their lives for a drink. Ranchers shoot to scare them away. Survival in such country is tough for everyone.

They choose a lunch spot at a place where a viewing platform overlooks a low-lying valley with a waterhole. They left early, and it's past midday. The chatter between the two up front has died down.

"Here it is!" says Lou when they're almost on the turnoff.

"A bit more warning, sis!" David breaks abruptly.

"It's hard to see from here," Lou replies, annoyed that she's being held responsible from the backseat. The narrow track leads into the bush. They leave the Nairobi road and follow it to a small parking area. Glad for a break and the distraction from her thoughts, Lou follows the others up faded wooden steps to the cafeteria, her body stiff and scrunched from hours in the car.

They buy Fanta and lemonade from a woman with a huge smile that reminds Lou of Grace. The only food is a selection of greasy snacks, though the kitchen is surprisingly clean, without the habitual flies.

"I've forgotten my sunhat!" says Lexi.

"It's a shaded platform," replies David and he steps toward the nearest table.

"No, I must have it to protect my skin. I need you to come back with me."

Lou follows Carla up to the wooden platform by the café.

"I'm sorry my sister has been a bit of a princess on this trip," says Carla.

"It's all OK. Don't feel bad!" replies Lou. "I'm so grateful you talked me into the dive course."

"I knew you and Steve would hit it off!"

Lou guesses Carla knows nothing about her sister's other boyfriend. *What would be her take on it?* But Lou is not about to bring it up. They're alone in the viewing space where a panorama opens across the valley, the savannah seemingly endless, uninterrupted by roads or settlements as far as the hazy horizon.

Just ahead of Lou, Carla leans over the drop-off for a better view and then frantically beckons her to hurry up.

"Quick, you're going to miss it!"

Lou runs the last few steps. Opposite the platform is a family of thirsty elephants emerging in a single file through a gap in the scrub. They cross the clearing below, the herd so close they must sense humans nearby. But the elephants appear unconcerned as they continue toward the muddy waterhole. Obviously excited by the sight of water, a few of them make low rumbling calls as they share and communicate their pleasure. As they hurry to keep up, the young ones flap their ears and flail their tiny trunks. They shamble along close to their mothers, the enthusiasm of the grown-ups infectious.

Close to the bank, the family members spread out to follow various trails down the slippery slopes. In awe, Lou watches their evident happiness as they wade out toward the deepest spot.

A mud-bath party begins as the elephants fill their trunks and blast cooling water over themselves and each other. The gray liquid splatters back and forth, and the waterhole turns thick and muddy. It's deep enough for them to submerge completely while they wallow. Occasionally only the tip of an elephant's trunk remains above the churning surface. No skin parasites could survive such an onslaught. As they stand back up, rivulets of mud run off the deep wrinkles of their pachyderm hides. They seem to be in elephant heaven.

Enthralled, Lou hangs over the railings, anxious not to miss a moment. The energetic elephants have a purpose but are also having fun, taking pleasure in the water. Clumsy youngsters submerge and frolic alongside the adults. Their skinny trunks swing busily back and forth as they copy the adults. Occasionally a mother nudges her calf toward the safe shallow spots along the edge. Though aware of humans just above them, they seem at ease. Lou is glad the herd considers this a safe place. At least some elephants are lucky enough not to associate the sound and smell of people with danger.

"Ground hornbills out to the left!" Carla grabs her elbow. Through her binoculars, Lou watches the ungainly black birds waddle along the edge, their large bills a startling orange against their glossy bodies. Apparently unworried by the heaving mass of gray giants only meters away, the hornbills search for food along the water's edge. Lou snorts with laughter as an ungainly hornbill jumps sideways to avoid a swoosh of flying mud.

When Lou refocuses back on her favorite animals, only moments of the bath remain. The spectacle is over as unexpectedly as it began. The largest female hauls her mass out of the mud and uses her trunk to push her teenage calf ahead of her. Gray sludge slides from an expanse of skin as she climbs out. A second adult follows and then a third. Calves gambol erratically alongside their parents, determined to keep up, their trunks twisting as they balance on the slippery surface. One after another, the remaining elephants follow in quick succession.

The giants vanish as quietly and quickly as they appeared, leaving the clearing through a belt of acacias. Their passage through the invisible gap is so seamless it's hard for Lou to believe what she's seen. Once the trees have swallowed them, all that remains is a trampled expanse of mud and water. It would be difficult for anyone not on the viewing platform for those few minutes to imagine what they've missed.

Her spirits high, Lou checks for her brother. He'd have loved it. She hears lively chatter followed by laughter that grows noisier until David and Lexi reach the platform, out of breath from the climb.

"You just missed a mob of elephants having a mud bath!" An uncharacteristic hint of exasperation has crept into Carla's tone.

"It happened too fast to get you," Lou apologizes.

"Never mind. I've seen plenty of elephants," David replies, utterly nonchalant. Lexi, flushed and giggly, heads off for the bathroom without a comment.

"How about we eat?" David turns to Lou. "Then we must get a move on. We've a way to go after we drop the girls off in Nairobi." He hardly glances at the deserted space below them.

Lou eats slowly and watches out across the empty waterhole, her mind initially on the elephants, and then the last two weeks. She feels less gutted after seeing the antics of the herd, but it's a pity neither Steve nor her brother saw it. Not that her brother cares. Lou wonders if he ever discusses Masaranga's elephants with Lexi. For some reason, she hopes not.

Lexi returns, blonde hair freshly twisted into a coil off her face, new eyeliner and lipstick applied. She glides gracefully into the seat next to David, obviously playing up to the way his smiling eyes watch her every move. He breaks off a conversation with Carla, who winks at Lou and then rolls her eyes in tolerant amusement. *How would it be to have Lexi as a sister?* Often Lou has wanted a sister to share stuff with. She suddenly realizes you can never tell what hand you might be dealt.

The sky is dark when they hit Nairobi's outskirts. Outside Sara's gates, the familiar tree looms inky black. The night watchman emerges warily, alert for trouble. He recognizes the car and smiles, his gapped teeth bright in the headlights as his hands fumble on the padlock, and the gates swing open.

They stay only long enough to briefly chat with Sara and unload bags by torchlight. The night watchman waits to re-open the gates.

"Lexi's a great girl!" David comments somewhere on the endless final leg home. Lou, too tired to hide her feelings, says, "I prefer Carla. She's a whole lot more real and interesting as well."

"Carla's no fun. She takes herself too seriously. The two of you are as bad as each other!"

Thirty-Four

The bull elephant Tembo curves his trunk up high to test the breeze. He's recently joined a herd and become attached to a young female, who mirrors his movements as she waits close by. She, too, detects the ominous tang of human sweat. Uneasy, Tembo sways his massive head to locate its source, and as his agitation builds it transmits to his female. But the scent is downwind and hard to pinpoint. Tembo swings slowly around to again face the breeze.

The bushland seems deceptively quiet. A hornet hovers briefly over Tembo's forehead and then lands between his intelligent eyes. Irritated, he swats it aside with his trunk. Its sting won't penetrate his thick hide, and he's preoccupied with the potential threat. He recognizes that dangerous stench.

Tembo has been shot at by poachers before. The first time was when he roamed alone across the savannah. Explosions deafened him and the inexplicable pain that followed made him fear predatory men. Stored in his long memory is an exhausting escape, when he fled through Mopani scrub. As blood poured from his leg, an armed man closed in from behind.

But today, the scents from the herd dilute the human sweat stink, moderating its acridity. It's hard for the bull to locate when his senses are also assailed by the ready-to-mate female that drew him to these mothers and calves. He's also tired from chasing her and slower to react at the first sign of trouble, a potentially fatal mistake.

The size of his tusks bears witness to Tembo's usual caution. Out here, elephants don't survive long enough to grow such trophies unless they're smart and wary. That time he was shot, the bullet lodged deep in his left thigh, and the wound festered. He became slow and sick, and pain throbbed up through his leg until his entire body hurt. Toxins seeped into his blood, and he was cranky for weeks. Only because he was young and vigorous was his immune response able to expel the bullet. When the abscess broke open, the gaping hole healed well. Fresh granulation tissue sealed it from flies and ants. After that, Tembo confined his solitary existence further within Masaranga's boundaries.

In his youth, elephant country extended past Masaranga's borders. The female elephants who cared for Tembo as a youngster found food and raised him out of harm's way. He gamboled and played without an ever-present sense of fear emanating from his adult caretakers. Now he's contained without true refuge, his nomadic instincts curtailed. Despite the official protection of the park, the threat from mankind is ever present. This island of wilderness is surrounded by an exploding human population, whose subsistence cultivations merge into each other.

Close to Tembo, another female rips up tufts of brown grass. Sensing danger, she stops chewing with the desiccated stalks still in her mouth. It has been hard for her to make enough milk for her first calf. Gently, she nudges her baby out of the way as the bull completes another circle, his trunk still high in the air.

At her mother's touch, the playful calf gambols out of Tembo's way. For her the world is still new and exciting. Born late last season, she senses only her mother's familiar hulk. The herd's youngest, she's only partly aware of the meaning of close-by predators. Her mother's ears waft air over her body, making the calf reluctant to move too far from shaded security. At her mother's urging, she moves closer to the safety under her neck. Suddenly, she senses the herd's agitation.

But it's too late. Explosions rip through the herd. The poachers are too close and their attack is savage, as they unleash one round of bullets after another. Without time to comprehend an escape, the elephants trumpet with terror and then scream in agony. There's no chance to save themselves.

The first bullets are aimed at Tembo, but the young mother falls instead. At the last moment, she wraps her trunk protectively around her calf, who tumbles with her. Others attempt to escape as they crash away through the bush, unsure where their murderers are hidden. The stampede is chaotic, filled with raw panic and screams. One by one, the elephants stumble and fall onto the ground for the terrifying last few moments of life. As they go down, gunshot drowns out the moans of the stricken, and rounds of bullets tear through new flesh, indiscriminately maiming and killing.

The calf pushes against her inert mother, scared to leave the only safety she's known. The mother's pulse is weak, but she's aware of her baby. For the first and last time, the calf smells the bitter gunshot and the acrid odor of sweat. The shouts of excited men draw closer. Terrified, the calf senses their menace as they approach her. To these killers, all *tusks are worth the carnage. A dead elephant represents money, and the real cost means nothing to them.*

Frozen by fear, the calf leans hard against her dying mother, who extends the tip of her bloodied trunk to give her daughter a final fleeting touch. Her calf won't survive out here without her.

The first man arrives at the massacre and shouts instructions at the rest of the gang. He urges them to hurry. To him, the calf is nothing but a nuisance. It will interfere with their next job, which is to hack off the spoils, the so, so very precious ivory. His gun is newly loaded, ready to destroy any impediment to his progress. He raises it, aiming more carefully now he's so close to his prey, and empties it into the doomed elephant calf. With her last breath, the mother screams out her anguish. Her calf dies only seconds before her.

Thirty-Five

Birdsong. The cooing of doves pulls Lou from an underwater world seamlessly back to the bush. The anticipation of returning to Masaranga kept her motivated through university. As the first rays of light penetrate her room, Lou wonders how the elephants have fared. She arrived home too late last night to ask.

Grace is already in the vegetable garden, and Lou helps her pull up potatoes, the earth crumbling through her fingers.

"Already awake, Lou. You came home late!" Grace's tone is suspiciously light, and she fails to hide her tension behind a smile.

"Yes late! Where's everyone?"

Mostly Lou means, "Where's Peter?"

Peter's enthusiasm for the anti-poaching unit worries Grace. It's risky, but he's deadly keen, and his mother can't stop him.

"Bwana and Peter left early. Very sorry news. More poachers."

"How many? Elephants or rhinos?"

"Not sure, Memsahib Lou. Many elephants, I am thinking."

The joy of home shudders into oblivion. Instantly in overdrive, Lou feels her chest constrict, as what she wants to forget smashes back into awareness. A tide of emotion slams through her.

The smell of coffee brings Lou out of her trance. Grace is next to her, mug in hand.

"I am also sad, but you are tired. Best to stay here today."

Lou's first impulse is to try to get a call through to her supervisor at the university, just to talk. But nothing anyone says or does can help without facts. It would be self-indulgent to offload and waste her mentor's time.

"My study achieves nothing," she says.

"No, Lou. Not so! But you are impatient!" Grace's soothing tone does not help.

"And look at what happens when I'm patient!"

Lou empties her cup in a couple of gulps, swallowing the bitter grounds. For Grace, she walks calmly away. Out of sight, she races down the back steps, three at a time.

A painful knot has clenched around her heart. She struggles not to imagine the elephants' terror as poachers gunned them down. Does David distance himself from Masaranga to avoid being consumed by this? Her desire to help is stifled. She's stuck at home with the horses, almost on ground zero, but unable to help in any useful manner.

A halter slung over her shoulders, Lou strides toward the paddock. When their bellies are full of grass, Oliver and Roma groom each other meditatively, but right now, they look forlorn in their usual hangout at the back of their enclosure. Here, a slow leak from their battered water trough feeds a patch of greener grass, alongside a shady stretch of bougainvillea. As Lou approaches, their tails flick away the pervasive flies.

Before Roma's arrival, Oliver spent more time by the horizontal bough close to the house, where Lou brushes and saddles him. He craved the company of people with their molasses and rolled oats.

Oliver greets Lou with a soft nicker and allows the halter to slip on over his velvety skin while he nuzzles for food. She wonders which direction the men took. She's tempted to follow.

Oliver's habits changed the day her father brought the half-tamed filly home. Roma's eyes were wild as Lou unbolted the borrowed horse float. It was hard to entice her into unfamiliar territory.

"Transport for Peter!" her father cheerfully replied to the question in Lou's eyes.

"Great!' Lou examined the highly strung horse with trepidation, but she called softly to her. "Come on, big girl."

Roma was going to be a handful. She edged off the float, her gray haunches flecked with sweat. Today, she's tinted dusty-orange. Oliver is sensible and low maintenance. His chestnut coat disguises dust and protects him from sunlight.

Wary of his new companion, Oliver drew his body up, flattened his ears, and flared his nostrils. The moment their noses touched, both horses squealed and recoiled. For a week, they eyed each other with suspicion. After that, they banded together, and Oliver lost some of his attachment to humans.

"Hello, you two. Are you bored?"

They watch Lou move around them. Roma stamps a hoof on the ground in a gesture of defiance. Even with the molasses bucket as a bribe, she will be hard to catch today.

Kind Oliver is straightforward, unlike haughty Roma. If his exuberant prancing unseats Lou, he's never mean enough to follow through and throw her, as Roma does on a bad mood day. Before they learned her tricky ways, Roma often bucked riders off.

"Your Oliver is a gentleman!" Peter once said, with a rueful chuckle, as he dusted off his clothes. "This Roma. She has a temper!"

Lou places the halter on Oliver, and he follows her across the paddock, his neck stretched and his tongue rasping on the sides of the molasses bucket. A few steps behind, Roma follows just out of catching distance. She extends her neck cautiously, scenting the sweet, sticky smell. But when Lou extends her hand, the mare pulls back and snorts disdainfully.

"Oliver, you lovely fellow, have some more!" Lou ignores Roma and lets him have the bucket as she leads him along. He's so close, his halter rope hangs loosely. Roma trails at a safe distance and nickers when she loses ground. Lou's breaths come hard, and the exercise dissipates the emotions swirling underneath.

When Lou saddles Oliver up. Roma overcomes her fear of entrapment and accepts the halter. Lou feels slightly better, more human. A strange expression, to equate feeling better to being human. Do people actually feel better than animals? If only she had Grace's ability not to worry about what she can't fix.

The horses' concerns are immediate, their outlook simple. Lou rides Oliver, and Roma follows on her halter. Along the tracks outside the park, they pass villages, where the kids run out, eager to see the horses. They shout and urge their friends out to see the mzungu, the white person riding by.

Lou comes this way often, but they seem as excited as if it's her first time past.

Later, as Lou brushes the horses, a blanket of depression again descends. The death of more elephants breaks her heart. The needy work for the greedy to extricate the last precious animals. Lou likes the way that rhymes but hates how crops and towns have overrun nature, and how human needs combine with human failings to form a chain of corruption.

People often ignore things they'd change if they could. They imagine their influence insignificant and dissociate from what matters to them. In her more futile moments, Lou completely understands this more comfortable path, especially considering her present ineffectiveness. She returns past the weaverbird nest. All the vehicles are still out. To be considered a liability rather than useful doesn't help her. Lou eats alone at her desk and waits for the men to return. Doggedly, she sorts data for scientific presentation, her aim to earn credibility. Asleep at her desk when the men return, her neck and back are cramped as if she spent the night in the patrol vehicle.

Days and weeks pass painfully. Sometimes they remove traps and intercept lone poachers, whom the police question and let go with a warning. More often, they find carnage and evidence of a poaching gang long gone. The tight, sick knot becomes a persistent presence in her chest. And their rhinos are too thin on the ground to find a mate. Their last calf died soon after her mother was poached. How could she raise money to capture the remaining rhinos and employ a guard?

Her father's frustration makes him ill-tempered.

"This gang does have a sixth sense," he says. "They're elusive, but we always catch them in the end."

"And there are always more," Lou replies. "And we're out of time."

"Not yet," her father replies.

Lou had vowed not to voice such negativity. He's right not to speak his doubts. Such admission is to lose hope, though last time Steve promised a visit he told her that "hope is not a strategy."

Though her thesis seems like squandered time, Lou frantically pursues her tedious paper trail. She's aware how many animals die unseen. A small carcass like a skinned leopard would be quickly cleaned up by scavengers, leaving no time for the vultures' spiraling silhouettes to alert anyone.

"Come and eat dinner. Get back to that later," her father says, and she obeys. But even as she gains scientific credibility, it's as if the destruction has accelerated.

Thirty-Six

Recently, elephants have become elusive and hard to locate. Today is no different and Lou is downhearted as she sits on a fallen tree trunk by the dirt track. She left her Land Rover to check a pile of elephant dung, which is the closest she's been to an elephant since a glimpse of a retreating haunch yesterday morning.

Perhaps it's time to call it a day? Lou sighs and continues to watch an industrious dung beetle excavate balls from the pile and drag them backward across the cracked earth to its burrow. The beetle is on its third trip harvesting the digested plant material, when an unfamiliar birdcall sounds from the nearby stretch of riverine forest. But the call was all wrong. Any other wildlife appears to have gone to ground in the heat, apart from the beetle that molds another sphere and then uses its weight to roll it to the underground stash, the hot sunlight glinting off its black back.

Another low whistle sounds, and Lou cups her ears to locate its origin. *Someone's mimicking a birdcall. Who could be so close?* The only access to the river is the overgrown track that Lou followed this far. Hardly anyone knows it exists, and she saw no tire marks on the way in.

Quietly, Lou eases to her feet and absently rubs the tree-bark indentations on her legs while she listens. Yet another higher-pitched whistle emanates from a stretch of meandering forest along the nearby river. She returns to the Land Rover, pulls the rifle from behind the seat, and then closes the door gently, afraid to make a noise.

Though it would be perilous, intrepid birdwatchers could be on a cross-country chase after secretive bird species that hide in dense vegetation. They'd keep quiet so as to not alert any birds. Park rules forbid tourists to leave their vehicle outside the campgrounds, but birdwatchers are often overly determined to tick species off their must-see lists, a photograph a bonus, their goal to record, not destroy, unlike trophy hunters with their misplaced efforts to prop up fragile egos.

However, birdwatchers can be inclined to push their luck. Unwitting and naive, they often use hippo paths to reach the water near the deep sections of rivers. Occasionally, when they surprise wildlife, they're trampled to death by animals defending their territory. Although tourists are warned to stay safe in their vehicles, the less rule-abiding ones often end up in serious trouble.

Lou knows the dangers, but the only way to progress is on foot. It's a bit risky out here alone, but her rifle is a safeguard. She follows the neglected track under thick-leaved trees toward the river and doesn't come across any human footprints. Cautious and careful not to tread on sticks or break branches, she follows the calls. Long ago, Peter taught her to tread lightly through the bush. Small creatures skitter away through the undergrowth ahead of her. Sweat beads on her arms. Lou crouches instinctively when she reaches the riverbank.

The river is dirty and its flow slow. Motionless, Lou listens to the random sounds of the bush and swirl of the muddy water below. Her senses on alert, she waits. It's quiet now, except for a sudden loud growl from her stomach that reminds her how long ago she left headquarters.

At last, a high-pitched whistle from upstream. Half crouched, Lou moves toward it, the rifle tucked under her arm. She ducks further into dense vegetation right on the bank, where vines twist down from tall trees and wrap through the saplings. They catch at her as she struggles on and it's impossible to disentangle herself quietly.

After a scramble over a series of fallen branches, Lou is faced with a slippery mudbank at a bend where the river narrows and deepens. The only way forward is to hang onto a vine and climb. It's too dangerous to stay close to the water. Even though there's no sign of hippos, a crocodile on the bottom would be invisible.

As Lou hauls herself up the muddy bank, her feet skid and slide. Tree roots and vines slip through her fingers. Now almost at the top, she's panting and only too aware that all her noise would alert anyone of her approach. She looks up for the last handhold to find a gun muzzle in her face.

"No. Wait!" Lou gasps and she falls back to her last handhold. Her heart pounds wildly in her ribcage. Blood roars through her ears. She almost lets go. Her instinct is to roll back into denser vegetation. "Don't shoot!" Lou shouts as she twists away from the gun.

A brief silence, then a man's voice. "Memsahib Lou?"

A flood of relief washes through Lou. *He knows me!* The man steps out from the shadows above her and lowers his gun. She recognizes Paul, one of the new rangers, who extends a hand to help her. He watches sheepishly as Lou scrambles over the top. Her chest heaving, Lou brushes leaves and dirt off her clothes.

"I heard your bird whistles," she gasps. "What are you doing here?"

"I was calling John. We came from the crossing to check along the river for snares."

It's a plausible explanation, though Lou had no idea her father sent rangers this way today. At least they're keen to do their job. That they've walked this far shows determination. Paul turns and whistles upstream, and Lou hears a higher-pitched whistle reply. What a relief it's the rangers rather than poachers. Had Lou encountered armed strangers, she'd have made a more perilous mistake than the time when she left her crashed car.

"You gave me a big shock, Memsahib Lou," says Paul. "I thought you were a hyena coming up the bank!"

She laughs, relieved.

"And I thought you were a poacher ready to shoot me! I didn't expect anyone to be here."

"Now that we have come to help, Bwana says patrols must cover all areas."

John seems to have almost caught up. He approaches quietly, his progress hardly disturbing the vegetation. He calls out a few words in a language Lou guesses is Kikuyu. She knows their sound, but not their meaning. Paul shouts back and an exchange follows. Lou reflects they could be polite enough to use Swahili and not cut her out.

"Hi John," she calls as he approaches. "You both frightened me!"

She grins as he pushes past vines and into view. John returns her smile but says nothing, always the retiring one.

Lou tells them she'll return alone to her Land Rover, but they follow her. Paul insists it's dangerous to walk unaccompanied. Someone might shoot her! The truth is that until now, she was warier of wildlife than of being shot. Lou hears an edge to Paul's voice as if he's annoyed to find her here. That's not surprising considering she was unexpectedly in an area they're supposed to patrol. Perhaps he got a bit of a fright as well. Lou tries to joke, saying that they seem to be the ones most likely to shoot her. Paul manages a smile, but she gets the impression he doesn't find it all that amusing.

The walk back seems easy now there's no need to creep along with her senses on edge. Lou gets into the Land Rover, the overheated air inside suffocating.

"Thanks for walking with me. I'll give you a lift back to the crossing," she says.

"No, we are OK. We can walk back."

"I don't mind."

"No, Memsahib, no problem. We are not finished yet."

Lou arrives home to find Grace washing out clothes, methodically beating them against the old stone sink.

"Bwana has gone to Nairobi," says Grace. "He says he will go stay with Sara if you need him."

"What's called him away this time?" Lou asks. "Another meeting with government?"

But Grace only shrugs and her smile is complacent.

"I wish he'd let us know his plans!" replies Lou. She'd have liked to have seen Sara and also her thesis supervisor.

The evening stretches out ahead with no one to discuss the day's unexpected events. Lou would tell Grace, but suspects she'd get a gentle telling off. Come to think of it, her father mightn't be pleased either about her solo walk along the riverbank. It's not so long since she backed her Land Rover over an embankment. If she's not careful, he might insist she never go out alone. It's probably best to say nothing until she can tell Steve about it. At least he seems to take her seriously.

Lou raids their reference library and eats heated-up stew as she researches dung beetles. It's pleasant to be reminded of the role played by seemingly insignificant creatures.

Thirty-Seven

To Lou's delight, Steve finally arrived this morning! As he drives the Land Rover along the rough road toward the southern waterhole, it rattles horribly and Lou is acutely conscious of how old it is. Behind them, a red plume of dust obscures the thorny scrub in her side-view mirror. In this dry, distances seem to stretch out, and Lou's memories of the green coastal plain appear as if from another world. They stop by a clearing to watch a giraffe nibbling leaves from a high branch. Almost as they pull away, Lou spots a buffalo hidden further back in the vegetation that she'd have missed had she been driving.

Steve winks at her and slows again, his eyes briefly off the narrow track. He pulls up close to the cranky old bull, and then moves on when the buffalo lowers its head and advances toward them. Potholes loom. Steve concentrates on the uneven road and covers the harsh terrain comfortably as if used to it. *How did he get so confident?* A trickle of sweat crosses his forehead, and Lou resists an urge to wipe it away. Sweat snakes down her own back and beads on her arms; the drying moisture cakes with dust. Her face is coated red, and her hair tangled from the open window. Typically, Lou doesn't worry about how unattractive she must look, but today is an exception.

With his hair cut short, Steve seems altered. A few months ago, it was fashionably long, and he merged perfectly with the tourists at the coast, relaxing after their safaris. Lou remembers how they overheard a group of satisfied sightseers during their cocktail chatter discussing how they'd "done" Kenya in two weeks.

"That pompous lot don't know much about 'doing Kenya,'" Steve had whispered in her ear. "They act as if a couple of weeks here makes them experts!"

Lou had laughed. She couldn't have put it better.

Somehow, Steve seems different today, though at least he turned up. *Best to never assume anything.* Lou restrained her surge of enthusiasm when he phoned to say he was on his way. Her ingrained strategy has become to expect little and avoid disappointment. So, she's glad he came, though Lou is not immune to the warnings about men who work with tourists and their many brief affairs. Memories of how her first boyfriend went overseas permanently don't help either. She wants to avoid all that.

The bush opens up to reveal herds of Thompson's gazelles grazing in open clearings. As the vehicle jolts past, the slender antelopes lift delicate heads, alert, but dependent on the reaction of their social network to alert them of real danger.

"I don't think I've seen one of those before," Steve says.

"They're common in Masaranga," Lou replies. "Their horizontal black stripes distinguish them from Grant's gazelle."

Lou flips open her *Guide to East African Mammals* on the antelope section and holds up the page to show him.

Another bend. The vehicle frightens another small antelope, which swings quickly around and leaps away into a dense thicket.

"That's a duiker," she says. "They're solitary and wary."

"Sounds a bit like you then!"

Lou feels her jaw drop but he grins and winks again.

Close to the southern waterhole, the acacias grow taller. The grass in the clearings is longer. Wildlife becomes abundant. Warthogs dig in mud holes by the track. As the Land Rover lurches by and interrupts their foraging, the inquisitive hogs raise intelligent eyes toward the noisy vehicle. Lou loves to see their strange, tusked faces.

Almost at the waterhole, Steve slows to negotiate puddled potholes and muddy verges. Whenever the vehicle slides sideways, his reflexes spin them back out of trouble. They emerge onto an open plain alongside an expanse of cracked mud. Ahead, a gray lakebed stretches out below an empty sky of steel—a desolate beautiful scene.

Far out from where they've stopped is a puddle of shallow water and, beyond that, a faint shimmer.

"It's pretty dried up. Probably a mirage out there." Steve pulls out battered binoculars.

"Hopefully, not yet," Lou replies. "There was water last week when Peter and I walked out to check."

They'd chosen to walk because there was a risk the Land Rover would break the surface and get bogged.

"Hot old walk!"

"Not so bad. It was late in the day."

"You're both crazy! Was it worth it?"

"Just a couple of herons and elephant tracks from the west, over that way." Lou points, her eyes squinting against the sun as she searches for signs of life.

He hands her his binoculars. Their field of view is narrow, but the image is sharp, considering the heat rising off the lakebed. She hopes some water still remains for the wildlife.

When Lou returns the binoculars, she's suddenly self-conscious that he's been watching her.

"It's so dusty!" she says and wipes her shirt sleeve against her face. It's weird to be so scrutinized. Again, Lou imagines how unattractive she must look, and then reminds herself that this is who she is.

"We better keep moving," she says. "We've quite a way to go!"

As they drive on, Steve chats away about how the business keeps him busy at the coast. "To be honest, I'm a bit anxious about it all," he admits.

"What stresses you most?" asks Lou, but he's suddenly silent on the matter and she doesn't want to pry. He can tell her when he's ready.

They sit quietly for a moment.

"The road crosses the south boundary about forty minutes from here," Lou says. "The far side is a bit boring, but the road loops back into the park. It's the shortest way home."

"You know this place well, don't you?"

"I've been here for a long time."

There are no markers at the boundary, just the sudden appearance of human habitation. Dwellings cluster along the dirt road, and occasionally people on errands walk barefoot across the scorching ground. Lou waves to women who stride along with baskets of firewood balanced on their head, while Steve slows to minimize the vehicle's wake of choking dust.

A sudden sickness hits Lou hard in the gut as they cross back into Masaranga's open savannah. Ahead, dots soar high in the sky, then descend in a spiral. Lou points and calculates the vultures are on their way toward a small waterhole frequented by shyer animals. Even while they watch, the spiral thickens. *What's died this time?*

"Want to check it out?" Steve gestures skyward, and Lou nods.

"This track will probably get us most of the way," she says.

Though she knows the rutted road, it takes many more turns than she remembers to draw close. At the dried water source, they turn off and track cross-country past where three gorged vultures rest on a bare branch. Steve picks his way through the bush, the risk from predators making it impossible to continue on foot.

Black-trunked trees and spiky bushes make their progress agonizingly slow. Thorns squeal against the Land Rover's doors. On their final circuit, vultures glide low overhead. Lou wonders if the vehicle will get stuck, or if they'll run out of daylight and get lost in the dark. But at last they push through a thicket and find the distended carcass on the edge of a clearing.

Lou expected the worse, but she's still shocked to see the male rhino, his body full of bullet wounds, his belly disemboweled by scavengers. His size and location suggest an older rhinoceros, one of the last in the park, whose name was Shida, the Swahili word for trouble. He was a bold rhino and would spin confidently to face vehicles that approached too close. But far more terrible trouble has found him than he ever gave anyone else.

A gouge remains where his horn was sawn off, his defense against predators but no match for bullets. Like dark tears, streaks of congealed blood cross his face. Poor Shida, his life lost to greed and ignorance, a savage sacrifice to satisfy impotent strangers too caught up in their inadequacies to appreciate or care about the real cost of their purchase.

A pair of silver-backed jackals slinks off as Steve pulls up. Several bald-headed vultures tug at fleshy wounds. Their stringy necks extend as they swallow chunks of Shida. Others, already gorged, fly heavily away from the disturbance. Overweight, they flap forcefully toward the lower branches of dead trees.

Lou follows Steve out of the vehicle.

"These bastards need severe punishment!" he growls, visibly shocked, and Lou realizes he's never seen poaching carnage before. Still fresh in her memory are the last month's dead elephants, their heads hacked by machetes.

"It's almost impossible to catch them, never mind get justice," she answers, aware of his hand on her arm. Numb and spun-out, she calculates when Shida was killed and what sort of head start the poachers have. From here, it's a short getaway to the park boundary.

"Sometimes, I think it won't end until all the wildlife is gone," she says, her voice tired, as Steve circuits the mound of dead flesh, checking bullet holes. "The poachers will be long gone. It takes a while for so many vultures to find a carcass."

They search for tire tracks, the escape route easy to spot, but already overlaid with jackal prints. It's late, and more scavengers will soon find this food. Jackals are nervous and not a problem to humans as they warily defer to other predators. But the hyenas are different and will even challenge lions at a kill if hungry.

"We better get home and let Peter know," she says.

Dinner is hard to swallow, though it smells good. To improve their low spirits, Grace killed a chicken and used vegetables from the garden to make stew.

"Take more!" Grace chides her, and Lou complies with another spoonful.

Her father is late for dinner.

"Dad, this is Steve!"

"Sorry, I wasn't here to meet you earlier," replies her father. "It's good to have some male company. Grace and Lou tend to boss me around a bit!"

Steve grins at Lou's incredulous expression. Nothing could be farther from the truth.

They discuss entry points into the park and the poachers' inexplicable efficiency.

Her father describes the entire situation for Steve's sake, including how elephants and rhinos are so always under threat that they've become too stressed to breed. Before long, the men are in a drawn-out discussion.

But Lou can't get the slaughter of Shida out of her mind. Now just a carcass, he was a gorgeous creature in his prime. Tonight, hungry scavengers will gnaw on his bones and reduce him to nothing. All the talk adds to her sense of desolation. Shida is the final straw. They've covered this territory all too often, and it's hard to imagine more discussion might unearth answers.

How to turn the tide against such catastrophe? The apparent enthusiasm of the new rangers has failed to help, and the staff is demoralized. Shida died close to park boundaries, and the poachers had a head start. Lou doubts the police will do much to find them. His horn is ridiculously valuable, considering it consists of keratin just as fingernails do. The fact that rhino horn is peddled for its supposed aphrodisiac quality is ludicrous. This theory extended would indicate that nail-biting also cures impotence! But ignorant men want a quick fix. As Lou listens to the discussion, the rangers' inefficiency bothers her.

"How many rhinos do you have left?" Steve directs this at her father but catches her eye at the same time. Perhaps he's noticed her mind is elsewhere.

"Twenty-two as far as we know. Twenty-one now." Her father chucks his napkin on the table. "Only black rhino now. We lost our last white rhino two years ago."

One of Lou's fellow researchers, Stan, worked on a project where a small breeding herd of white rhinos had a full-time guard. This expensive venture had relocated rhinos that were isolated due to poaching. One morning she got a call.

"All my rhinos are dead," Stan said and promptly started to cry. Too choked up to continue, he called her back later.

They never found out whether the guard was murdered or given a cut of the deal to vanish. Stan was too dispirited to remain there and returned to university to study vet science and upgrade his skills. Cynically, Lou wondered whether a military school might be more useful.

"I couldn't bear seeing my rhino friends dead and butchered," Stan told her. "They were family!"

At the time, the efforts of his team to bring the remaining animals together seemed to add up to nothing. Stan's defeat alarmed Lou as well as the deaths of the rhinos. But now, she feels just as beaten.

"Soulless humans and corruption are scourges on the planet!" Her father's voice contains a mixture of anger and disgust. It's a relief for Lou to hear the old fire back.

"Corruption is ingrained here. Not much happens until the right palms are greased," replies Steve.

"Favors are too easily bought. It makes the greedy and ignorant unstoppable!" her father replies, on a tirade now.

They all know business as usual often implies corruption. Even driving licenses are bought in this manner.

One way or another, nature pays when people care only for themselves. Rare rhino blood carelessly spilled on the dirt is just another aspect of human mistreatment of the planet. Too many self-centered humans consider the natural world merely as a source to plunder.

To slow her father's rant down, Lou brings out crackers and chunks of cheese.

"Have another Tusker." Steve offers Lou the bottle, but she refuses. Another one and she'd rest her head on the table and pass out. She'd like to go to bed, but she wants to hear Steve's angle.

At the moment, their problems are exacerbated by water scarcity that concentrates the wildlife closer to where poachers can find their prey. Hides are always strategically placed to observe animals at water sources. Lou often uses them at dusk, a favored time for elusive creatures to slink silently down to the water.

Once, a leopard came so close to the hide where Lou hid that, as she lowered her dappled face to drink, Lou saw her emerald eyes reflected from the still surface. For a split second, the cat's face touched her mirror image before the ripples broke the spell. The cautious leopard never dropped her guard. Lou held her breath, determined to keep the moment safe.

"What's your opinion, Lou?" Steve's voice brings her back to the present. The men are looking at her. She smiles, the leopard still in her thoughts.

"Sorry! What did I miss?"

Her father raises exasperated eyebrows. "Nothing that's fixable tonight," he says. "I think we all need some sleep." His chair scrapes back as he bids them goodnight.

Lou leads Steve to the guest room across the courtyard. Her feet are bare on the stone floor as she pads along, acutely aware of him a few steps behind. An owl calls from a high perch outside, but otherwise the night is eerily quiet.

She opens the guestroom door and flicks the light switch to reveal wooden furniture and batiks of tall Masai warriors.

"You won't need your mosquito net," she says. "That's one benefit of no rain!"

"Hey, thanks!" Steve touches her shoulder lightly. It's hard to raise her eyes to meet his. She feels unhappy and awkward and steps away into the corridor, but his hand moves from her shoulder to her face, his touch electric against her cheek. The thrill runs along her neck. Incredibly lightly, his fingers encircle her, lifting her face to his. He kisses her, and she moves into him, kissing him back, seeing the desire in his eyes. Their bodies come together naturally, rediscovering each other. For moments, she sinks into the sensation, wanting more.

Then Lou pulls back and he lets her go. As they separate, a shock wave passes through her, though it's she who's retreated.

"Better get some sleep." Her words are said before she articulated them. There's no chance to guess his thoughts because he's already turned away.

"Goodnight then." The door clicks quietly behind him, and she's lost her chance to say any more.

Lou returns past the courtyard to her room and stands for a moment, staring blindly at the wall. Why does she feel so alone? Especially when much of it is of her own doing, her own fear!

In the morning, Steve leaves for a visa appointment in Nairobi.

"You have to go so soon?" She tries to keep her tone light to hide her disappointment. *He's only just got here!*

"I told you. Hence my haircut! It's just slipped your mind."

Lou can't find the courage to tell him how she feels and it seems the wrong moment anyhow. Now she's angry at herself. She wonders what he sees in her. Is that appointment real, or is he just mad at her?

To distract herself, she feeds Zebu, the horses, and the chickens. What made her pull back from Steve last night? She regrets it. Her distraction with Masaranga made her forget his interview. What are his thoughts right now Gnawing anxiety underlies her questions. Everything seems to be broken. If only someone could tell her how to handle it all.

The doves are still cooing when she returns from her errands. Life continues as usual, no matter where the mind is or how chaotically the thoughts run. Eventually, the doves soothe her like nothing else, their calls more effective than any pragmatic attempt to rationalize.

Another grounding force is Zebu, who shakes off dust and bounds toward Lou from the shadows, her morning bone destroyed. Expectant doggy eyes indicate that it's time for a walk. Her tail speeds up when Lou clicks her tongue, and her jaw opens in a smile, the ivory reflecting sunlight. Though named after the drought-hardy cattle, Zebu has hyaena jaws. She's a top watchdog with a placid temperament.

Lou ducks away to avoid a kiss and grimaces.

"Yuck Zu, don't breathe all over me!"

Lou wraps her arms tightly around Zebu's soft neck for a few seconds. If only she'd had the courage to hold onto Steve this tightly. Lou wishes he'd not left.

She's discouraged him with her lack of communication, and it will be near impossible to contact him in Nairobi. Her chance has gone to tell him she misses him. But now she's failed to get it right, it's time to shake off this headspace and get on with her work.

Zebu follows her into the kitchen, a dog no-go zone, but Grace is not here to shoo her out. A fresh fruit scent hangs in the air. The click of toenails follows Lou. She slices pawpaw wedges with Grace's dangerously sharp knife.

"You won't like it, Zu!"

Zebu waits patiently until Lou offers her a piece. A cautious sniff, and hope turns to suspicion. An expression of dog disgust as Zebu pulls back from the offering. For the first time today, Lou laughs. Zebu drops clumsily onto the floor with a huge sigh, keeping a sharp eye out. Perhaps another bone is imminent.

Outside, the bougainvillea is again laden with purple flowers, startlingly beautiful against dark green leaves and the clear sky. Lou is aware of the morning air in her lungs for the first time today.

Zebu watches her with mournful eyes, and she sighs sadly until Lou opens the fridge to release the enticing scent of her reward for being a good dog. Then her tail thumps, and she jumps up with an expectant yawn.

"Take it gently! Mind your manners," says Lou. She laughs as Zebu slinks off like a wild dog with its kill.

Thirty-Eight

Her shins scraped from the hike, Lou stops to catch her breath and wait for Peter. Ahead of her is a small clearing dotted by massive termite mounds with more scrub beyond. Though they're lost and tired, this scenario is preferable to yesterday, when Masaranga supplied another lunch for visiting officials, whom they're unlikely to ever see again. Their visit seemed particularly hollow, and their lack of promises regarding change demoralized Lou more than ever.

"Thank the Lord that is done!" Grace said under her breath as the convoy pulled out. Relieved by the sight of the departing vehicles, Lou grinned at Grace and rolled her eyes. These intrusions might be a necessary pre-requisite to keeping government on side, but they stretch Masaranga's scant resources.

So today Lou beat a hasty escape with Peter at her side. She was keen to do some field work, but nothing has gone to plan. Their task was an overdue survey of a little-visited part of Masaranga's wilderness. They accessed it by an overgrown track that looped in from the north. Lou's original plan had been to bring Steve here.

The walk from the end of the track proved longer than Lou anticipated, an obstacle course of boulders and thorny trees. Initially, a day seemed time enough for this survey, and they'd even planned to visit a waterhole afterward. But the landscape misled them. They followed a seemingly sensible trail that led them off along a riverbed. Surrounded by thick scrub, it took a while to realize their mistake. After that, Lou and Peter hiked past scattered rock formations for some time before they got their bearings. Now almost out of daylight, they've finally reached the main outcrop. Ahead is a bush-bash around its massive base to reach the Land Rover somewhere behind it.

Lou uses the clearing to approach the rock face and then follows its edge, occasionally scrambling up cracks between boulders to search for shortcuts over the high ridge. Behind her, Peter whistles to attract her attention, and she hears branches being pushed aside. Perhaps he's scouted out a way back.

But when Peter catches up, he's obviously frustrated and cusses as a thorny shrub tears at his shirt.

"No luck?" she asks. Wordless, he shakes his head.

Lou begins to hurry again. They must find the Land Rover before dusk when predators start to prowl.

As the heat wanes, birdsong starts up in the nearby thickets, an unnecessary reminder of the time. Automatically, Lou notes the species contributing to the chorus.

"You spent too much time writing!" Peter's tone is critical rather than teasing. He's being a pain. She only took thirty seconds to scribble the names down. Though recently, this endless fact-gathering seems of little value. A little direct action would make her more useful.

"You're right," Lou replies. "I just don't know how else to do things."

Again, Peter fails to reply. Lou knows that shifting weather patterns and ongoing human-related damage mean many facts will have changed by the time her thesis is complete. *Does Peter also think these records represent wasted time?*

Nature can be hard to pin down and write up, and the miracle of rain still seems far off. In the past, wildlife readjusted when droughts broke; now, with dwindling wildlife populations, it's a harder recovery process. Though water shortage is a built-in variable, the unrelenting onslaught from poachers is a whole different problem. Often, Lou agrees with Peter's bemusement about white man's compulsion to order, label, and list every last thing. But people want to control things. When a certain politician commented that nature cannot be left to run wild, Lou thought it a pity his own changeable political opinions were not more subject to control. It's become impossible for nature to self-regulate and maintain as it did before human overpopulation destroyed the balance. Lou catches her thoughts mid-stream, suddenly aware of her distraction from the situation at hand.

This gorgeous boulder-strewn landscape reminds Lou of the desert country in the north of Kenya, near Marallel, where she saw women wearing impractically tall necklaces to stretch their necks. Those exploratory trips away from home seem long past. She wonders if Steve has ever been up that way. Probably not.

At least she's not alone today, although Peter seems unusually withdrawn. Lou has been focused on navigation and only now does she notice how little he has to say. Lou makes a mental note to work out what's bugging him, once they're closer to safety. The hike has become easier with the evening breeze cooling her skin. She trudges along the base of the outcrop, still on the lookout for a shortcut. The boulders space out, leaving shady gaps. In the shelter beneath an overhang, they slow again to search for a route to scramble further up the steep slopes. Lou gasps at the new beauty of the cracked domes that line the skyline, now burnished by the flaming ochres and yellows of sunset, their edges sharp against the vast indigo sky.

Undistracted by their splendor, Peter points out a landmark. "I see a way through past the big rock like an elephant's back."

Lou grins at his description, and she quickly spots the relevant outline.

"OK. Let's try that way."

From growing up with Peter, she's aware his navigational skills far surpass hers.

The climb is a challenge, and Lou's boots dislodge loose shards splintered from the boulders. But the expanding view more than compensates for the harsh terrain. Close to the summit, they slip through deep patches of shade behind the high rocky domes. A surreal and beautiful landscape opens up.

Lou stops to catch her breath and waits for Peter to catch up.

"All OK with you, Peter?"

"Yes, Memsahib."

"Peter, please don't memsahib me!"

"Bwana David says it is respectful."

"But we are friends!" Lou sighs openly at her brother's influence.

She continues to climb with determination.

"You are very quiet today," she says over her shoulder.

"Yes, Memsahib."

If he doesn't want to talk, then he won't; she must accept this right now. It's more important they move along quickly. But Lou misses how things were. None of them seem happy these days.

"Shall I tell you what it looks like under the ocean near Mombasa?"

"OK, Memsahib." His tone suggests he acquiesces because he feels duty bound.

Lou talks, between gasps, often out of breath as they climb again. Her boots dislodge fragments that roll noisily down rock faces behind them. They reach a high stony plateau and start across the undulating surface. Peter punctuates her descriptions of coral walls, anemones, and the workings of scuba equipment with "Yes, Memsahib." Doggedly, she ignores his obstinance.

They skirt past isolated boulders perched like giant glowing marbles on an uneven rocky table. Up here, there's no vegetation to slow them. Spectacular savannah views stretch all around, the features picked out by golden light. There's no time to stop and soak up the scenery or to search for wildlife through her binoculars. Steve will love this place, though they'd be lucky to catch such stunning light again. In daylight, this height will make wild animals easier to spot. Lou imagines that any person able to see this view should want to protect its inherent beauty. She knows it was a mistake to follow that dry riverbed when they could have climbed straight up here.

Lou moves fast, the sound of Peter's boots behind her. She turns a sharp corner, her movement ahead of her mind. Abruptly, in mid-step, she leaps sideways and twists mid-air to face the danger. Only now, as Lou lands away from a pile of rocks, does the image of the snake's writhing coils coalesce in her mind.

From a safer distance, Lou remains motionless, her heart pounding. Two meters away, the cobra's head rears above the ground, alert and ready to strike if threatened further. But her heart slows now she's no longer a menace to it, or it to her. She takes another cautious step back out of strike range and releases a sigh.

A few steps behind, Peter waits, crouched, rifle raised and ready, the snake still invisible to him. Lou beckons him sideways, her finger on her lips. He lowers the gun and creeps away from the rock wall. Lou wants the cobra to stay so he can see it. But it drops down and its coils shift and unravel as it retreats hastily into a pile of rocks.

"It's gone. Sorry. A cobra!"

They move cautiously towards where the snake vanished.

"It sat up like this!" Lou holds her arm and fists up to indicate the snake poised to protect itself.

"I thought it was a leopard! You were fast, my sister!" Peter cheerfully slings his gun back over his shoulder.

Lou is thankful her reflexes worked well to save her.

"Let's keep going! I don't want to meet another one in the dark." She starts off ahead.

"Hey, Lou. My turn to walk in front!" he replies, the memsahib forgotten.

They grin at each other for a moment, and he takes the lead with his first decent smile all day.

Thirty-Nine

Steve has to agree with Lou. Even in this drought, Masaranga is impressive, and he understands why she's attached to the place. Its wild beauty shows up the ugliness of cities with their hard, concrete edges and congested streets. But, more and more, he understands how Lou became so independent. There's not a whole lot of help for anyone out here. It's great to be with Lou again. Steve thought he'd be tougher, but he realizes he's already hooked enough not to want to leave the country without her.

The boulder-strewn outcrop up ahead has a harsh, spectacular beauty that's entirely different from the lush green of the coast. Lou is spot-on to guess he'd enjoy a hike up those gorgeous rocky domes. It's just what he feels like after the long drive out past straggly dust-blown settlements. He wants to climb to the highest, most isolated spot, take Lou in his arms and make love to her up there under the vast African sky.

Apparently, Lou almost stepped on a cobra somewhere near the top. Sometimes, it's as if she has no idea of personal safety at all. Obviously, she's completely her own person, but Steve wants her to be his as well. He likes that she's so focused and passionate about the elephants, but, at the same time, somehow manages to have a left-field sense of humor. You never know what she's going to say next. To some extent, her unpredictability blows his mind, though Steve's opinion is that Lou really needs someone to protect her from the dangers she exposes herself to.

It was an exhilarating drive out, and Steve has now got the hang of the old Land Rover. But, as he pulls around into a rocky gorge, his enthusiasm plunges horribly. It's instantly replaced by disgust at the sickening sight ahead. A rhino has died in a snare, and the signs of its struggle are all around.

Its body lies contorted among broken branches, the wire sunk into the flesh, a gouge where the horn was hacked off. A couple of satisfied vultures linger by the maggoty carcass.

Seriously! Steve can hardly believe this replay of his previous visit! Does nothing ever change around here? By now, he's able to read Lou well enough to see her heart plummet. He can even pick the moment when it hits rock bottom with a thud. Lou looks utterly destroyed as she assimilates another loss.

Steve was looking forward to the day out and the climb up onto the high plateau. All that is now ruined. A dead rhino was not part of the plan.

"I don't know how you do it!" He's angered both by the mess in front of him and what it signifies.

"Do what?" she replies.

"Deal with this; deal with having to see this all the time." Steve fails to keep the frustration out of his voice. He knows it's unfair to Lou, as she obviously feels terrible enough already. The unintended judgment in his voice doesn't prevent her from speaking her mind.

"The facts don't go away just because people can't stand to look at them!"

Steve does not take her anger personally. It's aimed more at those queasier folks who prefer not to deal with what really goes on, who, given the choice, ignore the underbelly, their attention straining toward easier, more enjoyable distractions.

It must hurt Lou more than he can imagine, this rhino that she knew now a butchered carcass.

"You must be used to such sights?" Steve asks. He keeps his voice emotionless and says it almost like a statement. He's surprised when she suddenly starts to open up.

"My eleventh birthday was the first time," she replies. "Dad took me on a day safari, and we stumbled on a dead elephant with its face hacked up."

"A bit of a shock at that age. Something so big. I mean, we all see dead birds." Steve tries to cast his mind back to how he'd have reacted at that age.

"Yes. It was confronting. I was so sad. Only hours before, it was a healthy elephant, not harming anyone." Lou seems equally sad now, as if ready to talk about traumatic events from her past.

"Surely your father would have hated to expose you like that. He'd have shielded you from a dead person." Steve has no idea why he's gone down this track, but for some reason it seems relevant.

"My mother once had to!" Lou replies. "A taxi rolled off the highway and spun over and over down an embankment, right in front of us."

"Your mother?" Steve is surprised at her mention. Any discussion of Lou's mother is usually taboo. But she seems on a roll now, caught up in contemplation.

"Yes. My mother didn't stop to check the upturned vehicle. She just drove to the nearest police station instead. She couldn't do much to help the trapped people with us kids standing by. But, all the same, she felt guilty."

"How do you know?"

"I don't. I wondered about those people. The outcome would probably have been the same, even had we stopped."

"Perhaps you felt guilty, not her."

"Maybe. I don't know. But for ages, the memory made me sick. The driver was so reckless with those lives. He overtook at high speed, and then his wheels caught a rough edge up ahead. I remember exactly how that car spun crazily out of control."

"No wonder you get so depressed!" Steve says, caught between her words and the scene in front of them. "It's appalling. I'd personally like to kill whoever's responsible for this!"

He wonders who he'd have to kill. Who precisely is responsible in the chain of people behind this action? The rhino horn trade is fueled by misguided men who pay highly to stave off impotence and keep their egos intact. Fed fallacies, they're too ignorant to know the horn won't help. Next are the greedy dealers who live well, but never did an honest day's work in their lives. Behind them, corrupt officials are bribed to turn a blind eye. A few probably also help deal the goods for a more significant cut. The poachers on the ground take the immediate risk when they brutally kill the precious wildlife. They're tainted by real blood, their hands actually dirty. But everyone in the chain is equally to blame in Steve's opinion. He's been here long enough to get the picture.

The young men who've directly killed may one day consider their actions and suffer misgivings when they are older and hopefully wiser. But the hidden others are detached from the crime and don't seem to care how they acquire wealth. Steve doubts they bother themselves with consequences except to themselves. Too many really don't care. Lou is naïve to think people change much. Enough of them are born and brought up too self-centered to care, and they remain that way unless some drastic life event takes them close enough to the edge to self-examine.

"You OK?" Steve puts his arm protectively around her and pulls her against him. But nothing can protect her from being sad.

"I'm sorry about today, but I'm grateful you're here with me," Lou says.

Steve finds it incredible she's apologizing considering where she'd be at!

"I asked if you're OK?" He tries again.

She nods and lies that she's OK.

"I'd no idea this would rile me so badly!" he says after a moment. "You poor thing. I can't believe you're so used to seeing this sort of stuff."

"I think this young female is about eighteen months old. She's so mauled, it's hard to tell." Lou seems keen to change the subject now.

"A loss of new breeding stock then," Steve replies to distract her.

"Yes. If I'm right, this rhino was a calf alongside her mother not that long ago."

Lou sounds forlorn. It's suddenly patently evident to Steve how little time is left to save the rhinos. Will they cease to exist outside zoos unless someone stops this? Faced with the evidence, the imminence of such a tragedy seems even more real to him.

His arm still protectively around Lou, Steve steers her towards the Land Rover. For once, she allows him to take control as if glad of the support. He's relieved to distance himself from the sight of the mangled creature.

They're quiet on the drive home. Steve's thoughts churn along, as he turns options over in his mind.

"There are other ways of dealing with all this," he says suddenly.

"I've never known how to cope with that." With a flick of her head, Lou indicates what they've left behind.

"No, but there must be better ways to get on top of what's going down here."

"Do you have any ideas?"

"Don't worry about it now," he says, aware that this is not the time to discuss ideas for how Lou might fight from a safer distance, instead of being stuck here at ground zero.

She frowns, an expression he rarely sees from her.

"I'll talk to you about it another time," he says.

Steve leaves it at that. It's hard enough dealing with his own headspace. Right now, he doesn't need to either explain himself or convince her of alternative ways to use her intelligence. The ride home takes ages, the old Land Rover rattling in sympathy with his thoughts. Lou seems lost in reflection. Obviously, that stuff about her mother still bugs her.

Later, as the shower water runs off Steve, and he watches it swirl away down the plughole tinted orange from the dust, his thoughts swing back to a solution for Lou's dilemma. She only seems to understand half of her troubles. It's admirable that her life's purpose is so focused externally, but Steve thinks she needs to look after herself as well. It's not something she pays enough attention to. You can't save something else without looking out for yourself a bit.

Lou's father took the news of the rhino badly. His shoulders visibly sagged, and his eyes registered exhaustion and frustration as if he's already experienced too much and been defeated. It's a shock for Steve to suddenly get just how dire things have got. Everyone is used to hearing about the slow attrition of the wildlife by poachers, but it must be quite something else to live in the thick of it, day after day. Despite the discovery, Steve is glad he came. It's given him a whole new insight into what Lou's life is like, isolated out here with almost no help. No wonder she gets so emotional! He can see how it will slowly destroy her to keep losing animals that she knows well enough to have named, one after another. A newfound determination to help solidifies inside him.

Forty

A week after the second dead rhino, Lou is awake before dawn, her mind in overdrive, Steve's absence an empty gap beside her. Already back in Mombasa, he's probably waking to the sun rising over the ocean. Life is not always bad, and that's a welcome thought after the depressing depths of her sleep.

A cough from her father's room reminds her how gaunt he looks recently.

"It's just a cold, Lou," he always says when she suggests a medical check-up.

As Lou struggles not to rehash recent events, the usual mix of emotions floods back: sadness and surges of anger, all that she's tried to control that helps neither her nor anything else. Only action will suffice. Steve is right, they need another approach. She must brighten up and disentangle herself from her anguish. Only then will this terrible inertia lose its grip on her.

Lou titles her page— "The effect of another loss: Two breeding-aged rhinos taken out of the equation"—and then describes everything relevant to their deaths. Just before sunrise, she hears Grace set the stove in her room. Each day before dawn, tendrils of woodsmoke rise from the chimney as the first light touches the landscape. Grace hangs on to many of the old ways despite a changing world. The smoldering wood with its familiar smell has won again over the gas cooker. The age-old routine of going to sleep early and being awake for sunrise seems to connect people with the land that sustains them. Lou's thoughts settle as her hand moves across the page. Paragraphs form as the smoke drifts toward her from Grace's fire.

Then, on the edge of her vision, Lou notices a movement by her father's office. *Why didn't I hear him get up?* Typically, she'd hear his boots along the corridor. *Why is he over there so early?* And his light's not on.

But someone's there! A figure stops by the bougainvillea and then slips around the back of the building. The person reappears, half hidden in shadows and impossible to identify. Definitely not her father.

With a gasp, Lou pulls back from her desk and runs silently down the corridor, slowing briefly outside her father's room. His low snore is almost drowned out by the pounding of her heart. She sprints to the living room for a closer view of the office and waits there, out of sight.

But the intruder has vanished. Nothing now seems different as Lou searches the shadows along the hedge by the office. She leans back against the curtains and watches. Her heart slows as the minutes pass. Now she doubts herself. Even at the best of times, her imagination tends to run wild.

Then her breath catches as the office door swings slightly open. From inside, a man's head and shoulders emerge cautiously. He stops momentarily to check the coast is clear, then steps out and quietly pushes the door closed behind him.

Lou runs the few steps to the glass doors. Against the predawn silence, they squeal and bang as she throws them open and sprints across the veranda and down the steps. Her legs carry her full pelt toward the office. The man slips behind the building, and she follows. But seconds later, when she rounds the corner, he's disappeared, presumably through the hedge. In a frenzy, she searches for a way through. His escape route must be close by. One section seems more open. Spikes jab at Lou as she forces her way through the bougainvillea. He can't be far ahead.

"Lou. Lou!" Her father's voice booms from behind, perceptible above her racing heart and a rip as her bed shirt tears. His boots are heavy on the ground as he covers the distance between them and takes advantage of her momentary indecision to grab her arm.

"What are you doing?" Her father gasps out each word as he attempts to catch his breath.

Underneath his alarm, Lou hears his exhaustion.

"A man broke into your office. He escaped through here."

Exasperated, she indicates the sparser section of hedge. How did he get through so quickly? It's as if he's just vanished.

"You sure?"

Not waiting for her answer, her father lets her go. He covers the few yards to the office and tries the door.

"We need to follow him!" Lou shouts. She searches along the edge of the hedge, dismayed that the chase has already been lost.

"It's locked," he says.

"It's easy to lock on the way out!" she calls, irritated by his disbelief and the way he's stopped her in her tracks. Discouraged, she follows the hedge as far as the staff quarters. It's already too late, and her father obviously has no intention of searching further.

When her father returns with the keys, the sun has broken the horizon. High in the sky, a lone cloud glows yellow out toward the eastern waterhole.

"Let's see if anything's missing!' he says and opens the office. Quickly, Lou flicks all the lights on. They stare at the maps on his desk, the filing cabinets to one side, the painting of the rhino in a backdrop of long yellow grass.

"Doesn't look as if anything's disturbed." His tone is skeptical. As her father checks the safe, Lou takes a good look around. It's all as she left it.

"You sure you saw someone?" he asks her again.

"I know I did."

"You and I are the only people with the key."

"I know, Dad!"

"He was probably snooping around the compound, after something to steal."

"I swear he came out of here before I chased him."

"There's not much to steal here. I doubt anyone's been inside. And please don't ever follow an intruder again, real or imagined."

Lou manages to restrain her frustration to a heavy sigh. It's quite evident that any protest on her part would be futile.

Forty-One

Hesitantly, Lou dials and waits. After the phone picks up, there's a moment of silence as if Colin Graham waits for callers to reveal themselves first.

Finally, an older man's voice, shaky with age, but brisk and confident. "Yes, hello?"

"Mr. Graham?" asks Lou tentatively.

"It is he."

"Oh, good. My name is Lou Hopkins, I'm—"

"Lou, my dear. Will's daughter, I presume?"

He knows her! Pulled up mid-sentence, Lou searches unsuccessfully for a memory of him. She recalls only an old photo of her parents and him in a Nairobi restaurant.

"What can I do for you, Lou?"

A deep breath, and the tension leaves her chest. Colin seems friendly rather than indifferent, as she'd worried. Her father described him as abrupt and arrogant and used this as an excuse against asking his advice. Uncomfortable for doing just this behind his back, Lou suffers a tinge of guilt. But her father's attitude toward her has been dismissive, and his disbelief about the intruder has left her frustrated.

"Sorry to bother you out of the blue like this," Lou says. "I'm studying the elephants and—"

"Of course, my dear."

His upfront reception disarms her. Does he mean of course he knows, or of course, that's what Will's daughter would be doing?

"You need advice?" he asks in a precise British accent.

"Um, well." Exposed and pre-empted, Lou replies, "To be honest, yes perhaps I do."

"We can meet at the Tusker Bar for a drink at sundown. Does that suit you?"

"Yes, of course!" It sounds like an apt place to meet, and Lou conceals her ignorance about where to find it. She's astonished the meeting was arranged so quickly.

To seek Colin's advice does feel like a betrayal. Her father's lack of trust in many people makes him old school and he prefers to gather his own facts. Lou is unsure how well her father knows Colin, and already she hears him telling her to pull her horns in. *Pretty pathetic horns.* Lou feels hesitant and out of her depth, but it's time to toughen up. Too often, her imagination creates mountains where only molehills exist. As her stomach cramps, Lou wonders what exactly she expects to gain from this.

Her father also thinks that Colin no longer holds any influence, and that, although Colin worked in the same offices as Fred Lonnegan, it doesn't mean he can help. Perhaps Masaranga's issues will mean nothing to Colin, and their need for help guarantees neither interest nor sympathy. *Will he be apathetic, but listen politely because he knows her father?* Lou shelves these thoughts—they only drain her confidence. Right now, he's a useful contact.

The Tusker Bar is at the edge of town, and it's busy but reasonably quiet inside. As Lou enters through the swinging door, Colin waves her over as if confident of who she is. Wiry and tall, he watches with piercing blue eyes as she dodges stools and glass-topped tables to reach him. He indicates for her to sit next to him on a high window seat, which has a lovely view out across bushland.

"Hello, you look just like your mother!" he says, which immediately puts her on a back foot.

Lou smiles to conceal her disquiet. She's quite sure she doesn't resemble her mother at all!

"Hello, Mr. Graham!"

"Please call me Colin. No need to be formal!"

"I'm glad you recognized me." Now Lou also vaguely remembers him from years ago.

"Easy enough, my dear. Your father showed me a photo not so long ago."

"Really?" She's incredulous her father carries a photo of her with him.

"Yes. Graduation day at Nairobi University, I think."

"Oh! I'm post-grad now. But I mostly work from Masaranga."

"Pretty isolated out there?"

The comment is almost as familiar as the back of her hand, and Lou grins. "Yep, that's the upside!"

He snorts with laughter.

"You might look like your mother, but you're your father's daughter."

Happy to have an audience, Colin launches into a description of his semi-retirement. As he talks, Lou wonders how secure his government connections are. It's easy enough to just listen and answer an occasional question about her work. Lou politely avoids the topic of her mother, which he skirts around a couple more times. Without reasons for the desertion, she feels reluctant to discuss her mother with a virtual stranger. A bizarre fear of exposure discourages her from the topic, and opening up about it to Steve just recently was unintentional.

Instead, Lou tries to engage Colin around the supposed help they've so far had from the ministry. Colin should know Fred and Sam well enough to throw light on such matters. But whenever she tries, Colin seems guarded and dismissive as if he prefers not to divulge the inside workings of his old office. Reluctantly, Lou is forced to ask the question outright. Colin's opinion matters to her as she's lost any confidence in Fred.

"Do you know Fred Lonnegan well?"

"Fred's not such a bad chap, and he's a shrewder man than most," answers Colin.

"Shrewd in what way?" she asks.

"Well, he's obviously an ultimate diplomat to keep his position when the rest of us were moved along years ago."

Colin seems reluctant to say more.

Is Colin envious of Fred's ability to retain his position? Or is there something else?

"The rangers they sent us have not helped," says Lou. "The poaching has worsened."

"If that's the case, I'd find an excuse to send the rangers back then!" Colin replies.

His answer surprises Lou. *Surely, any help is better than nothing.*

"If you want to fix things, don't rely on the system!" Colin says suddenly.

Lou feels she's touched on a nerve. Almost anything she says now will seem utterly out of line.

"Focus your energy elsewhere," continues Colin. "Dealing with government is an obstacle course. At best, you'll only delay the inevitable."

Lost for words, Lou considers his fatalistic angle, while he returns to the bar for another drink.

Lou wonders where she might find motivated allies. She guesses Colin knows more than he's prepared to let on. He's definitely hesitant on the topic of Fred Lonnegan. This meeting mightn't have told her much, but it's definitely not been a waste of time.

Forty-Two

The impala is instinctively cautious, but life has also taught her survival skills. Like a human, she learns from her mistakes. The golden sunset reflects off her horns as she steps through the sparse undergrowth. Delicate hooves disturb wisps of red dust. Scattered close by, other herd members approach the waterhole together. A social creature, the impala feels safe in the presence of her own kind. Dusk can be dangerous and a time to be on high alert. It's when the big cats like to hunt and when she lost her last calf. Fear is necessary to ensure her survival, and right now she tests the breeze for any unusual scent. Trouble is rarely far away.

Though this impala has no name, other herd members know who she is. Her timid nature allows her to take only a few short steps at a time, broken by periods of stillness as she gauges the situation, all senses tuned. An awareness absorbed from her own kind alerts her of the danger associated with strange acrid scents. Like a person, she stores information pertinent to her survival.

Curved scars cross her flank, where a lion's claw raked through her skin but failed to hook deep enough to throw her off balance. The well-camouflaged cat hid behind a stand of yellowed grass, but the impala spotted her movement and darted away, just in time to evade death. Though the lion turned and lunged again, it had lost the advantage of surprise. Had she been a second slower, the cat would have pinned her down with its teeth latched onto her jugular. The impala wouldn't be here now, alive and always on watch. The memory of narrow escape now embedded within her cells gives her an edge in the daily game of survival.

Has a dangerous scent unsettled the herd? Does tension jump from one antelope to another? Creatures accustomed to being prey must always be on guard. In measured bursts, the antelope closes the gap between herself and the waterhole. The relentless heat and desiccated grass make this drink essential, and the moist muddy smell pulls her closer.

The impala's world is more fraught with real danger than the one humans inhabit. She notices any change in the bush's familiar patterns. Men with their weapons are now top of the food chain. For creatures lower down, water sources are places where life is as simply taken as given. When ephemeral sources dry, impala are forced towards the remaining waterholes, and these become sites of risk. Armed with guns and lethal snares, predatory men kill prey such as the impala for bushmeat.

On the cracked edges of the mudflat, the impala sees an exposed stretch ahead of her, where the only water for miles glimmers. She senses safe, natural movement out there, and other grazing animals are silhouetted ahead of her. Striped zebras seem to float above the ground, their legs lost in the heat haze.

A measure of tension leaves the impala as she steps from the cover of the bush into the open area where other wildlife is more visible. The ground becomes less dusty so close to the water and has lifted into cracked red ridges that she high-steps over. Now she's like a person released from fear. Occasionally, one of her hooves breaks through the mud crust, and she sinks slightly through to the sticky underside. Momentarily, this feels dangerous. But other herd members are even further out, and this encourages her. Less graceful now, her neck stretched for balance, she crosses the irregular surface to reach the water's edge. If she were human, she'd be elated at having ventured into new territory.

Forty-Three

Words, maps, charts, more words. Lou drains her glass of lukewarm water. The ice had melted while she edited a section on elephant behavior during droughts. Pen and paper take so much of her time, and for what? This approach is too slow, far too cautious. Another day at her desk, the room dark compared to the intense sunlight outside.

"You finished yet?" asks Grace.

"Nearly. Do you need help?"

"No. I'm just checking." Hands on her hips, Grace waits by the door.

Lou looks up from a map and smiles at her. "Another ten minutes, then I'll feed Zebu and the horses."

Vibes of disapproval emanate from Grace, who does have a point. A niggling voice tells Lou that these pages achieve nothing compared to tangible action, and that it's time to venture into new territory. Certain judgments directed at her also seem accurate. She should lighten up and enjoy life more.

As Grace clumps off down the corridor, Lou sketches a last elephant trail onto a map. The smell of posho wafts through the open window, along with the sound of relaxed chatter from the rangers' quarters, a sign the day is at an end.

Lou wishes she didn't miss Steve this badly. About now, he'd steer his boat into shore, with waves breaking alongside. The divers would help unload scuba gear, watched by curious onlookers. Lou wants to feel the ocean breeze against her skin and smell saltwater, to sink her feet into the sand and watch the foam swirling in the shallows. A pang of longing washes through her, and she wants to wrap her arms tightly around Steve and soak up his strength and reassurance. Briefly, the image anchors her.

But Lou also worries if Steve has other distractions, and this grounds her another way. It prevents her from finding an excuse to leave for the coast right away, as she considers the possibility of being less welcome than anticipated. He seemed so distracted last time they spoke.

"I must lock the shop up now. They were burgled down the street last night," he'd said.

Lou had never heard him sound so stressed.

"Did they lose much?" she asked.

But he was in too much of a hurry to tell her more.

It's time to stop anguishing and get busy.

"Where are you, Zebu?"

The dull thud of a tail precedes a dust cloud. Zebu rouses and shakes herself, and her ears flap noisily. Slow and hot from a long snooze, she stretches into a down-dog posture.

Lou vaults through the open window and lands beside her.

"Honestly, Zu. Look at the dust on you!"

Her arms wrap tightly around Zebu's contented body.

"Coming for a walk?"

Zebu grunts her approval and yawns noisily.

Five years ago, Zebu was a starving, hairless stray on the outskirts of the nearby village, and Lou had never seen so many ticks on a puppy. Gray masses of parasites hung off her, and she scratched continuously at the infected scabs that covered the exposed skin.

"Who owns this dog?" Lou asked a few of the villagers.

"That's just a shenzi dog. The boys throw stones to chase her away," replied a teenage girl. No one objected as Lou approached the hungry half-grown pup. To ascertain her age, Lou checked her teeth and found the gums anemic from blood loss.

Dejected but hopeful, the nameless stray watched Lou warily, with a half-trust born more from the anticipation of a food scrap than a reason to put faith in people. Lou thought it a sad predicament to be reliant on scraps scrounged from humans. Although generations of faithful dogs have stood guard in exchange for mere morsels of food and warmth, strays get little help here.

The puppy wolfed down a sandwich as Lou pulled a few turgid ticks off her, and then jumped back to safety. She wagged her tail sheepishly when Lou coaxed her back.

"Come on, little girl. Be good. You'll feel better!" Lou gently reassured her. But the puppy whined pathetically and objected as Lou removed more ticks.

Mindful the ticks might infest headquarters, Lou still took the puppy home and poured horse dip over her. The pungent chemical made Lou think of nature's gentler pest control, the ox-pecker birds that clean ticks off the hardy Zebu cattle. This puppy would grow big and gentle like a Zebu calf and the name stuck.

Zebu shadows Lou past the house. The living room light is on, her father inside with an evening drink at his side. Now Lou gets up earlier, she often finds a whiskey bottle by his leather armchair. Because Grace clears up, Lou has never noticed this before, and she's alarmed that her father regularly stays up late drinking.

"Do you throw away many bottles like this?" she asked Grace.

But Grace just shrugs her shoulders. In this, she won't be disloyal to the Bwana.

Lou's resolution to wake early and achieve more has backfired. Her father is supposed to be dependable and stable. This discovery makes Lou nervous and doesn't improve her outlook. This morning, she felt as cold as the empty bottle in her hand. Though, at breakfast, he was no different from any other day. What else has she missed due to her lack of attention?

She has to visit her thesis supervisor, who's an intellectual rather than an activist. Now, as Lou passes the weaverbird nest, she also considers combining this with another visit to the ministry. Her conversation with Colin has made her warier of Fred Lonnegan. He definitely left something unsaid and thought they should send the extra rangers packing. If this made Fred seem suspect, would time alone in his office help solve why? Perhaps even after everyone has gone home. Security wouldn't be tight, and the night watchmen are unlikely to be super vigilant. Lou decides not to dwell on the consequences of being caught, nor will she put anyone else at risk by asking for help.

Late to bed, Lou listens to the bush outside, but tonight the sounds fail to settle her. Another restless night passes with her thoughts in overdrive as she jumps erratically between scenarios. Common sense tells her to get up. She should read or write, do anything but this, but she doesn't.

Fitful dreams take over. Shadows of elephants and rhinos now gone. A leopard hunts through the darkness of her mind. Lou drifts between these creatures and an awareness of her bedroom as the night sounds enter through her window. Dawn takes forever.

Before daybreak, a commotion from the rangers' quarters. Lou wakes abruptly and runs down the corridor to get a better view outside. But their voices quickly die to a murmur. Whatever disturbed them is gone, and the night quietens. Perhaps a snake was seeking shelter, or a hyena came through in search of food scraps.

Eventually, she falls into a dreamless sleep, until the birdsong wakes her. Exhausted, she forces herself out of bed, her heart heavy. Today she will organize a visit to Nairobi and then throw herself into useful physical activity. Then, with any luck, sleep will come easier tonight.

Forty-Four

As her taxi catches up to a battered truck, Lou sucks in a lungful of moderately clean air, between gray belches from the rusty exhaust pipe ahead. The fumes enter through the open windows and engulf her, the acrid tang burning her nose. Inside the overcrowded taxi, she again holds her breath.

Evidently impatient to reach Nairobi, the driver's haste puts them at risk, and Lou's nerves are on edge. A stream of potentially car-mangling trucks bears toward them from the opposite direction. The road is dangerously overdue for repairs, but nothing deters the driver from tackling it head-on. He speeds scarily along the potholed tarmac as if riding a horse, leaning into each bend. To make matters worse, many other drivers along this highway seem equally hell-bent on their destination.

Firmly wedged in the backseat, Lou catches the eye of the plump woman next to her.

"Sorry. I'm not used to driving so close to the car ahead," she says to her companion, who seems amused at her breath-holding.

"Yes. These taxi-drivers are always so impatient!" The woman's smile is stoic as she fans away a gust of diesel fumes.

Lou endeavors to calm down, but the driver suddenly pulls out in a reckless attempt to overtake. Immediately, he encounters a large truck ahead coming from the opposite direction, brakes hard and pulls back behind the fumes. Lou releases her breath and inhales cautiously. The fumes sting as they slide into her lungs.

Asleep on her other side is a middle-aged man, oblivious to discomfort. Almost upright, he begins to snore, and his head lolls her way, whiskey on his breath. She's too frightened after the near-miss to care, and the alcohol fumes are less awful than the exhaust fumes.

Squashed between the others on the back seat and away from the open windows, Lou banishes the thought that If they crash, she'll be cushioned here between the others, but unable to get out. Long-haul share-taxis are just something to be endured as the locals do regularly. However, crushed here inside its sweaty interior, Lou vows, should she survive this time, never to repeat this. She left the Land Rover behind as Steve will have his car with him, and Nairobi traffic is a nightmare she wants to avoid.

Once more, the driver decides to overtake, and Lou's heart plummets. As he pulls out, there's a blind bend ahead, and the engine roars as the driver rises to the challenge. Lou hangs on to the seat and braces—as if doing so would change anything. A car appears around the bend, and there's no time for retreat. His foot hard on the accelerator, the driver attempts to complete his maneuver. They're going to be out of space. At the last moment, the oncoming car veers wildly onto the gravelly verge. Lou glimpses shock on the face of the displaced driver, who gesticulates angrily as their taxi speeds on past the spot where the crash would have occurred. Their driver appears oblivious, intent only on his progress over the cracked tarmac.

Eventually, Lou surrenders to potential disaster and relies on her reflexes to minimize the choking fumes. The traffic thins, and she distracts herself with the scenery, though the landscape is monotonous with shacks and scrubby plants. She contemplates possible alternatives for her visit to the minister's office.

Close to Nairobi, the taxi screeches to a halt on the verge. The snoring man, now propped against Lou, fails to wake. Passengers leave, and half-spaces open up for others to take. The friendly lady on her other side gets out.

"Goodbye. Enjoy Nairobi!" She gives Lou a last smile, then waves and walks away along a track between rows of maize.

At a collection of dilapidated buildings by a crossroad, the driver shakes the whiskey-breathed gentleman awake. There's a period of relative comfort after he leaves, with room to stretch cramped limbs. But, all too soon, they stop by another scraggly village, and a young woman with a baby squashes in to fill his space.

"How old is she?" asks Lou.

"Two weeks!" The mother whispers her answer and is too shy to talk much. She settles her baby in as comfortably as possible.

Mother and child lean up against the window, and, in no time, both are asleep. The contented baby reminds Lou how early in life tolerance to adversity starts. No wonder people grow up resilient here. The apparently happy, smiling faces of so many suggest her own perspective is all wrong. Lou is painfully aware of how many people would regard her life as enviably comfortable.

🐘 🐘 🐘

The morning traffic roars past as Lou steps onto the curb by the imposing building. She's ahead of time for her appointment, but still hurries along the main corridor toward Fred Lonnegan's office. The pretty secretary, busy behind a typewriter, lets her fingers come briefly to rest as she again sizes Lou up.

"Mr. Mkomo will stand in for Mr. Lonnegan today," she says and gestures for Lou to sit and wait.

Lou hopes this Mr. Mkomo might hear her out. Perhaps, he'll be able to influence Fred. Frazzled from yesterday's taxi-ride and today's rush to make it here promptly, Lou is glad of the time to reassess her pitch. But an hour later, Lou begins to lose confidence and decides to have a scout around instead. For an excuse, she asks for directions to the bathroom.

It's a while after Lou returns from reconnoitering the building before the thick-set Mr. Mkomo arrives with a briefcase tucked under his arm.

"I'll be with you soon!" he says and pulls his office door half-closed behind him. Already Lou knows she's going to be late for her rendezvous with Steve, and there's no way of letting him know.

Between lengthy phone calls, Mkomo emerges to flirt briefly with the secretary. He sends her out for coffee and then disappears into his den again.

Eventually he asks Lou in.

"Fred is sorry to miss you. A last-minute problem demands his attention," he says.

Lou has a bad feeling neither statement is true.

"Thank you for seeing me," she says politely, keen to use the opportunity. "I'm here to discuss the escalation of poaching in Masaranga."

"Ah, yes. You are here to fix our poaching problems. Quite a challenge!" Mr. Mkomo replies in an unsympathetic tone as if he considers such an idea ludicrous. Then, disconcertingly, he smiles.

"I'd like to at least find a reasonable solution for Masaranga," she answers.

"And what did you have in mind?"

"Real penalties, not just a slap on the wrist, for poachers and anyone connected with the ivory or rhino horn trade. That would be a start. Perhaps an advertising campaign that makes people think twice. At the moment, all they get is a rap over the knuckles."

"A rap over the knuckles. Such a British way of putting things. You are English, I presume?"

"Originally yes, though I grew up in Kenya." Lou nods. She is not immune to his suggestion that her opinion has no place here. Mr. Mkomo might officially be a public servant, but she guesses he's more interested in serving his own needs than the public's. Lou makes an effort to suspend her own judgment. Fred's absence is probably not his fault, so he deserves the benefit of the doubt. Most likely, he knows nothing, so she explains the situation from scratch, careful to summarize to keep it brief.

But Mkomo makes no effort to feign interest. Halfway through, he gives a huge yawn and says, "Fred has already been generous enough to supply two extra rangers. At some cost to the department!"

"For some reason, they've not been effective. That's why I'm suggesting a revised approach."

"I see," he says. "A terrible situation, of course. One of many we are faced with daily in these offices."

The detached smile on his face suddenly leaves her cold as a knot clenches around her heart. Lou finally grasps his complete lack of interest.

For a while, she persists, but he's evasive, and her attempts fail to engage. It all seems so entirely futile. She tries to decipher if he's hostile or would rather just be elsewhere?

"I saw an elephant once," he suddenly comments. "It was quite scary!" He giggles—a surprisingly high-pitched sound.

"They're not naturally aggressive, but they will defend their families," she answers. Her words dry up as she again notices Mr. Mkomo glance out through the window and dab at the sweat on his face. His absence of interest would embarrass her if she weren't so crushed.

Her consolation is that at least she took a good look around. Her trip won't be wasted, and the building's layout is simple enough. Although Mr. Mkomo wasted both their time, her visit wasn't a pointless waste of effort.

"How will you spend your time in Nairobi?" he suddenly asks. "I know a good restaurant. Perhaps, I could show you around town a bit later."

Is he asking her out? What a surprise, after his indifference to what matters to her! Lou conceals her rush of anger with a smile. The hand clenched around her heart warns Lou to stop. Say nothing she'll later regret. Being angry never gained her anything. Best to keep a lid on how badly his complete lack of interest elsewhere grates.

"I'm afraid I've already too much to do this trip. Perhaps another time." With considerable effort, Lou smiles again. If only he knew how she now plans to spend some of her time here.

He's hardly pretended to hear her out. As his own department sent the new rangers, their progress, or lack of it, should be of interest. However, she must keep her reservations under wraps, otherwise his department will become even more stubborn.

"Can you put my suggestions to Fred on his return?" she says. "Perhaps he might take a phone call from me."

"Most certainly. I look forward to our discussions when you have time to see Nairobi!"

Mr. Mkomo leans back with a self-satisfied air. Does he seriously think a night on the town is an option? The interview leaves Lou utterly disillusioned. How can he offer to show her around when he appears to despise what she represents? Is her opinion worthless, no matter how long she's lived here, how much her heart is here?

"Perhaps I could show you Masaranga?" Lou asks him this partly to hear his excuse to decline.

"Anything is possible! We can discuss it on your next visit to Nairobi."

What made her imagine he might want to help? At the very least, lost wildlife means lost tourism for his country. It would upset him if his own welfare were directly involved. He'd care if he thought poaching directly affected him, and he's too ignorant to appreciate that, in the end, it does.

A wave of negativity threatens to swamp Lou. Is she jumping to conclusions? His non-participation without a date seems unfair and she'd be a fool to tread such a dangerous path. This failure only fuels her frustration. Lou stands up, ready to leave, daunted by the other approach she must take. Clearly, this interview is over.

"Thanks for talking to me, Mr. Mkomo."

"My pleasure. Here is my card if you need me for anything. I've written my private number on the back." His chair scrapes against the ground. Again, he smiles widely. Lou shakes his proffered hand.

Resolutely, Lou ignores the secretary's curious glance as she exits under the sign "Assistant Minister for Environment" with its artistically etched animals, the real ones supposedly protected by this department. She's incensed that artwork and old photos may one day be all that remains of those animals.

Although short on time, Lou doesn't immediately leave the building. She walks the corridors briskly, as if she has a legitimate reason to remain. The offices are surprisingly quiet now, so her surreptitious return past the janitor's room goes unnoticed. It's on the first floor, and it looks as if it's been a while since the dirty blind across the small window was opened. Careful to leave the cobwebs undisturbed, Lou slips her fingers behind the blind. She releases the latch and eases the window slightly open. This definitely can't be discussed with Steve when she meets him later.

Outside in the heat, people jostle along the pavements. Cars honk their horns, and the smell of curry and frying samosas hangs in the haze. Lou's cynicism smolders. It's time to get real about how things are. If she shook off her pessimism, life might be more comfortable, but the reality is all-pervasive. One step at a time, one problem at a time, is the best tactic. If she dwells on the scale of the problem, there's a risk of surrendering to the belief that her pathetic efforts are pointless. It's essential to avoid an apathetic mindset. The knowledge that men like Mkomo regard her merely as an amusing annoyance riles her.

Suddenly hungry, Lou buys a samosa from a stall. Bony fingers expertly toss the triangle from the sizzling pan into a brown paper bag that darkens instantly with the excess grease. The Indian youth grins at her, briefly catching her eye as he exchanges the samosa for a shilling. He's skinny as if he doesn't consume many of his own samosas. Lou eats quickly as she walks, hardly tasting it, aware only of the heat from the spice. From habit, she saves the pastry edges and tosses them toward a skeletal street dog. The starving creature gulps the scraps down and looks up for more. Saddened by the sudden hope in its eyes, Lou crosses the street and rushes on through the crowd.

Hopefully, Steve won't assume her lateness means she couldn't make it for a drink. What a long wait to then have Mr. Mkomo so casually brush her off. The memory of how he made time between calls to flirt with the secretary suddenly aggravates her further. She hates the congested city and how people become when they are packed too closely together. There's barely time to get across town and meet Steve.

The crowded streets seem suddenly stifling, the air pungent with sweat, spices, and grease. To avoid the throngs, Lou drops off the pavement and walks on the edge of the road. Cars pass within touching distance. Traffic, pedestrians, and food stalls force her to dodge up and down along the sidewalks. She flags a taxi.

At last, a cab not already loaded with people. As the driver pulls over, bystanders jump out of the way. Lou gets in quickly and slams the door to escape an overly persistent street vendor, who now holds an elephant carving against her window.

"You like?" he mouths at her through the glass. She made the mistake of a second glance, which the vendor instantly spotted. His persistence is determined, but Lou shakes her head and averts her eyes to reaffirm her lack of interest. The cab pulls away, and the vendor drops back, still waving wildly in a last attempt to convince her. The stuffy taxi is more suffocating than the street, but it's a relief to escape the crowds. Lou winds her window down to let some air in and sighs with relief as they begin to thread through the streets. The driver watches her through his rearview mirror, but his attention doesn't much unsettle her. Being a relative outsider has inured her to the intense observation of curious people. Whether she likes it or not, she's considered a stranger.

Lou shifts across the seat to remove herself from his view. She reruns the meeting a sentence at a time to confirm what transpired. Her perfect memory of dialogue often infuriates her brother when his version of shared conversations differs. She re-evaluates Mkomo's stance while it's fresh in her mind, wanting to dissect through the details before she asks for Steve's take on events.

Did Mkomo conceal anything from her? Definitely not his indifference! Why pretend to listen when he could have just sent her away? Why act as if possibly sympathetic when he was obviously bored by her requests? It's true his department has much to deal with on limited funds, and that solutions are hard to find. His suggestion he could take a personal interest that would involve other considerations returns to mind. Lou is not sure she wants to know exactly how the process might be eased. Those slippery words made her uneasy. She feels queasy now and wishes she'd given the oily samosa a miss.

Steve has chosen an open-fronted bar to meet. It's high above the street, away from the fumes of the slow-moving traffic. Flowers and greenery grow in pots on the veranda. Lou hugs him quickly, sure he'd be embarrassed if she threw her arms around him and hung on tightly.

"At last!" he says with a grin.

"Sorry, my appointment was unreasonably late," she replies. "I'm so glad to see you!"

They order Tusker beer which arrives refreshingly cold. Steve looks great. His hair is longer again, and she'd almost forgotten how gorgeous his eyes are. He's managed to blend in quickly here, a newcomer, able to adapt like a chameleon. So many people stay a few months, and then decide it's too hot and uncivilized and that they miss home. Steve seems different. Lou hopes he won't develop such a mindset anytime soon.

She drinks thirstily, the beer intoxicating. The cold liquid radiates warmth out from her stomach. Already, she feels better.

"You drank that one fast!" Steve exclaims and shakes his head in mock disbelief. He grins at her to soften the blow, and Lou laughs to cover her embarrassment.

"Sorry, that wasn't lady-like!"

"It was obviously medicinal. You looked pretty stressed when you got here!" he says, and laughs cheerfully.

She's so glad to see him and grateful that his Nairobi trip coincides with hers. It's been three months, and apparently he's forgotten his annoyance from last time. The chemistry is the same as always. Steve kisses her as they wait for the second beer, and nothing's changed. Her relief and the beer combine to make her light-headed and slightly giggly. The anger and tension of the morning dissolve.

"I won't drink too much. I want to tell you about my meeting today," Lou says, ready to unload.

"You can tell me later. Actually, in the morning. A day makes no difference to anything. Come to that, a month wouldn't either. Nothing happens in a hurry around here!" Steve kisses her quickly on the lips again.

He's right, but his opinion is important. At least her mind has settled, the thoughts no longer coming thick and fast. Sometimes, Lou wishes she could just ignore it all. Time with Steve is what she needs. Just the fact he's around anchors her. It gives her something to hold on to when there's no one to talk to back home.

On the crowded street below, a squabble breaks out, and angry shouts erupt over the constant honking of horns. Lou leans over the balcony and sees a man attempting to upend a flimsy food stall. The vendor holds on to the structure and pacifies the angry customer. Money passes hands, and the outburst is over. The aggressor shouts abuse as he stalks off. A path opens up in front of him as curious onlookers give way. Nobody wants trouble here. Few can afford the bribes necessary to prove their point of view. Steve's arm is around her now that the commotion has died. He kisses her again. Suddenly self-conscious, she's glad the bar is almost empty.

"I wish you could come to Masaranga for a few days," she says.

"Better if you come down the coast. Your father might not be delighted to see me too often."

"He wouldn't mind. He likes you!"

"Him liking me and me stealing his daughter away are entirely different things. You're his only company since your brother left."

Her brother again, always there on the edge of her existence.

"Dad has more contact with David than I do," she says.

"Why don't you spend more time away?" asks Steve.

"Dad thinks it's dangerous for a single female."

"So, you're expected to remain there forever."

The sudden anger in his voice surprises her, and Lou pulls back to examine his face.

"Nobody makes me stay. It's my choice to study there!" For the first time, she wonders where else Steve judges she should be.

"Come on," Steve replies. "Let's get out of here. Enjoy the bit of time we've got. No serious talk till tomorrow when we're both completely sober." He leads her downstairs and out onto the street.

The hotel is on the outskirts of Nairobi, encircled by bright bougainvillea hedges similar to home, except that the lawn here is watered and mown. The guard recognizes Steve.

"Bwana Steve, good afternoon, a man is waiting to see you."

Steve frowns slightly as if he's forgotten about a visitor. Lou hopes this won't take long.

"Go to the room and pour us a drink. I'll be there soon." Steve gives her a key and indicates one of the circular thatched bungalows set among the gardens. He disappears into the shaded reception area. Lou wants to follow, but, instead, walks between sprinklers and lets herself into the cool interior of his bungalow. It's delightful inside. She runs her hands along the polished wood surfaces and stone benchtops. Inside the fridge is a bottle of gin, and the citrus tang of lime and tonic wafts out with the cold air.

Forty-Five

Lou wakes with Steve asleep next to her, liking the experience, though they only have a day together. After he leaves for Mombasa tomorrow, she intends to break into the ministry offices.

Her defenses were down last night, and she almost confessed her plan. It would be a relief to confide in someone, and his often-helpful advice might have been handy. The whole scheme seemed less crazy than it does now. But fortunately, she wasn't quite tipsy enough to imagine he'd consider her plan sensible. Now, as he stirs in his sleep, she's glad she kept quiet. It would be painful to spend all day listening to him talk her out of it. Instead, they plan to visit an orphanage where baby elephants are reared until old enough for release.

As Steve stirs and rolls toward her, his arm reaches across her belly, his hand stroking her hip, pulling her toward him. Lou goes without resistance. She kisses him back, and giggles as his hands run along the back of her thigh, all thought abandoned. With no words spoken, she slips back against him and surrenders blissfully to his insistent body. Only half awake, they make love slowly, not urgently like yesterday after so many months apart. For a while, her thoughts and worries are suspended.

"Come to Lamu with me," Steve says quietly in her ear afterward, his arms still holding her tight against him.

"You never told me you were going there," she mumbles, snuggled against him, her eyes closed. Lamu has a special meaning for her, so it's strange he's asked her to go there out of the blue.

"I hadn't planned to," he replies, "but it's supposed to be an interesting place. I've no bookings next week. Come with me to Mombasa. We can follow the coast north from there."

"Mm." Wide awake now, Lou considers there's no real reason not to go, and she's wanted to see Lamu for years. She searches for an excuse not to go straightaway, needing to buy another day alone in Nairobi.

"Great, so you're coming?" he asks, cornering her into an immediate decision. It's an easy one. Lou nods and grins. The details will work themselves out. She will find an excuse to stay here a couple of days longer. Realistically, an extra night should be all she needs to follow through on her plan.

"We have some elephant calves to visit!" she counters to distract him.

Not far from where Nairobi gives way to open country, the orphanage seems small and inadequate compared to the size of the problem. Here, a few dedicated people make a difference for elephants against tremendous odds. Lou pays double the requested donation and reads about how the initial funds for the center came from a family passionate about Africa's wildlife, who wanted to create a safe haven for elephants orphaned by poaching.

From the front counter, Lou glimpses the daytime enclosure, where the rambunctious orphans play. Their cheerful caretakers hose and scrub them down and are almost as muddy as their charges. Sensibly clad in overalls, they dodge around shallow puddles and gamboling calves. The chief handler, Asha, is gorgeous, her dark hair braided back to accentuate high cheekbones. She smiles and hands Lou a bottle of milk replacer. "Try and feed that one there," she says. "His name is Marco Polo."

Lou runs her hands over Marco Polo's bristly gray skin. It's not hard to entice him to drink, and she laughs happily as he guzzles the thick liquid down and then wraps his trunk around the bottle. Holding it upside down, he chases the last drop, and then transfers his attention to Lou's pockets.

"The name suits him! He's definitely an explorer!" she says to Asha and then giggles, ticklish while he inquisitively investigates with his trunk.

The other orphans frolic around the enclosure in search of rations and trouble.

"This lot are a handful!" says Steve as he jumps out of the way of an exuberant calf that swats him gently with its trunk on the way past.

The keepers coax and bribe the calves toward an area shaded from the sun. Although babies, they're too heavy to be pushed or pulled along and have to be cajoled. Marco Polo doubles back from his handler and heads toward Lou, keen to search her bag one last time. She laughs and holds the strap tightly, resisting the force of his trunk.

"He's sure he's missed something!" she says and tries unsuccessfully to push the inquisitive baby away.

Out of breath from chasing calves around the enclosure, Asha tugs at his trunk and manages to unwrap it from around Lou's bag and onto her own arm.

"Our explorer is very cheeky and hard to discipline!" She dangles a banana in front of Marco Polo and bribes him back toward the shelter. Lou walks alongside to encourage the calf to behave.

The shelter smells of fresh dung, but there are no beetles here to roll and store balls of manure underground as part of nature's plans. A young man passes them, carrying a shovel.

"What about her?" Lou asks and points to a small calf, who seems shyer than the others and has stood slightly apart, to one side of the group. On becoming the center of attention, the calf backs a few steps away and watches them warily, without the confidence of the other youngsters.

"Our Mtoto is new here. Rangers found her beside her mother's body a week ago," replies Asha. "They said she screamed when she was taken away from her dead mother. Poor Mtoto is still very nervous."

"Elephants have long memories. I wonder how long it will stay with her," Lou says.

"Oh, I'm sure she'll never forget such a traumatic event. But she will be a strong one, our Mtoto. We must find her a safe place to live, where she can have her own babies!" Asha sounds confident and matter-of-fact as she hands the banana to Marco Polo. "Come and make friends with your new sister," she says to him. "Mtoto is part of your family now!"

"You should visit Masaranga," says Lou. "I'll take you to see our elephants, and you can stay with us."

"Yes, I would like that. When Mtoto is older!" With a shy smile, Asha pushes a braid back off her beautiful face.

When finally they drag themselves away from the orphans, Lou scrawls her contact details on the back of an orphanage pamphlet and hands it to Asha.

"Don't forget to come. Please make the time. If you need, I can organize a lift from Nairobi for you."

Lou worries that Asha won't come, that she's an introvert, like Mtoto, and might be too shy. But she seems a kindred spirit. One day they might work together or at least swap stories and information.

"Come on. We should get a move along. What plot are you hatching now?" Steve grabs her hand and leads her out. "I'm starving. How about you?"

Lou nods to agree. The shadows around them have lengthened, and it's ages since brunch.

Forty-Six

er senses are on high alert as Lou creeps along the dark corridor. Terrified, she vows this diversion better pay off! The fact she's broken the law and entered these offices illegally disturbs Lou even more than she bargained for. The consequences of being caught seem worse than any dangers she faces in the wilderness. This morning when Steve left, Lou almost confessed her intention. To be honest, she'd have welcomed an excuse to ditch this stupid idea and go directly to the coast with him.

In theory, all the public servants should have gone home long ago, and Lou saw no signs of life from the outside. Now she's within its dark interior, the place seems like a meerkat warren. As the hairs stand up on the back of her neck, Lou reflects that wild predators frighten her less.

Step by careful step, Lou silently navigates the dark corridor, her body taut and ready for anything. A scuffle to her right, and Lou waits frozen, ready to bolt back through the darkness. But it was a mouse or cockroach exploring a waste paper bin. Lou rationalizes to regain a modicum of control, and wills her heart to slow. It's unlikely a straggler remains hidden in some back office. After another deep breath, she takes a few more steps, her hand against the wall to guide her. Apart from the muffled sound of a siren outside, the building is deathly quiet.

The fifth door on the left. This should belong to the Assistant Minister for Environment, a hypocritical title considering it doesn't relate to Fred's interests or knowledge. Lou wonders whether these positions are not just cushy jobs for pushy people. She runs her fingers across the door and up to the carved sign above it. A quick flash of her torch confirms she's in the right place.

With any luck, the nightwatchmen are still distracted outside. Lou waited for too long at a food stand across the road, and had almost given up when a lady selling drinks stopped to chat with the men. Lou took her chance to slip around the back of the office block and searched there, using planted shrubs as cover, for the window to the janitor's room. It wasn't exactly where she'd thought and took a while to find. Her hands shook uncontrollably as she tugged it open with gloved fingertips. Thank god it came quietly. As it hadn't been opened for a while, she'd envisioned it would come with a noisy squeal. Another five minutes and she'd have abandoned this madness.

After the dark corridor, the room seems bright, lit by moonlight. Instinctively, Lou crouches the moment she enters. Stacked on the desk are uneven piles of folders, and the top drawer of the nearest filing cabinet is open. *Where to start? Masaranga should warrant a file of its own, with documents about the extra rangers. Or would they come under general employment?* Lou begins to scan through everything she can lay her hands on. Somewhere here, there might be relevant information on why their poaching problems have worsened since this department became involved.

Her torch on low beam, Lou squats below the desk and begins to pull down folder after folder. Though the window is above street level, her light must remain invisible when the nightwatchman circuits the building. It would be safer if the blinds were down as they were when she sat opposite Mkomo. Stupidly, she'd envisaged them closed. Perhaps the cleaner opened the room up. It smells of disinfectant, and the cabinets glint in the moonlight as she rifles through their drawers. Lou considers closing the blinds but fears the change might be noticed from outside. She shudders involuntarily as images arise of how they'd deal with her if she was caught.

But the mounds of paperwork reveal nothing relevant. Lou continues to skim documents, drawing from years of practice at scouring academic papers. The time that's been spent recording valueless information confounds her. *Does anyone ever read or use this stuff?*

Footsteps crunch on the gravel path outside, and Lou flips the torch off. Motionless, like a frightened impala, she listens. The watchman's torch beam searches methodically as he pauses for a moment, and then passes. Lou's heart races horribly as she crouches, her chest ready to explode. But the footsteps recede, and she resumes her search with trembling hands.

An hour later, with another pass by the watchman, Lou is severely discouraged. Much of the material pertains to events headlined in newspapers years ago that should have been archived. Little seems relevant to the present and, so far, nothing relevant to Masaranga. At first impression, the office appears busy, its owner overwhelmed by the responsibilities of a demanding portfolio, but that perception now seems a far cry from reality.

Yet another hour and Lou is hunched on the floor, her eyes tired as she flicks through the last folder. Still nothing of interest, the risk of coming here unwarranted. About to call it a night, she hears a shifting, sliding sound from down the corridor. Lou's only escape route is the window, and her body recoils as she crawls toward it and listens intently. The sound subsides and then, when it repeats, she realizes it's from overhead. What's up on the next level? As the sliding grows insistent, her thoughts coalesce. This is the top floor with only rooftop overhead. *Thank god, it's probably not human. Maybe a python hunting for rats.*

Again, Lou forces herself to be rational and breathe slowly. To find nothing and get caught doesn't bear consideration. On her knees, she reaches the window and peers out into the moonlit courtyard. Just a gust of wind catches the high naked branches of a frangipani tree. As its silhouette shifts eerily against the stars, a chill runs along her spine. The nightwatchmen should have passed the window again by now. Lou imagines one stealthily stalking down the corridor, the other hidden in the shrubs below this window, ready to block her escape. With a sharp intake of breath, she moves away on all fours and crawls to the door. She eases it open and peers into the dark corridor.

The window frame rattles as the wind gusts, perhaps the first signs of an anticipated storm. The frangipani shakes a menacing hand against the moonlit sky. Lou's mind reels as she huddles on the floor by the door, her spine against the hard wall, and gathers her thoughts. Logic tells her she's alone. She must leave before panic completely takes hold. What a fool she's been. The watchmen are probably sharing a cigarette out the front, but, if not, she's put herself in a dangerous position for nothing.

Lou shifts again along the wall, ready to crawl back to the window to check outside again. A small bookshelf blocks her way. Her fingers run over the volumes. A flash of her light shows papers stashed under the bottom shelf. She sweeps her hand underneath and finds another folder.

Its contents relate to a visit to Malindi by the president's son, the material of no interest. Impatiently, Lou flicks through the pages. With every passing moment, she wants to get out of here more. Sandwiched right at the back of the file is a line-up photo, including the president's son at a glamorous outdoor function. Expensively dressed people smile and pose with drinks held high. Behind them, palms grow alongside a swimming pool with a waterfall. An unremarkable photo of affluent people, but Lou's attention catches when she recognizes Sam Watchiri, one arm around a tall, heavily muscled man, who seems out of place in the group. On the other side is Fred Lonnegan. The photo is worth keeping, and she slides it into her inside jacket pocket. Seconds later, she slips back into the dark corridor.

Minutes later, Lou pushes the window that she broke in through hard shut behind her. If the janitor is observant, he might notice the signs of disturbance, the lack of cobwebs around his neglected blind. Once on the sidewalk again, Lou strides along, as unhurried as she can manage. At the first corner, a watchman approaches from the opposite direction. Instinct tells her to turn and run, but Lou forces herself to continue toward him. No choice but to bluff it as she couldn't outrun a couple of fit security guards. As the gap closes, Lou keeps her pace constant and pretends to check her watch.

He slows as she approaches, his eyes on her face and then her jacket, the photo hidden in its folds. Lou tightens the garment around her chest, and counters by shivering, in a motion to indicate she's cold out here at night.

"Habari?" he asks, his voice soft. Does he want to know how she is, or is he just suspicious and slowing her down?

"Mizuri sana!" Lou assures him all is well and does not slow, as if she doesn't expect to be held up. He lets her pass, and she imagines his head turned to watch her as she continues, one step after another, without allowing herself to look back.

Forty-Seven

ou wakes from a dream of fighting to escape dark enclosed spaces. If only she'd seen sense and gone with Steve, they'd have almost reached Lamu by now. In one swift motion, Lou swings her legs over the edge of the bed and takes in her surroundings with a sigh of relief. Even without Steve, it's a treat to wake up in this peaceful bungalow. From outside comes the sound of someone sweeping the covered walkways, and through the windows are views of watered garden beds. Steve insisted on paying an extra night so Lou could stay here. Now alone in Nairobi, she desperately wants to confide in someone sensible, and Sara seems a logical choice.

But the moment Lou's taxi pulls up by the big jacaranda tree, her instincts warn her to keep quiet about her escapade. It would alleviate her qualms to confide in someone she trusts, but now, as Lou waits outside the security gates, she's unsure a confession will help anyone. What excuse will she now create to explain this surprise visit? The guard appears quickly, and his face relaxes into a broad grin the moment he sees her. She has little time to worry about excuses as he immediately throws the gates open. The gaps in his teeth make Lou wonder about his age and how long he's worked for Sara.

"Habari?" he asks, and his keys jangle as he locks the gate behind them.

"Mesuri sana," Lou answers and grins, happier already, as she inquires after his family and then Sara.

With a skinny arm, he points to where the garden slopes off and the view opens across the valley. Sara is halfway up from the lower garden beds, flanked by a sleek adult Doberman. A half-grown puppy gambols alongside, obviously a replacement for the dog lost to a snake. It's a sensible move considering the need for security.

The Dobermans desert their mistress and bound over to Lou. The puppy immediately puts her paws against Lou's leg and gazes up, eyes expectant.

"Hello, Sara. Sorry to surprise you at the last moment. I didn't think I'd have time this trip!"

The truth is, Lou hates to intrude, and Sara seems tired and drawn, not the beaming hostess of previous visits. Soil stains her shapeless shirt, and vegetation has caught on her sleeves. Sara tosses her spade onto the ground and hugs Lou.

"What a pleasant surprise!" she says and gestures for Lou to follow her back to the house. "Visitors are a rare event these days. Everyone seems to have sold up and left."

Her dejected voice concerns Lou. Sara is usually so confident.

"What about the girls? Don't they visit?" she asks tentatively.

"Oh, Carla's gone to Tanzania again. She's forever collecting material for her thesis."

"I know how that feels! And what about Lexi?" Lou asks, mostly in the hope of news of her brother. Sara's grimace, a mixture of exasperation and resignation, comes left field. "Is she OK?"

"Yes, she's better now. It's been bad for her. But I can't believe she's chosen to continue her affair with that awful man."

For a moment, Lou is lost for words. A sick sensation wells up from her guts. An image of Lexi hanging off David's willing arm is displaced by the memory of her crossing the Mombasa bar with someone else. It's suddenly necessary to find out.

Before Lou decides how to ask, Sara blurts out, "Why she has anything to do with him beats me, especially after his insistence on an abortion!"

Sara's distress is so evident that Lou is taken aback. This is the last thing she'd expected. Lexi's situation must have been foremost in Sara's thoughts for her to launch into this so quickly. Usually, she'd usher a visitor in, send off for tea, and ask about the relatives. On a couple of fronts, Lou is shocked. Despite the heat, a cold knot begins to tighten around her heart. Abortion!

Lexi pregnant while she's been with David. But why is she so surprised? Who's the father? Sara continues on, oblivious that all this is news to Lou.

Lou manages to hide her reaction only because Sara is on a roll, unaware of her ignorance. Sara obviously assumes Lou and Lexi are close enough to have shared this information. Now all Lou can do is repeatedly nod, partly to cover her disbelief as well as to agree with Sara's tirade. It's much too late to say she's not in Lexi's confidence.

"What a bastard!" continues Sara. "He flatters her with fancy presents and the high life, and then insists on an abortion!" She stops for a moment to think, then adds, "Though I do admit, it's probably for the best." Her voice becomes more reflective.

Lou loses track as Sara continues. She wonders if her brother knows. At least he doesn't appear to be the father. If David knew about this, he would surely stay away from trouble. Perhaps he's blissfully ignorant. But then again, Lou thinks, her mind doubling back, maybe he'd not be hurt as badly as she assumes.

Sara leads her to the living room, where Lou sits uncomfortably on the edge of a sofa. A zebra skin hangs on the wall behind her host, and its black and white stripes move in and out of focus as she listens. Lou remains sympathetic and manages to expresses disgust at the lover's behavior. Poor Sara has either forgotten or was unaware of Lexi's involvement with David. Otherwise, she surely wouldn't have confided in Lou like this.

The barrage of words, all of Sara's dismay, halts. In the silence, Lou searches for words.

"I'm so sorry," she says and means to stop there, but part of her must have it confirmed. "Remind me what department he works in."

Sara has started again on how she never imagined anything like this could happen. She pauses as the question sinks in.

"Oh, he's high level. Environment and Tourism. Sam travels on official tours, so he has plenty of excuses to spend nights away from home when it suits him," she answers.

The knot wrenches tighter as Lou remembers her suspicions it was Sam Watchiri, the smooth talker. When she met him at their Masaranga lunch party, he seemed so considerate, and at his follow-up visit he was just as charming. Had she not been so distracted by Steve, she might have paid more attention in Mombasa and not let her suspicions slide.

The fact that Sam is the father infuriates Lou for several reasons, not least of which is that David deserved to know, and she failed to tell him. Why didn't she just follow her hunch up? Was it because she felt unsure of David's reaction? Or perhaps she was just too distracted and self-absorbed to pay proper attention.

The black and white bars of the zebra skin come back into focus as Sara goes quiet. Lou drags herself from her private reverie.

"I'm awfully sorry about all of this," she says again. After all, it's the truth, and Sara is almost in tears. "Is she OK now?"

"As good as can be, all things considered," says Sara. "But I'm sorry to unload on you. You don't need to hear a mother's rant. How are you, Lou?" Sara bravely attempts a smile.

"Not bad," says Lou, using her standard reply. "We're not on top of the poaching. It's got worse than ever."

The conversation turns, and Lou no longer has to hide her reaction. Neither has she needed to invent an excuse for her visit.

"Have you been able to work on your thesis?" Sara asks.

"Yes. I want it over and done with now. I think I'm close—unless my supervisor insists on a lot of revision." Her words come quickly now, and Lou is relieved by the shift to a safer topic.

"I doubt you will have to change much," Sara replies. "I've been told you're remarkably focused."

Focused? The description doesn't seem to fit her. Lou knows how much she misses in regards to the people around her, and, recently, she's been pretty scattered. And her future is anyone's guess. How would anyone see her that way? Now, so close to the end of her research, it's difficult to imagine her way forward. If Sara knew about last night, she'd definitely drop the compliment.

"For a long time, my thesis has been the goal. Now it's almost completed, I can't see past it," Lou says.

"What do you want to see?" asks Sara.

But Lou has no answer. She's so close, and everything seems unclear. For sure, her thesis will be an achievement, a sort of milestone, but the ongoing loss of elephants torments her. How to help best afterward? To some extent, she's applied the brakes to keep the future at bay.

"I wish I could see an obvious way forward, but I can't make anything take shape!" she says.

"The future rarely shows itself. It just happens!" replies Sara. "Don't take it too seriously!"

But if her path were more apparent, Lou feels she'd be stronger. All she has are ideas, along with an unwelcome dose of reality, and her fear that the problems aren't fixable.

"I feel pretty useless at home these days," she says.

"Then it's time to give yourself a break and follow your instincts!" says Sara.

Lou hugs Sara, and her thoughts track off again. To follow her calling and protect the elephants, she must avoid distractions. If the situation at Masaranga settled, she'd be able to learn and become useful in other ways. Life at home has built-in difficulties, and she's proven ineffective so far. Even her misguided attempts at detective work have failed.

It suddenly occurs to Lou that if this business with Lexi changed David's opinion about Nairobi's attractions, he'd probably become more available to help out at Masaranga. Just this bit of hope opens up new possibilities. Lou hugs Sara again, tighter this time. A trickle of relief enters the constricted knot inside her chest and she tastes the salt of her tears. But she's also sad for Sara, and when she lets go and stands back, they both have tears running down their cheeks.

Forty-Eight

The island of Lamu at last, and Lou is keen to explore. Clearly Steve is nowhere near as enthusiastic.

"You're always so restless!" he complains.

Half asleep, he sprawls across the low bed in their cozy room with its rugs and wall hangings, the lights charmingly muted by Arabic lampshades.

"I'm thrilled to be here," she replies. "I'll just have a quick a look around to get my bearings."

"We've driven for hours on a dirt road, and then been cramped on a crowded dhow, and now you want to check out town as well?" An expression of disbelief crosses his tired face. Lou can see he's about to crash.

"Go to sleep for a bit," she says. "You're tired from all the driving."

"You need to be careful in places you don't know. Wait, and we'll go together later," he replies grumpily.

A look of irritation crosses his face as he pulls a pillow over his head. Lou takes a last glance at his fit, lean body, half under the sheet, and then clicks shut the door quietly behind her. When she returns after a quick scout around, he's fast asleep, so she lets herself out again.

When Steve suggested this trip up Kenya's coast, Lou agreed without hesitation. She even splurged out and flew down to Mombasa to make up for her extra time in Nairobi. Years ago, her mother bought her a unique chest that now sits in the corner of her room back home. Her mother's descriptions of Lamu's ancient trading port sowed seeds in her imagination. Now finally here, Lou wonders what took her so long. It's a revelation to her how much her first impressions differ from her mother's account and her own vision of how it would be.

In high spirits, Lou follows the tucked-away lane until it joins the crowded main street. It's incredibly busy. As she steps into the fray, throngs of people push and shove around her, all caught in the hustle and bustle of private thoughts and errands. There's no choice but to be carried along by the crowd, and, before long, Lou begins to lose track of time and landmarks needed to retrace her path. Finally, two women begrudgingly let her through, and she manages to ease her way onto a slightly quieter side street.

Grateful to escape from the congestion, Lou slows down and takes in the high balconies and walls that reach above the cobbled shadows toward the pale-blue sky. She hopes Steve is still asleep. If he wakes to find her gone, he'll probably be worried and annoyed. She should have left a note before she crept out alone. But an even narrower side street beckons, and Lou shelves her concerns to wander a little longer. Then she must return.

Lamu was once an essential port for Arab dhows that sailed along Kenya's coast. Lou senses the generations of people that have lived and engaged in myriads of trades inside these crowded alleys. She passed stands sagging under the weight of exotic foods. Precariously balanced volcanoes of orange and yellow spices spill over ledges, the bare earth below streaked with their hues. Rich aromas of spicy food fill the air. Multi-colored kikois hang along sidewalls and shop fronts.

A different artistry exists here from elsewhere. Lou lingers at stands to run her fingers over the different textures and patterns. But she already owns too much stuff and fends the vendors off with a smile and a quick negative headshake.

Too many previous acquisitions are hidden away at home, stored by Lou until space becomes available for their display. When treasures are cheap, she's tempted to own more than necessary. The excess items crowd her limited spaces, and little is left for clothes and essentials. One day this private collection will decorate her own place, though Lou can't imagine how or where that place will be. Life seems so indefinite. If they're forced to leave Masaranga, she may have to ask Sara if she can store some of her precious treasures there.

"Memsahib, you like? Just look, please!"

Lou hurries quickly past a determined man selling batiks. From ahead is the smell of spicy hot samosas mingled with the fresh, sweet scent of sugarcane juice. All around, street vendors call out, and children run wildly through the alleyways, laughing and screaming. The ancient town overflows with life, past and present, its air heavy with memories. The dwellings seem always to have been here. A woman sits in a doorway, her baby cradled sideways. She waves to catch Lou's attention and then extends an arm to show her a carved rhino.

"Please. You buy? Very special!"

Lou's carved chest came from the window display of an antiques shop. She understood it was a precious gift, which her mother probably couldn't afford. It was not her birthday and seemed to have come to her for no apparent reason. Though delighted, Lou was perplexed as she ran her fingers over the garden scenes.

"I may not always be around to look out for you," her mother said in a matter-of-fact tone. Childishly, Lou interpreted this to mean one day, in the far-off future, her mother would be old and die before she did. As the concept was not immediate, she didn't dwell on it. When her mother left a few months later, those words returned, suddenly unwelcome. The warning that accompanied the chest taught Lou how people close to you keep secrets.

Years ago, an artist carved Lou's chest here, and it found its way to her. Strangely, this thought brings tears to her eyes. It bugs Lou that the concept makes her sad, not happy. Why can't she be a bit less sensitive? Lou quickly wipes the tears and swats the memory away. She won't return to the hotel looking dejected. How would she explain that to Steve?

He was right in that their trip was uncomfortable. The wooden dhow with its cargo of sweaty humans seemed hardly seaworthy, and the crossing took twice as long as the ticket sellers promised. On the top deck, Lou watched the rough swell and searched for manatees on the edges of the mangroves, though the likelihood of spotting one was slim. Few such sea cows would survive the pressure of human hunters, and they're close to extinction.

"How often do you see manatees?" she asked an old man, who was returning home to Lamu.

"I was a young man last time I saw one!" he replied with a laugh and shrug of the shoulders.

Again, Lou hopes Steve is still asleep. Her walk has taken her further than she planned.

"Would you like to see my shop?" The words are virtually whispered into her ear as if she's to be let in on a special secret. Automatically, Lou shakes her head and refuses to give the man even a sideways glance. She wants to be left alone.

"I have many special things you can't find anywhere else. The best ivory carvings!"

"My husband and I are here on business. We're not tourists," she says to discourage him. The threat of a protective husband close by often keeps hassles at bay. Anyhow, Lou doesn't want to see dead elephant merchandise, no matter how beautifully carved.

"Perhaps you prefer whole tusks! What business do you have?" the man asks, his tone insistent.

Lou turns to look at him, sorry she answered at all. It's made him more persistent. He looks Arabic. She's about to decline more assertively, but he's faster than her.

"I have whole sets of tusks for sale."

"You must have a huge shop!" she replies evenly, her disgust carefully hidden.

"The sets are stored elsewhere. They are too large, even for my shop."

Calculations work inside his dark eyes. He peers down at Lou over a beaked nose and sizes her up. Thick lips twist into a smile, exposing teeth, yellow and cracked against his dark skin. Is she being assessed as a potential buyer or as a lone female? Either disconcerts her, but he has her attention. Her gut instinct says to stay clear, but perhaps she'll learn something about the ivory trade from this interaction. On impulse, she decides to go and see the tusks.

"How many sets do you have?" Lou forces the best smile she can with her heart so heavy. "Are they massive tusks?"

"Oh, yes, they are magnificent sets. I will show you." Behind his self-satisfied smile is a wheedling tone of anticipation. Lou immediately reconsiders her decision. He doesn't seem at all trustworthy. Also, Steve might be awake wondering where she is.

"Perhaps another time," Lou backtracks. "Give me directions, and I'll come tomorrow."

"My warehouse is hard to find. If I show you the way now, you can return another time."

"OK, as long as it's close, then I'll bring my husband tomorrow," she agrees against her better judgment.

Lou follows him past tourist stands. At a colorful clothes stall, he turns into a quiet side street, and then down a narrow, winding alley that seems deserted. If Steve saw her now, he'd be angry, and he'd have a point. The dirty stone walls seem older back here, stained with grime and bird droppings, a stark contrast to the newly white-washed walls of the streets frequented by tourists. Lou is about to call it off and turn back when he stops by an uneven set of steps that descend toward heavy wooden doors.

"This is my warehouse!"

When Lou peers down into the shadows, she sees flaked red paint and a shiny modern lock. The man goes ahead. Halfway down, he turns and beckons impatiently. Tentatively, Lou follows. At the bottom, he pulls a key from his pocket and slides it into the padlock. The massive doors of a dingy cellar swing open. Sunlight pierces the darkness. Uneasy, Lou moves out of his way as he steps back against her and a dank, musty odor spills from the warehouse. Lou glimpses rows of white curves balanced against a wall. To the side, a massive storage crate is open, the top at an awkward angle as if someone forgot to tidy up.

"My god!" Lou can't keep her dismay to herself. She's aware she should make a show of detached interest, but the man's hand suddenly clamps onto her arm.

"You don't like?" he says.

Lou tries to twist sideways as she jerks back toward the steps. His grip tightens, vicelike.

"No, let go!" She throws her weight against him. Miraculously his sweaty grasp lets go and she bolts up the steps. He chases, only a step behind. He's fast. Her foot catches, tripping her hard against the cracked stone. Lou hears her own ragged breaths and she almost manages to recover, but he's got her again now, one hand locked onto her arm, his other around her waist. The acrid stink of his sweat engulfs her.

In slow motion now are the sounds of their struggle, her panicked gasps, the man's grunts, aggressive and angry. Held sideways against the steps, Lou suppresses a scream and instead flings her strength into a wild, well-aimed kick as he forces her around. Her heel slams into the softest spot of his body, and, mercifully, his grip loosens. He moans and drops to his knees on the steps below her. His hands between his legs, his focus lost, he curses her, his voice guttural and menacing.

Lou rolls off the step into a defensive crouch, her shin bloody, her shoes ripped off. Her assailant lunges again, his eyes furious, driven by pain. He'll be cruel If he catches her. Half on her knees, she scrambles up the last steps ahead of him.

At the top, she's barefoot, her chest heaving. Not wasting time to look back, Lou runs in the direction she came. Turning down the first alleyway, she almost crashes into a stray dog that yelps and leaps sideways. She stumbles but uses the momentum to propel herself faster. Fortunately, barefoot has never been an issue. When she stops to catch her breath, he's nowhere to be seen. People stare curiously at her.

"Mzuri sana," Lou says to the question in their eyes. She's safe. Of course, he wouldn't chase her so far, or be seen running a tourist down.

Lou leans against a white-washed wall to gather her thoughts, still ready to run if necessary. The onlookers talk among themselves, their language unfamiliar, then lose interest and move on. Her heart slows, but she's still trembling.

Still with an eye out for him, Lou starts to walk. Attempts to rationalize fail to settle her and she's still quavering. Her arms are bruised, and Steve will be annoyed she took an unnecessary risk. There must be a tourist bar somewhere along the way to get a drink. She can also use the bathroom to clean up her legs.

Forty-Nine

Steve wakes up to find Lou gone. The air is muggy with heat and humidity and his watch says he's slept for three hours. *How long ago did she leave?* He has no idea but hopes the sound of her departure was what woke him. His thoughts are scattered, and his mind tracks back to his Nairobi meeting with the prospective partner. The idea of another partnership worries him, even after the trip here, and now his concern about Lou. *Where has she gone?*

Partly as a distraction, Steve takes a shower. The cold water across his skin sharpens his awareness as he mulls over why it's a dumb move to get financially entangled with a person he hardly knows. It took Steve a while to get a grip on how the system operates here, and an unknown business partner anywhere is always risky. The man never let on where his money came from and avoided any serious discussion regarding his other business concerns, which was a pity as he appeared well-heeled. Could be a black-market punter trying to look legit for all Steve knows. Plenty of them in Mombasa as well as Nairobi. His gut instinct is to let the option go, even though it's a ticket to stay. The offer he's had back in England has become more enticing, though cold-water dry-suit diving will take some getting used to again. Steve grins as he remembers how Lou correctly envisages the miserable British weather. *Where is she?*

Perhaps she's just gone to buy water for all he knows, so no point worrying. The trouble is, he's anxious about Lou. That look on her face earlier said she's heard him, but will make up her own mind anyhow. He knows her well enough by now. That fiercely independent streak means she hates being managed. It's not something you'd pick up immediately about her, though. In many ways, she comes across as keen to please. That smile of hers hides a lot. And why didn't she just take a ride from Nairobi down to the coast with him? It would have been a whole lot simpler.

Even after Steve has dried off and thrown on some boardshorts, there's no sign of Lou. Apparently, the Indian guy at the front desk saw her leave.

"How long ago?" asks Steve.

"I'm not sure, sir. Quite some time ago, I am thinking!"

"About how long?" Steve tries again. The man gives him a worried head wiggle in reply as if he might be held responsible and wants to keep out of it.

She wouldn't just vanish for too long. Or would she? Steve takes the path that leads down to the beach as the most logical place she might go. The sea has come up, and the waves roll in, one after another, crashing and foaming across the sand. It's one of his favorite sights, and he waits for a moment as their sound and the spectacle of the drifting bubbles settle his thoughts. Where to look next? This beach seems to be a haunt for locals rather than tourists. Not that Lou likes to be classified in the latter group, but her skin and eyes prevent her from ever being a true local, whatever she thinks; however much she kids herself.

He suddenly realizes he's been in love with her since the day they snorkeled in the current along from the headland. It was fair ripping along, but she never missed a beat. Steve liked that fearlessness, though he's not so sure about it now. He blames most of it on the way she was allowed to run wild as a kid.

His anxiety ramps up as he climbs the path back to town and takes the main street toward the market. He's annoyed to find himself like this. Anything or absolutely nothing could have happened. Partly he's angry that Lou didn't wait for him. Sometimes she has more energy than is good for her. When he gives the street vendors a description of her, they shrug their shoulders or give him a vacant stare as if unsure how to deal with his distress. He starts to check side alleys. They narrow down fast and become pretty squalid. He hopes her exploratory tendencies have not taken her down one of these. Surely not? The thought she might venture to such places sends his anxiety up yet another notch. Over an hour has passed since he first woke up.

Steve decides to return to the hotel and insist that the bloke at the front desk at least answer him and allow him to use the phone. As he runs up the front steps into the foyer, the Indian waves his arms excitedly, his face a beaming smile.

"Sir! She has returned."

"Lou's back?"

"Yes. Just a few minutes ago."

A flood of relief washes through Steve as he hurries along the corridor to their room. When he bursts in, Lou is splashing cold water over her face, a strange look in her eyes. All trace of anger drains out of him.

"Where have you been? What happened?" he asks.

A smile, but those eyes tell him otherwise.

"It's all OK," Lou says.

Obviously, it's not. He can see her hands shaking.

At first, she resists telling him, but Steve insists and manages to get it out of her. Apparently, she followed some unsavory man back to his ivory stash and almost got raped in the process. Jesus!

"What the hell did you think you'd achieve?" he asks, aware how terse his voice sounds.

"I'm not sure. I wanted to see where the ivory was stored."

"So, what now? Will you report him for having a go at you, or for dealing in ivory?"

"The ivory, of course. Maybe report the attack if it helps. I don't know!"

"Probably not. I'll deal with the bastard myself on that score. Could you find the place again?"

"I'm not sure."

Steve is sure she could. She's far too smart not to have kept track of the warehouse location.

"If that's the case, the whole thing has been pointless and dangerous!" he replies, careful to tone down his reaction. It takes all his self-control not to demand Lou lead him back there. She seems close to tears and doesn't defend her actions.

"Sorry," she says.

"Yeah, me too. You poor thing!" Steve's voice softens as he puts his arms around her.

His guess is that part of her reluctance to tell is because she's afraid he'll ask her to take him there. On reflection, perhaps she's not quite as reckless as he thought. Right now, he'd kill that guy if he could lay hands on him. When Lou's guard is down, he'll get the information out of her another way.

Still, Lou's recklessness worries Steve. She may be competent and have a sharp mind, but those elephants are like some sort of roaming pet dogs to her. She's so attached and emotional about them. Her passion is terrific but frightening at the same time. She can't expect to save them all from poachers. All that energy of hers needs to be better channeled. As if he didn't have enough to worry about without all this!

"Let's find somewhere to eat," he says.

"Yes, I'm starving!" says Lou, and he laughs.

The girl is always starving, it seems. His last girlfriend hardly ate anything and spent too much time worrying about her figure and how she looked. She was rarely up for anything new that might take her out of her comfort zone. Sure, it was nice that the other blokes were envious whenever they saw him with a glamour-girl on his arm, but it would never have worked out; in fact, it didn't. He wanted someone to share experiences with, go places with. The gorgeous stay-in-town girl turned out not to be his type after all.

With Lou it's a whole different worry. Talk about the opposite end of the spectrum. Lou would look great in high heels and a strapless dress, but Steve suspects he'll have to wait a while to see her dressed so alluringly.

There's an Indian place near the waterfront area frequented by locals. As Steve leads Lou back down that way, he's already forgiven her for the turmoil she just put him through. What happened to her is a lot worse than his moments of panic, and she's not complaining or blubbering about it. It's a measure of her strength. People need to be strong to survive in a place where they're in the minority. Lou even cracks a couple of tongue-in-cheek jokes over dinner, and Steve finds himself laughing despite everything. She's probably using the humor to distract herself as much as him from the day's events. None of this surprises him. If he's learned anything about Lou at all, it's that she's an expert at keeping things close to the chest.

And from what Lou tells him, he gets a pretty good idea of where to look for that sleazy bastard. There wouldn't be many places in the vicinity fitting her description of those steps. When the chance presents itself, he'll make it his turn to scout around alone and see what he comes up with.

Fifty

In high spirits, the poacher reaches the top of the rocky escarpment. His heart pounds from the exertion and his clothes are sweat-slicked onto ebony skin, outlining bulky muscles. He has slung his gun casually across broad shoulders, and it glistens after his strenuous climb to this incredible vantage point. Slowing his pace, the poacher scans the expanse of savannah below, and a powerful sense of exhilaration rushes through his veins. He's used to having his way, and this raid will earn him more than enough to make it worth the effort. Up here, with the world at his feet in every way, he's massively satisfied at how far he's come.

He crouches slightly to remain inconspicuous and follows a precipitous ledge. Alone and up high, there's no real need to conceal his whereabouts. But the force of habit is hard to break, and he tends to lie low when possible, though there wouldn't be another person for miles apart from his gang of men, left below to saw the ivory from the morning's kill.

It's been a while since he exercised so hard, but he's young and has an underlying fitness from a life on the edge. He stops for a moment and absently massages the scar on his thigh. As leader of a gang from an impoverished village, he's certainly well set up for this sort of pursuit. While he respects the dangers of the wilderness, it doesn't frighten him much.

Lately, life has been kind to him, and his bank balance exceeds his wildest expectations. For the last couple of years, ivory has allowed him to savor the advantages of an affluent lifestyle. Only a previously poor man like himself could really appreciate such indulgences. Those pampered city folks have no idea. As the poacher recalls more recent pleasures, he considers what a pain in the ass it is to be out here in the desolate scrub, while only last week he was living it up in Nairobi, hob-knobbing with highfliers.

Though, truth be known, the poacher feels more affection for his present gang of armed men than the movers and shakers who run the country. As far as he's concerned, those city dwellers are mere pansies. Their ability to slither past the dangers of life at the top and their streetwise tactics disgust him. His own direct approach is more brutally honest.

But the rewards outweigh his misgivings. Apart from the unbelievable money, the fringe benefits of his present revamped life include the liaisons he enjoys with the city girls. Luckily, the attractive, leggy ones generally hang out with the wealthy men that he now rubs shoulders with. Surrounded by so many new-found friends, his diversions are endless, especially regarding those gorgeous, well-groomed women. He'd be a fool not to take advantage of the situation. Most of the ladies regard him merely as a diversion, but he doesn't care. For the moment, their agenda suits him well. It's hard for them to ignore how he stands a head taller than their Nairobi wimps, and he enjoys the way they give him the eye straightaway. It won't be long before he's as wealthy as their husbands. Once he's bought a fancy mansion close to Nairobi and acquired a beautiful trophy wife, he might curb his other liaisons, at least for a while.

The poacher stops in the shade of a twisted tree clinging to a cliff edge and checks the bush far below for tell-tale signs of elephants, or, better still, a rhino. As he searches the landscape, his thoughts remain elsewhere. He smiles as he recalls how Serena couldn't resist his obvious charms that night a week ago, though she took a risk, considering her husband was with her at the party.

"You are so tall, and you look so strong!" she said to him, once he'd maneuvered through the crowd to stand right next to her. Obviously, she was wondering how it would feel to be taken by a real man.

When he selects a wife, she will be a pretty and shy woman, not bold like Serena. In the meantime, the thought of Serena's supple body, and the memory of her back, arched in ecstasy, has him rock hard in anticipation of more.

They can't resist him, those girls, who've only known scrawny city slickers. Out here, their men would be clueless, unable to survive the harsh wild country. They couldn't hunt dangerous animals through lion-infested bush, or hold a gun straight and fire a round of bullets into the heart of an elephant. Ironically, those same individuals are perfectly content to remunerate him to perform their dirty work. This serves him well, but he despises how they hide behind the scenes and leave the real job of killing to him.

Even that big-breasted girl Lexi with long blond hair has her eye on him. So far, he's been cautious. His chance will come, but not just yet, as she's presently the mistress of a government official who pays him generously. Though such a gamble would be an adrenaline kick, this one could threaten his chief source of income. It would be stupid to take such a risk. He reins himself in around her and restricts her to the pleasures of his imagination. Often, he fantasizes how good it will be the day he makes that conquest.

He treads a dangerous path out here and back in town, and it keeps him honed. Those city sleazes suffer no qualms about paying one man to murder another. If Serena's husband ever catches on, there will be more to worry about than lions and elephants, but that's a challenge he'll deal with when the need arises. He's not so easily scared.

The poacher sights the gray back of a solitary elephant far below and refocuses on the present as he hurries along the escarpment. A last kill for the road would be a bonus. Up ahead is a steep trail back down that will bring him closer to his prey and, by his estimations, closer also to where his men are cleaning tusks by the camouflaged jeeps.

Many elephants have died at his hands, and the poacher intends to kill plenty more here in Masaranga, while the pickings are reasonable. Fresh territory will be found once this place is cleaned out. But first, he's vowed to take out a certain bull, whose tusks would have grown larger since their previous encounter. Back then, the poacher was raw enough to be insanely confident, and he aimed from an impossible angle. It was unnecessarily risky to fire those random shots, and, though the bullets met their mark, they failed to kill. The wily bull rampaged toward him, but his last-minute shot frightened the beast and it veered away just in time. Shaken but uninjured, the poacher still felt beaten, and he's never forgotten it. His pride severely damaged, he vowed to have the final say. The experience taught him not to hunt alone. How many times has he rehashed the memory of that first failure?

Those tusks were only temporarily lost to him and that animal's time will come. Begrudgingly, the poacher admires the wild cunning of that elephant, a reminder of his own ability to survive situations that daunt lesser men. Since then, the bull has roamed Masaranga free and unhindered. An intelligent elephant like that one would only need to fear an astute man such as himself. As the poacher descends the steep trail, his anticipation rises at the prospect that the lone elephant below could be his adversary. Again, an invigorating surge of adrenaline rushes through his arteries.

Fifty-One

In the early hours, gunshots ring out not far from Tembo's favorite waterhole, and he flees immediately across the savannah, the memory of previous occasions firmly etched in his mind. Despite his size, the wary elephant covers the ground rapidly as he travels through territory well known to him.

The size of his tusks testifies to his survival through many perils over past years. A remarkably intelligent individual, he's a lone survivor from a herd savagely massacred by poachers. Experience has taught him how predatory humans arrive in noisy vehicles and chase elephants deep into their own terrain. The armed men rarely venture close enough to risk their own lives, and their dangerous weapons allow them to annihilate their prey from a safe distance. On two occasions, Tembo has escaped such killers, and memories of their malevolence are hardwired into his cells.

His first flight was from a lone hunter, when he learned how puny men damage other creatures without risk to themselves. At the time, the explosions and searing pain triggered Tembo to charge in self-defense, but he's not made that mistake twice. These days, he understands the danger of the unfair fight and knows to get away as fast as possible.

After the first attack, sickness forced Tembo to take refuge in the riverside scrub. Flies explored the wound as it festered. He entered a toxic and feverish state and hallucinated for days, but he was young and healthy. The abscess discharged liters of pus that carried the bullet out of him. With the poison gone, he was rejuvenated and ravenously hungry. Suddenly his life held interest again.

As the abscess healed, Tembo scraped its itchy scab against a tree and exposed a knob of proud flesh. It contracted and hardened into a gnarly callus to match the mental scar that has protected him this far through life. The injury shrank inside the increasing bulk of his maturing body. Had he been human, he would most likely have forever carried a grudge and vindictive hate.

More recently, a herd he joined was massacred. Imprinted in Tembo's memory is their mortal panic. On the far side of their group, Tembo was briefly shielded from the initial onslaught. He'd smelled danger moments before the men opened fire and managed to get away just as a young mother took a swathe of bullets. She fell onto the dirt beside him, her anguished trumpeting audible above the gunshot. The death screams of other mothers and calves merged with another deafening round of bullets. Flooded with fear, Tembo smashed away through the undergrowth. The sound of the tragedy chased him as he fled, hard and fast through the bush. The herd's bellows of pain are forever with him. When he reached Masaranga's boundary, human habitation prevented him from getting further away.

🐘 🐘 🐘

An observer would see this nomadic bull roaming across the plains, splendid against the savannah scenery. Tembo follows a well-worn path among a network of trails that fan out toward the edges of the plain, and then fade where grassland gives way to woodland. As he walks, his tusks move rhythmically and glint in the pale evening sunlight.

An onlooker would also see the ambush Tembo inadvertently approaches. Tired from putting distance between himself and the waterhole since dawn, he mistakenly senses danger to be far behind. Until now, a mix of luck and caution has kept Tembo safe from poachers, and a wariness from early experience has kept him alive. His quiet passage across the plains should have carried him far from the killers.

But today, fate does not favor him. After the armed men failed to kill at the eastern waterhole, they took an alternative track, skirting the edge of the plains to decrease their risk of detection. They stumbled over a small herd and instantly opened fire. Now busy hacking the ivory off their victims, they are concealed ahead of the doomed elephant.

Tembo moves slower now as he enters acacia woodland. Weary from his walk, he's more at ease shielded by trees. He continues below a rocky escarpment. The evening breeze gives relief after a hot day as the sun descends toward the horizon. Those gorgeous tusks, his protection and downfall, gleam yellow. On them are the markings from half a lifetime of use. When he was toxic and discharge oozed from his leg, the tusks kept lion and hyena at bay. Those creatures slunk in at night, only brave to approach so close because they smelt sickness. But he was resilient and still dangerous enough to fend them off. Daily they came to check his defenses and then left him alone again, turning their efforts toward weaker prey.

For centuries, this was life on the African plains. The strongest survive, the weak are sacrificed, and balance continues. Even the men, presently invisible to Tembo, were once a part of a natural cycle. But then outsiders brought guns and a type of greed that arises from the ability to amass wealth. Equilibrium was lost. Lethal weapons allow men to kill without a fair fight and create distance between them and the death they deliver.

So now, angry, impoverished men are easily transformed into killers, controlled by cowards without values, men too gutless to do the dirty work. Elephants and rhinos die from greed rather than a necessity, defenseless against well-armed poachers. The avaricious benefit from the destruction at a massive cost to all else.

These six men, illegally in the park, have plenty to eat, and greed is now their main motivation. Downwind from the fleeing bull and unaware of him, they wait by their camouflaged vehicles and argue as they wait for their boss to return.

"It is time we took a bigger cut of the profit," says the smallest, most quick-witted of the men." His words are directed to anyone prepared to stand with him. Sweatband around his forehead, he turns toward his most likely ally and challenges him with his eyes.

"Yes. Did you see that house he just bought? He receives more than he tells us." His ally is quick to back him up.

Thirsty from his long walk, Tembo approaches a waterhole near the men. Their present load of tusks is from immature animals, not yet old enough to reproduce.

"Let's offload the ivory and demand a higher cut!" says the man with the sweatband.

"Don't be so impatient. We will deal with this once we have more ivory. First, we camp out and continue our raid."

The only thing they all agree on is that they don't have enough decent-sized tusks, and they're not being paid enough.

As Tembo moves into the clearing, their leader returns from the escarpment, so quietly they miss his approach.

"Get off your lazy asses. Can't you see the bull with the tusks!" Their boss man drops to a crouch as he hurries past them toward the prey. In an instant they follow, guns ready to kill, all arguments forgotten. Their teamwork is smooth and well-executed from much practice.

"There it is," they whisper, eager for a kill. "A big-tusked bastard!"

Hardly able to believe their luck, they move toward the doomed bull, who is upwind from them, and unable to pick up their scent.

For a moment, Tembo stands motionless as the dangerous armed men line up, voracious for more. His trunk rises to test the air as if he's finally sensed their presence. For that last moment in the fading light, he stands magnificent for a few seconds. Somehow, he perceives the wrongness of it all.

Then bullets rip the air apart. In shock and terror, Tembo holds his head high and trumpets his anguish. This time, he knows it's over and his agonized screams fill the air. In slow motion, his hind legs buckle and sway. His body sags. As he jerks sideways, his tusks rear toward the sky for a second before he hits the red soil so hard the ground vibrates under the men's feet.

The poachers hear his screams, but the sound means nothing to them. Too full of the exhilaration of his death and what it will buy them, their exuberance overrides all else. They move in closer to await the end and calculate how much more will be due to them now.

Fresh red blood streams across Tembo's gray hide. Rivulets of his life spill into the dirt and dust. The men huddle excitedly. They ready their guns as he attempts to rise, but his legs fail him. He swivels on a tusk and falls back, his legs at impossible angles. Horror fills his eyes when he lifts his massive head off the dirt one last time. Obscured by blood from his forehead, his last vision is of excited men coming in for the kill. Crimson streaks flow down his face and stream over the white ivory. As his vitality drains away and life recedes behind his eyes, they dilate and dull.

🐘 🐘 🐘

Circling vultures alert Lou and Peter, and they come the last kilometer on foot, aware they're too late again. Wheel tracks from the poachers' vehicles tell part of the story. As Lou stands next to the ravaged carcass, a sense of devastation floods through her.

"Oh no, Peter," she says. "See the scar on his thigh. It's Tembo, the one who forced me off the road. Not for a moment did he consider harming me." Lou has followed this elephant in her dreams, and his death weighs too heavy for her to bear.

Fifty-Two

At sunrise, they pull up beside the impala. As Lou squats beside it, she sees its dulled eyes still open, and her grief wells up. So soon after her elephant! Blinding headlights caught this poor creature unawares, and then a dull thud as hard metal smashed into living tissue. The death is recent and vultures haven't yet arrived, although a scavenger has left a gouge along its flank.

Lou hopes this antelope went quickly. She winces at the prospect it was left in agony, alive but unable to escape predators. A quick death, like when a leopard drops stealthily from a tree, or after a short chase by a pride of lions, couldn't be so terrible as to lie injured and frightened, while the scavengers move in. Nature, too, can be indifferent. Lou places her hand on the still-warm body, and scans the surrounding bush. She's aware that their engine could have just frightened a hyena off.

No sign of any other life close by. Lou thoughts roam through the spectacular savannah, this stunning battleground. People are protected from nature as a result of generations of human collaboration, and unlike wild creatures, they rarely live in constant fear for their lives. Ironically, these days, the predatory humans in a big city are more dangerous than predators encountered on a wilderness safari, though nature's beauty and savagery are best viewed from safety. Present day survival for man would be difficult without the inventions of a few geniuses. Not so long ago, human existence was equally hard, each day's existence a feat.

"You ready, Lou? Leave the carcass for the scavengers!" Peter interrupts her thoughts, and Lou turns to see him already back in the driver's seat.

"OK, I'm coming."

Still cut up, Lou fights off the wretchedness brought on by the dead elephant, followed by this antelope. Jobs wait for her at headquarters, hours away. New high-detail maps have arrived.

"Let's go home and try to work out the easy off-road access points into the park," she says. "We can stop at the escarpment and check for elephants from there."

Past that, the road drops steeply, and the thick bush makes wildlife hard to spot.

From the lookout, the drought's hold is especially evident. Lazy eddies of red dust swirl across the plains and leave a haze over everything. In her hands, the binoculars are hot from the sun as Lou searches the landscape. Occasionally, she stops to check an outline below. Dust obscures the detail and alters the perspective. Its tiny particles infiltrate every space in this endless gritty heat.

"There's a herd over there. See their ears moving!" Lou points to far below, where a family of elephants crowds together. The patch of shade hardly covers them.

"Yes, they are far away," replies Peter with a distinct lack of enthusiasm. An untrained eye would have passed them over. He hands her a water bottle through the vehicle window. It's warm, but Lou swigs it down gratefully.

"Why did we come out here today?" Lou asks Peter. "We're not getting anywhere." She wants to let him know she's also bored and despondent. He hasn't even bothered to get out of the vehicle. With his elbows on the window ledge, he half-heartedly searches the savannah. It's been an unproductive day, which is hardly surprising, considering the heat.

The elephants below are their first today. The direct approach path is rugged and involves traversing a sandy riverbed that divides the valley. It's too late to follow an alternative bush track that winds south before kinking back.

"Think we should go home?" she asks Peter.

"Good idea, Memsahib Lou!"

Lou would berate him, but neither of them is in the mood. Frustrated and still thirsty, she stretches. Her body feels tired and stiff from hours of jolting along bush tracks.

It's then that she spots a new line of dust, cutting a swathe through the natural eddies, beyond where the elephants wait in the shade. It's hazy, but through her binoculars the vehicle seems more substantial than the usual four-wheelers, and the canvasback is enveloped in a dust-cloud.

"Hey, Peter?"

"He's driving very fast!" replies Peter, his voice no longer bored.

A sudden sense of dread grips Lou. She tries to rationalize. Though there's reason to be paranoid, it's most likely an overland tourist vehicle. Even poachers don't venture out in this heat on hot, unproductive afternoons. Perhaps a tour group has run out of time and the guide is on a mission to return home, but already Lou envisages other scenarios.

Peter frowns and lowers his binoculars. A knot forms in Lou's stomach.

"Who do you think they are?" she asks.

"Maybe tourists. Perhaps poachers with guns to kill our elephants."

"Can we cross there?" Lou points to a narrower section of riverbed far below.

"Only if you want to get stuck in the sand."

On their own, it's foolish to follow. There's virtually no chance of catching the vehicle, and, even if they did, they've only got the one rifle between them.

"Let's get back and let headquarters know!"

Even before Lou slams her door shut, Peter begins to accelerate.

Fifty-Three

The corrugations suddenly jar harder through the seat as a flat tire slows the descent from the lookout. The delay wastes precious time as they sweat and grunt with the spare. Uncharacteristically, Peter cusses vehemently. Lou's panic escalates as she tightens the bolts. The sun is almost on the horizon when they finally reach headquarters. Sweaty and dusty, Lou hastens across the hard-baked ground toward the office. But this late, she's downcast. At least her father shouldn't yet have left for the evening patrol.

Keen also to collect the day's elephant sightings, Lou hopes to confirm which individuals she saw from the escarpment. Tourist and ranger observations help her keep track of the herds. A trail of smoke trickles across the yard as she hurries toward the office. Grace prefers wood to the free fuel provided by the park, but today the familiar smell doesn't settle Lou's agitation. The fire just reminds her how late it is.

Lou hears her father talking inside the office, and she hesitates with her hand on the doorknob, not wanting to interrupt. His voice seems muted, and Lou waits, momentarily indecisive. She must alert him about the speeding vehicle. A piece of peeling paintwork dislodges just as Lou realizes it's not her father. The voice pauses, and she waits for a reply. Nothing for a moment and then the voice continues. Her father is not even in there! Someone has snuck into the office to make an unauthorized call.

Another short silence ensues. Alarmed but unsure, Lou glances around. She feels strangely guilty for eavesdropping. Especially if this call is legitimate. Apart from the now upward spiral of smoke, there's no movement anywhere around. Lou puts her ear against the peeling paintwork. Who's in there? She hears a few words of Swahili, plenty of yes, yes, then

OK, not sure. A location is described with exact directions, a region on the far side of Masaranga.

Lou recognizes the open stretch of savannah being indicated. Only yesterday, Peter spotted her favorite herd up there, the Mbane females with calves of various ages. The matriarch's calf is skinny and may not survive in this drought, though she's popular with the grown-ups. They attend to her frequently with gentle touches of their trunks as encouragement when she lags behind. Lou knows the Mbane elephants well and was sorry to have missed seeing them.

Frozen to the spot, Lou strains to hear more. Her heart races as terror begins to grow. Instinct warns her that this information exchange is a betrayal, especially after today's vehicle sighting. This person is a threat to the elephants, but it's hard to hear his exact words, and some of the Swahili is beyond her ability to interpret. No one enters this office uninvited, and the phone is out of bounds for social calls. Now the intruder's voice lowers insidiously, audible only in snippets, but enough for Lou to know he's describing the Mbane herd.

Cold tentacles of fear clutch her as she hears the intruder describe individual elephants. There's a silence and then answers to questions. Lou leans harder against the door. Who is in there? His answers become shorter and affirmative as if responding to instructions. The conversation is being wound up. Uncertain, Lou backs off a couple of paces.

Instinct prevents Lou from surprising him. It's essential to get the facts right and not be caught listening. A few seconds later, she slips back into the house and sprints to the same spot she used to watch the office a month ago. On that occasion, it was dark, and her father wrongly assumed she was mistaken. Now hidden from view, Lou waits impatiently for the intruder to leave, aware that the night patrol could leave anytime now.

Before long, the office door opens slightly, and the intruder surreptitiously checks the coast is clear. As he slips out and shuts the door quietly behind him, the man again scans the compound cautiously before scurrying away from the office.

Surely it can't be Paul, one of the new rangers? The same solid build and slight limp. But of course, who else! Lou recalls Paul's amusing description of a fall from a horse. He speeds up toward her. As she ducks behind the curtain, she catches a glimpse of his wide cheekbones and deep-set eyes. Then he turns sharply onto the path that leads toward the rangers' accommodation.

Once safely away from the office, Paul slows to his typical sauntering, asymmetrical gait. Had Lou just spotted him, she'd assume he was on his way to his quarters, though he's supposed to be on the evening patrol. As he turns past the house, Lou's hands ball into fists.

What do they know about Paul, so recently sent courtesy of the Environment Minister? Who is he? To whom was he speaking? If his actions were legitimate, he'd have no reason to sneak around or risk losing his job. The fact he snuck into the office during the day, with a reasonable risk of being seen, means he considers his report on the Mbane herd urgent.

What a betrayal! Lou begins to shake. But beneath her anger is a terrible sense of dread. She dry retches. Paul just secretly advised an unknown outsider about elephant locations, and Lou's immediate fear is for the Mbane herd. Her father must be told so he can focus tonight's patrol to the north, where the herd was.

And he may have already left. Lou sprints down the corridor. On her way through the kitchen, she collides with Grace, who starts to laugh but catches herself when she sees Lou's urgency.

"Sorry!" Lou shouts her apology and takes the back steps three at a time. On her way past the ranger's quarters, she imagines Paul inside, watching her hurtle past.

Out of breath, Lou reaches the impossibly calm scene where rangers prepare for night patrol. Golden light slants gently through the tall acacias behind the vehicle sheds. The sound of dove-calls contrasts starkly with her runaway thoughts. Everything seems unreal, and, for a moment, she fears her imagination is just working overtime. Lou forces herself to walk the last stretch. She catches her breath and gathers her thoughts.

"Habari, Memsahib? How are you?" Paul's off-sider, John, greets her by the main shed, a smile on his face, his rifle already slung over his shoulder.

"Mizuri sana. I'm very well!" Lou forces a smile to disguise her distress.

Less panicked now, she searches for her father. He's preoccupied with a last check of the spare fuel. Usually, Lou wouldn't bother him because that expression on his face would make it pointless. That look indicates he's stressed and busy enough already, without time for anything or anyone else. Out of the corner of her eye, she notices Paul arrive and go immediately to help John with a load of spotlights.

"Dad, I need to talk to you for a moment!"

"Not now, Lou! The new boys have held us up enough. We need to reach the Napane River before nightfall."

It's not what she wants to hear. The Napane flows far away from where her favorite herd is in danger. He must cover the area she mentioned in the suspicious phone call. If he changes his plans now, it'll be too late for Paul to report back to his contacts.

"I must talk to you now!" she says.

"Get Grace to prepare a late dinner. We can talk then. I don't have time!"

"Please, Dad, now!" Her tone is insistent enough to get his attention. There's a sudden lack of activity around her. She's aware of eyes on her, and of Peter watching it all.

Her father's look of irritation softens to include concern. Her resolve is unusual. Briefly, she's surprised that this is all it takes to get his attention.

He motions for Peter to load the fuel containers, then shrugs, and follows her to where the doves still coo from the shade of the acacias.

"Lou, I hope this is important."

Relief floods through her. Her father has not brushed her off and driven away in his usual hurry. Unexpectedly, the weight of his arm rests across her shoulders, suddenly grounding her.

"Yes, Dad, it's important. Tonight, please focus on the Mbane herd up north."

"That's not what I had in mind. It's a long way after this late start."

"You want me to talk now or later?"

"Ok, let's make it later. When it comes to the elephants, you do have a sixth sense. I'll take your word for now."

"It's more than a sixth sense!" she insists, but can't tell if he heard. He's already halfway back to the waiting men.

After they leave, Lou lets herself into the office and stands there for a while. What would she do if she came here, snooping for information? None of the filing cabinets is locked because, until now, no one thought it necessary to hide anything. Her father's desk stores all the documentation needed to run Masaranga. Lou is guilty of hardly paying attention to such mundane logistics. Perhaps she should have. Wildlife records are stored in a cabinet by the main window, where Lou can see out as she sits and sorts data. It's often a lonely task. Post-grad students work on similar projects elsewhere, and these long-distance friendships lessen her isolation. But phone calls are difficult to put through, and she only makes them when it's essential.

She opens the top cabinet, then the next and the next. Everything seems just as she left it. These records are of her observations and those from rangers and tourists. Some have notes to indicate the reliability of the sources. Occasionally, other researchers come through and use the sightings to search likely locations of big cats, elephants, and rhinos.

Lou's heart sinks at the sudden knowledge that Paul checks these for information on wildlife unfortunate enough to have beautiful skins, horns or tusks. Anxiety sets in as Lou imagines how he uses it. She now bitterly regrets keeping these records here. Her first impulse is to remove everything and leave the folders empty. But that might alert Paul.

Bleakly, she absorbs the impact that such records may have harmed rather than helped the wildlife. Her files are not stored elsewhere because she's never considered it necessary to screen them from employees. Quite the opposite, in fact, as rangers are encouraged to develop their knowledge. Her father also focuses his patrols based on this information. The data is for those keen to conserve, not for self-interested people that might use it for nefarious purposes.

Had Paul asked, he'd have open access to it. The fact he reads and reports it secretly leaves her with no doubts that he's traitorous. A rush of anger toward him is followed by one at herself for failing to predict this possibility.

Will Paul connect her determined attempt to talk to her father with the change in tonight's patrol? Now over her initial panic, brought on by visions of bullets decimating the Mbane herd, Lou realizes how cautious they must now be to best use this discovery.

Outside the office, the sun sits low on the horizon, and the dark silhouettes of trees are lined with gold, but Lou is blind to their beauty. Nor does she notice the mousebirds as they raid the fruit trees. One by one, she rehashes her interactions with Paul, with a whole new slant on the day she bumped into him on the remote riverbank. He always appeared so motivated, and his corruption is a bitter thing to swallow.

She removes only the most recent sightings as if she needs to work on the data. From now on, any new observations will be replaced by fake notes that send prying eyes along false trails. Perhaps Paul can work unwittingly for them instead of against them.

The men return after midnight with little to report—a regular night apart from the direction change. Peter thought the Mbane mothers and calves seemed restless, but a search of the area was unproductive. He agrees to return with her at daybreak. She almost cries with relief.

"You absolutely sure about this? It was definitely Paul?" her father asks.

"Absolutely," she replies.

"I never particularly liked him, but he's the small fry in all this," he says. "I'll leave you to supply the misleading data, and I won't discuss patrols with the men until we're almost on the road."

"At least we know where the problem lies," she says.

"We know only part of it. Paul could lead us to the higher levels of corruption. We'll continue as if unaware of his agenda."

Her father has taken it more in his stride than she imagined. Lou herself feels gutted. One unchecked person can inflict so much damage.

Fifty-Four

At daybreak, Peter drives out with Lou to recheck the Mbane elephants. "They have vanished!" he says after a while as they search along the bush tracks.

"No vultures circling?" Lou asks. His use of "vanished" makes her heart lurch.

"No, I mean they have moved on."

"OK. Let's go home. It seems we've got nowhere."

But the deskwork achieves nothing either. Tired and agitated, Lou hunches over maps of Masaranga until her eyes blur. The fan circulates hot air. Is there a direct connection between Paul and the speeding vehicle? Abruptly, she pushes her paperwork away.

Though all this data has value for the right people, Lou is appalled that her research has inadvertently aided the enemy. Their resources are already lean enough. The present lot of poachers could possibly be led into an ambush, but that won't get the syndicate behind them. Too much of her time has been spent mapping these elephant trails between watering holes and feeding grounds when she should have been involved in direct action.

Lou drains her glass of water. A second glass goes down just as fast. Her dehydration headache eases. All afternoon, her theories have run circles, always returning to her fear for the Mbane elephants.

She named one of the younger females Tumaini after the Swahili word for hope. Now Lou hopes the matriarch will lead Tumaini and the herd to a safe place away from poachers. The Mbane herd is her favorite; they've always trusted her enough to let her close even during this poaching crisis.

The reason elephants got under Lou's skin is partly because their behavior reflects the best side of people while omitting the worst.

From the activity outside, Lou deduces that Peter has been assigned night patrol again, though he's worked with her half of today. Never mind. He's itching to prove himself. Their oldest ranger complained of being overworked and asked for time off, so Peter now drives the back-up vehicle.

The rangers' guns, once used as protection against rogue animals, are now used as a defense against armed poachers. Lou watches as her father runs a weary hand through his hair. He heads off, ahead of him another long drive with spotlights wielded to search the savannah. Again, Lou wishes she was allowed along, but the patrols are considered men's domain.

The rangers chatter as they walk past. On the roof, doves coo as if they have no cares in the world.

As her father's Land Rover pulls out, Lou makes a split-second decision to go. Damn the consequences! She sprints toward the backup vehicle that starts to move as she yanks the back open and hoists herself inside. Lou slams the doors shut behind her and takes a seat alongside the startled rangers. None of them say anything, so her impulse goes unchallenged. Peter heads the vehicle off across the savannah. To avoid any interaction with the men, Lou remains quiet, her attention focused on the passing landscape.

On the rough road, the vehicle rattles and sways. Along slow stretches, where the road winds tightly, the dust catches up. Through invisible gaps, it infiltrates their enclosed back section. Whenever the speed picks up enough, the men open their windows and blast the dust out. Their resilience reminds Lou of the taxi ride, as she holds tight to the hard seat. Even so, whenever Peter brakes, the force throws her forward.

"The seats are too hard!" Paul shouts over the vibrations to make himself heard. Lou holds her tongue and nods her agreement.

"He wants to go back to the city!" says an older ranger. Oblivious to the conundrum, he winks at Lou and then playfully pats Paul on the shoulder.

Despite their discomfort, they all settle in stoically for the long ride. There's plenty of time for Lou to reflect both on Paul and the fact her father will be furious to find her here.

Against all odds, her headache clears. Exertion and adrenaline replace internal tension and conflict. The soft evening light has fallen across the savannah outside, and a huge orange sun sets slowly over the Western Ranges. The last rays linger, silhouetting the wide-boughed acacias. An auburn glow tempers the browned grass of the plains. Impenetrable hollows form in the shadows.

Across the grasslands, massive termite mounds stand sentry, like large tombstones. As the light fades, they resemble the backs of elephant calves hidden in the long grass. Lou suppresses her gloomy thoughts about graveyards, aware that a morbid mental state won't help anything. This surreal scenery has her unwilling to let her struggle spoil the beauty the wilderness holds. Soon, the night creatures, the hyenas, and the leopards will stir from the safety of their lairs.

Fifty-Five

Like a stowaway, Lou scrunches on her rear seat. She faces inward, the place opposite her empty. Because these back seats take more impact, they're the most avoided. Outside, the rusty haze of sunset gives way to a black starry night. Sand replaces dirt on the road and their progress becomes quieter. The rangers murmur quietly among themselves, while Lou's conscience keeps her silent. Her surprise appearance seems to have made the men cautious. As their vehicle turns onto the shortcut to the northern waterhole, the corrugations return, jarring relentlessly through the seat. Cramped and uncomfortable, Lou absorbs the impact through her thighs until they ache. Eventually, weariness takes hold of her. She gives in to the vehicle's motion and lets her body lurch along with it.

Upfront, Peter slows the Land Rover. Immediately, Paul hoists a spotlight into position.

"Make the beam wide," the older ranger instructs him. "Then you will see more!"

For a while, whenever the bush opens up and the vehicle slows, Paul sweep-searches the savannah.

"Let me take it." Impatiently, the older ranger takes over, his technique expert. The beam of white light bounces eerily off tree trunks and penetrates patches of low scrub. It catches surprised creatures previously hidden in the dark. Ahead on the road stands a tusked warthog, red-eyed and frozen in fright. With a loud grunt, it plunges abruptly into a thorny thicket. Twigs snap noisily as it disappears into the darkness.

This old, slow vehicle is the one Lou uses, and they're some way behind her father. She's grateful for the gap. The separation allows the dust to settle.

As they pass, new clouds billow up behind them. The distance also delays the moment her father overreacts on discovering she's along uninvited. Peter has conveniently chosen to ignore her. Lou hopes he considers it's fair she came. After all, she was the one who spotted the suspicious vehicle yesterday. Peter has always tried to protect Lou from her father's wrath.

Lou would prefer that Paul were not here in the back with her. So far, she's managed to more or less avoid catching his eye. Her distrust and disgust must not show. They've misinformed Paul, and therefore his contacts, of where tonight's patrol would focus. They need to bide their time, but his presence twists a painful knot tighter inside her chest. To control her growing agitation, Lou tells herself that tonight's patrol is merely a routine circuit, with only her father's anger to fear. But that's not entirely true, and the night has a disturbing quality. She watches, expectant, while the lights pick out shapes across the dark savannah.

"No elephants tonight," John says in an attempt to engage her.

"Not yet. It's a pity. I like to see my friends," Lou replies. She wonders if he knows about Paul. Were they friends before they came out to Masaranga? If only she'd paid more attention. Far from their real homes, they may have developed a close relationship.

The chatter between the rangers settles. Between the sweep-searches, they seem mesmerized by the section of road highlighted by headlights. Lou loses track of exactly where they are. It can't be far now.

Up ahead, Peter hunches over the steering wheel, his eyes focused ahead, determined to miss nothing. He drives skillfully and avoids the worst potholes, while maintaining enough speed to skim the tops of the endless corrugations.

Paul and John seem impassive and uncomfortable now. They rouse as the vehicle slows. John takes his turn to wield spotlights and search the darkness. The established rangers switch from Swahili to English when Lou loses track of the conversation. Paul and John use Kikuyu when they talk together as they did when she surprised them on the remote riverbank. The other rangers probably don't understand them either.

Wearily, Lou again wonders about the sanity of her impulse to come along. Exhaustion from hours of rough traveling overrides all thought.

Fatigue numbs her mind, and the tight knot in her chest sinks below her awareness.

Though she's been holding out for it, it's a shock when they pull up. After the engines cut, the silence seems uncanny, the bush strangely empty of sound and movement. Through the dust, their headlights reveal the open back of the lead Land Rover.

"OK, we're here. Let's get to it!" Her father's voice breaks the eerie quiet outside.

Peter jumps down and opens the rear doors. "Paul. You come with me," he says.

He then instructs the other rangers and acts as if Lou is invisible. Rifles knock against the sides as the men climb down. Their boots thud dully on the dirt track. Once they're out, Peter shakes his head at her and opens his hands in an expression of disbelief.

Paul and John converse privately, and Lou's anxiety returns. The rest know the drill and follow instructions, all very matter-of-fact. A moment of hesitation and then Lou jumps down behind them, her joints and muscles cramped. She twists her torso from side to side and stretches her legs to improve her circulation. To the north, the dark outline of familiar hillslopes tells her they're close to the waterhole.

Her father covers the distance between the vehicles. With a sweep of his arm, he indicates the direction they're to take. His gesture is mimicked by his shadow, magnified and oversized in the yellow headlights. He notices her and stops in mid-sentence.

"Louise. What the hell are you doing here?"

"I thought I might—"

"Get back inside the Land Rover and stay there. I can't imagine what's got into you!"

He grabs her arm hard and forces her along toward the open back doors.

"Lie down and stay in there. You're on your own. I can't spare anyone to look after you." His voice sounds less harsh now, more tired and stressed. It doesn't enter Lou's mind to do anything but obey. She half-crawls back in and lies along the length of the seats, leaving the rear doors open. She watches the men organize themselves in the pool of light around the vehicles. Their voices are subdued as they prepare to track toward the waterhole. Just as they leave, Peter pulls her rifle from behind the front seat and quietly slips it into the back with her. Neither of them speaks.

Then the lights are cut, leaving only the pale moonlight on the landscape as the men slip off quietly to the north. Lou stashes her rifle lengthways alongside her on the seat. It's supposedly her protection though she only uses it for target practice. Outside, the bush remains quiet, as if the disturbance has silenced the nocturnal creatures. Lou listens for their sounds but hears only the footfalls and low voices of the rangers that fade as they move off into the still night.

Her mind wanders as she waits and listens. Her ears are more useful than her eyes now, as the shapes outside are blurred together and difficult to distinguish. It's a favored time for predators when the senses of their prey are confused. That rustle nearby could be a lizard or a leopard. A hyena laughs briefly in the distance, the sound eerie though Lou knows it well. Out here, animals hunt quietly. They kill for food and take enough to survive. Only men greedily go after more than they need. Paul has become linked with malevolence and greed. Here in Africa, the corrupt bribe small men into decimating their heritage. They turn them into indiscriminate killers, who take what they can in exchange for rewards from gutless men, whose dirty hands remain deceptively clean.

As Lou loses track of time, she senses it stretch out. For the elephants out there, those gray ghosts in the night, their size is no protection from man's bullets. Her thoughts drift into a half-sleep tangled with an awareness of her surroundings, where she fears it's too late to save the elephants and that Peter will be caught in the crossfire and killed.

Then comes a sound too immediate to emanate from her dream. Gunshot splits the night open. Instantly awake, Lou rolls into a crouch, the rifle under her arm, ready for the next shot. It's nearer than the last. Shakily, Lou positions herself on the floor between the seats and watches through the open back, the metal floor cold against her body.

The road behind is moonlit. On one side is a high bank, on the other the track dissolves into the scrub. Lou hears distant shouts, then a yell nearby. Vegetation is smashed back. Another two shots blast out, and now there's a man running toward her along the dark road. His outline looms closer and his boots pound toward her. As the distance separating them shrinks, Lou flattens her body against the floor, her rifle ready, the butt against her shoulder. She can't tell who the lone figure is as it closes in fast. Is it one of the rangers or a poacher?

The silhouette looms against the moonlight, suddenly larger and more overbearing than any of the rangers. As it advances, Lou steadies her rifle on her elbows, her target lined up. The man keeps coming as if he's after a vehicle for a getaway. *Would he take her hostage or just kill her?*

Another distant shot off to the left, too far away to help. Alone with the stranger almost on her, Lou sees his gun held ready to shoot. He lopes toward her, closing the gap. Her rifle tightly in place, Lou lines him up. She can't let him reach her. Her heart pounds harder as she aims, her focus on the sights, her grip amazingly firm. For a fraction of a second, Lou hesitates and then she releases the trigger. The rifle kicks back into her shoulder, and its retort obliterates her gasp as the bullet meets its mark.

The man hits an invisible wall that tips his body sideways. His legs buckle. The deflected momentum from his speed lifts him from the ground. But the man's reflexes are fast. As his torso twists into an oblique arc, he aims a shot toward Lou. The air explodes and the Land Rover jolts. A second later, he hits the ground with a guttural scream.

The rifle warm in her sweaty hands, Lou quickly lines him up in her sights again and waits, terrified he'll get up and come for her, even as she's paralyzed by the conflicting fear that she's killed him.

Branches crack in the bush, high on the left bank above the track. Another figure pushes out from the vegetation with a flash of torchlight. Lou instinctively realigns her rifle. Her hands are steady again as she lines up his head.

Fifty-Six

The blinding glare of a spotlight sweeps the track and alights on Lou. She quickly realigns the rifle sights, but the beam moves on toward the inert man on the road. With a jolt of recognition, Lou realizes it's Peter up on the bank, his headband lined up in her sights.

"Lou, you OK?" he calls urgently.

"Yes. I'm fine!" Lou shouts back, her voice strangely disconnected.

"That's one of our poachers. See any others?"

"No. Only you."

Lou watches as Peter scrambles down the scrubby bank. Halfway, he launches out and lands with a thud on the track. She lowers her gun with shaky hands. Has she killed him? Lou is uncomfortably aware of how close she was to pulling the trigger on her friend.

Peter approaches the man slumped on the ground, a few hurried steps at a time, on alert for any other disturbance.

"Is he alive?" Lou shouts as Peter reaches the still form, her voice wavering. No answer. That other fear, the one of doing wrong, floods her with dread, its source different from her previous panic. She should have let off a warning shot. But the man did instantaneously return fire, so that might have worked out even worse.

The sound of rangers crashing through the bush contrasts bizarrely with the alarm and silent disbelief inside her. Lou waits, incapable of movement, while Peter squats by the form on the track. A surreal haze of dust rises through his spotlight beam as he moves around it.

Someone is shouting, but Lou is only able to make out the eerie shadows of surrounding trees. She suddenly understands that Peter needs her help. Her rifle still ready against her shoulder, she's frozen still like some incompetent.

Instantly, with a newfound focus, Lou grabs a rope and flips on the rear spotlights. She runs toward Peter and the body. Her shadow bounds ahead like a determined demon, huge in the spotlight, with coils of rope flying and leaping alongside as it races her along the dusty track.

Facedown, the poacher seems inert, but when they attempt to roll his heavy body over, his muscles jerk into life. There's a moment when Lou is glad that he's alive, for a fraction of a second, until a massive arm swings back to grab her. Peter dodges just in time, knocking the arm sideways, while Lou launches her weight against the man's torso. She hears his grunt of pain from the force of the impact.

"Face him back down!" Peter shouts. He lands hard on the man's back and wrenches the flailing arm behind the bulky body. Lou seizes the other arm, and together they pin him to the ground. As she attempts to wrestle the man under control, she's aware of his ferocious strength. All her weight is on him and she uses this advantage to maintain her hold, but not for long. His arm gains against her, and the fingers twist around and lock onto her hair. Her head snaps sharply back and a tearing heat burns through her scalp. Lou gasps noisily.

A sideways blow from Peter breaks the vicious grip. Sudden relief is replaced by fury. Lou strikes the poacher. Pain radiates along her arm as her fist connects with hard muscle. Under different circumstances, she understands that this man would effortlessly smash her to the ground.

"Get on his back!" shouts Peter.

Her hands sticky with congealed blood, Lou throws her weight higher to immobilize the torso. The poacher rocks aggressively from side to side, but fails to dislodge them. Her breathing ragged, Lou struggles against the brute strength of the man as she forces his chest hard against the ground. He shoves fiercely back against her weight and throws her forward onto the dirt. Immediately, his freed hand latches onto her leg, and she feels its grip tighten with a savage strength. Pain jabs up through her thigh.

Lou grabs a rock off the road and uses it to strike his hand so hard she feels the impact through her leg below. As his fingers loosen, she yanks them back to break his grip, so that, at last, Peter is able to get a loop of rope around the arm and secure it tightly against the other. Some of the fight leaves the poacher, though he again begins to roll from side to side as if to test his chances of breaking free.

As he seems almost subjugated, Lou rolls upright, her entire weight now on his back. A gritty dusty sensation threatens to choke her.

Out of breath from exertion, Peter deftly lashes a couple more knots. The poacher moans and stops struggling. A moment's reprieve. Then his knees come up abruptly, and his weight throws her sideways again.

"Hang on!" gasps Lou, as sharp rocks cut her skin. On her shins, she spins and launches hard back against his legs. The man's agonized wail is followed by a Kikuyu curse as a dark stain expands over his thigh. The darkness spreads as new blood oozes from the bullet wound. Lou notices her hands smeared with it as well, and there's plenty congealed with dust on the road. Taking no more chances, Peter loops the rope around both legs and yanks brutally.

"Do it the hard way, if you like!" he says under his breath as a stream of curses erupts from the poacher.

Lou wants to scream at the poacher. That this is the pain elephants feel when he fills them with bullet holes, and the anguish he inflicts as their life drains out with their helpless calves close by. She feels no empathy although only minutes ago her worse fear was that she'd killed him. The anger that drives her now rages stronger than her fear of his dying.

As Peter has him roped under control, Lou backs off a few steps and takes a moment to absorb the situation. *Is he losing enough blood to kill him?*

"I'll get the bandages," she says, and sprints back toward the glaring spotlight from the Land Rover.

The first-aid kit is stashed under the seat. She throws it open, and her hands shake violently as she finds swabs and bandages. When she returns, the man has relinquished all hope of escape. He lies motionless, his face sideways in the dirt, blood everywhere, much of it caked on the dusty ground.

The poacher's leg spasms as Lou applies a pressure bandage above the bullet hole. It's too late to worry that his blood is all over her as well. She secures a final wrap around the injury as Paul arrives ahead of the others. He steps in to help Peter lift the poacher. The bandage in place, Lou is suddenly no longer needed.

Only a few minutes ago, the poacher was bearing down on Lou. A cocktail of fear and anger, adrenaline, and exertion runs through her veins, and she suppresses an urge to throw up.

One after another, the rangers return. Lou hears them crash through the last stretch of the scrub and then down the bank. Their shadows stretch behind as they hurry toward Peter, who instructs them as they hoist the subdued man to his feet. He's handled this well, better than her. Lou feels her resilience has all but vanished.

"Louise, get back into the vehicle!" The anger in her father's voice takes Lou by surprise. She'd all but forgotten about him and knows any reply would be pointless, even had she one. Defenseless, Lou strides back towards the vehicle.

"Don't let me see you back out again till we get home," he adds, and mercifully returns his attention to his men, without another glance her way.

Cowering inside, Lou is relieved to escape the scene outside. The last few minutes are hard to absorb. Would it have worked out better had she stayed home? Her father is as furious at her as if she were still a child. Undoubtedly, she's asked for it this time. *How will he react when he discovers who fired the shot?* But she did stop the poacher from escaping. Will her actions get her locked up? She has no idea. Crazy visions of courtrooms and prison cells run through her mind.

The poacher is marched toward the vehicles. A head taller than anyone, he gasps at each step. His legs are now freed, but he's flanked by rangers. Ahead of them, her father passes Lou and throws the rear doors of his Land Rover open.

"Tie him tightly to a seat between you. Restrain him properly and don't take your eyes off him," he growls.

The poacher lurches past Lou's open window. The close-cropped hair exposes the broad lines of his face, backlit by the spotlight. A glimmer of recognition suddenly tugs at Lou's memory. Those compressed thick lips give him a sullen expression that doesn't fit her memory of that face. Though she doesn't know him, he's familiar as if she's seen him somewhere. Her skin crawls in recognition. What's her association with that face? A sudden raw fear washes through Lou that she's bitten off more than she can chew.

This poacher was in the photo she stole that night from Fred Lonnegan's office. He stood a head above the others on the edge of the image. On his face was a confident smile, though he seemed out of place, as if slightly uncomfortable in his stylish clothes. *Is the man tied up in the front vehicle, a bullet in his leg, that same man?* A little more clearly now, Lou remembers the proud smile and square face, caught by the camera on that celebratory occasion. Right next to him, looking entirely at ease, was Sam Watchiri, one arm casually draped around the poacher, the other around the president's son.

Peter leans in to grab her rifle, and the déjà vu disperses. A minute later, he climbs in ahead of the rangers and flings himself on the seat opposite Lou. Why hasn't he taken the driver's seat? Then, as if reporting to her, he says, "The poacher came straight toward me with his gun ready. I had to shoot him first!"

His words sound strange and all wrong.

"But you didn't shoot h—" Lou tries to correct him.

His reply cuts through her words. "Yes, please listen to me. I shot him." His voice is urgent as he reiterates.

Lou recognizes that determination.

"Yes, I shot him," he says again, "and you bandaged the wound. He gave me no choice. I had to shoot him."

His expression is only half visible in the dark. The other men chatter excitedly as they climb in. Their estimates of the size of the gang vary depending on where they were when the chase started. The man they've captured seems to have been the ringleader. Their camaraderie is infectious as they congratulate Peter loudly and slap him cheerfully on the back. Even Paul performs as if ecstatically pleased.

Lou sits back, outwardly silent, confused by this change to the truth on top of everything else. Peter wants to protect her, but she can't allow that. When she again goes to speak, he raises a finger, a quick angry gesture toward his lips to silence her. The rangers are too distracted to notice. True, it's less complicated if a member of the anti-poaching unit pulled the trigger. The manager's daughter probably wouldn't fare so well. Lou's mind spins at the implications. Too strung-out to think straight, she quietly absorbs this new turn of events.

Peter gives her a last resolute nod and returns to the driver's seat. At her first chance, she must catch him alone and talk to him before they come clean with her father. Lou is also eager to first take another look at the photo to be absolutely sure. They may be onto more than they realize here, more than just the seizure of a gang leader. Her gut feeling of having bitten off more than she can chew returns with a vengeance.

But at least tonight was not for nothing. In a churn of conflicting emotions, Lou's spirits lift. Whatever the fallout, she's made connections. So, perhaps her other unauthorized, night-time excursion to the ministerial office wasn't wasted either. A shiver runs through Lou. She needs some quiet and a clearer mind to think it all through.

The sound as the vehicle starts to move hardly registers with her. They return through the night, back the way they came, over endless potholes. From the corner of her eye, Lou watches Paul, whose countenance seems hardly different from the others. In contrast, her own reality seems irretrievably changed.

Fifty-Seven

Lou beats a hasty retreat as Peter returns the vehicle to its shed. Back in her room, she smooths the bent corners of the stolen photo. Their poacher smiles confidently back at her, unmistakably the same man. Alongside is the handsome Sam. Lou stares at the image as her thoughts gel. No longer surrounded by his fancy friends, the poacher showed a different face tonight. *How many elephants has this one man killed?* The smug expressions of the people in the photo make her feel sick and empty. *How could I have been so naïve?*

Mostly awake for the rest of the night, Lou tosses restlessly as recent events run back and forth through her mind, now seen in a whole new light. Piece by piece, her perspective alters. Minute details of her visits to Nairobi return. Inadvertently, she's aided these people, who, under the guise of governing, profit from the destruction of Kenya's legacy.

Just before dawn, Lou drops into sleep scenarios as convoluted as reality. Woken by the roar of vehicles from the compound outside, she's relieved to escape the nightmares. Car doors slam, and loud male voices bring her wide awake. For a moment, Lou lies on the bed, pervaded by a sense of loss, her eyes fixed on the ceiling.

The curtains billow, and Lou squints against shafts of bright light. It's late and the doves' chorus finished hours ago. Is her father back from delivering their poacher to the authorities? She wants to be spared from the sight of the man who massacred so many elephant families. Last night, he fought hard, like a man with a lot to lose.

But it's not her father. Two burly policemen have come for Paul. Lou considers it about time he was dragged off to be questioned. She watches him resist as he's pushed unceremoniously into their van.

As Lou follows Grace down the back steps, the police hardly glance their way.

"Good thing my son was with you last night!" mutters Grace under her breath. Evidently, she's already heard Peter's account.

"He saved my skin again," replies Lou.

Paul attempts to get back out of the police van.

"I have done nothing wrong. You cannot take me!" he says to the officer, who shoves him back down into the seat. "You are mistaken!" he protests more vehemently. "The Bwana has caught his poacher. He will be angry if you arrest me."

The other officer chats with Peter, who looks exhausted. Lou eavesdrops as she prepares the horses' breakfast.

The car door slams behind Paul, his pleas ignored by the officer. He obviously hopes that because his hands are literally clean, he's somehow blameless. But not being present at the crime scene doesn't erase his guilt. Lou knows her attitude is hard, but she's angry enough to give it full rein. There should be enough evidence to put Paul away. He's a forlorn sight, but she can't feel sorry for him. A decent job was not enough for him. Lured by easy money, he chose to be a traitor and took the wrong path.

Will Paul guess she overheard him the night she pulled her father aside? Right now, he seems unaware of what they have on him and how badly his cover has been blown. Lou wonders how many times he's betrayed them all. They were successful last night mostly because they misinformed Paul, and therefore his contacts, about the locations of the elephants and the focus of the patrol.

Mixed emotions swirl through Lou: anger and resentment, her fear of being questioned over the shooting, and, through it all, relief that they've saved the Mbane elephants. For now, the herd is relatively safe from slaughter, their lives not lost to supply ivory to ignorant humans on the other side of the world. Lou reflects that the wealth of the guilty and gutless can often literally be measured in bones. For many, ownership of ivory is a mere ego-boost, but their self-delusion is as lethal as murder. Perhaps a few are truly ignorant of the damage done, but most are not and they don't care as long as they prosper. Meanwhile, the loss instigated by their money can't ever be replaced.

"This is the first time my son shot a man," Grace says to Lou. "But it was for a good reason. I helped him clean the wound before Bwana took the poacher away."

That such consideration was shown is more than he deserves, thinks Lou. No doubt, his first stop was a doctor. She quickly quells her indignation. Considering her part in his injury, it's not the time to express her outrage.

Peter stares grimly toward where Paul sits hangdog in the backseat. Lou wants a private chat with him, though apparently there's no trouble brewing over the shooting. Guiltily, she watches the scene unfold as if she had no part in it.

The same people Lou asked for help are the ones from whom the elephants needed protection. Now sure of this, the knowledge appalls her. Not only has she failed, but she's aided them. Never again will she be so ingenuous. To think she even fancied Sam.

Government involvement makes it imperative to remain quiet about the details. If guilty officials could accuse her of a crime, her father's employment might end. Neither she nor her father are citizens, and they can't afford to lose the privilege of living here.

"Do you think Paul influenced the other rangers?" Lou asks Grace. She needs reassurance. From early on, Paul was often the center of rowdy laughter and joked a lot with co-workers. Though irreverent, his humor seemed harmless.

"Just because a man can make people laugh, does not make him a good man!" replies Grace. "They are not stupid. Now they will see who he is!"

Briefly, Lou wonders whether he was threatened or maneuvered into his dirty role, his motivation fear rather than greed? She judges not. Paul is far too confident for that and just managed to slip under their radar. Lou feels mortified by her part, and by how many elephants and rhinos no longer roam the wilderness as a result of his subterfuge.

A measure of trepidation shadows Lou's relief at the overnight gain. But the adrenaline has run its course, and she wants the oblivion of real sleep. Perhaps this victory will carry them through previously invisible barriers.

As the police prepare to leave, Zebu pushes up beside Lou. Her coat is soft as she rests against Lou's leg and then becomes more persistent, leaning harder as if sensing her mistress's strange mix of emotions. Lou wraps her arms around her bulky body and Zebu grunts appreciatively.

"Morning, snuggle bug Zu!" Lou says and ducks sideways to avoid a kiss. Zebu's doggy affection is always reliable, whatever the circumstance.

When the police leave, Lou steps forward to shake hands.

"Kwaheri." The officer bids her goodbye and his rough hand briefly grips hers.

"Kwaheri. Asante sana!" Lou thanks the officer, who turns immediately toward Peter and gives him an affectionate pat on the back. Evidently, she plays no part in the equation. Such invisibility might be infuriating in different circumstances, but not today. The vehicles leave, and Lou turns to Peter. She's ready to talk, but he's already made himself scarce and is nowhere to be seen.

Zebu follows Lou faithfully to her desk. She's supposed to stay outside, but today she senses things are different. Lou watches her sniff around the room and then settle down with a contented sigh. Seconds later, Lou puts her head down on her desk and immediately falls asleep.

When the smell of woodsmoke wakes her, Lou looks out to see an expanse of orange sky streaked with delicate pinks. For the first time in ages, her mind is empty of thought, and her body calm. It's a rare special feeling, and Lou remains utterly still for a while. She holds on to the sensation and breathes it in, hoping to make it last.

Fifty-Eight

The poacher can't fathom how he got into a situation where he's tied up in the back of this vehicle with a bullet in his leg. These park ranger bastards were supposed to be on the opposite side of Masaranga. He'd anticipated taking out an entire herd, and his men were excited. They planned to work uninterrupted through the night and be well on their way with the ivory haul by daybreak. Once past Masaranga's boundaries, bribes to their police contacts made it unlikely they'd be detained, even should they be stopped.

When the raid caught them out, he was separated from his gang and toward the front of the herd, ready to shoot and scare the elephant back toward them. But before he had a chance, his men spooked and took off with the vehicle quick smart, and he suspected they'd not be in a rush to return for him. Recent mutterings of dissent among them indicate that he needs to erase a couple of troublemakers.

The poacher's immediate escape plan was to steal a Land Rover and get himself to the nearest main road. A bold solution for sure, but he considered it preferable to a long walk and possibly being eaten by a lion along the way. Their informant said the patrol vehicles were left unattended. And if necessary, he had no qualms about shooting someone to enable his own escape.

The poacher's adrenaline pumped full-bore as he doubled back past the rangers toward their access track. He ran along it for a while until he spotted the glint of moonlight off metal up ahead. The vehicle was not lit from inside, and the coast seemed clear, his escape route open. Childhood practice meant he could start anything without a key.

The bullet was an unexpected surprise and it caught the poacher mid-stride. Quick reflexes allowed him to return fire toward the Land Rover, but he was moving fast and felt his body being slammed sideways. The adrenaline briefly delayed the onset of pain. Male and female voices, unintelligible at first, came in as a blur through the shock. Then, as he struggled to get free, there came the satisfaction of feeling the hair tear, and the realization that it was probably her who shot him. An overriding fury surged through him, and that was enough to mask the pain. The white bitch would pay for this. As they half-carried him past the rear vehicle, he glimpsed her face, pale in the moonlight.

Now, the poacher's anger flares as strongly as the pulsating throb of his wounded leg. The bitch's time will come once his connections get him out of this mess, as they undoubtedly will. A severely painful glitch is all this will prove to be; no more than a time-waster. He's pissed off that an uncomfortable night in a jail cell awaits him. These guys have no idea who is behind him, nor what they're up against.

It's a long way back with plenty of time to mull it all over. The poacher's thoughts distract him somewhat from the dull ache in his thigh. He's frustrated at the loss of tonight's haul, the Mbane elephants, according to their informer. Amazing how they bother to name them. For fuck's sake, it's as if they were pet dogs rather than dangerous wild animals, of no use except for their ability to grow ivory. He never liked dogs much, and these days the elephants even less. They were just cunning, wily beasts. When the elephants and rhinos run out, he'll move on to something else; pangolins perhaps, something less challenging when he's older. There's no end to what people will pay for. In the meantime, his operation is about to be put back weeks, months even. The poacher considers that the time needed to sort this mess out would be better spent stockpiling wealth. That inside informer should pay dearly for this. As far as he's concerned, nothing less than a bullet will suffice.

The Land Rover takes a sharp turn, and his wounded leg knocks against the metal division. He swears vehemently. The ranger seated opposite him shifts his rifle yet again, and the poacher detects a glint of amusement in the man's eyes. Low-life bastard. The poacher would like to smash the weapon over his head. But he'll not allow them to see his pain again. They are merely pawns in a corrupt system, too stupid to make it on their own.

He'd like to get a good look at the white bitch in the other vehicle. That will help him decide and relish how he'll privately deal with her—a longer-term plan to look forward to. But when they reach the headquarter buildings, that vehicle separates off. The one in which he's imprisoned stops long enough for his wound to be rebandaged—not so gently either. Then another endless drive. The bullet is removed at a hospital, which he finds as crude and basic as the one nearest his home village. The backward bush facility seems totally unacceptable, since he's now used to the best Nairobi doctors.

The poacher's fury flares again, despite the dead exhaustion that threatens to send him to sleep, just when he needs to be hypervigilant and watch for any chance to escape. But even in the hospital, no opportunity presents. The bastard ranger never misses a beat. With the right pressure, the man could be a good recruit when he replaces the insurgent men in his own crew. The hospital staff inject him with something that numbs his consciousness at the same time as it eases the pain. The drugs send him on a ride where even his anger is a distant entity. At first, he fights the sensation. It scares him to lose the fury that has infiltrated every part of his existence. Its power has gained him so many material things.

When the strangely blissful stupor wears off, the poacher wakes in his prison cell. A guard shakes him, the grip rough and hard. A visitor already? Two stony-faced men handcuff him and lead him away. He's suddenly hungry and thirsty.

"I need water and food," he says.

"After!" replies one of the men. "You are lucky. Someone has done you a favor and sent a lawyer."

"Then you will bring food and water immediately. Otherwise, the lawyer will find how you've mistreated me." The poacher feels a potent surge of confidence, bolstered by the speed with which his allies have responded.

Fifty-Nine

Lou's father paces the room like a caged animal. One minute he curses Paul's duplicity, the next himself for not having seen this possibility. Lou is sure that even If her mother suddenly appeared, he'd hardly notice.

"Evil bastards! Our request for reinforcements has us double-crossed. Corrupt scum! We'll expose them whatever it takes."

A wave of panic washes over Lou. "Let's wait until we know more. If government is involved, they could get nasty and terminate your contract and replace us with corruptible people."

"If we worry about that, we become powerless to do anything!" he replies angrily.

Lou feels her father's frustration, but his rationale worries her. They need to tread gently if they're to follow this to its end.

"Where would we go if we're forced to leave? Who would look after Masaranga then?" she asks.

Lou tries to imagine life somewhere less wild, a "developed" place defined by concrete and hard straight lines.

"Lou, I haven't always lived here." He almost smiles. "Other places do exist!"

But she can't shake her visions of urban sprawl, cultivation and what would happen to the elephants if they left.

"Damn!" His fist hits the dining table.

"I hate all this!" Lou's words burst out abruptly. Tears prick her eyes. Through their haze, her father sags visibly as the rage drains from him. He puts his arms around her. Lou can't help it; she starts to cry, her tears coming unchecked.

It's strange to be suddenly held by her dad. Lou needs to wipe her eyes, but she's caught in his hug. Her tears run instead into his shirt.

"Sorry, my gorgeous girl. Sorry about everything."

She pulls back a little and is surprised to see tears in his eyes for a second before he recovers.

"I need a drink. What about you?" says her father.

"Dad, I have a photograph I need to show you. It explains a few things, but you can't ask how it came into my possession."

🐘🐘🐘

If people understood how the system dupes them, they'd rise up and change it. From behind thick walls, the corrupt control the resources. There is little fair play. Others are bribed or bullied while the greedy enslave the poor. Few have either the means or energy to rise against the system. Lou dreams of such a revolution, but, in her nightmares, the opposite plays out.

Names roll through her mind, and Lou wakes slowly through the dullness of disrupted sleep. The dark hours carried her no closer to resolution. She spent them entangled in endless futile effort.

Her mind heavy, she's glad to escape her nightmares. Bands of yellow light penetrate the curtains of her bedroom. Lou pictures the fat, fluffed up doves on the roof above, their wings warm from the first sunlight.

Her earlier dreams resurface: African cities overflowing with people, images of smiling faces despite the poverty. The smells of street cooking and samosas, right next to hunger and destitution. People without power to influence events because they're too busy surviving. How can they be helped to bypass the old deadly ways? Few have the education to understand their connection with all life. They need to understand that their wildlife is worth more alive than dead and that their heritage is being stolen.

Even if tourists leave without a backward glance, their money raises the value of wild creatures in people's perceptions. In the sad world of the dollar, their wildlife creates wealth only if it remains alive. Dead it lines the pockets of a corrupt few. Lou is finally prepared to discuss wild creatures in financial terms, despite her conviction of their inherent right to exist.

Unable to lie still with this overload of thoughts, Lou rises early.

"Morning, Grace," she calls on her way out, in an attempt to sound more bright and cheerful than she feels. "Our world is about to change!"

"Our world is always changing," replies Grace.

Lovely Oliver nickers as Lou steps out into the soft dawn light, a mug of coffee in her hand. In the sky are high white clouds that almost promise rain. Zebu lies quietly in a patch of sunlight. It's another deceptively peaceful morning. Lou reflects that her actions of breaking into the government offices and then later of jumping into the patrol vehicle at the last moment have achieved more than all her hours of research. She's still surprised that her father has not yet demanded to know where the photo came from.

She loves the research, and it's so necessary, but her role needs to be one of action as well. A bit of activism must be combined with the academic; otherwise, the research achieves little. Only when activists distract people from their artificially busy lives can they imagine and be enabled to become part of the change.

Vulnerable and a little frightened by her future, Lou feels her anger drain. A space opens up inside her chest. She sits by Zebu and snuggles into her rough coat. It's as if she's only just starting to fathom reality. Zebu stretches and yawns appreciatively in her arms.

Her father steps out, and Zebu struggles free to greet him, her body swinging from side to side.

"Morning Zebu, you hairball!" He pats the dog absently and looks out across the valley. "All OK?" he asks.

"Sort of."

"Sort of what?"

It's unusual for him to ask, so Lou has to think for a second.

"Sort of sad. Sort of depressed."

"Best not to dwell on it," he advises.

That's the truth of it, but Lou can't free her thoughts. Tears of relief and sadness well up. Lou gets up quickly, and, so that he doesn't notice, she heads off on her errands.

"I better feed the horses," she says over her shoulder.

Sixty

Despite a slight limp from his bullet wound, the poacher strolls jauntily along the final stretch of his journey home. He's been advised that a visit to his parents would be an excellent diversion considering the circumstances. His Nairobi friends prefer he keep a low profile until free from the scrutiny of authorities. Although the syndicate has suffered a setback, it will remain intact, provided they're careful. Once the right hands are greased, and his trial is over, he'll take up where he left off. Most likely, they'll target another park, but he doesn't mind now he's taken down his nemesis, that bull elephant. His leg has healed well, and Sam promised everything would be taken care of.

"Don't worry, my friend. Before long, it will be business as usual!" Sam said on their only opportunity to talk secretly.

The poacher has chosen to walk and surprise his family rather than take a taxi right to their door. It's sensible to remain inconspicuous, and the exercise has helped him let off steam after his incarceration. His parents couldn't afford to visit him in the lock-up, and know only the basics of his crime. Their lack of funds does cause him a twinge of guilt, considering how much he's stashed in a hidden account. Distracted by his new-found life, he forgot to send money to his mother. Otherwise, she might have bought him some decent food.

He leaves the dusty road and takes a shortcut to his childhood village. Truth is, he'd rather be in Nairobi, with Serena on his case. His arrest has deprived him of female company, and he's not had a woman for ages. To pass the time, he fantasizes about a wild session with Serena. It would invigorate him and release some of the tension. On the other hand, since her husband arranged the bribe for his release, it seems sensible to avoid temptation.

As he passes behind the only house near the shortcut, the smell of cooking posho hangs in the air. Repulsive stuff, but it does remind him of contented childhood days before the endless procession of hungry new siblings forced him to leave and find his own way. Then came the run-in that gave him his first real scar and a first taste of how to survive. He won't eat maize meal now, not even to keep his mother happy.

He clears a fallen log and strides alongside a vast field of maize, planted since his last trip home. All this land used to be a forest where he played with his mates and learned his bush skills. He liked it better then.

He's sure his mother's face will light up when she sees him. It's been a while, and this also gives him a mild pang of guilt. She knows little of his present life, though his father may guess how he lives. The word around the village used to be that his father was a bit of a wild man before he settled down with the prettiest girl for miles. He owes them this visit, just in case he's forced to do jail time.

If he were due for a long incarceration, he'd jump bail and disappear. But his connections assured him he's safe as long as he keeps his head down and follows instructions. His punishment will be minimal, if any. The syndicate needs him more than he needs them. But he owes his mother a visit after such a long absence, and, right now, he has nowhere else to go. No doubt she'll be delighted when her number-one son walks through her front door. He should have brought her a gift, but it's too late now, and he has little cash on him, the rest being stowed safely. Until all this inconvenience blows over, he won't draw attention by accessing the account.

The exercise has made his wound ache slightly, and, although it was treated promptly, he's irritated not to have got top medical attention. He can afford the best care, and it angers him not to have access to it. His thigh still throbs sometimes at night, and the new scar needs plastic surgery. While it might work to brag of his exploits to village girls, the city ladies are less impressed by ugly disfigurements.

He's still bothered by the way he was shot. The bastard ranger took credit for it, but he saw the girl in the Land Rover, which is where the bullet came from. She took a good look as he passed as if she recognized him. He'd never seen her before, and she was attractive, so he'd remember. When his case comes up, he will ensure the lawyer uses this information to bring the white bitch to her knees. The best legal help is on its way, though it will cost him dearly in ivory when the time comes to repay the debt.

The poacher had swigged down the last of his soda and thrown the plastic bottle into the bushes a mile back. Now he scrambles down an embankment to a creek, where the water used to be drinkable. The water seems murkier than he remembers, but the strip of vegetation along the river is shady and refreshing. Thirstily, he drops to his knees and scoops up mouthfuls of water, at the same time splashing his face.

At the last moment, he notices the shadow, his warning of someone on the bank behind, an acquaintance perhaps from his village. But it's strange they didn't call out a greeting. As he turns, a bullet enters the left side of his rib cage. He'd protest at the mistake, but his killer is a professional, and able to fix inconveniences without aggravation.

The poacher falls face down into the water. He struggles briefly though violently while blood gushes into his lungs with each more erratic heartbeat. His mouth is open as he strains for air, but water enters instead. He fights against the current, and twists away from the vice grip that holds him below the surface. As his arms scrabble and lose strength, the stranger's hands push down, forcing him deeper.

Sixty-One

Outside, Grace calls the chickens and clangs metal buckets, while Oliver and Roma nicker for food. The world seems on hold, and Lou feels oddly disconnected from routine activities. These sounds, the markers of daily life, seem a world away from recent events. She wanted someone to talk to and finally got a call through to Steve, who was keen to visit, but talked of competing errands, which made her reluctant to assume anything. She's impatient for news on how the prosecution progressed, hopefully today when her father returns from Nairobi.

As if someone has ventured too close to their nest, the weaverbirds' calls intensify, but when Lou leans out to check, all she sees are a few Thompson's gazelles. Always wary and ready to flee, the gazelles nibble at the grass with their ears alert for Zebu's sporadic barks, though they've learned she's unlikely to disturb them.

High in the pale morning sky is a single cloud, its feathered edges dissolving into the blue. A welcome breeze billows the curtains, and patterns of sunlight dance against her elephant painting, highlighting tusks against the shadows. His arid landscape seems somehow less severe. The world has shifted, the air seems softer, more forgiving, as if it contains a touch of moisture.

Lou's urge to rush ahead has dissipated, despite her mental task list. Her reality seems altered, its focus changed. The worst of her emotions have evaporated. After a few hours at her desk, she falls into a dreamless sleep, her head cushioned by a pile of journals. A whine from Zebu pulls her back through layers of sleepy resistance before the kerfuffle of male voices jolts her awake. It's almost midday. Hurriedly, she splashes cold water on her face.

On the horizon behind her father's vehicle, low purple clouds chase sunlight off the savannah.

Dark smudges under his eyes accentuate his age and his face crinkles into a smile when he sees her.

"Hello, darling!" He hugs her. "We've made passable headway in Nairobi."

What's with the darling bit? He must be in an exceptionally good mood.

She follows his gaze out toward the thundery sky. He's certainly cheerful about the oncoming storm. Zebu is equally enthusiastic and bounds around the greeting party, making it hard to unload supplies.

"So, they're treating it seriously?" asks Lou, with some trepidation.

Her father smiles and nods. She knows that's enough information for now. The rest will come in good time.

"Rain at last," Lou says instead. "It'll be on us soon!"

The inky clouds and darkening sky fill her with newfound optimism.

"See those flocks of birds flying ahead of the front!" As her father points to wavering lines of minuscule dots, Lou hears a trace of the old enthusiasm that used to inspire her.

The men chatter cheerfully until the storm front is almost on them.

"Slow down! I'm not getting any younger," complains her father, his tone jovial, as he helps Peter drag an old engine under cover.

"You finished that thesis of yours yet?" he calls out to Lou. Then, with jobs to do, he heads off toward the storage shed. Lou returns to her notes and watches the sky from her editing desk. Her project definitely contains material that will help protect this amazing place, and she's virtually wiped the voice that insists her work is a waste of time. Its power to insinuate she's done more harm than good has been expunged. A long-awaited tide of change waits on the horizon.

After the judgment of her thesis, and an inevitable revision, her choices are about to open up. Now less deterred by life's uncertainty, Lou wonders how she might help while at the same time dealing with her own survival. Surely it can't be so hard. Even her supervisor commented on how her outlook had adjusted.

"Many roads lead to Rome!" he said. "It's not essential to fight the battle at ground zero."

"I've just got to get this done and to you first. Right?" Lou replied.

"That's right!"

Her soul might be here, but a parallel path is preferential to hanging on here like a limpet until change forces her out. Another level of work awaits her.

Of course, her father will stay as long as he's permitted, but Lou's input will change. She'll fight from the outside, while her father and his staff fight on the ground. To save her world, she must leave it and learn more about the forces that destroy places and people.

A few early beads of rain displace puffs of red dust. At the sound of the first heavy drops against the roof, Lou runs barefooted outside to watch the clouds spill their contents.

"Grace. It's raining!" she shouts.

Fresh raindrops plop against her skin. All around her, they pepper the earth with dark red dots. In a moment of suspended time, Lou waits, the dusty ground soft under her feet, her face upturned, arms extended, exhilarated and expectant. This fantastic landscape will make use of every last drop of rain as if it were a dehydrated animal.

After a few seconds of slow rain, the deluge arrives with such force that it's impossible to keep her face upturned against it. Drops coalesce into curtains of unexpectedly cold rain that stick her thin shirt against her skin. Grace's face breaks into a beaming smile at the kitchen window.

Roof gutters overflow, spilling over the sides of buildings. In a newly saturated world, Lou stands drenched and delighted, water puddled around her. Now at the backdoor, Grace laughs at her rapture. As puddles join, the groundwater amasses and flows down the slopes toward the waterhole, which is enveloped in sheets of rain. Muddy channels of water join in the valley below and flow toward its cracked banks.

Shivering, Lou returns to the veranda, where drops explode across the polished surfaces. The surreal drumming of the rain carries her toward a far vaster reality than her everyday existence.

Sixty-Two

At breakfast, Lou's father reads a newspaper article aloud. A body has been dumped not so far from the Lake Naivasha property that she knows so well. Birdwatchers discovered it in the rocky hills behind the lake. The group diverted their hike to follow a descending spiral of vultures, and discovered the corpse before the scavengers cleaned it up.

"Evidently, the assassins were keen to hide the evidence to have picked such a remote spot!" he says, briefly glancing at Lou.

"How do they know it's murder?" Lou asks.

"Hands and feet cut off. Cleanly, probably with pangas, not just chewed by predators."

"Perhaps the victim had something on them," she says.

"Pretty good chance. It would take at least two men to haul a body up those steep slopes."

Lou knows that, even using animal trails, that terrain is rough. Had the birdwatchers not stumbled on it, the corpse would never have been found.

"Doesn't the loss of hands and feet signify some sort of dishonor or disgrace?" she asks. Precisely what eludes Lou for the moment.

"It'll be a tribal thing," he answers. "They certainly dealt with him severely!"

"It must have been premeditated," Lou says, more interested than she wants to be. "To mutilate him and then have the resources to dump the body on a remote hillslope."

But her father has already flipped on to the next article.

Left with her thoughts, Lou's stomach turns. There are reasons why murderers mutilate bodies. One is to prevent identification. She tries to shake the image, but her thoughts continue to niggle away. Lou would read the article herself, but her father is maddeningly slow with the newspaper, and she has work to do.

All day, her mind circles back. Though acclimatized to animal carcasses, Lou has never seen a dead person, never mind a hacked-up corpse. She recalls that another possible reason for the mutilation is that some tribes believe the deceased can't pass safely to the next realm unless their hands and feet are intact. As Lou measures out the horse food, she's too distracted to be aware of their bad behavior.

Naivasha sits on the Rift Valley fault line, her slopes part of the escarpment. Many times, over the years, Lou has stayed at the Chellis' gorgeous hexagonal guesthouse. The retreat sits on a rise, and the main windows open onto expansive views across the lake. Last visit, Lou was alone and she compiled a bird and wildlife checklist for their family friends, the Chellis, who planned to rent the place to tourists.

In the mornings, Lou sat outside the guesthouse on the grassy slopes high above the lake—an idyllic outlook. It felt surreal to sip her wake-up coffee and watch the dawn hues mirrored by the lake's calm surface. Hippos lazed in the water below, the sun glistening off their backs. Through her binoculars, she could sight animals usually hidden by lakeside reed-beds. Closer to her, birds flitted through high treetops, and the high-pitched calls of waders added to the serenity. When the sky was cloudless, the yellowing hillslopes accentuated the emerald lake surface. Occasionally a hippo would snort and exhale a cloud of mist into the still air. Now, with this new information, these memories seem contaminated.

When Lou returns from her errands, the newspaper waits on the breakfast table. It's only two days old. She flips impatiently to the article, which tells her that scavengers damaged the victim enough to make identification difficult. A shiver runs down her spine. The incident disturbs her more than it should, as if she's connected to it. Why does she feel like this when the victim is unknown to her? Resolutely, she resists her instincts. But all day, a sense of foreboding sits beneath her busyness. It makes a strange change from anger and despair.

That night, Lou dreams of searching for something hidden under the reed-beds along the lake. At dawn, she remembers the python coiled around a warthog, and afterward how Joshua taught her to rehabilitate the injured snake. She also recalls how Joshua told her his tribe had those beliefs about the passage into afterlife.

When she dials his number, it takes the operator several minutes to connect her, which is not unusual. As she waits, her fingers work impatiently, drawing circles within circles on a notepad, while the usual sounds down the line, the clicks and buzzes, go on forever. *Could Joshua be in trouble because he helped me? Would they know I called Joshua after they captured the poacher?* He'd seemed jumpy and professed to know nothing. But her initial interview with Fred Lonnegan was made possible by Joshua pulling a favor. *Would they suspect he'd helped in other ways, even though he didn't? Or is it my own paranoia sending me off the deep end again?*

When, finally, Joshua's secretary answers, she's unable to help. "Sorry, Joshua is on leave. Shall I write a memo for when he returns?"

"No. I'm a friend of his. Is there another way I can contact him?"

"That's not possible. Joshua is away for another week."

Lou leaves a message anyhow and then impatiently searches the directory for a home number. A softer female voice answers, and when Lou introduces herself, Joshua's wife explains he's not there either.

"He's depressed. I sent him to visit friends and cheer up," she says. "He doesn't like his job but we need it. We want our children to go to a decent school."

It's not the reassurance Lou was after. Briefly, she chats about his Masaranga visit so as to not transmit her alarm.

"I have an injured python and was hoping for some advice," Lou lies, as an excuse for her call. Joshua's wife promises to get him to phone her as soon as he's home.

For the rest of the day, Lou tries not to worry. At one stage, she gives in to her concerns and phones Steve. Amazingly the call goes straight through, but he advises her to settle down and not allow her imagination to ferment. The fact Joshua pulled strings doesn't put him in danger. Steve is right. Her reaction is way over the top. A discussion with her father would be met with a similar response. She's paranoid and just making mountains out of molehills. Steve's advice to wait a day or so and call again is plain common sense.

Sixty-Three

It was a long drive up from Mombasa and Steve is tired, even with a stopover for a business meeting in Nairobi. On the drive out to the waterhole, he listens while Lou pours out her thoughts in a jumble of words. He agrees and sympathizes, but has no immediate help for her. She probably thinks he should be more empathetic, but it's hard to know how to assist or console her.

Now inside a hide by a lake, they talk in whispers so as not to disturb the wildlife. A herd of zebras approaches, and the first takes a cautious drink. Steve is angry, though not particularly surprised by Paul's betrayal. He points out that it happens sometimes. Rangers' salaries are low compared to easy black-market money.

Poor Lou. She's a few years younger than he is, and has less concept of the wide spaces that separate how different people think. It's an absolute tragedy that elephants she's so attached to have been murdered. Steve has only just started to learn how social and family orientated elephants are. It's not until you've spent a bit of time with them that you get an inkling of their intelligence and intuition. No wonder Lou gets so heartbroken.

Steve considers her lucky and unlucky to have connected with such unique animals. Few other people would directly experience the massive loss she does when elephants are murdered. But mankind seems greedy for ivory. The less of the commodity left, the more valuable it becomes.

"I wish David were home to help," Lou says, and launches into a tirade about the betrayal.

Steve is reminded of something Lou's brother once said about how single-minded she can be. "You've got way too serious!" The moment Steve blurts the words out, he wishes he'd stayed silent. It's unfair of him to accuse her of being too intense. But the whole situation frustrates him so much.

At the water's edge, a cautious zebra spooks and moves away. Steve can tell his accusation hurts, but part of him agrees with her brother on this one.

"Let's go home," she says.

As they close the hide and start home, Lou seems absent and caught up in her thoughts. Steve is about to apologize when she asks, "Too serious for what? For you, or just generally?"

"I don't like to see how it eats you up so badly. That's all!" Steve replies, aware he's on shaky ground.

Steve lets the vehicle gather speed until the wheels catch in a pothole and throw them sideways. He straightens them up, and they come free at the last moment, avoiding a slide into a ditch. The sudden adrenaline jolt sends them into a fit of relieved laughter.

"Bloody terrible roads you've got out here!"

"Doesn't seem to slow you down!" retorts Lou.

Steve grins, glad to change the subject. "Sorry, but we need to hurry. We've promised your father sunset drinks. Remember?"

She's obviously forgotten.

"It's unusual for Dad to plan ahead for such things," Lou replies.

"You get it from him!" Steve says.

"Get what?" she asks.

"The too serious bit." Steve keeps his tone light and teasing now.

Lou laughs along with him now. She's fun when not on one of her depressive rolls.

"What will it be for you? A gin and tonic, my dear?" Steve affects a respectable upper-class accent, and she hits his arm playfully with her hand.

"Don't be mean! Dad doesn't sound like that."

"No, he doesn't, actually. It's the colonials who have airs and graces."

"We're not colonials."

"No. And thank god for that!" says Steve.

"Anyhow, gin makes me depressed." Lou changes the subject.

"And we don't need any more of that!" he replies, and starts to laugh again.

Lou grins and giggles.

"At least you've got a good sense of humor," Steve says.

"What do you mean, at least?"

Oh god, he thinks, suddenly on rocky ground again.

Over drinks, as Steve chats to her father, he notices Lou sitting on the edge of the veranda and hopes he didn't hit a nerve too hard earlier. Lou probably just needs time to herself, though Steve's guess is she gets plenty of that. Will is certainly not one for idle chatter, and his daughter seems to have inherited the trait. Lou does, however, have an excellent memory for conversations, which might prove incredibly handy. To a certain extent, Steve doesn't mind that she's so introspective. He's had to learn to lighten up a bit himself, so that side of her is no real mystery to him. Easing up on life is hard at first because you feel as if you're faking it, but after a while you actually do feel better for it.

Out on the edge of the savannah, the sun glows huge and orange on the horizon, as the last ice blocks melt in their glasses.

"So, how's business?" asks Will.

"Business is good. It's just running it in this damn place!" Steve answers, and they chuckle together.

Steve becomes so caught up in the discussion, he misses the rest of the sunset.

Out in the darkness beyond the reach of the veranda lights, Lou's dog wanders in the shadows and explores new smells. Zebu comes to life when it cools. Apparently alert to hidden danger, she sniffs out a world of scents. As Zebu wanders over to her mistress, Lou extends a hand to her. Steve likes how they interact, the way Lou wraps an arm around her big old dog, who stops for a moment and then returns to her rounds. As the dog passes him, Steve clicks his tongue at her and gets a quick tail-wag in return.

When Will leaves, Steve goes and sits with Lou.

"How's Zebu," he asks. "She doesn't look as if she's getting any younger."

"She's just fine, thanks, with many more years to go!"

He laughs. "OK, have it your way."

Steve sits on the stone steps next to her, and together they look out into the impenetrable night. He does not feel the need to say anything. As the moon moves out from behind a cloud and casts its glow across the

waterhole, Steve takes Lou's hand in his. Far below them, an impala steps
out into the moonlight, less cautious than it should be. He wonders what it
is that makes that one a little bolder than the rest of its herd.

Sixty-Four

Let's go explore outside the park," Steve says the following morning.

"There's not a whole lot to see," says Lou. Only yesterday, she'd complained to him about the endless snares set by villagers for bushmeat. She's not excited at the prospect, but is happy to go along, if only to turn his mindset around. He's still a bit grumpy today, and it might cheer him up to have his own way.

Lou answers Steve's many questions about the nearby villages, until he insists that they stop and explore a maize plantation. Now on foot and surrounded by the swaying rows, Lou is reminded of the trees that once grew here. The previously verdant patch of forest, with its noisy birds and secretive antelopes, was a favorite childhood haunt.

The villagers felled the trees for firewood, and their repeat maize crops have almost depleted this soil. Today, in stark contrast to the previously cool undergrowth, a hot breeze rustles through the dry leaves and dangling cobs. Lou curbs her urge to reach up and pluck a heavy, ripe cob from its protective cocoon, aware that a farmer would sell her one for almost nothing.

She finds it hard not to reminisce. "At boarding school, some of us used to break bounds and cross through the maize fields on our way to the plains," Lou says.

"You had a different sort of childhood to most!" Steve replies.

For a short while, Lou became best friend with two sisters who moved into her dormitory. Their school sat on a high ridge, and, on weekends, the three of them ran wild through the savannah below.

"We were a bit unruly when I think about it," Lou admits. "An escape from the landscaped grounds broke the monotony. To escape, we had to shimmy down the sides of an eroded gully, behind a patch of prickly pear trees."

Strangely, the schoolmistresses never caught them out. How they managed not to get caught, Lou has no idea. With the arrival of the sisters at the school, previously dull weekends suddenly gained a whole new purpose.

At the start of one memorably miserable term, Lou arrived to find the sisters had unexpectedly left Kenya with their parents. No one knew where they'd gone, and she never heard from them again. Without any way to track them down, Lou badly missed their company.

These days, Lou has little reason to venture between the corridors of maize. Often as she drives past, there's a scent of sweet ripe corn and glimpses of ramshackle houses set back among the crop. At the mercy of the sun's heat, the villagers eke out existences in their corrugated iron houses. Absently, Lou wonders how such a life would be.

"Watch for snakes!" she cautions Steve. "Vibrations from our footsteps should scare them away, but keep an eye out anyhow." Lou finds it weird to be in these surroundings with a mature mindset. In her younger days, she worried less about such threats.

Lou is so distracted by her thoughts, she trips into Steve when he stops without warning. He catches and briefly holds her, then laughs at her surprise. His mood has improved, and he kisses her, but she's hot from the walk and feels self-conscious. He kisses her again, and slides his arms under her shirt, pulling her against him. But as she relaxes into him, he suddenly lets her go and strides abruptly away, only to double back along the next row.

"Come on, let's get a move on," he calls back over his shoulder.

The plantation opens into a clearing, where a rough shelter sits alongside the trickle of a silty stream. Lou's instinct tells her to duck back into the crops. They're trespassers, and she feels exposed and guilty. But the gray-haired man resting against a bench outside seems not to mind. They stand, unsure what to do, as his face creases into a smile.

"Jambo!" he calls and waves them over. Neither angry nor indignant, the man seems mostly amused by their incursion into his peaceful territory. Lou's hesitancy evaporates.

Steve apologizes in Swahili and pretends they're lost. His fluency surprises Lou. It's not a hard language to learn, but he already sounds like a local. This reminder of his many abilities makes her think she should adjust and pay more attention to his opinions about life in general.

Recent events have changed some of her perspectives, and she's had to reassess some hard-held opinions. She understands that part of the solution to habitat loss is to educate people, like this man, to properly care for it. Perhaps then, what remains of the natural world might have a chance. Others will make their own judgments in different ways, from different headspaces, their opinions often at odds. But, if the planet is to survive man's dark side, those who understand and care about it must work together.

Steve and his new friend burst into boisterous laughter, but Lou has missed their joke.

"Once I was asleep," says the man. "A huge cobra came right past and woke me up!" He grins, and his gnarled hands demonstrate the actions required to dispatch such invaders with a swift cut from his panga. He proudly points out the shining implement hung casually on a hook right beside Lou.

"You keep it very sharp!" Steve whistles his admiration.

Such ever-present danger makes Lou grateful that Steve agreed to accompany her to the border country tomorrow.

Her supervisor requested a preliminary survey of elephant movement into Kenya from Uganda.

"What about the civil war after that crazy dictator's departure?" Lou asked, feeling queasy.

"I'm not suggesting you cross into Uganda!" he replied.

"Oh, that's alright then." Lou agreed with a touch of sarcasm that he failed to notice. She really didn't think it was completely alright. Rumors of murders came regularly from the Ugandan side. At one stage, Uganda's Asians were evicted, their permitted suitcase of packed valuables stolen at the airport as they left. Their syphilis-afflicted president headed a system of injustice that meant anyone out of favor could disappear.

As Lou listened to her supervisor's brief, her heart sank. He confirmed how severely the Ugandan wildlife has suffered under lawless regimes. Unregulated officers in army trucks used Uganda's parks for killing sprees. Unlucky wildlife anywhere within range was shot at random, often with machine guns, their deaths satisfying man's uniquely murderous streak.

"We need to assess the impact on local people when elephants cross boundaries," her supervisor instructed. "I know it's a bit off on a tangent, but you're the best person for this job."

"Are you sure?" she replied, hoping for a reprieve.

"Yes, I'm sure. Poaching is rife over there as well. The elephants that have survived attacks are frightened, split from family groups, and unfamiliar with the new territory. Their behavior may be similar to Masaranga's herds."

"OK." She'd sighed, not disguising her trepidation.

She knows how, when chased out of natural habitat, traumatized elephants create strife. With nowhere to forage, they may raid crops. When bulls at the top of the hierarchy are poached, younger males may become troublesome from lack of discipline. Clashes between elephants and villagers often end with elephants injured and dying slowly, and trampled crops make local people unsympathetic. The idea of involvement with such conflict dismays Lou.

"I don't suppose you know a friendly journalist," Lou had asked her supervisor. It was her initial reason for calling him, before he'd surprised her with his request. "We need to expose government involvement in ivory poaching."

"Possibly. In fact, yes! Leave it with me and we'll talk on your return."

As a final encouragement, he said, "An overview of a human/wildlife conflict situation would look good on your CV."

🐘 🐘 🐘

Just before daybreak, they leave for the border, the Land Rover loaded with camping gear and spare fuel. Lou wouldn't have agreed to this without Steve to accompany her. While he drives, Lou skims notes from her supervisor and navigates. It's wild country up ahead, and she hopes not to meet too many disenchanted people.

The intense heat persists. By midday, they cross only dry riverbeds. Villages shrink to sporadic clusters of shacks hunkered down in the open country. Lou swigs warm water to cure a dehydration headache. They've not seen a single elephant, or any other wildlife for that matter. She ruminates about the situation across the border.

"Good spot to camp?" Steve interrupts her thoughts and slows the Land Rover. Lou grins to see where he's headed—a solitary old baobab with a broad shadow, though its root-shaped branches are bare of leaves. The only obvious campsite for miles is under the gnarly arthritic limbs. There's no other shade as far as the flat, distant horizon. No water anywhere, but at least no thirsty animals either.

"Looks like that's our spot," she agrees ruefully.

"We'll have it all to ourselves!" Steve jokes, not doubting his prediction for a moment.

Under the aged baobab tree, Lou organizes the cooking area while Steve hammers tent pegs into the hard ground, making enough noise to frighten anything away. Not that there's much to scare considering the rocky, desolate surroundings. There's something special about the campsite, as if the baobab once stood sentry over a different landscape, and beneath the grooves and bark, its arched limbs store memories of better times.

The salty smell of simmering stew reminds Lou that she's hungry.

"Interesting idea of a good time," says Steve as they eat. He's developed the habit of teasing her along these lines.

"Give me a break!" she replies.

Exhausted, they crawl into their sleeping bags early, their bellies full. They snuggle together against the surprisingly cold night air.

In her dream, Lou is at Sara's place with her brother and a dog fitting itself to death. This time it's been poisoned, and the guards who are supposed to protect them mutate into bandits. Lou wakes in a lather of sweat to the sound of material tearing as the front of their tent is ripped open.

Outside, angry male voices shout commands in an unfamiliar language. For a moment, it seems still part of Lou's nightmare. But a flash of torchlight enters their tent, and the alarmed expression on Steve's face tells Lou otherwise. She squints into the bright light and cold fingers of dread clench around her chest. A gun muzzle appears through the torn tent flap, inches from her face, the stranger behind it invisible in the dark.

Steve's hand is on her arm, holding her steady. Trapped in the tent, half-blinded, she recoils from the gun and remembers her rifle, stupidly left in the Land Rover.

"Out! You come out!" the stranger barks the first words she understands.

"OK, yes," Steve shouts back, his voice tense.

He motions Lou to stay put and crawls toward the tent flap. Hands as dark as night reach in and haul him away from her. A crazy moment passes as her heart races madly, and Lou considers an escape out the back of the tent. Then rough hands clamp like vices onto her arms and hoist her out of the tent into the darkness. She suppresses a scream of terror.

Several men surround them.

"Get down!" shouts the man who grabbed her. He shoves her forward and forces her to her knees. Then the rough ground scrapes against her belly as she's pushed flat, next to where Steve lies with a gun against his head. Lou goes without a fight, aware it would aggravate the situation. Any hint of resistance would only make these men more violent.

Facedown on the hard ground, with a massive boot against her shoulder, Lou is sure she will be raped or murdered or both. She wants to run as fast and far away as adrenaline will carry her, but even if she could move, there's nowhere to go. Immobilized, she lies shaking, while the men argue among themselves in their own language.

"Why are you here?" After the foreign dialect, the English words sound out of place. The heavyset man looms over her, his eyes bloodshot in the torchlight as he leans closer. A gun muzzle remains pointed at Steve's head. Lou swallows and gathers up the courage to speak, but Steve answers first, his voice strained, but strangely calm.

"We are from Nairobi University. My wife is Dr. Louise Hopkins. The government sent us."

The man swings the gun muzzle over. He holds it by her head as if considering whether to shoot her first.

"My father is the Chief Boss at Masaranga Park. He's an important man. Everybody knows him."

"Then why have you come to Uganda?" the thug replies.

"We're not in Uganda!" Steve sounds indignant and outraged now. He rolls onto his side to face the man.

Lou is relieved they're having a discussion and have not yet been beaten up, or worse.

"Yes! You are here in Uganda!" the man yells suddenly. The gun muzzle swings back to Steve. Another man laughs, the sound insane in Lou's ears. A different pair of boots moves up close to her face, and she feels something hard against her back.

"Why are you in Uganda?" the first man demands.

"We are doctors studying the elephants. We are Kenyan. We are in Kenya!" Steve sounds assertive now.

Lou feels a rush of gratitude toward him for keeping so calm. He's doing better than her. She tries to control her trembling body. She wants to believe the situation is now less dangerous. At least there's doubt in the minds of these brutes. The interrogator's voice contains less of that self-assured aggression, as if he's lost confidence.

"Kenya is that way!" says the thug, and he steps back from Steve. Blessedly, the gun muzzle swings away to an invisible point off in the darkness. As her eyes adjust to the dark, Lou sees the others behind the bully, men dependent on his lead.

"We go back. We leave now," Lou suggests and pushes off the ground to face the leader. The boot doesn't shove her back down, though his gun angles back her way. With all her strength of will, she holds steady and avoids throwing herself flat to the ground again. Instead, she looks from one man to another. Now that the outlines of their faces have emerged from the black night, they seem marginally less terrible, although their dark eyes size her up dispassionately. Icy cold inside, she knows it would be a mistake to show weakness now.

They can't be allowed to push her and Steve around any longer. Lou senses the leader still measuring them up, the momentum of his aggression lost. She's sure he'd happily kill them if he could get away with it. But perhaps now he judges the repercussions too severe. These men wear uniforms and aren't complete outlaws; otherwise, this discussion would never have taken place.

"We are Uganda Army," their leader answers the question in her head. "And you are on the Uganda side of the border. Where are your passports?"

"Our passports are not with us because we don't intend to cross the border. All we have is some money. Perhaps we can pay you a fine?"

Are they after Ugandan fugitives? Why else would they be out here?

"We will go back!" Lou again tries to reason with him. "You can show us the way after we pay the fine."

"Yes, you will pay a fine, and then you can drive back that way. You will leave all this here." He indicates their camp with a flick of his head, as if angry that he has to let them go.

As he steps toward where the other men wait, Lou gets to her feet, aware of blood on her clothes. She crosses her arms protectively across her chest and walks slowly, so as to not appear frightened, away from them toward the Land Rover. Relieved slightly to be hidden from sight at last, Lou slides into the passenger seat while Steve negotiates the bribe. The kickback and the camping gear seem a small price for escape. She waits in the dark and tries to calm herself, taking big slow gulps of air.

Steve's face is white when he returns and wastes no time putting the vehicle in gear. As they drive away, a gun blasts off behind, and a bullet clips the roof of their vehicle. *Please, not a tire next time*, pleads Lou silently. A half-mile later, she breathes a sigh of relief, aware that only the threat of consequences curbed the men enough to grant them freedom. Otherwise, she shudders at the thought of how much worse things would have got.

Steve drives on through the night. It's a relief when dawn throws the first golden hues over the desert. Almost back at the last town before the border country, they stop by the roadside to brew coffee.

"Perhaps we could try and do some sort of survey further along the border," says Lou.

"You've got to be joking!"

Faced by Steve's incredulous expression, Lou keeps quiet.

"You're not!" he continues. "You must be out of your mind."

"Perhaps it's a dumb idea," she agrees. "We were just unlucky enough to have been in the wrong place at the wrong time."

"Don't you get it?" Steve retorts. "This whole bloody continent is a place where it's easy to be in the wrong place at the wrong time. What about what happened in Lamu?"

There's truth there too. Silently, Lou admits it. They sit by the Land Rover and sip coffee. The day begins to heat up. What will happen to her father, her brother, Peter, Grace, and Masaranga?

"OK, let's go home," she agrees.

"Good idea!" Steve replies angrily.

It's a long trip after a sleep-deprived night, while he complains about the corruption and about how hard it is to exist out here, and of unexpected dangers such as those they've just endured. Somewhere in the midst of his tirade, Steve reminds her there are safer places to live.

"Where?" she asks.

"Why not come back to England with me? We'd do alright there for a while," Steve replies.

Although he's hinted at it before, this is the first time he's asked her outright. She hopes it will be a while before he packs up shop and forces her into a decision.

Sixty-Five

In an uncharacteristic display of anger, Lou's father slams down the phone and smashes his fist against the wall. The body dumped at Lake Naivasha has been identified as their poacher, the man she shot. It's terrible news as there were to be further hearings and his evidence might have implicated other syndicate members. For some reason, he was released and has now been killed—probably to protect the people behind him. With the damage from her own bullet rendered insignificant, her reaction to his death swings wildly as the implications gel in her mind. Lou searches for a rational response, while her father paces the office like a caged animal. It's true that with this murder, they've lost potentially valuable information.

"Paul is still locked up. And he's as good as confessed," Lou says, to calm her father. His outward display of anger disturbs her almost as much as the news.

"This gives the hidden players time to cover their tracks!" he replies.

Lou imagines people further up the black-market chain slithering sideways as they attempt to distance themselves from past interactions with the murdered man.

"If they hadn't killed him, he'd be back slaughtering elephants the moment they released him!" Lou says, eager to point out the upside.

"You don't know that for sure. And there are plenty more similar men where he came from."

Lou doubts if there would be many men quite so capable of ingratiating themselves within the wealthier circles as this man did. Many ivory poachers remain at the bottom of a long chain of corruption and receive a relatively small share of the proceeds.

According to the authorities, the prisoner had permission to visit his family, an unusual privilege that probably involved higher dispensation. Initially, his disappearance was interpreted as an attempt to jump bail. However, instead of escaping justice, he's been murdered, a far harsher punishment.

"If they investigate who facilitated his release, it might help," says Lou. Surely the photo, now in her father's possession, should help lead authorities to whoever engineered his death. Along with Paul's evidence, Lou hopes this shouldn't be so hard. Only people with a lot at stake would risk such a boldfaced crime, Fred Lonnegan and Sam being the likely candidates. Keen to sink evidence, they'd offer their poacher protection or an escape route while planning his timely death.

At least her off-track hunch about Joshua was merely her overwrought imagination. Though she's tortured herself unnecessarily, Lou now understands why she felt connected to the Naivasha murder. Along with the photo, the accidental discovery of the well-hidden body could make the syndicate easier to track. As connections to his release are followed, others will be implicated, however fast they run for cover. The poacher's murder may be as much a win as a loss.

Already Lou has contacted a couple of journalists who should be sympathetic, suggestions from both Sara and her supervisor. If they are brave enough to expose the political situation, it would be a win in the war for the wildlife. Those who hide need to be eased out from their comfortable mansions. Like a spider's web, the network of deceit must be unraveled from the poachers on the ground to the driving currency at the far edges, the consumers of ivory, who are equally guilty and the reason the carnage exists. These unworthy aspects of human nature combine to deliver the nightmare. Though all involved will deny their part and escape down bolt holes of justification. When journalists uproot the invisible perpetrators hidden higher up the chain, the criminals won't have refuge from accusatory fingers. If that happens, then syndicates will find it hard to reemerge, employ new killers, and continue their ravages. At every level, journalists can help make the guilty responsible. Otherwise, those in the wrong will continue to excuse or justify their part in the immorality.

When Lou tries Joshua again, he takes a while to answer his phone and his voice sounds terribly cautious.

"Deal with your enemy from a distance," he warns her.

He advises her to tone it down. But how? She won't just shake her head in disbelief and walk away. It's merely a matter of getting this information into the right hands.

"They won't punish people enough to compensate for what they've done to the elephants!" she says.

"There's often not much justice in human laws!" replies Joshua.

"It's just that our elephant family units are so disrupted and damaged. They don't make more babies when they're too stressed," says Lou.

"Yes, I know. It takes a while for their herds to join and rebuild social structures. They are quite different from reptiles." Joshua's voice is gentle. "Perhaps that is why I stuck to snakes!"

Lou's unresolved frustration again tightens the knot around her heart. People, who are not indifferent to the wilderness need to be motivated to join forces. She will focus on this after they've put Fred and Sam away.

Despite a wall of issues that might obstruct progress, Lou won't let anxiety and fear sabotage her any longer. If she's determined and steady, any barrier can be pushed through. Her research will be aided by a healthy dose of activism. She refuses to watch in fear as the greedy continue to destroy. A few ideas have come to her recently, but with her insider's view only, and she needs to develop a comprehensive picture. The underbelly of human activity is something she must learn to navigate.

Peter is mentally stable. Already, Lou takes clues from how he survives adversity. She will follow his example and face each new morning with new hope, despite disasters.

One morning after a dead rhino day, Peter seemed his usual self.

"How come you're so cheerful today, Peter?" she asked, dismayed by his nonchalance when her own spirits were in shreds.

"I'm always like this, every morning. You know this!" he'd replied.

"You're not angry about the rhino?"

"Yes, I am angry, just as you are, but my anger will help me find the men responsible. It makes me strong!"

Lou grapples with how to learn to take the losses less personally. Each death is a loss almost as if it were her own dog killed. Each rhino is one of the last, with indefinable value. The slaughters seem to cut intrinsically right through to her core.

But she must leave her past unhelpful headspace far behind. Taking adverse events so personally fails to address the issue. Her depression won't rescue the elephants. Mentally stronger now, she'll make anger a productive force. Her resolve is to push past familiar territory and not waste time speculating on what's wrong with herself and everyone else. Smart people don't let knock-backs drag them down.

Nor will she detach completely. That also allows evil to continue. An effective fight needs emotional engagement without taking the losses personally. Then she will focus on one thing at a time and not imagine the broader problem insurmountable.

Peter's emotions don't eat him up. Earlier this morning, he was dead keen to help her trail four elephants they spotted moving south yesterday. But her father needed him for another errand. He headed off, cheerful and unfazed by the unexpected change of plan. She would do well to learn from his attitude.

Sixty-Six

Lou has use of the Chellis' Naivasha retreat again, and she plans to update her last species list though they've not asked. It's the least she can do. With any luck, she might sight a rare bird and encourage enthusiasts to book the place.

It's time out at last with Steve, a consolation for their hazardous drive to the Ugandan border. Lou feels almost guilty at having nothing to do but enjoy the breathtaking outlook from the pool. A crisp breeze carries the fragrance of flowering trees, and below her an arm of Lake Naivasha stretches toward newly green slopes. The dappled dawn light across the water's surface is particularly lovely, and its pale rays cast patterns along the reedy shores.

Like a well-heeled tourist in luxurious seclusion, Lou wanders the paths through the private grounds, her only concern when to eat breakfast or have a dip in the pool. It reminds her of how exclusive resorts shelter tourists from the country's underbelly, and how most tours deliver a disguised Kenya of select locations—a holiday shielded from reality, a detached experience. The truth would spoil things.

But the truth is occasionally best forgotten, and Lou banishes all thoughts about the body recently found on Naivasha's far slopes. The snorts of contented hippos divert her from her ruminations. Through binoculars, she spots their rounded backs as they wallow in the shallows below. Thick hides glisten in the morning light, and large implacable faces blast plumes of spray from upturned nostrils high into the air. Smaller similar outlines float alongside the five massive adults, and a couple of teenagers are close to the headland. On land, an adult male searches for food along the muddy bank, his bulky body nimbly carried by stumpy legs, his skin no doubt secreting its special sunburn protection.

Lou decides to let Steve sleep on. When she left him, he was sprawled under the fan, oblivious to the first light creeping into the room, and exhausted from his long drive down from the coast. She wants to show him the hippos, but they seem lazy and unlikely to move from view anytime soon. It's already warm, and Lou feels suddenly enthusiastic about everything. A wave of exhilaration spurs her on as she sprints down a path toward the pool, dives in and swims its length underwater in long smooth strokes. The cool water pulls through her hair and against her skin. It's all she could ask for after yesterday's long drive and too few hours of sleep.

Against a background of blue tiles, the sun's rays refract underwater into whirling yellow patterns that twist and curl around her. Lou surfaces at the shallow end, where tall palms shade her eyes, their shadows shifting with the breeze. She swims hard, completing several laps underwater, and emerges gasping for breath but energized. As a teenager, they came here often to spend time with the Chellis.

From one side of the pool, she's able to see part of the lake below, with its insidious endemics such as the bilharzia parasite, not to mention the larger scarier inhabitants. Yesterday, Steve mentioned the relative safety of English waterways.

"Yes, sure. But they're freezing cold and saturated with man-made pollutants!" she'd countered.

He laughed at her obstinacy.

In past times, when Lou visited, the indulgent Mrs. Chelli always hovered close. From her kitchen came vast helpings of pasta for everyone, including her two energetic sons. Right now, it's good not to be so smothered, though those generous doses were always welcome back then.

The Chelli boys attended the same boarding school as Lou. They seemed to like it better than she did. Lou pretty much hated it when first sent there after her mother's departure. Her dad's car broke down on the way, and she arrived late, which somehow made her a target for the kids in her dorm. For their first attack, they raided her half-empty trunk right in front of her and threw her few possessions around the dormitory. Maybe it was not so much the lateness, but just that they quickly spotted that she was weird, an odd one out. She sees that now.

It was a rush to get her ready for the start of term, and she arrived with only a fraction of the school's required list. Her father delivered the rest a week later. Lou returned from classes a few days later to find it piled on her bed. The way he'd dropped it off, without asking to see her, added to her sense of desertion.

However, the Chelli boys remained friends for years. Occasionally they'd accompany her on a boundary-breaking excursion through the plantations. Unfortunately, like many others, they left in a hurry for a new life in Italy long ago. But their grandparents refused to leave the country where they'd spent their whole lives. They stayed to manage the family ranch further along the Rift Valley. Until yesterday, when Lou picked up the keys, it had been a while since Lou actually saw them.

"The place is always empty!" lamented Mrs. Chelli. "We're too old to drive up there."

Her father reckons that the Chellis' days are numbered as the government has been reclaiming estates owned by Western farmers. He predicts that, as expelled landowners, they will receive minimal compensation. After they're forced to emigrate, their properties will be given away within the old-boy network, or split into maize plots for the Kikuyus.

A deep breath and Lou sinks back into the water. It swallows her up and closes quietly overhead. Her legs tucked tight under her chest, she pushes off the hard edge, and glides through the water again, her eyes open, the blue and white blurry lines of the tiles reflective all around her.

Once, she finished a lap like this one and surfaced face-to-face with a half-grown cheetah cub, the boys' new pet. It was found after the mother died in a poacher's trap on their ranch. The intense yellow eyes and whiskered face briefly frightened Lou. For a comical moment, both she and the cub started back. Then Lou giggled, and the cat nervously stepped forward and cautiously sniffed her face, curiosity overriding fear.

The playful furball that snuggled with the boys quickly grew into a gangling half-grown wildcat, its claws and teeth capable of severe damage. Before Lou knew better, she'd laugh at the sight of the cheetah chasing a football swung by the boys in circles on the end of a rope. Inevitably, the cheetah caught the ball and refused to give it up, which ended the game.

They learned this was the wrong way to raise a wild cat. Before long, the boys would immediately evacuate the sofa when the cheetah padded into the room, as she was protective of her favorite sleeping spot. The cheetah was subsequently released back at the ranch and fed for a few weeks near the homestead until she stopped visiting. Poachers probably killed her long ago—a half-tame cat with a gorgeous coat wouldn't survive the hungry eyes of certain villagers.

The idea that beautiful creature probably met a similar fate to its mother saddens Lou, though all that's history now, just another childhood memory safely sunk below the surface. Her reminiscences settle, and Lou climbs out of the water. Wrapped in a sarong, she follows a path to another outlook. Across the lake, flocks of birds have congregated along the shallow edges and reed beds. In cleaner water adjacent to a low cliff, more hippos bask, their legs visible below the water.

Now, as the heat begins to rise off the lake, the morning chorus ends. In its absence, a calming silence runs into Lou and expands to fill the space inside her, dissolving boundaries. A red-and-white fish eagle hangs briefly in the cloudless sky and then glides above where she stands, suspended in time. She senses how it would be to fly close to the lake's still surface and then soar high above the landscape like this bird of prey, whose high-pitched call suddenly breaks the silent emptiness, and drops her back to reality.

Then warm fingers cover her eyes, and she's being pulled backward. She giggles and tries to wriggle away from Steve, but his hands are around her waist, holding her tight, so she can't turn to look at him. He sounds groggy from sleep.

"You deserted me!" he complains, holding her firmly against him.

"Only for a swim! You were sleeping."

"So, you vanished. I can't let you escape that easily!"

"I'd never try to escape you!"

"You sure?"

"Of course."

"Come back to England with me then."

"Why?" she asks. "What do you want from me?"

"Everything, for god's sake. I love you! Don't you feel the same way?"

"Yes," she replies, tongue-tied, strangely unable to surrender to the truth and say the words back to him. She does love him, but it wouldn't ring true if she said the words right now after he's asked outright.

Instead, she leans her head back slightly and twists her face sideways towards his. His fingers move across her breasts, along her neck, then his lips are on hers, and she turns within his loosened grip. She feels deliciously giddy but frightened at what he's asking her to give up and leave. What about her life here in Kenya and the elephants? They need her help more. As she kisses him, she has no answer.

A loud snort sounds from the lake below. One of the hippos stirs, sending circles of ripples across the calm surface.

"He's disgusted!" Steve laughs, and his eyes leave hers to look out across the lake.

"Why do you think that?" she asks.

"Because you didn't properly answer me!"

He catches her as she tries to wriggle free again, still laughing a little, then says, "Please come!"

"I'm not sure. I've still got so much to do, and I hate to leave Dad on his own."

"He'll survive. He did when you were younger, didn't he? He's not made of china, you know. Neither is your brother!"

"What's he got to do with this?"

"Nothing and everything. I bumped into David in Nairobi, and we had a chat."

"What about?"

"Is this the inquisition or something! He's had a bit of a mental turnaround."

"About what?"

"Look, just rest assured, both David and your father are tough men. They need you less than you need them."

"What about my studies?" Lou continues her opposition, though she's partly distracted by conjectures about her brother.

"Haven't you got all the data you need? Haven't you done all the fieldwork?"

"More or less."

"Then bring it with you. You can finish the write up anywhere."

"I'll think about it." She hears the logic in what he wants.

"There's not much time left to think," he continues. "I leave in a month. My visas up and no amount of bribery will extend it this time."

A month. That's not long! Lou is sure he's not mentioned this timeframe before. She neither wants him to go nor does she want to leave. Balanced on an imaginary fence, she envisages the consequences of a jump either side.

"You okay?" he asks.

"Yes. Well, no. I don't know!"

She tries to laugh, to sound less heavy-hearted than she suddenly feels.

Steve lets go of her and steps a few paces away. Lou keeps her eyes focused out on the vista. The ground under her feet has warmed.

"I'll get breakfast. Aren't you starving?" Lou says. It's an excuse to escape and gather her thoughts. "What will you have?" she calls back over her shoulder.

"Whatever you want will do."

He sighs noisily, and when she looks back, his eyes are distant and focused on the slopes across the lake. Lou sees waterbirds gathering out there on the far bank, their black-and-white silhouettes contrasting proudly with the green vegetation.

For days, Lou considers the situation. Poaching has decreased with the syndicate busy on its defense case. But not for one moment does Lou imagine them permanently discouraged. The dark side of human nature shifts and reforms. Her resolution to be less attached to the elephants is a challenge. Perhaps a future when all is well, and everything safe, does not exist, and she must live with that reality. Self-focused man is slow to turn his gaze outward.

"Come home with me," Steve asks again, ten days before he leaves. "You'd find new ways to do the same job, and be safer."

"You think I'm still in danger?"

"Of course. You deliberately put yourself there!"

She frowns, a denial on her lips, but he'll say she's pigheaded if she answers anything but yes.

"Look what happened up on the border. And at Lamu before that!" he reminds her.

Perhaps he's right. But his exasperation gets Lou's back up. Can what she and Steve have together survive such massive changes of circumstance?

"Let's face it," he continues, "your father can't stay on forever. It's no longer his world."

Tears run down her face now. If only Steve could stay a few more months. How will she develop a view of life as full of possibility as so many others do? Without Steve's influence, she'll probably remain until circumstances force her out. That's what her father will do.

But it's time to extend her boundaries and become better educated in conservation, then other avenues will open. She'll return better equipped.

"OK!" she finally replies into the silence that stretches between them.

"OK, what?"

"OK, I'll think about it."

Lou can't help but giggle at the look of relief and surprise across his face.

Sixty-Seven

Steve can't believe they're unlucky enough to be confronted by this on the final stretch of the Nairobi road. Already stressed about leaving Lou here, he now has to deal with a roadblock that was hidden by heat-haze until the last moment. Up ahead, ominously spiked boards stretch across the bitumen. Steve takes a deep breath and glances at Lou, who rolls her eyes in dismay. She's no stranger to this either.

Two passenger-packed cars have been pulled up on the dusty verge behind a heavyset policeman, who strides out onto the road, confident in his power.

"Christ! We'll be here forever unless we cough up a bribe," Steve complains as he hits the brakes. The inevitable interrogation will be nerve-wracking, whether in breach of traffic laws or not. It's one reason why he hates Nairobi, though Mombasa is only slightly less frustrating. Rarely is Steve waved straight through and able to sigh with relief, and his heart sinks as the policeman indicates for him to pull over.

"No way I'm giving them money. I'm sick of the bullies!" Steve hopes this won't take too long, and he wipes perspiration from his forehead as they slow to a halt.

"Don't get cranky. It makes them worse." Lou eases binoculars and camera out of sight. "We need to reach the airport on time."

The boredom leaves the officer's face as he sizes them up. Most likely, he's deduced they're wealthy tourists carrying foreign cash. He peers in at Steve, and then boldly runs his eyes over Lou. As she forces a smile, Steve suppresses an urge to punch the man.

"Jambo. Habari?" *Hello. How are you?* The officer's voice seems innocuous, but his smile is cold as he weighs up what the situation is worth.

Steve watches Lou meet his eyes squarely, her probable discomfort well hidden. "Visuri sana," she replies, politely.

"Good afternoon," says Steve, forcing the man to address him.

Is the worst-case scenario merely to pay a bribe? The man would consider it a legitimate supplement to his meager salary. But Steve is rattled by the deliberate way he checked Lou over.

"Your driving license, please."

Unhurriedly, Steve passes it over. The man examines it upside down.

Lou has averted her gaze. Smart girl. It's best not to incense the officer in any way, particularly not by being amused. These policemen tend to have a nasty side.

Across the road, another uniformed man stops an overloaded taxi. He questions the uneasy passengers until the driver passes him a folded note. It's quickly slipped into an inside pocket, and the vehicle is immediately waved on.

"Where are you going?" The interrogation begins.

"To meet a government minister," says Lou. Steve is surprised at her answer, but she's on the right track. The pressure might come off if they're deemed residents who know the right people.

"Is this your car?" the man asks Steve as if she'd not spoken.

"It belongs to a friend." Steve sticks to the truth. The policeman's confidence seems to drop a notch as if now less hopeful of easy pickings. He checks the number plates, then moves over to Lou's side and squints at the registration stickers on the windscreen. At least they are the right way up for him to pretend to read.

"Your registration has expired."

He leans against Lou's window. Even from Steve's side, the sweat smell wafts in. Steve notices dark stains on the underarms of the man's khaki and how pockmarked his face is. He must be uncomfortable in that heavy uniform.

"The registration is OK, my friend. The owner is meticulous," Steve replies. The man has got to be bluffing.

Lou opens the door, which forces the man to step back. Immediately Steve does the same. He doesn't want her any closer to that man than necessary. They examine the circular sticker together. It's actually hard to decipher and different from his old Mombasa one. *Is it even a registration sticker?* Suddenly unsure if the vehicle is legal, Steve's anxiety moves up a notch. Offering a bribe for an imaginary infringement is entirely different from being guilty of a real offense. Surely his mate wouldn't be so careless.

"It's up to date, and we can't miss our appointment," he says. "The minister hates to be kept waiting!"

With sunlight directly in Steve's eyes and the registration questionable, the option of paying baksheesh suddenly seems acceptable.

"Bwana. You must pay a fine. Then you may return the car to your friend."

But Steve stiffens at the officer's tone, slippery and conciliatory at the same time. He mustn't lose his temper and inflame the situation. *What's the worst that can happen?* He remembers a dank, dingy jail he visited a few months ago. His incarcerated friend looked emaciated. He'd been slow to recognize a roadblock one night. At the last moment, he swerved to avoid the spikes, and, in the dark, accidentally hit a policeman.

The other officer crosses the bitumen toward them. A vehicle pulls out behind him, relief on the faces inside. A couple of cars flash by unstopped, belching black fumes in their wake. Perhaps a bribe would be a small price to get this over with. Steve indicates for Lou to get back in and notices her wince when the seat covers burn her legs. It's a pity she's wearing shorts, especially as the policeman is so leery. Steve wishes Lou hadn't got out in the first place.

"How many shillings would fix the problem?" he asks.

The request is exorbitant, many times the usual and out of the question. Between them, they'd not rustle up a quarter of it. The outrageous sum launches Lou back into the argument. This time she drops Sara's name as a well-known Nairobi figure. Time slips by. Steve stews silently as he listens to them. More cars pass by, unimpeded. The police aren't used to such a fight. To pay baksheesh is usual, but not at today's price. Their dispute continues. Steve notices their antagonist's hair sweat-slicked against his scalp at the same moment the man becomes belligerent.

"You must come to the police station," says the officer.

It's possible he might miss his flight. And these men could plant something on them. Steve envisages the plane, soaring to freedom while they wait inside a dingy office. Lou seems almost ready to somehow pay the bribe.

Steve abruptly flings his door open, forcing the officer to back off. Despite Lou's alarmed expression, he jumps out as if he might punch the man. Instead, he throws open the rear doors.

"OK. Get in. We'll sort this out with your boss!" he indicates the back seats with a decisive gesture. "Let's go."

It's a calculated risk. The station is the last place they need to go, but Steve's pretty sure it's not what this officer really wants either.

In the ensuing silence, Steve wonders why they didn't slip the man a smaller bribe straight up. Finally, the officer steps nervously back from the open door, a forced smile on his face. He seems to have come to his senses.

"No, Bwana. No need. You get back in the car."

Steve slams the doors shut. There's a worried look on Lou's face, and Steve has a feeling they're not off the hook yet. The officer instructs him to move the car across the road and to park on the other side. So that's his game.

The clutch clunks as Steve pulls the vehicle out. Lou coughs. Her throat sounds dry from the argument. He drives straight ahead towards an intersection.

"What are you doing? Park on the other side," pleads Lou. "They'll shoot us or something. We can't just drive away!"

She looks ready to duck when the shots start. Perhaps her mind is still illogical after that time on the Uganda border. Steve continues slowly ahead. He crosses the intersection, continues for a hundred meters, and then does a U-turn, returning to a point opposite where they were. A large truck roars past in a gust of diesel fumes.

"It would be our first offense if I'd U-turned this close to the intersection," he says.

When Steve parks as requested, the men seem nonplussed. Their eyes are red from dust and fumes as they talk between themselves in Swahili.

"Bwana Steve, please go collect the papers from your friend for us to check."

It's the man's way of saving face, even as he admits defeat.

"Yes, of course, his house is not so far away." Steve keeps all emotion out of his voice. He offers his hand through the window, and the man shakes it. They agree he's off to get the vehicle's paperwork. The officer seems crushed.

"Try to never let those guys get away with anything," Steve mutters under his breath as they pull out. There's no reason to return; it's not expected that they will. He takes a different route into town. No way will he drive past these guys again.

"Some aspects of this place just suck!" he grumbles. They're out of time, and he needs to hurry.

When Steve hugs Lou at the departure gate, she holds on to him after he lets her go. He's surprised how clingy she is, especially considering it was her who insisted he go home alone. At least it appears she's going to miss him. There's still hope she might come and apply her talents in a place where he can better look after her.

"I wish you were coming. You know it's not safe here anymore." Steve is suddenly anxious again. "I'm serious. Things are changing fast."

He doesn't want to add to her insecurity, but it's hard to disguise his concern.

Steve remembers the man's eyes running over her, and the jerk in Lamu who had a go at her. Had they not wasted their time at the roadblock, he was going to tell her about the official visit he's organized for the pervert. That will have to wait now. She'll be pleased that he's done his bit against the ivory trade.

"I need to get this thesis done—get my bit of paper," she says.

"You could transfer it to a UK university."

"We've been through this before. It won't work. Anyhow, Dad needs me."

"He's got plenty of help. At times you'd be more of a liability."

Lou drops her face, so Steve can't see her expression. Obviously, the truth in his words hurts, but she must understand it's still a man's world out here.

"Please think hard about it. Remember, you agreed!" he says, dejected rather than angry now their time is up.

"OK," she says.

"Here's so you don't forget me too quickly." Steve hands her the tiny wrapped package from his pocket.

"Of course I won't forget you!" she replies.

Steve walks slowly away towards the customs check post. When, at the last moment, he turns back, Lou looks about to cry. He shrugs his shoulders and waves. After their holdup, it's too late to go back and say anything more. Seconds later, he's through and has to hurry to the departure terminal.

Steve planned to tell Lou, over a beer at the airport, how her ill-advised interaction with the jerk in Lamu was not a waste of time, as he'd judged. It would have been a great farewell to see her happy at a small amount of justice being played out. Though angry at the risk she took, he begrudgingly admits she's exposed a black-market ivory dealer. A day ago, the police marched the man away in handcuffs. Steve only regrets he won't be around to follow the story through. He shouldn't have held out for the right time to tell Lou. A long-distance call from home won't have quite the same impact. He wanted to see her expression when she heard the news. There's a back-up plan if the bastard buys his way out, and Steve is sure that Lou's new journalist friends would love to follow up on such a story. There's more than one way to skin a cat—or a black-market racketeer.

On the flight home, part of his mind is on the underwater research project ahead. If Lou were with him, Steve wouldn't mind going home too much. The work will be interesting and well paid, even if it's a far cry from the sunny coral sea diving he's become used to these last couple of years. But right from the start, he knew the limitations of setting up shop in a foreign place. What he'd not bargained on was falling for someone like Lou. There's no end to what she'll do to save what's important to her, and he's worried. Not that for one moment he regrets meeting someone so passionate and single minded about something that matters. He just needs to organize a suitably tempting escape that doesn't take her away from her calling.

Steve wonders when she'll open her present. Inside is a necklace of silver elephants, trunk to tail the whole way around. His note says, "To match your lovely eyes. Please remember me when you wear it."

Sixty-Eight

The deluge that followed her father home a month ago was a false start to the wet season—a promise the drought won't last forever. Since then, nothing until now. On Lou's first night home after her return from Nairobi, the wet arrives with a sudden vengeance, and the sound of rain on her roof permeates through layers of her sleep, the first drops so spaced out she doubts them.

But the drops coalesce into a downpour. Wide awake now, Lou throws her bedspread aside and rushes to the window. As she leans out and stretches her hands into the suddenly cool night, streams of rainwater run down her arms and off her fingertips down toward the already sodden ground. She shivers with anticipation and the promise of change. If this continues, the landscape will quickly regenerate.

By morning, the dry earth has absorbed the stormwater, the moisture soaked into its infinitesimal structures. At dawn, the sun begins to reclaim the dampness, its blue intensifying, making last night's downpour too ephemeral to change anything.

But the blue darkens to a stormy gray. The smell of the moisture-laden air and the dark hues of the washed sky become as real as the drought ever was.

Four thunderstorms in as many days evaporate all doubt. Around Masaranga, new vegetation pushes through the cracked earth. Staff morale improves. Lou hears laughter as she does her errands.

Pale green shoots emerge across expanses of red dirt. Waterholes expand. Individual blades of new grass become seas of green. Antelopes are enticed out onto the plains. Zebras mingle with gazelles, their newly washed markings delineated and perfect. Herds of wildebeests congregate and graze hungrily. Nature makes up for lost time.

In bursts of sunlight between downpours, Lou wanders about in open sandals. Mud squelches between her toes as she crosses the horse paddock. She doesn't mind. The rinsed buildings seem newly painted. On high boughs and low shrubs, emerald leaves unfold against dark old vegetation. Between storms, plants reach towards the sunlight. Lou remembers how, only recently, life shrank beneath that same sun.

Gone is the stagnant world where life just clung on. Options expand. Amazed by the speed of change when one factor alters, Lou plans camping trips in the far reaches of the park, where rivers and waterholes overflow. Her fieldwork is done, and it's no longer necessary to go, but she's impatient for any excuse.

Intermittent rain continues, the sky heavy with clouds. Desert transforms into green plains dotted by red mud-holes and shady acacias. Water surges along previously empty riverbeds, and wallows are flushed clean. Strips of vegetation thicken along watercourses, and leaves multiply into every sunlit space.

Nature's turnaround invigorates them all. When Lou considers how they busted the poaching syndicate, a wave of optimism washes away her cynicism. Recent events have armed her to fight. She feels called to action. It's time to go to learn more and return fortified with new skills. Her role as a mere drop in a massive ocean no longer overwhelms her. Her mission is to do her bit. Evidently, she must go elsewhere to develop her strengths. Being closer to Steve is what she wants, but is not the reason for her decision.

The wet makes it harder for the poachers. Their tracks become easier to find, their access into the park muddied up. Pressure on Masaranga has already eased massively as implicated officials attempt to extricate themselves from trouble. Lou's blood boils whenever those traitors come to mind, but she's glad for breathing space before new syndicates organize. There's time to rethink strategies and be ready for any further attacks on the elephants.

The rigid lines on her father's face have eased. Occasionally, like now, he manages a smile as, without comment, he hands her a letter over the breakfast table.

"Will you be OK here, Dad?" Lou asks tentatively. She resolved to ask him this days ago.

"In what way?" he replies, nonplussed.

Her father glances briefly over the top of his newspaper. He returns to the article when she doesn't immediately respond.

The answer is obvious. Of course Dad will be alright. Why did she imagine anything else? Vanity, perhaps, makes her persist.

"Will you miss me? I mean, I have a purpose here, don't you think?"

"Of course! But there's nothing we can't handle while you're gone."

"Oh, that's OK then."

Why's she so surprised? Isn't she an integral part of the place?

"It's time you got away for a bit. Be good for you," her father replies, eyes still fixed on the newspaper.

So, it's that easy for her to leave, as far as everyone else is concerned. In a way, Lou is relieved. He doesn't mind. No one minds! It's really that simple. Her father looks up for a split second as she leaves the table, letter in hand.

"Louise!" he says. The use of her full name stops her just inside the door.

"Yes, Dad?"

"Don't doubt for a moment how proud I am of you."

"Really?"

"Those Land Trust people that Steve's on about will accept you. I know it."

She stands there bewildered as her father puts the newspaper down and then gives her a bear hug on his way past.

"Oh, by the way. I've worked out what happened that night we caught the poacher." He winks at her over his shoulder, and strides off before she has a chance to respond.

Back at her desk, Lou tears open another of Steve's short letters. Again, it's right to the point. Why has it taken her so long to visit? Best not to complicate his simple request. Recent experiences have taught her to ease up on assumptions. However, she misses Steve badly and also must reply to that letter from the Wildlife Land Trust, especially after the legwork he's done for her. No more heel-dragging! Direct action on her part for a change! Suddenly decisive, Lou sits at her desk within a yellow circle of lamplight and starts her letter to the Land Trust. It's time to act and explore alternatives to help her elephants.

Lou puts the completed letter on her desk beside her thesis. She's been bogged in a reassessment of the finer details of her own work. Only her reluctance to leave keeps her here, nothing else, not even the wildlife for the actual amount of help she contributes. But she's suddenly grateful for her life as it is. After hopefully minor changes, her thesis will be done, the qualification as good as guaranteed. A weird sense of disconnection washes through her as her guilt subsides, and she imagines time with Steve.

Outside, the bougainvillea has flowered again, and Lou lets her thoughts expand out past the hedges to the vast landscape beyond. It's strange and weird to have no other commitment. The other people in her life are quietly getting on with their lives as she must do. This isolation she loves has been her salvation and also her undoing.

Her thoughts on the future, Lou misses the hum of the Peugeot until it bursts into the compound. The bright red car is an unusual sight out here after the khakis of the usual four-wheel drives. There's no accompanying dust cloud today. Quite the opposite, in fact. The tires of the Peugeot 404 are coated with ochre mud from an earlier rainstorm. The passenger door opens, and David climbs out. Her brother is home!

"David!" Lou vaults through her window and her bare feet sink into the wet earth as she runs toward him. She's acting like a kid, but, to her amazement, he smiles broadly and opens his arms for a hug.

"How are you, sis?"

His old self?

"We weren't expecting you!"

Despite her smile, a twinge of anxiety surfaces.

"I'm dead tired of the tourists and a whole lot of other stuff. I thought Dad might need some help."

"What stuff? I wouldn't mind being paid to go on safari."

"Yes, that's one aspect, but it seems I can't hack the downside anymore. John gave me a last-minute lift." He gestures toward the driver of the Peugeot, who grins widely.

"Hello. I guess you're Lou. I've heard all about you!" he says.

The brother she remembers has returned! When Lou shakes John's hand, it's white against hers, without a trace of sun exposure. He's newly arrived from England. Lou imagines Steve enduring the northern hemisphere winter, his tan long gone

John looks around as if absorbing an alien world.

"You both staying?" Lou asks, and John shrugs his shoulders, uncommitted.

"Of course! I've got a lot of catching up to do," David replies and grins as Peter comes to greet them.

The bags unloaded, they raid the fridge. Lou hurries after the men onto the veranda, where Peter finds ice, and David pours gin into glasses. They chat about work, corruption, and the unstable life ahead of John, teasing him a little. Lou is delighted to hear David's new vehemence against bribery and fraud at high levels. Brushing up against hunting tourism must have taught him a thing or two. *Has he also caught on to Lexi's deception?* Below them, grazing herds of gazelles cross the lush plains. Lou watches the dots of life move across a vastly changed outlook.

The conversation moves to Paul's betrayal, and Peter can't help himself.

"I saved our sister from being kidnapped, maybe even killed!" he says, delighted to embellish. He catches her eye and winks at her conspiratorially as he describes how he protected her. Her hands are tied. Her father has already guessed, and it seems he'll let sleeping dogs lie. She will always be indebted to Peter.

As an outsider, John was unaware of the widespread poaching. He's thrilled by his Nairobi posting and, as yet, untouched by the probable difficulties ahead.

"So far, life here is fantastic. It's exciting and I love the place!" he says.

"Not much of interest in Nairobi!" says David. "It's great until you get a handle on what's really going down." He grins in response to an inquiring look from Lou.

On their second drink, Lou asks after Carla and Lexi, and David's answer surprises her.

"They're chalk and cheese, those two. And Lexi accidentally let slip some information about some of her Nairobi friends."

"Like what?" says Lou, keeping her voice light. She knows not to openly pry.

"Let's just say, I maintain a friendship now only for what I might learn. Two can play that game!"

Lou can hardly believe her ears. Is her brother seeking retribution? She wants to ask more, but now is not the time. Lou lets it go and instead listens to John expound on his plans for his life in Africa.

At sunset, mauves and pinks form streaky layers on the horizon. The last light catches the heavy underbellies of gold-rimmed clouds. Lou has forgotten how much she enjoys this sort of company after the solitude of the bush. The only thing missing is Steve.

In the early morning, they take John on a short safari. He encounters his first wild elephant just beyond a previously dry waterhole, and the actual experience is apparently worlds apart from any documentaries he's watched.

"Such a unique presence! I can almost hear his thoughts!' he says, obviously awed by the giant.

Lou knew this elephant as a newborn. Perhaps now he stands a chance of reaching maturity. She recalls Tembo with the scarred thigh. The day they killed him, he stopped walking through her dreams.

The elephant tugs at a bough until it cracks noisily. He strips the leaves and stuffs them contentedly into his mouth, his skin folds flushed clean by rain, his eyes bright. He regards them inquisitively. Incredibly, they've been allowed to approach him so closely. Recently, the elephants are a little less wary. Communication has passed among them that their park is now safer.

Lou lets the others leave for an afternoon safari without her. After they leave, she rushes around and organizes her paperwork. When John returns to Nairobi tomorrow, she will trust him to drop her thesis in to her supervisor. He can also post her letter seeing the Land Trust has shown interest in her work.

"Please look after it carefully!" she says and hands him the package in the morning. It's taken so much of her time and energy. This wad of paper represents years of effort.

"I'll guard it with my life!" John jokes as they walk out to his Peugeot. A surreptitious glance over his shoulder, and he drops his voice. "Be kind to your brother. He's furious with his ex-girlfriend, though you'd never know it. He even still takes her out for coffee occasionally!"

Lou feels indebted for the update. It seems David is relatively robust. What else has he discovered that Lou knows nothing of? He's been privy to a whole way of life that she's never closely experienced.

"Hope to see you out here again," she says to John.

Then David catches up, and they hold on to Zebu while the Peugeot leaves.

It's a relief to have her work finally on its way.

"Nice bloke!" Lou says to David, and he nods. "You staying for a while this time?" she asks.

He nods again and winks. "Apart from information-gathering trips to Nairobi, I'm here to stay."

A day out in the savannah has done him good. Lou guesses the difference he will make might be even more than she hoped. Her brother is hugely motivated when not distracted.

Will Lexi continue to see Sam as the system catches up with him? Lou imagines David will keep his fingers on the pulse. Cynically, she guesses that Lexi's decision depends mostly on how severe Sam's punishment is. On its own, the photo is not sufficient evidence, but it's damaging enough to put his career in tatters along with Fred Lonnegan's. In the meantime, there are other fish to fry.

David has his own lessons to learn, different from hers but with similarities due to an isolated existence that taught them little of human motivations. It takes a week to become entirely sure of what David plans, and, of course, it's Peter who fills her in.

"Good thing Bwana David has come home to stay. We missed him!"

Already fewer jobs and requests take her time. David is on a mission, and the rangers have caught his enthusiasm. Lou spends her newfound spare hours worrying about whether the panel likes her thesis and researching possibilities for the future. It's a while since she's had space to breathe.

"Perhaps I should visit Steve?" she asks Grace one day when they're slicing fruit, the tangy taste of mango in her mouth.

"It's about time you go and do that!" Grace replies sternly.

Sixty-Nine

Lou wakes to the smell of coffee and with the painful knot around her heart gone. An episode of her life is "kwisha kabisa"—utterly finished—as Grace often says. It's an eloquent Swahili expression that sums things up. With her anxiety gone, it's time to look forward to the possibilities ahead.

Of course, this respite won't last forever, but the timeout is welcome and especially vital for the elephants and rhinos. As their stress levels drop, they'll become fertile and raise young. Lou makes a pact with herself not to dwell on all the loss. It only causes her pain while achieving nothing. Anger no longer consumes her, and, when it rises, she directs it usefully without letting it drain her. With the pressure off, she now sees how her emotions held her captive.

This morning the air is fresh and crisp after the night's rainfall. Masaranga's landscape shimmers with temporary water, and migratory birds have already arrived to take advantage of it, the pink haze of flamingos setting off the emerald green of the new grasses. What have been small springs are now proper waterholes, where elephants wade, their flexible trunks tearing out vegetation to fill their rumbling bellies.

"Someone is popular!" David has been teasing her again, and today he grins at her what-do-you-mean expression. In front of him is a pile of toast. Not a shred of regret remains in his attitude. It's just as if he never took off on another tangent. Zebu lies on the ground beside him. Her tail bangs noisily on the ground, but she's reluctant to move in case she misses out on toast. The dog has her priorities right—she too needs to be adaptable.

On the breeze are the scents of warming bushland and the promise of more rain. The expansive valley below is dotted with wildlife, and a lone elephant drinks safely at the waterhole, the first for ages. Further along the bank, a family of energetic warthogs forages busily. But Lou is distracted by the two envelopes.

Both have British stamps, one with Steve's sideways scrawl across the front, the other typewritten. She turns it over to see the logo of the Wildlife Land Trust and feels a stab of terror at the prospect of rejection, her resolution to search for positives briefly forgotten. Unsure which to open first, she wavers. But her fingers have made a choice.

Steve complains that it's hard for him to tell if she's listening. Of course she is! She grins and tears the other envelope open. Francis, the project manager for the Wildlife Trust, likes her work. With her input, Masaranga might be suitable for a trial attaching radio-transmitters to the elephants. The trust can cover the necessary costs while she learns the ropes at their London office.

It's all she could hope for, and how things seem meant to be. Her coffee forgotten, Lou imagines two years of entrapment in the city.

"What did they say, sis?" asks David.

"Good news!" she replies and pushes the letter toward him. Without waiting for his reaction, she hurries back to her room.

Her chest is suddenly tight as she takes in her private space, the flowering bougainvillea outside her window. Absently, she runs her fingers along the curves of the hippo and calf that she found nestled in beach sand. Her negotiations failed to allow for the fact the calf had lost a piece of itself. She hadn't minded, and the missing bit didn't matter. When she wipes the dust off, the wood glistens darker.

Her painted elephant watches her vacillations from his framed landscape, as he's done ever since she hung him there. Lou vows to help his living relatives more than her efforts have so far. She recalls her fear as the poacher emerged from the darkness, her rifle blast, and its kick against her shoulder. A tear rolls down her cheeks, and her lips taste salty. This may not be her country, but her memories were made here. The skin, hair, and eyes of her family mark her as a foreigner. Her life here is impermanent, despite her African imprint.

For now, her future is to leave this harsh, beautiful country that she loves, and work on a parallel track in an alien cityscape. Lou fights the tears back, wanting to delay them until the men leave. She's loath to further expose any weakness.

A sharp bark from Zebu and the clinking of dishes return her to the present. Her father's voice, low and even, is followed by her brother's muffled reply, and both men laugh. They wouldn't consider any of this stuff to be a big deal. Just this fact makes her feel even more alone. An image rises of Steve pulling his boat off the sand and out into the ocean. Though London will lack the romance of the Kenyan coast, she manages a smile.

Another burst of laughter from the men on the veranda, and the scrape as chairs are pushed back. The voices become businesslike as they set off together.

After they've left, she takes her last chance to drive to a high rocky area bordering the park. When the road ends, she hikes up a ridgeline for an hour, her lungs and muscles pushed to their limits. At the highest vantage point, the landscape encompasses a wide valley. Pale new leaves are already visible, expanding up the ridges.

The spectacular panorama reminds Lou anything could happen, despite her crowded artificial destination. Many people would perceive a wild place like this as suitable only for brief visits, and too far from the safe trappings of civilization. But something inside her will always crave to be close to the wilderness. She will return better armed to protect places like this.

A glimpse of bright color below. Lou's binoculars reveal a person climbing the ridgeline. In years of visiting this spot, she's never met anyone here. There are no villages nearby. To quell her disquiet, she assures herself that if someone intended any harm, they'd be unlikely to follow her in full view all along the rocky ridgeline.

The stick figure becomes a tall woman, her movements strong and proud as she climbs. A bright scarf trails behind her head and shoulders, its colors shimmering in the sunlight.

The figure passes through a thorny thicket, and the scarf disappears for several long minutes. Briefly, Lou wonders if she were hallucinating, as all around the bush seems so silent and empty. Spaces seem to expand both outside and inside of her.

But the woman reappears. Her skin is darker and more wrinkled than Lou has seen before, and her face is enclosed by a scarf as bright as flamingo feathers. Considering the steep climb, the woman breathes easily.

"Jambo!" Lou greets her.

At first, the woman remains quiet as she chooses a flat rock close by and sits effortlessly on her heels. Her eyes search out the vista below. Her body is thin but not frail, and even her hollowed cheeks have an undefinable vitality.

"Habari?" she finally asks Lou, her voice serene, suggesting an internal strength.

"Visuri sana," replies Lou.

For the first time, the woman looks at Lou, her face a mass of amused wrinkles. "Visuri sana?" she asks, slightly tilting her smiling face, her expression almost mischievous.

Lou returns the smile. Inexplicably, she feels the woman deciphering her thoughts. What conclusions would she be drawing? They sit close together for a while. Nothing needs to be said. All around is calm and quiet until the woman stands up gracefully as if she's gleaned enough. She wishes Lou luck and vanishes quickly down an indistinct trail on the far slope.

Seventy

On Lou's last visit to Nairobi to finalize things with her supervisor, Sara throws a farewell dinner. Lou is greatly relieved by Lexi's absence. Apparently, she's indisposed and licking her wounds after dramas of her own.

"She's angry at the lack of support from us!" says Carla. "It's time she grew up and stopped putting our mother through hell."

Almost everyone Lou knows is there. Not a huge group but overwhelming enough! David and John arrive accompanied by Sara's journalist friend. And then her father!

"To my sister and her future success in saving us all!" David toasts her. Everyone laughs, and Lou feels herself blush.

"I'm having enough trouble saving myself!" she says.

"We all are!" replies Sara. "Congratulations again!"

"To my gorgeous daughter. She cares only about what's important—certainly not appearances and make-believe. And thank god for that!" Her father chinks his glass against hers, and everyone cheers. Now Lou is really embarrassed. She laughs and takes another gulp of her cocktail.

Late into the night, Lou sits out on the veranda with Carla and David, the stars bright in an inky sky. All this she's going to miss, but it's not forever.

Though they've already said their goodbyes, Lou calls Carla again on her last morning at home.

"You always were the determined one!" says Carla.

"I don't have any choice," Lou replies, and cuddles Zebu closer to soothe her trepidation.

"Will David take up some of the slack once you're gone?" asks Carla.

"He already is! You should visit. He needs company!"

The men leave for a run to a village on the southern boundary, partly in response to her suggestion of recruiting the villagers' help. Lou would have liked to go with them. She has new ideas about how to involve local people. If they benefited directly from the wildlife, they'd be more willing to protect the animals.

🐘 🐘 🐘

"Enjoy the big smoke!" says David and hugs her goodbye.

"Did you?" she asks and smiles at him.

He shrugs his shoulders and rolls his eyes. "Contact with the big smoke is going to be as necessary for me as you," he replies. "I intend to make full use of it!"

"We'll miss you," says her father. He takes her by surprise and holds her face in his hands for a moment. "You've done well. Just as I expected."

"Please remember to show Zebu some love. She's the one who'll miss me most!" replies Lou. His open approval fortifies her more than anything else could.

Is she more excited or daunted? Her learning curve will be in a place where only minuscule remnants of the wild remain, a concrete jungle occupied by crowds. At the moment, she's more useful there. With her opportunity inexplicably granted, Lou vows to learn quickly. Outside help might enable solutions as people work together to break the links in a chain of destruction. Wildernesses will never get more resources unless someone fights for them. Enough people care to help a little. Every contribution of time and effort counts. More people would become involved if they knew just how much their small part matters.

"I look forward to your stories when you return!" says Grace as Lou hugs her goodbye and restrains her tears. Then Peter eases the Land Rover out past the hedges. He drives slowly, aware it's good for her to see home shrink only slowly to a blur on the savannah. Usually she doesn't look back, but today she watches Masaranga diminish behind her. It hurts, but her inner landscape is already adapting as she alters her focus rather than her purpose. David is back with a vengeance, and Lou has lost any misgivings about failing to pull her weight. The men will stay and safeguard Masaranga, and their anger at being double-crossed will fuel them. Lou is grateful for another path. In many ways, it's a relief to no longer have to fight so ineffectively on the ground.

"This Land Rover is mine now!" Peter teases her as if ecstatic to have control of her vehicle. Lou remembers how he's protected her and allows herself to assume that underneath his high spirits, he's sad about her departure.

Stretches of the road are recently sealed, their artificial acrid smell already pungent in the morning's heat. Lou is reminded of the inevitability of change. Even since her last trip, new makeshift buildings have sprung up on the roadsides near Nairobi, to shelter an overgrown population. Low corrugated roofs sit on uneven planks of wood, bound together by plastic sheeting and old sacks. Skinny, ragged kids play with complicated wheel arrangements created out of twisted wire. A few smile and wave thin arms, as they shout noisily at passing vehicles.

At the concrete drop-off pavement outside the airport, Lou tells Peter that she will miss him.

"Also, I will miss you, but not for long. You will come back soon."

"I hope so, Peter."

"You won't rest until we have won! However long it takes. I know you."

"I have an awful lot to learn!" Lou replies. Not such a terrible prospect when she considers how she plans to use the knowledge. A surge of inspiration from that determined place deep inside takes her unawares. It's just what she needs right now. Without her mission, she would be lost and aimless.

There is nothing more to say as he unloads her suitcase onto the hot, bright walkway leading into the terminal. Suddenly Peter has her in a bear hug. Then, just as quickly, he's back in the driver's seat. The engine revs as he pulls away. A last wave out the window, and the airport traffic swallows him.

When her plane lifts off, the engines find little resistance in the hot air, and the ascent is slow. The newly green landscape drops away and loses detail. The view continues to expand far beyond the raggedy edges of Nairobi, out past miles and miles of settled land and occasional isolated wild patches. This country that has been her only real home shrinks and merges with the rest of Africa until Lou no longer recognizes landmarks. How long will she have to wait before she experiences this scene in reverse, the details growing back out of the expanse?

In the meantime, there's so much for her to do.

Epilogue

The Mbane herd has been settled for some time now, and two of the elephants are pregnant. For twelve-year-old Tumaini, the time to give birth to her first baby has come. Her inexperience is not a problem. The matriarch will guide her, and her herd sisters will help her through the experience. The calf will be protected and tended by the females until old enough to take on social responsibilities.

For twenty-two months, Tumaini has carried this calf, and her timing is perfect. An excellent wet season has passed. The vegetation is thick, and food is plentiful, so her body will be able to deliver the volumes of milk soon needed. At least two years will pass before the calf becomes physically independent. Her emotional dependence on Tumaini and the herd will last a lifetime. All being well, the mother and her daughter will live their lives out with their family.

Since early morning, Tumaini and her herd have been restless. As darkness falls over the plains, her sensory overload diminishes. Now she has time to focus on what is happening to her body. Subdued trumpeting from her sisters accompanies her final contraction as the calf drops with a thud onto the ground, the sac bursting on impact. Immediately, Tumaini swings around and sweeps the tip of her trunk over the newborn, pulling the sac away from the still inert body. Deep rumbles emanate from the rest of the herd, in a moment of concern. But then the calf blinks open her eyes and lifts her head to see her mother for the first time. Her legs kick in the air as Tumaini blows on her and throws pieces of placenta aside.

The other females come closer, greeting the newborn with low rumblings, their trunks extended to encourage the new arrival's first movements. They form a group around her, touching her repeatedly, never once stepping close enough to injure her. She will soon be an integral part of the herd, and they will help Tumaini protect her from predators. The support system of the closely knit family binds them together. It gives meaning to their existence, just as it does for humans, the similarities of their emotional lives far outweighing the differences.

The calf takes her first steps. When she stumbles, her mother and aunts are there, and their trunks help her support her baby weight of just over 100 kg. Healthy and already thirsty, she lifts her short trunk out of the way and latches onto Tumaini's teat. Her aunts stand back as she guzzles down milk. It won't be long before the matriarch will send out her "let's go" signal and then lead the herd away to safety.

Afterword

As a vet, I'm clearly animal orientated, and occasionally treat wildlife. My opportunity to work with elephants in South Africa was thwarted in 2020 by covid-19!

My father taught science at Njoro secondary school in Kenya for six years, so Lake Nakuru and her flamingos were conveniently close for a day of wildlife watching. We spent holidays camped out in wild places. It was never glamourous but gave me an early connection with wild animals. I loved the elephants, whose social life made them particularly endearing.

My book describes the 1980s, and much has changed regarding the ivory trade out of Africa since then. Massive demand from China and parts of SE Asia drove a new wave of poaching. For the first fifteen years of this century, elephants were decimated by foreign-backed syndicates that supplied high-tech equipment to poachers on the ground.

I wrote this book to bring the elephants story closer to my readers. The more awareness of their plight, the better the chances of long-term survival for these intelligent beings.

If you enjoyed Black Ivory, please leave me a review on Amazon, Goodreads, or wherever you can, or sign up to my mailing list on www.josquirewrites.com

I really appreciate your support.

Acknowledgements

Thanks to L J, Jewel, Helen, Joy and Werner who read the first drafts and were kind enough not to discourage me.

Also to Philip Newey, my editor for his insight and invaluable help.